中英對照

五千年中華詩詞精選

江紹倫 選譯

5000 Years of
Chinese Gem Poems
in English Rendition

Translated by Kong Shiu Loon

商務印書館

5000 Years of Chinese Gem Poems in English Rendition

中英對照五千年中華詩詞精選

翻譯：江紹倫

Selected and translated by：Kong Shiu Loon

責任編輯：黃家麗

Executive Editor：Betty Wong

封面設計：涂　慧

Cover Design：Tina Tu

出版：商務印書館（香港）有限公司
　　　香港筲箕灣耀興道3號東滙廣場8樓

Published by：The Commercial Press (H.K.) Limited
　　　　　　　8/F, Eastern Central Plaza,
　　　　　　　3 Yiu Hing Road, Shau Kei Wan, Hong Kong
　　　　　　　http://www.commercialpress.com.hk

發行：香港聯合書刊物流有限公司
　　　香港新界荃灣德士古道220－248號荃灣工業中心16樓

Distributed by：The SUP Publishing Logistics (H.K.) Limited
　　　　　　　　16/F, Tsuen Wan Industrial Centre, 220－248 Texaco Road,
　　　　　　　　Tsuen Wan, NT, Hong Kong

印刷：美雅印刷製本有限公司
　　　九龍觀塘榮業街6號海濱工業大廈4樓A室

Printed by：Elegance Printing and Book Binding Co. Ltd.
　　　　　　Block A, 4th Floor, Hoi Bun Building
　　　　　　6 Wing Yip Street, Kwun Tong, Kowloon, Hong Kong

版次：2020 年 12 月第 1 版第 1 次印刷
　　　© 2020 商務印書館（香港）有限公司

Edition：First Edition, First Printing, December 2020
　　　　　ISBN 978 962 07 0581 6

目　錄
Contents

030　序

036　Preface

第一部份　遠古時代（公元前一五○○年至公元六一八年）
Part A　Ancient Period (1500 BC–618 AD)

周朝 ZHOU DYNASTY (1122–256 BC)

詩經 **The Book of Poetry (c. 600 BC)**

風 Songs

3　周南・芣苢 Capital South – Gathering Plantain Seeds

4　邶風・靜女 Songs of Bei – Quiet Maiden

5　邶風・燕燕 Songs of Bei – Parting Sparrows

6　邶風・凱風 Songs of Bei – Mother as Gentle Breeze

7　邶風・谷風（節選）Songs of Bei – Voice of a Rejected Wife (selected part)

8　邶風・二子乘舟 Songs of Bei – My Sons on Boat

8　衞風・河廣 Songs of Wei – River Wide

9　衞風・木瓜 Songs of Wei – Papaya

10　王風・君子于役 Songs from the Capital – My Man Serves His State

11　鄭風・女曰雞鳴 Songs of Zheng – Love Abides

12　鄭風・有女同車 Songs for Zheng – Riding with a Maiden Fair

13　鄭風・搴兮 Songs for Zheng – Song We Together Sing

14　鄭風・東門之墠 Songs for Zheng – Lover's Murmur

15　鄭風・子衿 Songs for Zheng – a Scholar

16　檜風・匪風 Songs of Gui – Travelling East

17　豳風・伐柯 Songs of Bin – To Make an Axe Handle

18　豳風・七月（節選）Songs of Bin – Peasant Life (selected part)

18　魏風・十畝之間 Mulberries Grown on Our Ten Acre Field

雅 Odes

19　大雅・綿（節選）Book of Epics – The Continued Migration in 1325 BC (selected part)

20　小雅・甫田之什・鴛鴦 Love Birds

21　小雅・采薇（節選）Gathering Ferns (selected part)

22　小雅・鴻鴈之什・鶴鳴 Cranes Cry

23　小雅・南有嘉魚之什・湛露 Heavy Dew
24　小雅・南有嘉魚之什・菁菁者莪 Excellence in School
25　小雅・魚藻之什・隰桑 Mulberry Tree
26　大雅・生民之什・泂酌 Fetching Water

頌 Hymns

27　周頌・清廟之什・思文 Hymns of Zhou – To the Corn Lord
28　周頌・閔予小子之什・敬之 Respect with Humility
29　周頌・天作 Zhou Hymns – Sky Mount
30　周頌・有客 Zhou Hymns – Welcoming Guests
31　周頌・絲衣 Zhou Hymns – Formal Gown

屈原 Qu Yuan (332 BC−296 BC)

32　九歌・湘夫人 Madam Xiang River
34　九章・橘頌 Ode to Orange (A Gentleman)
36　九歌・雲中君 To the Cloud Lord

漢朝 HAN DYNASTY (206 BC−220 AD)

項羽 Xiang Yu (232 BC−202 BC)

38　垓下歌 Final Song

無名氏 Anonymous

39　古詩十九首（節選）行行重行行 (I) On and on away You Go (I) (selected part)
40　古詩十九首（節選）青青河畔草 (II)
　　Green Green Is the Grass by Riverside (II) (selected part)
40　古詩十九首（節選）涉江采芙蓉 (VI)
　　I Gather Lotus Blooms Wading through the Stream (VI) (selected part)
41　古詩十九首（節選）驅車上東門 (XIII)
　　I Drive My Chariot up Eastern Gate (XIII) (selected part)
42　古詩十九首（節選）生年不滿百 (XV)
　　People Live Not a Hundred Years Long (XV) (selected part)

樂府詩 A Han Dynasty Folk Song

43　十五從軍征 To Arms at Fifteen

劉徹（漢武帝）Liu Che (156 BC−87 BC)

44　落葉哀蟬曲 Song of Fallen Leaves and Plaintive Cicada
45　秋風辭 Song of Autumn Wind

蘇武 Su Wu (140 BC−60 BC)

46　留別妻 Adieu Dear Wife

曹操 Cao Cao (155−220)

47　觀滄海 Watching the Sea
48　龜雖壽（節選）Tortoise Longevity (selected part)

曹丕 Cao Pi (186−226)

49　短歌行 A Short Song on the Death of My Father

曹植 Cao Zhi (192−232)

50　七哀詩 Lament
51　七步詩 Written on Seven Paces by Demand
51　贈白馬王彪 To My Brother

六朝 SIX DYNASTIES (265−618)

陶潛 Tao Qian (365−427)

53　擬挽歌辭 (I) Elegy Song (I)
54　歸園田居 (I) Back to Nature (I)
55　歸園田居 (III) Back to Nature (III)
55　飲酒詩二十首 (V) Drink (20 Poems) (V)

無名氏 Anonymous (Six Dynasties)

56　敕勒歌 Shepherd Song

孔紹安 Kong Shao'an (577−date of death unknown)

57　落葉 Fallen Leaf

第二部份　唐朝 (公元六一八年至九〇七年)、五代 (公元九〇八年至九七九年)
Part B　Tang Dynasty (618−907) Five Dynasties (908−979)

唐朝 TANG DYNASTY (618−907)

虞世南 Yu Shinan (558−638)

60　詠螢 Firefly

王績 Wang Ji (590−644)
61 過酒家 Passing the Tavern
61 野望 Wilderness View

無名氏 Anonymous (Tang Dynasty)
62 金縷衣 The Golden Gown
62 雜詩 A Room

寒山 Han Shan (dates of birth & death unknown)
63 杳杳寒山道 The Cold Hill Way
63 無題 No Title

綦毋潛 Qiwu Qian (692−749)
64 春泛若耶溪 Spring Boating on the Ruoye Stream

布袋和尚 Cotton Bag Monk (dates of birth & death unknown)
64 農夫問道 A Farmer's Way
65 問答 Question and Answer
65 問法號 My Name

牟融 Mao Rong (date of birth unknown−79)
66 秋夜醉歸有感 Returning Home Drunk in an Autumn Night
66 寫意二首 Two Poems on Feelings

常建 Chang Jian (date of birth unknown−727)
68 題破山寺後禪院 A Chan Hall behind a Temple Ruin

李頎 Li Qi (690−751)
70 古從軍行 Ancient Army March
72 琴歌 Dulcimer Music

李嶠 Li Qiao (644−713)
74 風 Wind
74 中秋月 Mid-Autumn Moon

宋之問 Song Zhiwen (656−712)
75 題大庾嶺北驛 At the Post House up Dayu Ridge
75 渡漢江 Crossing the Han River

張旭 Zhang Xu (658－747)

76 春草 Spring Grass
76 桃花溪 The Plum Flower Stream

賀知章 He Zhizhang (659－744)

78 回鄉偶書 On Homecoming
78 詠柳 The Willow

張若虛 Zhang Ruoxu (660－720)

80 春江花月夜 A Moonlit Night by the River in Spring

陳子昂 Chen Zi'ang (661－702)

82 登幽州台歌 Ascending Youzhou Tower
82 送東萊王學士無競 Parting Gift

張九齡 Zhang Jiuling (678－740)

83 望月懷遠 Pining for You in Moonlight

王翰 Wang Han (687－726)

83 涼州詞 Up to the Front

王之渙 Wang Zhihuan (688－742)

84 登鸛雀樓 Ascending the Heron Tower
84 涼州詞〔又名《出塞》〕To the Frontier

孟浩然 Meng Haoran (689－740)

85 夏日辨玉法師茅齋 My Buddhist Teacher's Hut
86 宴梅道士山房 A Feast with Monk Mei up the Mountain
86 留別王維 Leaving Wang Wei
87 過故人莊 Visiting an Old Friend in His Farm
88 宿建德江 Mooring on Jiande River
88 春曉 A Spring Day Dawn

王灣 Wang Wan (693－751)

89 次北固山下 Passing by North Mountain

王昌齡 Wang Changling (698－756)

90 芙蓉樓送辛漸 Adieu Xin Jian
90 出塞 To the Frontier

90   塞下曲 On the Front

劉方平 Liu Fangping (date of birth unknown—758)

92   夜月 A Moonlit Night
92   春怨 Loneliness

王維 Wang Wei (701—761)

94   山中 In the Mountain
94   竹裏館 A Cot on Bamboo Hill
94   雜詩 A Recontre
95   九月九日憶山東兄弟 To My Brothers on Double-Nine Festival
95   終南別業 Retirement at South Hill
96   相思 Yearning
96   鳥鳴澗 A Dale Where Birds Sing
96   陽關三疊 To a Departing Ambassador
97   鹿柴 The Deer Place
97   酬張少府 A Response to Prefect Zhang
98   渭川田家 Home at River Wei
99   送別 Farewell

李白 Li Bai (701—762)

100   行路難 The Road of Life Is Difficult
102   宣州謝朓樓餞別校書叔雲 Farewell to Uncle Yun at Xuanzhou
102   峨嵋山月歌 Song of Moon O'er Mount E Mei
104   獨坐敬亭山 Watching Jingting Peak in Solitude
104   山中問答 Conversations in the Hills
104   春夜洛城笛 Flute Music in a Spring Night at Luoyang
106   望天門山 A View of the Mount Heaven Pass
106   下終南山過斛斯山人宿置酒 With Hermit Husi in the Zhongnan Mountain
108   月下獨酌 Drinking Alone in Moonlight
110   將進酒 Let's Drink
112   憶秦娥 Tune: Remembering the Palace Maids
112   送孟浩然之廣陵 Farewell to Meng Hao Ran at Yellow Crane Tower
114   早發白帝城 Leaving Bai Di Town at Dawn
114   自遣 Solitary Pursuit
114   菩薩蠻 To the Tune of Dancing Buddhists
116   靜夜思 On a Quiet Night
116   清平調詞三首 (I) Three Serene Tunes (I)
118   長幹行 Song of Wife in Chang Gan

120　秋夕旅懷 Thoughts away from Home on an Autumn Night

崔顥 Cui Hao (704－754)
122　黃鶴樓 The Yellow Crane Tower

儲光羲 Chu Guangxi (707－760)
124　釣魚灣 Fishing Bay
124　吃茗粥作 On Eating Tea Congee

劉長卿 Liu Changqing (709－780)
125　新年作 Written on New Year's Day
125　尋南溪常山道人隱居 Visiting Daoist Chang by the Stream

唐玄宗 Tang Xuanzong (712－756)
126　經魯祭孔子而歎之 Honouring Confucius at Lu

杜甫 Du Fu (712－770)
127　獨酌成詩 Written When Drinking Alone
128　秋興八首 (I)、(III)、(IV) Autumn Thoughts (I), (III), (IV)
129　天末懷李白 I Pine for Li Bai from this Earth's End
130　夢李白二首 Two Poems Dreaming of Li Bai
132　秋笛 Flutes of Autumn
132　歸雁 Homebound Geese
133　南征 Travelling South
133　麗春 Poppies
134　晚晴 A Clear Eve
134　蜀相 Prime Minister Memorial
135　田舍 My Cottage
135　卜居 Searching for a Home Site
136　春水 Spring Swells
136　登高 Up the Mountain
138　旅夜書懷 Reflections in an Inn
138　病馬 To My Ailing Horse
140　野望 Watching the Wilderness
140　兵車行（節譯）The Conscript March (selected part)
142　秋野 Autumn Wild
142　落日 Sunset
143　贈衛八處士 To Hermit Wei
144　江邊星月二首 (II) Moon and Star by Riverside Two Poems (II)

張繼 Zhang Ji (715–779)

145　楓橋夜泊 Mooring by Maple Bridge Overnight

岑參 Cen Shen (715–770)

146　輪台歌・奉送封大夫出師西征
　　A Sent-off to General Feng in His Western Expedition

148　走馬川行・奉送封大夫出師西征
　　Seeing General Feng off on His Western Expedition

司空曙 Sikong Shu (720–790)

150　雲陽館與韓紳宿別 Bidding Han Shen Adieu at Yun Yang Inn

150　喜外弟盧綸見宿 Enjoy Passing a Night with Cousin Lu Lun

152　江村即事 Village by Riverside

錢起 Qian Qi (722–780)

152　歸雁 The Returning Geese

154　湘靈鼓瑟 Musical Soul of the Xiang River

154　送僧歸日本 Seeing a Japanese Bonze off to Home

156　谷口書齋寄楊補闕 To My Friend Yang from My Study

156　與趙莒茶宴 A Tea Party with Zhao Ju

皎然 Jiao Ran (730–799)

158　飲茶歌誚崔石使君 Tea Drinking Song for Master Cui

160　飲茶歌送鄭容 A Tea Drinking Song for Zheng Rong

162　尋陸鴻漸不遇 Visiting Master Lu Hongjian to See Him Home

韋應物 Wei Yingwu (736–792)

163　賦得暮雨送李曹 To Li Cao in a Drizzling Evening

163　喜園中生茶 Happy to Grow Tea in My Garden

164　夕次盱眙縣 Mooring in Xuyi at Dusk

164　秋夜寄丘員外 To Master Qiu in an Autumn Night

165　寄全椒山中道士 To My Friend the Daoist Hermit

李益 Li Yi (746–829)

165　江南曲 A Song from the South

166　敦煌曲子詞：菩薩蠻 Lyrics from Dunhuang: Tune Buddhist Dancers

盧綸 Lu Lun (748–799)

166　送萬巨 Seeing Wan Ju off

168 塞外曲 (I) Frontier Songs (I)

孟郊 Meng Jiao (751－814)
169 烈女操 A Faithful Widow
169 遊子吟 A Roamer Sings

韓愈 Han Yu (768－824)
170 山石 Mountain Rocks

劉禹錫 Liu Yuxi (772－842)
172 秋詞 Autumn Song
172 烏衣巷 The Lane of Mansions
172 竹枝詞二首 (I) Bamboo Songs Two Poems (I)

李紳 Li Shen (780－846)
173 憫農二首 (I)、(II) Feeling for Farmers Two Poems (I), (II)

白居易 Bai Juyi (772－846)
174 食罷 After a Meal
174 夜聞賈常州、崔湖州茶山境會亭歡宴 A Tea Party at Tea Hill
176 大林寺桃花 Peach Blossom at Da Lin Temple
176 賦得古原草送別 Farewell by the Ancient Grass Plain
178 燕詩示劉叟 Swallow Song
182 琵琶行 Pipa Song
187 錢塘湖春行 Visiting West Lake in Spring
187 長相思 Tune: Eternal Pining
188 憶江南 Recall the South
188 望月有感 To My Brothers While Sharing the Moon

柳宗元 Liu Zongyuan (773－819)
190 溪居 My Dwelling by the Stream
190 登柳州城樓寄漳、汀、封、連四州刺史 To Friends in Exile
192 漁翁 Old Fisherman
193 飲酒 Drinking
194 江雪 River in Snow
194 晨詣超師院讀禪經 Reading Zen With Master Chao Early Morning

賈島 Jia Dao (779－843)
196 題興化園亭 Temple Garden

197　尋隱者不遇 Visiting a Hermit

元稹 Yuan Zhen (779−831)
198　遣悲懷 Remembering My Late Wife
200　離思 To My Lover
200　菊花 Chrysanthemum

李賀 Li He (790−816)
202　金銅仙人辭漢歌 From the Han Palace the Bronze Statue Depart

許渾 Xu Hun (791−858)
204　塞上曲 A Frontier Song
204　謝亭送別 Farewell at Parting Pavilion
205　秋日赴闕題潼關驛樓 Returning to the Capital in Autumn

盧同 Lu Tong (795−835)
206　走筆謝孟諫議寄新茶 A Note with a Gift of New Tea

杜牧 Du Mu (803−852)
208　贈別二首 (I) 、 (II) Parting Two Poems (I), (II)
208　題宣州開元寺水閣 Ruins in Splendour
210　江南春 Spring South of the River
210　清明 Qing Ming Festival
210　遣懷 Confession
212　泊秦淮 Mooring on River Qinhuai
212　寄揚州韓綽判官 To Magistrate Han of Yang Zhou

李商隱 Li Shangyin (812−858)
214　無題 No Title
214　無題 No Title
216　無題 No Title
216　嫦娥 To Cheng E the Moon Goddess
218　登樂遊原 To Ancient Tomb Mount
218　錦瑟 The Zither

溫庭筠 Wen Tingyun (812−870)
220　利州南渡 Ferrying South from Lizhou
220　西陵道士茶歌 A Tea Song of Daoist Xi Ling

222 更漏子・柳絲長
Tune: Water Clock Drips All Night – Willow Tendrils Lengthy
223 更漏子・玉爐香
Tune: Water Clock Drips All Night – The Jade Censor Fragrant Usual
224 商山早行 Early Departure
224 夢江南 Tune: Pining for Home in the South
226 河傳 Tune: from the River

曹松 Cao Song (828－903)
226 己亥歲感事 The War Years

羅隱 Luo Yin (833－909)
228 自遣 Relaxation
228 雪 Snow

皮日休 Pi Rixiu (834－883)
229 茶舍 Tea Hut

章碣 Zhang Jie (836－905)
230 焚書坑 Book Burning Pit

韋莊 Wei Zhuang (836－910)
230 章台夜思 Night Thoughts on Terrace Tower
232 荷葉杯 Tune: Cup of Lotus Leaves
232 菩薩蠻 Tune: Buddhist Dancers
233 金陵圖 The Ancient Capital
233 菩薩蠻 Tune: Buddhist Dance

聶夷中 Nie Yizhong (837－884)
234 田家 Peasants

張泌 Zhang Bi (842－914)
234 寄人 To My Love

崔塗 Cui Tu (854－date of death unknown)
235 除夜有懷 Thoughts on New Year's Eve

皇甫曾 Huang Fuzeng

235 送陸鴻漸山人採茶 Seeing Master Lu off to Pick Teas

五代 FIVE DYNASTIES (907–960)

顧敻 Gu Xiong (date of birth unknown–928)

237 訴衷情 Tune: Revealing Inner Feelings

鹿虔扆 Lu Qianyi

237 臨江仙（節選）Tune: Riverside Immortals (selected part)

張喬 Zhang Qiao

238 書邊事 On the Frontier

牛希濟 Niu Xiji (date of birth unknown–925)

239 山渣子 Tune: Mountain Hawthron

馮延巳 Feng Yanqi (903–960)

240 蝶戀花 Tune: Butterfly Loves Flower
240 南鄉子 Tune: Southern Country Song

李煜 Li Yu (937–978)

242 菩薩蠻 Tune: Buddhist Dancer
242 烏夜啼 Tune: Crow Cries by Night
244 相見歡・虞美人 Happily Together – Tune: Yu the Beautiful
244 清平樂 Tune: Serene Music
246 浪淘沙 Tune: Waves Refining Sands
246 相見歡 Tune: The Joy of Togetherness
248 虞美人・風回小院庭蕪綠
　　　Tune: Yu the Beautiful – Wind Returns to My Small Courtyard Deplete of Green

第三部份　宋朝（公元九六〇年至一二七九年）
Part C　Song Dynasty (960–1279)

宋朝 SONG DYNASTY (960–1279)

魏野 Wei Ye (960–1019)

253 書友人屋壁 Written on the Wall of a Friend's House

葉紹翁 Ye Shaoweng (1100－1151)

253　遊園不值 Visiting a Garden with an Absent Host

王觀 Wang Guan (1035 — 1100)

254　卜算子・送鮑浩然之浙東 Tune: Song of Divination – To a Departing Friend

潘閬 Pan Lang (date of birth unknown－1009)

254　酒泉子 Tune: Wine Spring

古成之 Gu Chengzhi (968－1038)

256　憶羅浮 Remembering Mount Luofu

范仲淹 Fan Zhongyan (969－1052)

257　御街行 Tune: Strolling on Royal Walk
258　漁家傲 Tune: Fisherman's Pride
259　蘇幕遮 Tune: Behind Silk Screens

柳永 Liu Yong (987－1053)

260　望海潮 Tune: Watching the Tides
262　憶帝京 Tune: Recalling the Imperial Capital
264　雨霖鈴 Tune: Bells Drowned by Rain
266　八聲甘州 Tune: Eight Beats from Ganzhou Music

張先 Zhang Xian (990－1078)

268　木蘭花 Tune: Magnolia
270　天仙子 Tune: Songs of Immortals

晏殊 Yan Shu (991－1055)

272　建茶 Jian Tea
272　蝶戀花 Tune: Butterfly Loves Flower
274　浣溪沙 Tune: Silky Brook Sands

張昇 Zhang Bian (992－1077)

276　離亭燕 Tune: Swallow Vacated Pavilion

宋祁 Song Qi (998－1061)

278　玉樓春 Tune: Jade Pavilion in Spring

余靖 Yu Jing (1000−1064)

278　雙松 Double Pines
279　暮春 Late Spring

黃龍慧南禪師 Huanglong Huinan (1002−1069)

280　趙州吃茶 Zhao Zhou Eat Tea

介石 Jie Shi (1005−1045)

280　歲晏村居 Village Life towards Year End

歐陽修 Ouyang Xiu (1007−1072)

281　踏莎行 Tune: Treading on Grass
281　浣溪沙・堤上遊人逐畫船
　　　Tune: Silky Sand Brook – People on the Dyke Follow the Ornate Boat
282　蝶戀花 Tune: Butterfly Loves Flower
282　夢中作 Written in My Dream

曾鞏 Zeng Gong (1019−1083)

284　寄獻新茶 Sending a Gift of New Tea

司馬光 Sima Guang (1019−1086)

284　西江月 Tune: Moon on West River

王安石 Wang Anshi (1021−1086)

286　漁家傲 Tune: Fisherman's Pride
286　元日 Lunar New Year's Day
288　勘會賀蘭山主 Meeting the Master of Mount Helan
288　對棋與道源至草堂寺 To My Friend on Chess and Dao
289　桂枝香－金陵懷古
　　　Tune: Fragrance of Laurel Branch – Pining for Old Capital
290　書湖陰先生壁 Written on the Wall of Master Hu Yin

晏幾道 Yan Jidao (1030−1106)

292　臨江仙 Tune: Immortals by the River
292　鷓鴣天 Tune: Partridge Sky

蘇軾 Su Shi (1037−1101)

294　滿江紅・寄鄂州朱使君壽昌 Tune: River All Red – To Officer Zhu
296　汲江煎茶 Ladle the River to Make Tea

298 望江南・超然台作 Tune: Viewing River South – Transcendent Platform

299 中秋月 The Mid-autumn Moon

299 東坡 The East Slope

300 紅梅 Red Plum Blossom

302 蝶戀花 Tune: Butterflies Love Flowers

302 題西林壁 Written on the Wall of Westwood Temple

303 念奴嬌 Tune: Charm of a Maiden Dancer

304 沁園春・赴密州早行馬上寄子由
Tune: Qin Garden Spring – To My Brother on My Way to Exile

306 行香子・過七里灘
Tune: Joy of Union Eternal – Passing through the Seven-league Shallows

307 江城子・乙卯正月二十日夜記夢
Tune: Riverside Town – Remembering My Deceased Wife in Dream

308 水調歌頭 Tune: Prelude to Water Melody

310 定風波 Tune: Calm Wind and Water

312 念奴嬌・赤壁懷古 Tune: Remembering Palace Maids Memory at Crimson Cliff

314 和子由澠池懷舊 A Duet with My Younger Brother on the Good Old Days

李之儀 Li Zhiyi (1038－1117)

314 卜算子 Tune: Song of Divination

黃庭堅 Huang Tingjian (1045－1105)

316 清平樂・晚春 Tune: Music Serene – Late Spring

317 水調歌頭・遊覽 Tune: Prelude to Water Melody – Seeing As I Go

318 踏莎行・茶詞 Tune: Treading on Grass – Tea Poem

秦觀 Qin Guan (1049－1100)

320 鵲橋仙 Tune: The Magpie Bridge Immortal

322 滿庭芳 Tune: Fragrant Courtyard

323 江城子 Tune: A Riverside Town

324 千秋歲・水邊沙外 Tune: Ten Thousand Years — At Water Front away from Sands

米芾 Mi Fei (1051－1109)

325 浣溪沙・野眺 Tune: Silky Sand Brook – Watching the Wild

賀鑄 He Zhu (1052－1125)

326 鷓鴣天 Tune: Partridge Sky

326 青玉案 Tune: Green Jade Server

周邦彦 Zhou Bangyan (1057−1121)

328 　西河・金陵懷古 Tune: West Rill – Remembering the Ancient Capital
329 　蝶戀花・商調秋思 Tune: Butterfly Loves Flower

朱敦儒 Zhu Dunru (1081−1159)

330 　相見歡 Tune: Joy of Meeting
330 　好事近・漁父詞 Tune: Happy Events Are Near – Fisherman's Song

趙佶〔宋徽宗〕Zhao Ji (1082−1135) [Emperor of Song Dynasty]

331 　宴山亭・北行見杏花 Tune: Hillside Pavilion – To Watch Apricot Flowers in the North

李清照 Li Qingzhao (1084−1156)

332 　訴衷情 Tune: Revealing Inner Feelings
333 　永遇樂 Tune: Eternal Happiness
334 　攤破浣溪沙 Tune: Silk – Washing Stream, Broken Form
336 　聲聲慢 Tune: Adagio
338 　一翦梅 Tune: A Twig of Mume
338 　如夢令 Tune: Like a Dream
340 　漁家傲 Tune: Fisherman's Pride
340 　醉花陰 Tune: Drunk under Flower Shade

陳與義 Chen Yuyi (1090−1138)

342 　臨江仙・夜登小閣，憶洛中舊遊
　　　Tune: Immortals by the River – Remembering Friends Travelling Together in Old Times

張元幹 Zhang Yuangan (1091−1161)

343 　賀新郎・送胡邦衡待制赴新州
　　　Tune: Celebrating with the Bridegroom – Seeing Hu Quan off Banished South
344 　更南浦 South You Go

楊無咎 Yang Wujiu (1097−1169)

345 　玉樓春・茶 Tune: Jade Bower in Spring – Tea

岳飛 Yue Fei (1103−1141)

346 　滿江紅 Tune: A River in Red
348 　小重山 Tune: Manifold Hills

陸游 Lu You (1125−1210)

349 　蘭亭道上 Flower Dock Tea from the Orchid Pavilion
350 　訴衷情 Tune: Of Innermost Feelings

350 十一月四日風雨大作
　　During a Storm on the Fourth Day of the Eleventh Moon
351 釵頭鳳 Tune: Phoenix Hairpin
352 詠梅 In Praise of Mume (Tune: Song of Divination)
352 示兒 To My Son

唐琬 Tang Wan (1124－1156)
353 釵頭鳳 Tune: Phoenix Hairpin

范成大 Fan Chengda (1126－1193)
354 冬日田園雜興 (III)、(IV)、(VII)、(VIII) Winter Songs (III), (IV), (VII), (VIII)

楊萬里 Yang Wanli (1127－1206)
358 戲筆 Brushing Fun
358 曉出淨慈寺送林子方 Seeing Lin off from the Temple in the Morning

朱熹 Zhu Xi (1130－1200)
359 觀書有感 Insight from Reading

張孝祥 Zhang Xiaoxiang (1132－1169)
359 西江月 Tune: Moon over the West River
360 念奴嬌 Tune: Charm of a Maiden Dancer – On Dongting Lake

辛棄疾 Xin Qiji (1140－1207)
362 西江月 Tune: Moon over West River
363 定風波 · 暮春漫興 Tune: Calm Wind and Wave – Late Spring
364 水龍吟 · 登建康賞心亭
　　Tune: Water-Dragon Chant – At Jiankang Riverside Tower
366 西江月 · 夜行黃沙道中
　　Tune: Moon over West River on My Way Home through the Yellow Sand Ridge
366 破陣子 · 為陳同甫賦壯詞以寄之
　　Tune: Dance of Cavalry in Response to Chen Liang
368 菩薩蠻 · 書江西造口壁
　　Tune: Buddhist Dancer – Written on the Wall of Zaokou
368 鷓鴣天 · 博山寺作 Tune: Partridge Sky – At the Bo Shan Temple
370 青玉案 · 東風夜放花千樹 Tune: Green Jade Server – Lantern Festival
370 西江月 · 遣興 Tune: Moon over the West River – Self-reflection

劉過 Liu Guo (1154－1206)
372 臨江仙 · 茶詞 Tune: Immortals by the River – Tea Ci

373   糖多令 · 重過武昌
Tune: Sugar Rich Song – Passing through Wu Chang Again

姜夔 Jiang Kui (1155－1221)
374   揚州慢 Tune: The Yangzhou Adagio

元德明 Yuan Deming (1156－1203)
376   好事近 · 次蔡丞相韻 · 中州樂府
Tune: Good News Near – Rhyme with Prime Minister Cai

崔與之 Cui Yuzhi (1158－1239)
376   揚州官滿辭後土題玉立亭 On Retirement from Office at Yangzhou

史達祖 Shi Dazu (1163－1220)
378   詠燕 · 雙雙燕 Tune: Pairs of Swallows – Swallow Song

劉克莊 Liu Kezhuang (1187－1269)
380   玉樓春：戲呈林節推鄉兄
Tune: Jade Pavilion in Spring – To Jester a Friend
380   西山 West Hill

吳文英 Wu Wenying (1200－1260)
382   八聲甘州：陪庾幕諸公遊靈岩
Tune: Eight Beats of Gangzhou – On a Visit to Star Cliff with Friends
383   風入松 Tune: Wind through Pines

魏初 Wei Chu (1232－1292)
384   鷓鴣天 · 室人降日，以此奉寄
Tune: Partridge Sky – To My Wife on Her Birthday

劉辰翁 Liu Chenweng (1232－1297)
385   柳梢青 · 春感 Tune: Green Willow Tendrils – Spring Thoughts

李刻 Li Yan (1232－1303)
386   唐多令 Tune: Vibrant Melody

文天祥 Wen Tianxiang (1236－1282)
387   除夜 New Year Eve
387   過零丁洋 Crossing the Lonely Ocean

張弘范 Zhang Hongfan (1238–1280)

388　南鄉子 Tune: Southern Country Song

劉敏中 Liu Minzhong (1243–1318)

388　浣溪沙 Tune: Silky Sand Brook

張炎 Zhang Yan (1248–1320)

390　八聲甘州——記玉關踏雪事清遊
　　Tune: Eight Beats of Ganzhou – I Remember Our Trip through Snowy Jade Gate

蔣捷 Jiang Jie (1245–1305)

392　梅花引・荊溪阻雪 Tune: Plume Melody – Strand at Jin Stream by Snow

馬致遠 Ma Zhiyuan (1260–1334)

393　天淨沙・秋思 Tune: Sky over Clear Sand – Autumn Thoughts

王實甫 Wang Shifu (1260–1336)

393　正宮・端正好・長亭送別 Tune: Calm Dignity – Parting

萬俟詠 Wansi Yong

394　昭君怨 Tune: Lament of Princess Zhao Jun
394　長相思・雨 Tune: Eternal Longing – Rain

第四部份　元、明、清朝（公元一二七九年至一九一○年）
Part D　Yuan, Ming, Qing Dynasties (1279–1910)

元朝 YUAN DYNASTY (1271–1368)

曾允元 Zeng Yunyuan

397　點絳唇 Tune: Rouge Lips

張可久 Zhang Kejiu (1270–1348)

397　山居春枕（二）雙調・青江引
　　Tune: Prelude to Clear River – Spring in the Mountain (II)

喬吉 Qiao Ji (1280–1345)

398　山坡羊・自警 Tune: Sheep on Slope – Singing to Myself
398　憑欄人・金陵道中 Tune: Leaning on Railings – On My Way to Jinling

薩都剌 Sa Dula (1308－1348)

399 　百字令・登石頭城 Tune: Hundred Words Song – Ascending Jin Ling City

高啟 Gao Qi (1336－1374)

400 　友之越贈以惠泉 A Gift of Hui Spring in Parting

釋中峯 Shi Zhongfeng (Yuan Dynasty)

401 　行香子 Tune: Fragrance Songs

李道源 Li Daoyuan (Yuan Dynasty)

402 　遊大理崇聖寺 A Visit to Chong Sheng Temple at Da Li

戴昺 Dai Bing (Yuan Dynasty)

402 　嘗茶 Savouring Tea

明朝 MING DYNASTY (1368－1644)

陸容 Lu Rong (1436－1494)

404 　送茶僧 For a Tea Connoisseur Monk

唐寅 Tang Yin (1470－1524)

404 　題事茗圖 For the Brewing Tea Painting

文徵明 Wen Zhengming (1470－1559)

406 　煎茶詩贈履約 Tea Making
406 　暮春齋居即事 On Simple Living in Late Spring

楊慎 Yang Shen (1488－1559)

408 　臨江仙 Tune: Immortal by the River

吳承恩 Wu Chen'en (1501－1582)

410 　樵歌子 A Woodcutter Song
411 　舟行 On a Gliding Boat
411 　楊柳青 Green Willows

戚繼光 Qi Jiguang (1528－1587)

412 　曉征 To War at Dawn

陳繼儒 Chen Ji Ru (1558–1639)

412 浪淘沙・茶園即事
Tune: Waves Refining Sand – On Scenes of Tea Plantation

劉維 Liu Wei (Ming Dynasty 1368–1644)

414 感通寺與僧舊話 Past Chats with a Monk at Gan Tong Temple

吳偉業 Wu Weiye (1609–1671)

415 意難忘・山家 Tune: Unforgettable Memory – Mountain People

竺庵大成 Zhu'an Dacheng (1610–1666)

416 伯勞 Swallow

永覺元賢 Yongjue Yuanxian (1576–1657)

416 臥 Lying Down

王夫之 Wang Fuzi (1619–1692)

417 更漏子・本意 Tune: Time Dipper Song – Real Intention

屈大均 Qu Dajun (1630–1696)

418 長亭怨・與李天生冬夜宿雁門關作
Tune: Parting Laments – Staying a Night at Geese Pass

清朝 QING DYNASTY (1644–1911)

廖燕 Liao Yan (1644–1705)

421 祝月 Moon Wishes
421 辭諸生詩 Bidding Farewell to Students

佷亭挺 Liang Tingting（1615–1684）

422 水檻 Rail by the River

納蘭性德 Nalan Xingde (1655–1685)

422 長相思 Tune: Longing for You
423 菩薩蠻・過張見陽山居賦贈
Tune: Buddhist Dancer – Passing a Friend's Mountain Home
423 浣溪沙・身向雲山那畔行
Tune: Silky Sands Brook – Towards Cloud Hills in Horizon
424 南鄉子・何處淬吳鉤 Tune: Southern Country Song – Ancient Battle Ground

426　金縷曲・慰西溟 Tune: Song of Golden Tread Comforting a Friend

428　憶秦娥・龍潭口 Tune: Remembering Qin Maiden – Black Dragon Pool

429　水調歌頭・題岳陽樓圖
Tune: Prelude in Water Melody – For a Painting on Yue Yang Tower

430　如夢令・萬帳穹廬人醉
Tune: Like a Dream – Ten Thousand Woollen Tents Make Us Feel Exhilarating

430　山花子・風絮飄殘已化萍
Tune: Mountain Flower Song – Petals Drift Like Water Lily

431　霜天曉角・重來對酒 Tune: Morning Bugles on Frosty Day – We Happily Drink

432　采桑子・誰翻樂府淒涼曲 Tune: Gathering Mulberries – Song of Misery

433　采桑子・明月多情應笑我
Tune: Gathering Mulberries – The Caring Moon Should Laugh at Me

434　清平樂・憶梁汾 Tune: Serene Music – Remembering My Friend

435　蝶戀花・出塞 Tune: Butterfly Loves Flower – Out the Frontier

436　蝶戀花・眼底風光留不住
Tune: Butterfly Loves Flowers – Happy Days Gone Cannot Be Retained

437　琵琶仙・中秋 Tune: Pi Pa Immortals – Mid-Autumn

438　尋芳草・蕭寺記夢 Tune: Looking for My Lover – Recording a Dream at a Temple

劉悟元 Liu Wuyuan (1673–1725)

440　悟道詩 A Poem of Insight

金農 Jin Nong (1687–1764)

440　憶茶 Recalling Tea

鄭燮〔鄭板橋〕Zheng Xie [Zheng Banqiao] (1693–1765)

442　雪景 Snow Scene

442　小廊 Small Chamber

442　寄松風上人 To Master Pine Breeze

曹雪芹 Cao Xueqin (1715–1763)

444　紅樓夢・黛玉葬花吟 (節譯)
From *The Saga of the Red Chamber* – Lin Daiyu's Flower Burial (selected part)

袁枚 Yuan Mei (1716–1797)

446　馬嵬驛 Beauty Legend

黃釗 Huang Zhao (1788–1853)

448　落葉詩二首 Falling Leaves Two Poems

文祚嫻 Wen Zuoxian (1812－1861)
450 　登大容山 Climbing Mount Darong

張佩綸 Zhang Peilun (1848－1903)
450 　晚香 Evening Fragrance

谷隱啟 Gu Yinqi (Qing Dynasty 1636–1912)
452 　興至 Interest Arrives

自聞宣 Zi Wenxuan
452 　風敲 Knocks

遠庵禮 Yuan Anli
453 　一樣 Same

撫松 Fu Song
453 　黃梅 Ripe Plums

靈潤機 Ling Runji
454 　一片 Sounds

笠山寧 Li Shanning
454 　涼夜 A Cool Night

江立 Jiang Li (1732－1780)
455 　憶舊遊・秋窗茗話 Tune: Recalling Old Travels – Tea Talks in Autumn

范學儀 Fan Xueyi
456 　登獨秀峯 Peak of Solitary Charm, Guilin

> 第五部份　現代（一九一一年至現代）
> Part E　Modern Period (1911－present)

現代 MODERN (1911–Present)

林則徐 Lin Zexu (1785－1850)
459 　高陽台：和嶰筠前輩韻
　　Tune: Tall Sun Terrace – Rhyme with Zhe My Senior

460　與纖 Tug Ropes

李鴻章 Li Hongzhang (1823−1901)
460　池上篇 From the Pond
462　入都 (I) In the Capital (I)

樊增祥 Fan Zengxiang (1846−1931)
464　中秋夜無月 Moonless Mid-Autumn Festival Night

黃遵憲 Huang Zunxian (1846−1905)
464　八月十五夜太平洋舟中望月作歌 Singing to the Moon from My Boat in the Pacific Ocean on the Fifteenth Night of the Eighth Moon
465　到香港 Visiting Hong Kong
465　夜起 Getting up at Night

丘逢甲 Qiu Fengjia (1864−1912)
466　春愁 Spring Sorrow
466　離台詩 Leaving Taiwan
466　元夕無月 A Moonless Lantern Festival
468　山村即目 Mountain Village

孫中山 Sun Zhongshan (1866−1925)
468　挽劉道一 (1907) Remembering a Martyr (1907)

梁啟超 Leung Qichao (1873−1929)
470　水調歌頭 —— 甲午 Tune: Prelude to Water Melody – 1895
471　自勵二首 (II)　Self-exhortation Two Verses (II)

吳佩孚 Wu Peifu (1874−1939)
472　春感 Spring Thoughts
472　贈楊雲史 To Yang Yunshi

秋瑾 Qiu Jin (1875−1907)
474　黃海舟中日人索句並見日俄戰爭地圖
Written on Board at Yellow Sea to a Japanese Friend Who Show Me a Map of Russo-Japanese War on Chinese Soil
474　有懷 —— 遊日本時作 Thoughts – Written in Japan
476　日人石井君索和即用原韻 Reply to a Japanese Friend

廖仲愷 Liao Zhongkai (1877–1925)

476 壬戌六月禁錮中聞變 (1922) Thoughts in Prison (1922)

478 留訣內子 To My Wife in My Imprisonment

胡漢民 Hu Hanmin (1879–1936)

478 秋女俠墓 The Tomb of Qiujin

480 哭執信 Weeping for a Martyred Friend

魯迅 Lu Xun (1881–1936)

480 無題二首 (1931) Two Untitled Poems (1931)

482 送增田涉君歸國 (1931) Seeing Hiloshi Masuda Home to Japan (1931)

482 一・二八戰後作 (1932) Written after the 1932.01.28 Battle (1932)

484 無題 (1934) Untitled (1934)

484 自題小像 Inscription on My Photo

蘇曼殊 Su Manshu (1884–1918)

486 春雨 Spring Drizzles

朱德 Zhu De (1886–1976)

486 古宋香水山芙蓉寺題詩 (1911) To the Hibiscus Temple at Fragrant Hill (1911)

488 望雨 (1963) Waiting for Rain (1963)

488 悼陳毅同志 (1972) Remembering Comrade Chen Yi (1972)

489 浪淘沙・雪中過邯鄲 (1954)
Tune: Waves Refining Sands – Passing Handan in Snow (1954)

蔣介石 Jiang Jieshi (1887–1975)

490 述志 (1909) My Determination (1909)

490 出發校閱撰歌二則 (1928) To Review My Army Force Two Poems (1928)

492 遊峨嵋口占二首 (1935) Touring Mount E Mei Two Poems (1935)

492 六三自箴 (1949) Reflection on 63rd Birthday (1949)

493 養天自樂箴 Nurture Longevity in Happiness

陳寅恪 Chen Yinke (1890–1969)

494 甲申除夕病榻作時目疾頗劇離香港又三年矣 (1945)
In My Sick Bed on New Year's Eve (1945)

494 庚寅元用東坡韻 (1950) New Year's Eve on Su Shi Rhymes (1950)

496 五十六歲生日三絕 乙酉仲夏五月十七日 My 56th Birthday

郭沫若 Guo Morou (1892−1978)

498 　歸國雜吟 (II) (1937) Random Thoughts on Way back to China (II) (1937)
498 　登南岳 (1938) Ascending Mount Heng (1938)

毛澤東 Mao Zedong (1893−1976)

500 　沁園春・長沙 (1925) Tune: Qin Garden Spring – Changsha (1925)
502 　采桑子・重陽 (1929) Tune: Picking Mulberries – Double Nine Festival (1929)
502 　憶秦娥・婁山關 (1935) Tune: Remembering Qin Maid – The Luishan Pass (1935)
504 　清平樂・六盤山 (1935) Tune: Serene Music – The Six-turn Mount (1935)
504 　長征 (1935) The Long March (1935)
506 　沁園春・雪 (1936) Tune: Qin Garden Spring – Snow (1936)
508 　水調歌頭・游泳 (1956) Tune: Prelude to Water Melody – Swim (1956)
510 　蝶戀花・答李淑一 (1957)
　　　Tune: Butterfly Loves Flower – Reply to My Friend Li Shuyi (1957)
510 　為李進同志題仙人洞照 (1961)
　　　Inscription on a Photo of Comrade Li Jin at the Fairy Cave (1961)
512 　卜算子・詠梅（1961 年 12 月）Tune: Song of Divination – Ode to the
　　　Plum Blossom (December 1961)
513 　水調歌頭・重上井崗山 (1965)
　　　Tune: Prelude to Water Melody – Revisiting Mount Jing Gang (1965)
514 　有所思 (1966) Desires for Change (1966)
514 　訴衷情・贈周恩來同志 (1975)
　　　Tune: Revealing Inner Feelings – To Comrade Zhou Enlai (1975)

葉劍英 Ye Jianying (1897−1986)

516 　油岩題壁 (1915) Written on Oil Cliff (1915)
516 　劉伯承同志伍拾壽祝 (1942)
　　　Wishing Comrade Liu Bo Cheng a Happy 50th Birthday (1942)
516 　遊新疆 (1956) Visiting Xinjiang (1956)
517 　長江大橋 (1957) The Yangtze River Bridge (1957)
518 　鹿回頭 (1959) At Deer Turn-head Point (1959)
518 　回梅縣探老家 (1980) Visiting Home at Meixian (1980)

周恩來 Zhou Enlai (1898−1976)

520 　送蓬仙兄返里有感 (1916) Seeing Peng Xian Homebound (1916)
522 　次皞如夫子傷時事原韻 (1916)
　　　Reply to Master Kao Ru Grieving over Current Events (1916)
522 　無題 No Title
522 　春日偶成（1914）Thoughts on a Spring Day (1914)

陳毅 Chen Yi (1901－1972)

524 憶亡 (1932) Remembering My Wife (1932)

525 三十五歲生日寄懷 (1936) On My 35th Birthday (1936)

526 佳期 (1940) Wedding Day (1940)

526 「七七」五週年感懷 (1942)
Thoughts on the 5th Anniversary of Japanese Invasion (1942)

528 祝朱總司令六旬大慶（1946 年 11 月）
Wishing Commander Zhu De a Happy 60th Birthday (November 1946)

528 長江大橋 (1956) The Yangtze River Bridge (1956)

蘇步青 Su Buqing (1902－2003)

530 南雁蕩愛山亭晚眺（1940 年回鄉）
Gazing Afar from the Love Hill Pavilion (Returning to Hometown in 1940)

530 憶秦娥：從台歸國 (1946)
Tune: Remembering the Qin Maid–Returning Home from Taiwan (1946)

532 望大小金門島 (1981) Watching the Jinmen Islands (1981)

532 世紀絕戀（寫於 2002 年百歲生辰）
A Century of Love (Written on My 100th Birthday in 2002)

534 浙江大學 Zhejiang University

534 悼亡妻 Remembering My Wife

羅元貞 Luo Yuanzhen (1906－1993)

536 懷故鄉諸老友 Remembering Old Chums Back Home

陶鑄 Tao Zhu (1908－1969)

538 登衡山祝融峯 (1961) To the Summit of Mount Heng (1961)

538 贈曾志 (1969) To My Wife from Prison (1969)

張學良 Zhang Xueliang (1910－2001)

540 無題 No Title

540 遊華山感懷 Touring Huashan

540 柳老渡台來訪 Elder Liu Visits Me in Taiwan

鄧拓 Deng Tuo (1912－1966)

542 一嵐清玩 To My Wife Yi Lan

542 魯迅兩週年祭 (1938) On the 2nd Anniversary of Lu Xun's Death (1938)

544 定情 (1942) Love Devotion (1942)

序

本書選收中國五千年以來的詩詞，以地道英語翻譯，獻給佔人類總和七成的英語和雙語讀者。在今天充滿分歧矛盾的世代裏，有助不同種族和文化的人認識自我，互相溝通欣賞和友好合作。這些詩詞包羅萬象，指引人和諧共處和活出創意。

詩為心聲。每首詩以音韻和語言打動心靈，代表着詩人的內在聲音，表達靈魂在特定時空、文化和生活奮鬥裏的呼喊，而這種聲音在另一個時空地域裏常獲得他人的共鳴。

傳統中國詩詞是龐大礦藏裏的寶石，誰奮力進去尋找，誰就得到豐盛回報。它們也像銀河的星宿，照亮最黑暗的夜晚。本書收錄的詩詞比銀河的星宿，數量微不足道，但裏面蘊含的熱情卻是巨大的，它們是我過去八十年來最喜愛的詩詞，在我行走世界時一直陪伴着我，讓我的心舒暢平靜。我選收這些詩詞在本書裏，中英並列，旨在表現詩詞之美。

中國人早在文字出現之前，已用各種口語抒發自己，釋放情感了。文字出現以後，古詩被收集整理，於公元前六世紀結集成《詩經》，其內容豐富，體裁成熟，用字靈活，意像神妙，顯示古代大眾詩人對宇宙人生觀察入微，了解和讚賞自然和人間景況，歌唱激昂。《詩經》的 305 首詩，按曲調和內容分為風雅頌三大類。簡括而言，"風"詩是各地民間的生活歌唱，純樸優美。"雅"詩顯露人們對宇宙和人生體驗的智慧，敘說上層人士和各朝代領袖的生活景況，反映歷史。"頌"詩歌頌歷代君主的功德和明智，表現大型歌舞和禮儀，用來教導人民敬祭祖先。同樣歌頌的還有神明對人的庇祐。通過這些祭祀的禮儀和歌舞，人們表現對生死意義的探求和尊重。

到孔子出現的年代，教育成為維繫社會秩序和繁榮進步的關鍵力量，而詩經是基礎課本。孔子深信精通詩詞的人也是擅長思考和溝通的人。

承傳着這樣豐盛的心聲清泉，屈原把詩提升上文學高台，被稱為"詩祖"。他學問淵博，想像寬遠，比喻情新，用字靈活，行文流暢。作為君主的密友和外交官，他盡忠職守，但最終他因失望跳汨羅江自盡。他寫的許多詩表現着他無限的智慧和未獲解決的困惑。

他精通中文，善用每個字描繪心靈和才智，他開創了一個新的詩歌傳統，就是重複用同一個字，使其聲義反覆觸動情感，並且發生回響。他也靈活運用暗喻，把人的情感與大自然的花草、樹木、雲彩、風雨、季節、河流及羣山聯結起來。他對宇宙萬物的統見寫照，給後世科學家提供劃時代的實驗設想，在 1953 年，世界和平理事會舉行一個活動，紀念"世界歷史上四位最偉大的文化人物"，屈原獲選為其中之一，他除了是一位偉大詩人之外，還是世界上舉足輕重的人物。

古詩簡而清和不設標點。一首五絕詩有二十個字，每字一音一義，足以表現大自然的壯美景象，或詩人情感的悲歡起落，興起讀者的反響及長久和鳴。不設標點的詩任由讀者自由斷句取義，加入或創造個人的心思和情感。如是，中國詩的讀者並不因循地讀詩，而是積極參予，緊貼詩人心聲而互動。正如孔子所言，詩是教育必備的材料。我在本書的英譯保留了這些特點。

我 1955 年初為人師，教小學四年級國文，內有一課李白的五絕《靜夜思》。十歲小孩認識生字後一齊大聲朗讀"床前明月光……"五次，然後各表心得。一位姓羅的學生問："那人是坐在床上，還是躺着？"

經過一輪討論以後，大家得出兩個推想：(一)"那人從外入房，看到滿地月照，坐床思鄉"；(二)"那人躺在床上，驟然看見月華闖入房間，坐起來望月，想起故鄉的親人。"我建議學生保持開放的心，接受兩個推想，詩歌可有多於一種闡釋。

二十年悠悠過去，我從 1972 年從多倫多大學近港擔任中文大學教育學院院長，翌年仲秋的一天接到該學生的電話約見。他熱誠告訴我他事業有成，被稱為"玩具大王"，家庭三代同堂快樂滿足。他說："老師，我十分感謝你教我們讀詩，使我們至今醉心於多位詩人的心聲。當年你引導我們認識人的情感與時間和空間的多重關係、豐富生活和生命意義。我當年很愛惜一隻寵物狗，因牠時常陪伴我。我叫牠即來，有時不叫亦來。那天下課以後，我唸着詩，感到李白的詩亦如寵物狗一樣可愛和順，經常出現在我心中。這樣，二十年來，我就與詩詞為伴，從來不感到孤獨。"

一起吃午飯的時候，羅生悠靜地背誦李白的《秋夕旅懷》，我問他故鄉何處。他說："我父母來自中國，我卻認為故鄉就是一種美好的回憶，不一定是出生的地方，老師，你和我們在香港仔官小度過一年，至今我們有七位同學經常說起，那是我們最快樂的時光，每次上課都有新的情感。童年就是故鄉，我沒說錯吧？"

"你全說對了。"他說的話令我感動。"是我應該感謝你們，小小年紀便認識又多又深，起於一首五絕。"

孔子認為，詩有興、觀、羣、怨四種作用。讀詩教人覺悟自己的身份和能力，用心聲感動他人互相合作，以及譴責不義不平的事情。儒家智慧崇尚禮樂，重視人際關係的和諧合作，建設眾人共享充足安寧的家園。詩是教育的中心經驗，赤子學習言行的清泉活水，心靈的食糧。中國詩更深染老莊和禪宗智慧。前者教人放下固執，擬蓄虛靜尊敬之心。後者慈悲為懷，關愛萬物眾生，圓和生命。

不過，傳統中國詩詞有一個不利因素。它們含有不常用字，其音意對一般讀者都深奧難懂，叫人望而生畏。不過，唐宋詩詞多數用字簡易，其數千萬，可讓今天的學生欣賞。

　　我用簡明易懂的英語翻譯了千多首最受人喜愛的詩詞，從其中選出最好的收錄在本書裏，用意是幫助英語讀者欣賞中國人的文化傳承，認清中國人及中華文化對宇宙人生的觀想，以"求同存異"和"共相生息"為生活指標。中國人素來依從"和為貴"的價值生活和創造，在當前充滿紛爭仇敵的國際形勢下，實在是人類尋求持續生存繁榮的主要動力。

　　從個人修養出發，我提倡讀詩安心，寄盼中國兒童青年在成長中多讀詩詞。為此，我的英譯兼有第二重作用，表現漢英兩種文字的融和美，英語同樣可以寫成字少意廣的詩句，同時可以不設標點而容許讀者自由運用創意解釋詩意。特別對於香港和新加坡的各級學生，以及世界各地具有雙語能力的人士，我建議大家在繁忙的日常生活中，給自己片刻安靜，大聲朗讀英譯詩句幾次，欣賞其簡而清的特質，咀嚼其意味音聲，再讀漢文原詩，循環欣賞兩種文字的意韻融和，像握手一樣，你一定會體驗到多重喜悅，身住審美情懷，融入自然的安寧和滿足。

　　人的好奇詢問、思想、心思和心意都借用語文呼喊出來，自聽和供他人聽見，寄盼共鳴。聆聽自己的聲音和他人的迴響和鳴，是人類心靈最佳的瓊漿玉液，可以解除寂寞、無聊和絕望。

　　根據世界健康委員會的調查研究，在近三十年間，智能手機及互聯網被普遍應用以來，信息泛濫與人的心理健康背道而馳，加速加深人們的"心盲"（Psychic Blindness），損害約四成人的健康，令人不安的是每十四秒都有人自殺。與此平行，暴力增加，造成社會不安。英國在 2019 年增設了一個專責解決國民孤獨問題的部長。在美國，第十九任衛生部部長在哈佛商業評論中，就這樣說："孤獨是一個日趨嚴重的流行病，危害健康。我們生活在歷史上科技最廣泛應用的時代，但自 1980 年年代開始，孤獨比率就已經增長一倍。"

面對這樣嚴重的消極適應狂潮，各種關注人類前途的國際組織竟然只有呼喊，沒有解救良策。哲學家、教育家和心理學家聯合研究，把問題核心總結為人們失去了自我認識和生命意義，受虐於心理壓抑 (depression)。這是當前人類文明的時代病。

讓我們了解一下甚麼引致目前的情況。從上世紀 60 年代開始，消費主義和抗爭暴力政治把世界推向一個不可逆轉的驚懼未來 (Future of Fear)，使每個人都成為不完整的 "碎片" (fragments)，隨風飄搖，不能立足大地，不能靠緊恆定的時空和倫常關係，不能掌握生命的自主功能，只是被動地過日子。如今，科技軍商更銳意開發人工智慧和自動化，要取代人們親力親為工作和生活所得到的滿足感和成就感，同時抹殺人類心靈的最高表現，就是幻想和矇矓的審美情趣。如是，人不再重要了，個人不重要，羣體都不重要。

早在上述我學生成長的年代，愛因斯坦已認定科學的片面性和詩歌的全面性，以及人的精神需要。他曾在文章裏說："我們的科技超越了人性，方法日趨完美，目標混亂，成了我們時代的特色。"他也提倡神秘經驗，並說 "我們可以經歷最美的是神祕的事，是真正藝術和科學發源地上的根源，誰要是沒有情感體驗，或不為它感到驚訝。就如死人一樣，眼睛閉上。"

1959 年，愛因斯坦和好友完形心理學創始人沃特海姆 (Max Wertheimer) 講話，提起他喜愛音樂和詩，並說明科學和藝術的不同。他說："我愛音樂和詩，因為它們是消滅我生命中寂寞的武器 (weapons)。它們內涵的想像力比知識更重要，因為想像推動無窮無盡的發問 (questioning)。"

我在此引述偉大科學家的思維和情意，旨在用他來並列我那位十歲學生愛詩的相同經驗。如他所說，一首《靜夜思》怎樣引起他當年的發問，以及他日後獲得詩的貼身陪伴，使他有愛有成。通過我的學生，即普通人的經驗和人生，讓我認識詩的真正魅力，在不同時空之間價值永恆。

詩是幻想和創造。詩人借助想像將我們的靈魂從現實的負重中解救出來。它表達生的訴求，人對美善和滿足的願望，一首詩能夠描繪個人的志向和抱負，他對美的追求，對浪漫、自由和自主的追求。詩表現人類的尊嚴和價值。

這樣，詩是在詩人與人羣之間，讀詩者與他朋友之間最有效的溝通媒介。不同母語的異邦人可以通過翻譯互相認識和合拍，古代詩人與今天讀詩的人可以互相唱頌和創造。這就是我寫本書的主旨和動力。

我教學六十年，與各年紀和種族的"學生"約五萬人都有互動經驗。除了一百位小學生外，其他都是大學生和社會開發者。我教心理學，主要教人怎樣認識自我和關愛他人。我喜歡引用《周易》說，意義的闡釋無限循環，任人自由合拍為一。"坤卦"是一首大地詩，由秋天代表深意，人們在豐收的田野間歌唱色彩紛繁無邊的情意，他們大聲表達深深的感恩，令人聽了沉醉。他們知道冬天會悄悄來到，給他們寧靜和安息。大自然的萬事萬物在人心裏都得到認同肯定。

我又愛引老子說，"人法地，地法天，天法道，道法自然。"說明人性是自然而然，是天地萬物的集合，由每個人自己選擇怎樣與他人和大自然互動，締造生命目的和意義。中國五千年的詩詞滿載這些中國人的智慧，期盼讀者閱讀我翻譯的詩時，可以仿照我學生的經驗，獲得詩歌作為畢生的心靈陪伴，積極圓和生命，在此我誠心祝禱。

江紹倫

多倫多大學榮休教授

2020 年元日

Preface

This book contains Chinese gem poems in a 5000-year heritage rendered in modern colloquial English. I present them to readers of the English world, including people who know both Chinese and English. They constitute possibly two thirds of the human family. In today's much divided and intensely conflicting world, when human beings of all races and cultures need to know who they are, to communicate and appreciate one another for harmonious cooperation and creative living, this is a signal endeavour.

Poetry combines music and language to touch the soul. Every poem represents the inner voice of a poet as he expresses the human spirit in the context of time, space, culture, and the strife of life. Such a voice often finds resonance in individuals living in another land and time.

Traditional Chinese poems are gems in a vast mine. Anyone ventures into them would be richly rewarded. They are also star constellations in the Milky Way, glittering to illuminate the darkest night. The poems presented here are like a constellation in the Galaxy, small in number, but prodigious in passion. They are poems I have loved in the eight decades of my life as I drifted around the world, providing me with comfort and tranquillity. They are presented here in both Chinese and English to provide a juxtaposition of the beauties of the two languages.

Long before the written Chinese words were invented, the many tribes living in North China were singing poems in their various vocal languages. These poems depicted a rich array of imagination and real life activities, from farming to courting to honouring the gods and immortals, reflecting artistic creativity and the unlimited potentials of the human mind. These poems were later collected and edited into the *Book of Poetry* (*Shijing*), appearing in the sixth century BC. The 305 poems were organized into three parts, namely, Songs, Odes, and Hymns. Regardless of type, the poems depict daily activities, human relationships, love, fear, and a sense of time and space as they impact on feelings of happiness, sorrows, fairness, injustice, longings, intimacy, aspirations, disappointments, and hope.

By the time Confucius came along, education became a vital force in keeping society in order, prosperity, and progress. The *Book of Poetry* was the basic text. Confucius was convinced that, a person well versed in poetry would be an effective thinker and communicator.

Qu Yuan (340-278 BC) inherited the very rich literary heritage to write the finest and most romantic poems. He is considered to be the Grandfather of Chinese Poetry. He was a man of diverse talents, with understandings and views of the universe as well as human affairs. He served his king as confidant and diplomat with a singular loyalty. He was disappointed. In the end he jumped into the Miluo Jiang , a disappointed soul. His many poems showed his unlimited intelligence as well as his unresolved bewilderment.

He was superb in the use of the Chinese language, showing the power of every single word in depicting the human heart and intellect. He set the tradition of using the same word in repetition, enabling its sound and meaning to pound on the reader's emotions and echoes. He also set the stage for the liberal use of metaphors, linking human moods and feelings with flowers, grass, trees, clouds, wind, rain, and seasons, rivers and hills to endear human beings with Nature. His descriptions of the cosmic signs contributed significantly to the theorizing of modern sciences. In 1953 the World Peace Council hailed an elaborate event to commemorate "the four greatest cultural figures in history to be remembered by the world". He was one of the four. Qu Yuan had since then become a man of the world in addition to being a great poet.

Traditional Chinese poems have two unique characteristics,

namely, they express clear meaning with few words, and they do not use punctuation. For example, a five-word quatrain has 20 words in four lines, each and every word has a sound and a meaning to describe the grand view of Nature or the expanding meanings of a thought or emotion. The purpose of not using any punctuation include getting the reader to put a comma or period where he chooses, and enticing him to participate actively in giving the poem his own meaning. Thus poems are essential materials for education, as Confucius had conveyed. I have kept these characteristics in my translation of all the poems in this book.

I began my work seriously some 30 years ago, inspired by a former elementary school pupil. I began my teaching career in 1955, teaching grade four "Chinese". One of the lessons in the text used was Li Bai's quatrain *Thoughts on a Quiet Night*. I taught the ten-year-olds the meanings and sounds of the single words, and asked them to read the poem aloud five times to feel its beauty. "Moonlight carpeted the floor in front of my bed ..." During the ensuing discussion, a pupil named Low asked, "Was the poet sitting or lying on his bed?"

The many opinions were summed up in two possible situations: a) he entered the room from outside and saw the floor flooded with moonlight, then sat on his bed to yearn for his homeland, and b) he was lying in bed, awaken by the moonshine entering through the window, and sat up to pine for his folks back home". I advised the class to keep the two positions and to live with a poem having more than one meaning.

Twenty years had passed. I was invited back to Hong Kong from the University of Toronto to take up the position of Director for the School of Education in 1972. I received a call one day in early autumn the following year by pupil Law for a get-together. It was a joyful meeting when he told me that he was a successful manufacturer of toys and satisfied and happy living with his parents and two sons. "I must thank you, teacher, for teaching us how to love poetry. You taught us when we were ten, to know how human feelings were closely related with time and space to enrich life with meaning and happiness. I had a pet dog then. I loved it very much because it was always with me, keeping me good company. I went home that day after learning Li Bai's poem, humming it with joy, and my pet dog came to me as usual. I realized that I had a new pet, the poem. It filled my heart with warmth and the satisfaction of being able to recite it fluently. It leads me to love a number of poets and their works. I've never felt lonely or sad ever since."

We had lunch together. He recited another poem by Li Bai on the homeland. I asked him where his parents' homeland was. "They came from China, Sir. But, I believe homeland is happy memory, not necessarily one's birth place. Indeed, the Aberdeen Public School where you spent a year with us is our homeland. Seven of our classmates still get together today to share how we loved attending your class, because there was always something new to learn, and easily learned. I believe childhood is homeland. Am I not right?"

"You are certainly right." I replied, touched by what he had said. "In fact, I am the one who should be thankful, that you guys realized so much and so deeply when you were at such a tender age; many profound ideas got into your little heads from a mere five-word quatrain."

Poetry was the core subject matter in traditional Chinese education. In addition to the wisdom of Confucius, most poems also reflect the wisdoms of *Laoze* and *Zen*. The former taught pupils to be broad minded in knowing and to accept a diversity of ideas. The latter harboured love and respect so people naturally care for all living things to *lead* wholesome lives.

However, there is a drawback in traditional poems, especially the ancient ones. They contain words with meanings and sounds not easily known to ordinary readers. Fortunately, poems of the Tang and Song Dynasties use ordinary words. Numbered in tens of thousands, they can be learned and enjoyed by even today's elementary school pupils.

I translated thousands of these poems using simple English. The best of them are presented here in this book. Through them I hope to help readers of the English world to understand and appreciate the Chinese people and their cultural heritage. We uphold the wisdom of "seek communality, respect differences" (求同存異) and "To grow up and enjoy life together" (共相生息) as we interact with people of different races and cultures, as well as the universe in its manifold features. We value the middle course in all life activities and aspirations. Amidst the perennial wars and competitions in today's world, our values and beliefs and actions should be a vital force in humanity, as the human family attempts to move forward in peace and prosperity.

In personal perspective, I advocate the reading of poems to engender tranquillity and security in modern life. I hope today's children and youth can enjoy poetry in their course of development. Thus, my English rendition carries a second mission, namely, to exhibit the parallel effect and beauty of both the Chinese and English languages. English can convey wide and deep meanings with the sparing use of words. English verses without punctuation allow readers to freely indent a poem for personal meaning or interpretation. This is particularly intended for students of Hong Kong, Singapore, and anywhere else who have dual linguistic capabilities. I suggest that they set aside an hour or so away from the hustle and bustle of their daily life to read a favourite poem or two in a quiet personal space, and to repeat their reading in English as loud as they can for heightened appreciation. Then, they can look up the original Chinese poem to see how the two languages shake hands in tonal and spiritual concords. In so doing, they will certainly feel multiple happiness, nesting in the bosom of aesthetic riches, natural satisfaction, and serenity.

Human inquiry, thoughts, and ideas all shout out with the use of languages, for self-hearing, communication, and possible echoes. Listening to one's own voice and the echoes of others is the sweetest nectar for the soul. It can help to eliminate loneliness, ineptitude, and despair.

According to the research reports of the World Federation of Mental Health Organization and related agencies, in recent decades when intelligent hand phones had become widely used, the flooding of information had triggered the rapid increase of Psychic Blindness in people everywhere, harming about 40% individuals of all ages and cultures. Alarmingly, it is announced that there is a loss of life in suicide every 14 seconds round the clock. The parallel development is violence, destruction, and social unrest, most prominently in wealthy and educationally advanced countries. The United Kingdom created a Minister of Loneliness in 2019. In the United States, the 19th Surgeon General wrote in the Harvard Business Review that "Loneliness is a growing health epidemic. We live in the most technologically connected age in the history of civilization, yet rates of loneliness have doubled since the 1980's."

No organization or agency has come up with a solution, despite loud alarm calls. The joint research efforts of philosophers, educators, and psychologists resolve that the central problem lies in the general loss of self-recognition, coupled with the absence of life meanings. Depression has become the sickness of our age.

Let us have an understanding of what have led us to how we are. Beginning in the 1960's when consumerism and warring-to-win world powers had jointly created for the human race an irreversible "*Future of Fear*", and reduced human existence to *Fragments*. People are deprived of their referent anchorage of time, space, and ethics. They drift like petals in the air. They have no land to stand on. They spend their days passively responding to orders and prescribed routines, away from initiatives and purposeful actions. And now, the high-tech driven businesses are developing higher power artificial intelligence and automation, which will replace human beings' work satisfaction, accomplishments, and happiness. Thus, human beings are no longer important, as individuals, and as a whole.

About the time when pupil Law was growing up with poems

as his companion, Albert Einstein wrote in his essays that "our technology has exceeded our humanity, and that the perfection of means and the confusion of ends seem to characterize our age." He also advocated the experience of mystery, saying, "The most beautiful thing we can experience is the mysterious. It is the source of all true art and all sciences. He to whom the emotion is a stranger, who can no longer pause to wonder and stand rapt in awe is as good as dead, his eyes closed."

One day in 1959, Einstein had a chat with his friend Max Wertheimer, father of Gestalt Psychology, about music and poetry. He said, "I love music and poetry, because they are weapons which eliminate my loneliness in life. Their inherent imaginative powers are more important than knowledge. Imagination propels endless questioning."

I present the thoughts and feelings of the Nobel Laureate for Physics here for a single reason. So I can juxtapose them with the experience of my ten-year-old pupil whose questioning has the same powerful effects to lead him to a life-long love of poetry and a successful and happy life. Through these common experiences I learned the real charisma of poetry, and how its power permeate through time and space to show eternal value.

Poetry is imagination and creation. The poet uses imagination to liberate our souls from the drudgery of ordinary life. In turn, he also presents the meaning of life to nurture the soul. A poem can describe a person's aspirations and strivings, his wishes for beauty and satisfaction, his cravings for romantic ventures, for freedom and self-determination. Poetry platforms the dignity and worthiness of mankind.

Thus, poetry is the most effective medium of communication, between the poet and people at large, among readers and friends. People of different cultures and languages can exchange views and feelings through renditions, and today's readers can understand the beauties and imagined realities in ancient poems. These possibilities in connecting people across space, time, and cultures provide the impetus for me to work on this book.

I have taught for sixty years, interacting with some fifty thousand students of all ages and nationalities. Except for a hundred elementary pupils, the rest are people in universities and leadership positions in social development. My main subject is psychology. I teach people how to know themselves and care for others. I love to refer to the wisdom of *Book of Change* that the interpretation of an idea reverberates without limit. It is up to an individual to synthesize the various interpretations into a concordant one. The *Kun Gossip* is a poem of our earth, with autumn as its vivid representation. Folks harvest and sing in fields to celebrate the manifold colours of nature. They call aloud their deep sense of gratitude. They know that winter will follow in quietude, to offer them the comfort of repose. Everything in Nature is recognized freely and naturally in the human heart.

I also like to refer to the wisdom of *Laozi* who taught that human nature is seen equally in the cosmic sphere, made up by the collective gifts of sky, earth, and all living things. It is up to a person to choose all there is to construct the meaning and purpose of his or her life. The poems of five thousand years of Chinese history reflect the total wisdom of our heritage. For readers of this book, if their experience in reading my translated poems would echo pupil Law's success and contentment in the fellowship of his beloved poems, I offer my eternal prayers.

Kong Shiu Loon
Professor Emeritus,
University of Toronto.
1st January, 2020

1

第一部份

遠古時代

公元前一五〇〇年至公元六一八年

Part A

Ancient Period

(1500 BC−618 AD)

周朝
ZHOU DYNASTY
(1122–256 BC)

詩經

The Book of Poetry
(c. 600 BC)

風
Songs

周南·芣苢	*Capital South* – **Gathering Plantain Seeds**

采采芣苢　　　　Plantain seeds we gather
薄言采之　　　　Gather them with speed
采采芣苢　　　　Plantain seeds we gather
薄言有之　　　　Gather them for keeps

采采芣苢　　　　Plantain seeds we gather
薄言掇之　　　　Pick them up quickly
采采芣苢　　　　Plantain seeds we gather
薄言捋之　　　　Shake them down plenty

采采芣苢　　　　Plantain seeds we gather
薄言袺之　　　　Fill them up in our skirt folds
采采芣苢　　　　Plantain seeds we gather
薄言襭之　　　　Bring them home bagful

邶風・靜女　　　*Songs of* **Bei** – **Quiet Maiden**

靜女其姝　　　A maiden quiet fair and tall
俟我於城隅　　She waits to meet me by the city wall
愛而不見　　　Evasive her love for me is not seen readily
搔首踟躕　　　Scratching my head I approach her awkwardly

靜女其孌　　　My quiet maiden so cute
貽我彤管　　　She gives me a crimson reed as lute
彤管有煒　　　The crimson reed makes me happy and bright
說懌女美　　　I love both my maiden and her reed so fine

自牧歸荑　　　My maiden returns delightfully from the mead
洵美且異　　　She gives me a beautiful reed unique
匪女之為美　　'Tis precious not for its rarity
美人之貽　　　'Tis my love's gift for eternity

邶風 · 燕燕	*Songs of Bei* – **Parting Sparrows**
燕燕于飛	A pair of swallows fly
差池其羽	Chasing one another front and behind
之子于歸	My sister is marrying far away
遠送于野	I see her off on her way
瞻望弗及	When I see her no more
泣涕如雨	My tears like rain heavily fall
燕燕于飛	A pair of swallows fly
頡之頏之	From the ground they soar high
之子于歸	My sister is marrying far away
遠于將之	I accompany her all the way
瞻望弗及	When her image disappeared
佇立以泣	I stand still my face washed by tears
燕燕于飛	A pair of swallows fly
下上其音	Their songs reverberate far and nigh
之子于歸	My sister is marrying far away
遠送于南	I see her off at South Gate
瞻望弗及	When I watch and see her no more
實勞我心	I grieve my heart is very sore
仲氏任只	My sister is capable and responsible
其心塞淵	Her thoughts and feelings considerable
終溫且惠	She is loving and gentle
淑慎其身	So kind and so noble
先君之思	Do remember our late father so kind
以勖寡人	She left words for me to follow behind

邶風 · 凱風   *Songs of Bei* – **Mother as Gentle Breeze**

凱風自南   From south come breezes gentle
吹彼棘心   Warming jujube trees little by little
棘心夭夭   The trees thrive giving fruits many
母氏劬勞   Our mother toils and nurtures us diligently

凱風自南   From south come breezes gentle
吹彼棘薪   Mature trees offer firewood plenty
母氏聖善   Our mother understands and lets us free
我無令人   We feel sorry good kids we could not be

爰有寒泉   Love from a cool spring steady
在浚之下   Its source in Jun County
有子七人   We are seven brothers strong
母氏勞苦   Mother toils for us on and on

睍睆黃鳥   Yellow birds sing merrily
載好其音   Their songs comfort us tenderly
有子七人   Alas we seven brothers cannot bring
莫慰母心   Comfort and songs for mother to sing

| 邶風 · 谷風 | *Songs of Bei* – Voice of a Rejected Wife |
| (節選) | (selected part) |

習習谷風	Gusts in the valley rampant
以陰以雨	Clouds grey and rain incessant
黽勉同心	I try my best to keep you and I in unity
不宜有怒	Not to allow anger to interfere life in simplicity
採葑採菲	Like gathering a radish root and all
無以下體	Root and leave together grow tall
德音莫違	Remember our vows together
及爾同死	To grow old till death divides us forever

行道遲遲	Slowly I will be on my way
中心有違	My heart aches as I sway
不遠伊邇	I shall not be too far away
薄送我畿	Will you bid me adieu at the doorway
誰謂荼苦	Who says tea broths are bitter
其甘如薺	To me they are sweet as warm comforter
宴爾新昏	Seeing you two sweet on wedding day
如兄如弟	Like loving siblings naturally affectionate

邶風 · 二子乘舟　　*Songs of* **Bei – My Sons on Boat**

二子乘舟　　My two sons board on a boat
汎汎其景　　Rapidly downstream they float
願言思子　　How I miss them seeing them no more
中心養養　　My heart quickens like torrents pour

二子乘舟　　My two sons board on a boat
汎汎其逝　　Swiftly in a distance they float
願言思子　　How I worry and deeply worry
不瑕有害　　Let no danger awaits them for company

衞風 · 河廣　　*Songs of* **Wei – River Wide**

誰謂河廣　　Who believes the Yellow River is too wide
一葦杭之　　On a reef raft you reach the opposite side
誰謂宋遠　　Who says Song is far and unreachable
跂予望之　　You just have to watch it on tip-toe

誰謂河廣　　Who says the Yellow River is too wide
曾不容刀　　Crossing it takes only a boat ride
誰謂宋遠　　Who believes the land of Song lies too far away
曾不崇朝　　I can reach it in half a day

衛風 · 木瓜

Songs of Wei – Papaya

投我以木瓜	She sends me a papaya for food
報之以瓊琚	A green jade I give her for good
匪報也	'Tis not for retribution
永以為好也	But to generate enduring affection
投我以木桃	She sends me a peach for fruit
報之以瓊瑤	A pure jade I give her for good
匪報也	'Tis not for retribution
永以為好也	But for lasting relation
投我以木李	She gives me a plum to eat
報之以瓊玖	Jasper chains I have her worn on her feet
匪報也	It is not an exchange of gifts
永以為好也	But for love firm and never shift

王風 · 君子于役　　*Songs from the capital* – **My Man Serves His State**

君子于役	My man is away serving his state
不知其期	I know not how long he will be away
曷至哉	Or whence he will be on homeward way
雞棲於塒	Good fowls roost in bushy nests
日之夕矣	The sun sets west
羊牛下來	Sheep and cows are home to rest
君子于役	Knowing my man is away
如之何勿思	How can I not miss him night and day
君子于役	My man is away serving his state
不日不月	I know not until what month and day
曷其有佸	Or when we will be united again
雞棲於桀	Good fowls roost in homely nests
日之夕矣	When the sun is already set
羊牛下括	Sheep and cows are home to rest
君子于役	My man is away serving his state
苟無饑渴	Spare him from hunger or thirst I pray

鄭風 · 女曰雞鳴

Songs of Zheng – Love Abides

女曰雞鳴	Hark crows the cock maiden says
士曰昧旦	'Tis not yet dawn man says
子興視夜	Why not rise to watch the night sky
明星有爛	And see stars shining bright
將翱將翔	Wild geese and ducks soar and fly
弋鳧與雁	I will bring them down from high
弋言加之	Shooting games you are good
與子宜之	Cooking them I'll make fine food
宜言飲酒	Together let us share this wine
與子偕老	Together we will grow old so fine
琴瑟在御	With zither by our side
莫不靜好	Harmony we shall abide
知子之來之	I know you will tenderly care
雜佩以贈之	Pearls are yours to wear
知子之順之	I know you will willingly obey
雜佩以問之	How could pearls ever repay
知子之好之	I know your committal love
雜佩以報之	Nothing more shall I ask

鄭風 · 有女同車　　*Songs for Zheng* – Riding with a Maiden Fair

有女同車	Riding with me my fair lady
顏如舜華	Her face shines like a floral glory
將翱將翔	We ride happily as if in flight
佩玉瓊琚	Pendants amend her lovely glittering bright
彼美孟姜	A beautiful girl from the Jiang family
洵美且都	Graceful and elegant people envy
有女同行	We go forward to the same destination
顏如舜英	Her face blossoms in fascination
將翱將翔	We walked and hopped hands glasping tight
佩玉將將	Her pendants dangle like music chime
彼美孟姜	A graceful girl going quietly
德音不忘	I vow to love you eternally

鄭風 · 蘀兮

Songs for Zheng – Song We Together Sing

蘀兮蘀兮	Leaves how ye yellow
風其吹女	Leaves oh leaves blow
叔兮伯兮	You dance with winds so
倡予和女	Cousins young and old
蘀兮蘀兮	Leaves how ye yellow
風其漂女	Leaves oh leaves blow
叔兮伯兮	You dance with winds so
倡予要女	Cousins all in company

鄭風 · 東門之墠

Songs for Zheng – Lover's Murmur

東門之墠	Wide on East Gate grounds
茹藘在阪	Beautiful wild flowers abound
其室則邇	Your home is so close to me
其人甚遠	Far away you always seem to be

東門之栗	Besides the chestnut tree by East Gate
有踐家室	Lives a family not so great
豈不爾思	How can I not yearn for you dear
子不我即	Why would you not come to love me here

鄭風 · 子衿　　　　　*Songs for Zheng* – a Scholar

青青子衿　　　　　Your identity marked by a shirt blue
悠悠我心　　　　　Day and night I think of you
縱我不往　　　　　Although to reach you I'm not free
子寧不嗣音　　　　Why do you not send words to me

青青子佩　　　　　Your identity marked by a jade belt
悠悠我思　　　　　Is my thinking for you felt
縱我不往　　　　　Although with you I cannot be
子寧不來　　　　　Why don't you try to see me

挑兮達兮　　　　　How urgent I long for company
在城闕兮　　　　　I pace on the city wall longingly
一日不見　　　　　When for a day I see you not dear
如三月兮　　　　　It feels like three months to me

檜風・匪風　　　*Songs of Gui* – **Travelling East**

匪風發兮	Winds a fierce gust
匪車偈兮	Carriage runs flying fast
顧瞻周道	I look back the road travelled
中心怛兮	My heart sick and sorrow
匪風飄兮	Winds a whirling blast
匪車嘌兮	Carriage runs wild fast
顧瞻周道	I look back the road travelled
中心吊兮	My heart grieves unusual
誰能亨魚	Who can cook a fish for me
溉之釜鬵	I will fetch the cookeries
誰將西歸	Who is going back west
懷之好音	Please relay home a safety message

豳風 · 伐柯　　　*Songs of* Bin – **To Make an Axe Handle**

伐柯如何	To make an axe handle
匪斧不克	One needs an axe with handle
取妻如何	To marry a good wife
匪媒不得	I need a betrothal
伐柯伐柯	To hew and to carve
其則不遠	The model is in my grasp
我覯之子	To know my newly-wed
籩豆有踐	Appreciate food on the table set

豳風・七月   *Songs of* Bin – Peasant Life
（節選）   (selected part)

六月食鬱及薁	In the sixth moon plums and grapes come along
七月烹葵及菽	In the seventh we cook beans and mallows so fond
八月剝棗	In the eighth moon we collect dates to treat
十月獲稻	In the tenth we harvest rice fragrant and neat
為此春酒	We use rice to brew wine the best
以介眉壽	To wish our elders long life happiest
七月食瓜	In the seventh moon we eat melons every day
八月斷壺	In the eighth with gourds containers we make
九月叔苴	In the ninth we put hemp seeds away for the year
採荼薪樗	And cut firewood and gather tea leaves
食我農夫	These are provisions of farmers as we wish

魏風・十畝之間   Mulberries Grown on Our Ten Acre Field

十畝之間兮	Mulberries grown on our ten acre field
桑者閒閒兮	Our planters are able and skilled
行與子還兮	Home we go feeling fulfilled
十畝之外兮	Beyond our fields of mulberries
桑者泄泄兮	Our planters feel merry
行與子逝兮	Please come to my home happy

雅
Odes

大雅・綿	***Book of Epics* – The Continued Migration in 1325 BC**
（節選）	**(selected part)**

周原膴膴	The plain of Zhou fertile and a huge sweep
堇荼如飴	Tea plants are seen their leaves sweet
爰始爰謀	He asked his followers to speak their minds
爰契我龜	They used tortoise shells to implore the divine
曰止曰時	You can happily settle the gods say
築室于茲	And build homes here to create a new age
乃慰乃止	Together they settled in the land
乃左乃右	And strived to cultivate and to plan
乃疆乃理	They surveyed the area and divide and share
乃宣乃畝	And cultivated and dug ditches to irrigate
自西徂東	From east to west a fine farmland became a reality
周爰執事	The whole community got busy to promote productivity

⋯⋯

小雅・甫田之什・鴛鴦
Love Birds

鴛鴦于飛	Love birds fly in pairs no separation
畢之羅之	We catch them home to signal good fortune
君子萬年	To wish you live long and healthy
福祿宜之	Together in caring and lasting company
鴛鴦在梁	On the river dam love birds rest
戢其左翼	With beaks tugged in feathers they nap
君子萬年	We wish you to live long and healthy
宜其遐福	Young and old in a loving family
乘馬在廄	In the stable steeds are kept
摧之秣之	With grain and hay fully fed
君子萬年	May the master live in longevity
福祿艾之	Blessed with good luck and family
乘馬在廄	The carriage steeds are ready to go
秣之摧之	Well fed and trained they willingly go
君子萬年	May the bride come home safely
福祿綏之	Husband and wife grow old and happy

小雅 · 采薇（節選）

Gathering Ferns (selected part)

昔我往矣
楊柳依依
今我來思
雨雪霏霏
行道遲遲
載渴載饑
我心傷悲
莫知我哀

When I left here
Willows lingered and shed tears
Now I've come back
Rain and snow seen everywhere
Long long have been those days
Suffering thirst and hunger always
Grief in me launch and o'erflow
Who knows who cares to know

小雅 · 鴻鴈之什 · 鶴鳴
Cranes Cry

鶴鳴于九皋	From a distant marsh cranes cry
聲聞于野	Their voices heard in the wild
魚潛在淵	In the deep fishes hide
或在于渚	They also swim around the isle
樂彼之園	Happily this garden is mine
爰有樹檀	Shady sandal wood trees stand high
其下維蘀	Fallen leaves beneath smell fine
他山之石	Mineral rocks from yonder hills valuable
可以為錯	They can be turned into gem cutters useful
鶴鳴于九皋	From a distant marsh cranes cry
聲聞于天	Their songs heard in high sky
魚在于渚	In the shallows fishes glide
或潛在淵	Down adjacent deeps they leisurely lie
樂彼之園	Happily this garden is mine
爰有樹檀	Elegant sandal wood trees standing formal
其下維穀	Below are mulberries red and eatable
他山之石	Gem stones from yonder hills memorable
可以攻玉	They can be made into jade jewels

小雅・南有嘉魚之什・湛露
Heavy Dew

湛湛露斯	Dews heavy cool and nice
匪陽不晞	They disappear after sunrise
厭厭夜飲	We feast and drink all night
不醉無歸	Drunk we go home fine

湛湛露斯	Dews heavy cool and nice
在彼豐草	They help grass to thrive
厭厭夜飲	We feast and drink all night
在宗載考	In the temple our ancestors abide

湛湛露斯	Dews heavy cool and nice
在彼杞棘	Date trees and willows thrive
顯允君子	Our guests noble and gentle
莫不令德	They are virtuous and honourable

其桐其椅	The forest contains plane and jujube
其實離離	Their fruits juicy and free
豈弟君子	Our guests are happy and at ease
莫不令儀	Drunk we are merry and at peace

小雅 · 南有嘉魚之什 · 菁菁者莪
Excellence in School

菁菁者莪	Finest tall grass grow lushly
在彼中阿	Along the mountain valley
既見君子	When I see these fine personalities
樂且有儀	Happy showing propriety
菁菁者莪	Finest tall grass grow lushly
在彼中沚	On the river isle vividly
既見君子	When I see these fine personalities
我心則喜	My delights are many
菁菁者莪	Finest tall grass grow lushly
在彼中陵	On the hills wooingly
既見君子	When I see these fine personalities
錫我百朋	Good friendship in bounty
汎汎楊舟	A boat of willow easily floats
載沉載浮	Following waves high and low
既見君子	When I see these fine personalities
我心則休	My mind peaceful and happy

小雅 · 魚藻之什 · 隰桑
Mulberry Tree

隰桑有阿	The lowland mulberry a beauty
其葉有難	Leaves lush and plenty
既見君子	Behold my man gentle
其樂如何	I am happy and settled

隰桑有阿	The lowland mulberry a beauty
其葉有沃	Leaves green like water flows wavy
既見君子	Behold the man of my dream
雲何不樂	My feelings delight and keen

隰桑有阿	The lowland mulberry a beauty
其葉有幽	Leaves grow thick and dark daily
既見君子	Behold my man extraordinaire
德音孔膠	My heart hung dangling in the air

心乎愛矣	I love him more than I know
遐不謂矣	Why do I not tell him so
中心藏之	Better keep it deep in my soul
何日忘之	To rejoice and grow

大雅・生民之什・泂酌
Fetching Water

泂酌彼行	Water fetched from afar
潦挹彼注茲	Pour into vessels to carry here
可以餴饎	Millets and rice steam cooked
豈弟君子	Our Prince understands people's outlooks
民之父母	Like a father he helps them realize hopes

泂酌彼行	Water fetched from afar
潦挹彼注茲	Poured into vessels to carry here
可以濯罍	Gold vases are polished clean for the rites
豈弟君子	Our Prince understands people's needs
民之攸歸	People revere him and his advice

泂酌彼行	Water fetched from afar
潦挹彼注茲	Poured into vessels to carry here
可以濯溉	Water plenty to irrigate growth in fields
豈弟君子	As our Prince's affection to ease ills
民之攸墍	Like water we live here with satisfaction

周頌 · 清廟之什 · 思文
Hymns of Zhou – To the Corn Lord

思文後稷	O Lord of Corn on high
克配彼天	Your deeds signal god's advice
立我烝民	You keep us in sufficiency
莫匪爾極	Everyone enjoys your benevolence
貽我來牟	You provide us with seeds of grain
帝命率育	Providence helps us consume and train
無此疆爾界	Growing knows no territorial border
陳常于時夏	We all thrive in good order

周頌・閔予小子之什・敬之
Respect with Humility

敬之敬之	Respect and revere
天維顯思	He has Heaven's ways and sensibility
命不易哉	Opportunities slip by easily
無曰高高在上	Even the gods abide by this
陟降厥士	He rules over our rise and fall
日監在茲	And watches how things go one and all
維予小子	Behold a young king here I stand
不聰敬止	I revere wise people with skilful hands
日就月將	And watches events evolve in days hence
學有緝熙于光明	I will learn to do what is right
佛時仔肩	Assist me to do my duties efficiently
示我顯德行	Show me virtue and dignity

周頌 · 天作

Zhou Hymns – Sky Mount

天作高山	This high mount is heavenly sent
大王荒之	Ancestor kings tilled it to make land
彼作矣	Houses built
文王康之	King Wen praises folks so skilled
彼徂矣	More people came to settle
岐有夷之行	Roads and paths level to go
子孫保之	Future generations will thrive for sure

周頌 · 有客   *Zhou* Hymns – Welcoming Guests

有客有客	We welcome our guests alight
亦白其馬	They come on steeds white
有萋有且	A large noble company
敦琢其旅	Many wearing colourful accessories

有客宿宿	They mean to stay overnight
有客信信	We have them stay many nights
言授之縶	Ropes are well provided
以縶其馬	Steeds harnessed right

薄言追之	We wish them well bidding adieu
左右綏之	Helping them readying to leave
既有淫威	How noble our guests be
降福孔夷	How we wish them a pleasant journey

周頌 · 絲衣　　Zhou Hymns – Formal Gown

絲衣其紑　　　Silk robes colourful and bright
載弁俅俅　　　Noble caps donned for the rite
自堂徂基　　　We gather before the temple hall
自羊徂牛　　　Sacrificial sheep and cows and all

鼐鼎及鼒　　　Urns and tripods arranged fine
兕觥其觩　　　Rhino horn vessels filled with wine
旨酒思柔　　　Ah how plentiful wines in barrels
不吳不敖　　　We drank joyfully forgetting sorrow
胡考之休　　　To wish gods and people eternal

屈原 Qu Yuan (332 BC－296 BC)

九歌・湘夫人　　Madam Xiang River

帝子降兮北渚	On Northern Islet you descend my dear
目眇眇兮愁予	Burdened by grief my eyes can't see clear
裊裊兮秋風	Ceaselessly blow the autumn breezes
洞庭波兮木葉下	On Dongting Lake flow fallen leaves
登白蘋兮騁望	Standing on White Clover I gaze afar
與佳期兮夕張	Awaiting to meet you at twilight hour
鳥何萃兮蘋中	Could birds freely glide amid dense reeds
罾何為兮木上	What can nets do amid trees
沅有茝兮澧有蘭	In green creeks orchids thrive so meek
思公子兮未敢言	I pine for thee daring not to speak
荒忽兮遠望	Looking yonder I reach for my love of old
觀流水兮潺湲	I see but ripples gently flow
麋何食兮庭中	How could deer find food in closed doors
蛟何為兮水裔	What could dragons do when grounded ashore
朝馳餘馬兮江皋	Along riverside at dawn I hurry my steed
夕濟兮西澨	At dusk to ride the rapids I heed
聞佳人兮召予	Answering your call I've come today
將騰駕兮偕逝	Together we ride on clouds away
築室兮水中	In midstream a palace shall be made
葺之兮荷蓋	Its roof shall have lotus weaves for shade
蓀壁兮紫壇	Up its purple terrace thymes will wall

播芳椒兮成堂	Fragrant pepper plants will spread in the hall
桂棟兮蘭橑	Cassia pillars will stand like orchids upright
辛夷楣兮藥房	And rooms smell herbal fragrance of clover white
罔薜荔兮為帷	I shall make ivy weaves for window screens
擗蕙櫋兮既張	And cover the floor with leaves green
白玉兮為鎮	Cornerstones shall be made of white jade
疏石蘭兮為芳	In the air orchid fragrance shall never fade
芷葺兮荷屋	In lotus houses let vetch be found
繚之兮杜衡	With fresh azaleas blooming year-round
合百草兮實庭	Let the courtyard be filled with herbs of various kinds
建芳馨兮廡門	And corridors be frequented by learned minds
女嶷繽兮並迎	I will invite the gods of mounts nine measures high
靈之來兮如雲	To set my soul free aboard clouds in the sky
捐餘袂兮江中	I jump into the water awake from my dream
遺餘褋兮澧浦	With clothes sleeves and all in the stream
搴汀洲兮杜若	I pick sweet flowers from the landing in the bay
將以遺褋兮遠者	To comfort whoever living far away
時不可兮驟得	Time lost can't be regained free
聊逍遙兮容與	Let my heart roam intensely feeling for thee

九章 · 橘頌   Ode to Orange (A Gentleman)

後皇嘉樹	A blessed tree between heaven and earth
橘徠服兮	The noble orange stands
受命不遷	Destined to thrive in the south
生南國兮	'Tis not intended for any other land
深固難徙	Roots firmly entrenched
更壹志兮	Your will a single strand
綠葉素榮	Green leaves enshrine glorious blooms
紛其可喜兮	A sight in colourful beam
曾枝剡棘	On branches grow protruding thorns
圓果摶兮	Glittering round fruits adorn
青黃雜糅	Green and yellow a mix of harmony
文章爛兮	Flowery words sing verses of fine melody
精色內白	External colours fine
類任道兮	Internal purity divine
紛縕宜修	A thousand charms inculcated
姱而不醜兮	Not a single shade of ugliness imbued
嗟爾幼志	You are out of the ordinary
有以異兮	Even young you are exemplary
獨立不遷	Independent will so free
豈不可喜兮	We watch in glee

深固難徙　　　　　　Roots firmly entrenched
廓其無求兮　　　　　You seek nothing unneeded
蘇世獨立　　　　　　You proudly guard your virtue and vision
橫而不流兮　　　　　Distancing vulgarity in all seasons
閉心自慎　　　　　　Discreet and cautiousness you keep
不終失過兮　　　　　No wrongs could you creep
秉德無私　　　　　　Virtuous and selfless
參天地兮　　　　　　In heaven as on earth you show uniqueness

原歲並謝　　　　　　Willingly fade in year's end
與長友兮　　　　　　I should like to be your friend
淑離不淫　　　　　　Fair and upright
梗其有理兮　　　　　Your trunk grows right
年歲雖少　　　　　　Your age though few
可師長兮　　　　　　Even old folks may learn from you
行比伯夷　　　　　　An example so inspiring
置以為像兮　　　　　All humble folks admiring

九歌 · 雲中君　To the Cloud Lord

浴蘭湯兮沐芳	Perfumed in an orchid bath you appear in view
華採衣兮若英	Your clothes brilliant in varying hues
靈連蜷兮既留	With fleecy locks you race to reach unlimited heights
爛昭昭兮未央	In colourful splendour you skilfully paint the morning sky
謇將憺兮壽宮	Your many radiant faces thrive at high noon
與日月兮齊光	Your whiteness pure and bright matching the sun and moon
龍駕兮帝服	By your side the dragon glides in formidable attire
聊翱遊兮周章	Your wandering movements so free in spirit we admire
靈皇皇兮既降	In silvery drops you descend on mother earth in rain
猋遠舉兮雲中	On wind's wings you rise ever so high again
覽冀洲兮有餘	Seeing all continents at ease in a single sweep
橫四海兮焉窮	You float across the four seas to survey their deeps
思夫君兮太息	To show my longing for you I could but sigh
極勞心兮忡忡	My heart belongs to you however high you fly

漢朝

HAN DYNASTY

(206 BC–220 AD)

項羽 Xiang Yu (232 BC—202 BC)

垓下歌

Final Song

力拔山兮氣蓋世	My will transcend I can pull up a mountain with my might
時不利兮騅不逝	When fortune wanes even my steed refuses to fight
騅不逝兮可奈何	I care not if the steed is afraid to die
虞兮虞兮奈若何	I love to care if you know my mind

古詩十九首 Nineteen Ancient Poems
（節選） (selected part)

(I) **(I)**

行行重行行	On and on away You Go
與君生別離	Separated more and more we both
相去萬餘里	With you living ten thousand *li* away
各在天一涯	We are each on a different geo-sway
道路阻且長	The road between us is blocked and far
會面安可知	We can't tell whence again we could be together
胡馬依北風	Hungarian steeds love to gallop in northern winds cold
越鳥巢南枝	Southern birds choose to nest on warm trees old
相去日已遠	Each day farther from me you stay
衣帶日已緩	My clothes get more loose around the waist
浮雲蔽白日	Floating clouds veil the sun during the day
遊子不顧返	My wandering husband returns home in no haste
思君令人老	Yearning for you I become old speedily
歲月忽已晚	And my days and years get fewer steadily
棄捐勿復道	Please say not you are forsaking me
努力加餐飯	Remember to eat well and stay healthy

(II)

青青河畔草
鬱鬱園中柳
盈盈樓上女
皎皎當窗牖
娥娥紅粉妝
纖纖出素手
昔為倡家女
今為蕩子婦
蕩子行不歸
空床難獨守

(II)

Green Green Is the Grass by Riverside
Lush lush the garden willows stand with pride
Fair fair is the maiden on the veranda up high
She appears by the window her skin so white
Pink pink is her dress bright as she stands
Stretching out gracefully her slender hands
Born from a mother in a low vocation
Now a wife of a loiterer with no fixed location
Away he wanders with no care for home
She grieves in her empty bed alone

(VI)

涉江采芙蓉
蘭澤多芳草
采之欲遺誰
所思在遠道
還顧望舊鄉
長路漫浩浩
同心而離居
憂傷以終老

(VI)

I Gather Lotus Blooms Wading through the Stream
Fragrant plants fill the thriving swamp in beam
To whom I wish to present this beautiful bouquet
My love who is roaming so far away
Towards my old village I turn my eyes
The way back there is far and wide
In separation our hearts are same as one whole
In grief we will console each other till we grow old

(XIII)

驅車上東門
遙望郭北墓
白楊何蕭蕭
松柏夾廣路
下有陳死人
杳杳即長暮
潛寐黃泉下
千載永不寤
浩浩陰陽移
年命如朝露
人生忽如寄
壽無金石固
萬歲更相送
賢聖莫能度
服食求神仙
多為藥所誤
不如飲美酒
被服紈與素

(XIII)

I Drive My Chariot up Eastern Gate

And look north to gaze far at the graves

Solemn aspens stand guard and shade

Pines and cedars line up the broad way

Beneath laid the remains of people who died long ago

Timeless they stayed in a permanent darkhole

Resting in sleep they stay in the Yellow Spring below

For thousands of years they don't wake or know

Grand are the transpositions of day and night

One's fleeting life transpires like morning dew

Life is but temporal transition

While longevity last shorter than rocks and metals

Living to a hundred years people still say adieu

Even saints and sages are not exceptional

If by eating you seek immortality

There is no elixir for infinity

It is better to enjoy the best of wine

And dress in satin and silk as you like

(XV)

(XV)

生年不滿百	People Live Not a Hundred Years Long
常懷千歲憂	They worry how life goes a thousand year strong
晝短苦夜長	Days are too short as nights too long
何不秉燭遊	To enjoy life why not light candles to play along
為樂當及時	Seize the moment to be fun and gay
何能待來茲	Leave the future alone however it may
愚者愛惜費	Only fools choose to live frugally
但為後世嗤	And keep their wealth for posterity
仙人王子喬	The immortals may like to level with mankind sometime
難可與等期	To ascend to heaven is difficult as to leave earth behind

十五從軍征　　To Arms at Fifteen

十五從軍征	At fifteen I was drafted to fight in a war
八十始得歸	Coming home my age is of four-score
道逢鄉裏人	On the way I ask a man from my village I used to know
家中有阿誰	Who are still living inside my family window
遙看是君家	O'er there he pointed you will find your home
松柏冢纍纍	Resting amid pines and cypresses are your ancestors' tombs
兔從狗竇入	Inside my empty house I see a hare entering the dog hole
雉從樑上飛	While pheasants fly over the roof to and fro
中庭生旅穀	Wild grain stalks cover the central court densely
井上生旅葵	Around the well mellows thrive happily
烹穀持作飯	I take some spring grain to cook for rice
採葵持作羹	And boil mellows for a gruel suffice
羹飯一時熟	Both rice and gruel make up the finest home fare
不知貽阿誰	But there is no one here with me to share
出門東向望	Facing east outside my door I look for an answer clear
淚落沾我衣	My face furrow my clothes wet with tear

劉徹（漢武帝）Liu Che (156 BC—87 BC)

落葉哀蟬曲　Song of Fallen Leaves and Plaintive Cicada

羅袂兮無聲	Her silky sleeves rustle without sound
玉墀兮塵生	The marble steps gather dust around
虛房冷而寂寞	Empty is her bower cold and dreary
落葉依於重扃	Fallen leaves outside pile up in heaps hilly
望彼美之女兮安得	How I look for you my love only in vain
感餘心之未寧	How could my heart rest and be rid of pain

秋風辭

秋風起兮白雲飛
草木黃落兮雁南歸
蘭有秀兮菊有芳
懷佳人兮不能忘

泛樓船兮濟汾河
橫中流兮揚素波
簫鼓鳴兮發棹歌
歡樂極兮哀情多
少壯幾時兮奈老何

Song of Autumn Wind

Autumn winds rise to help white clouds glide

Yellow grass wither to send geese southward fly

Orchids display their elegance and mum's sweet scent

My love how I pine for you when you are out of sight

On a bark to cross the river I hurry to be with you

At midstream ripples turn white and keep my boat behind

The rhythm of drums and pipes sound the rowing song

When spent excitement subsides as sad feelings rise

The time of youth will cede as old age surely arrive

蘇武 Su Wu (140 BC—60 BC)

留別妻　Adieu Dear Wife

結髮為夫妻	We vowed to be husband and wife for life
恩愛兩不疑	Our loving relationship is true without guess
歡娛在今夕	Let's love one another even more tonight
嬿婉及良時	Let's make the best use of time for ecstasy
征夫懷往路	To embark on the far off journey I have no fancy
起視應何其	I get up from bed to check the hour of night frequently
參辰皆已沒	Stars in the dark night are giving way for dawn to be
去去從此辭	And I must leave home now and part with thee
行役在戰場	From this moment on my life will be in battle ground
相見未有期	We must believe firmly our reunion will come around
握手一長歎	Holding your hand I could but sigh and again sigh
淚為生別滋	Letting go I pledge to keep our love in mind
努力愛春華	Let's do our best to keep alive our love for spring
莫忘歡樂時	Let's remember the happy times our togetherness bring
生當復來歸	Whence alive and sound I'll be with you certainly
死當長相思	Even in death our souls will be one eternally

曹操 Cao Cao (155－220)

觀滄海　　　　　Watching the Sea

東臨碣石　　　　From the Rocky Hill on eastern shore
以觀滄海　　　　I stand to watch the sea in awe
水何澹澹　　　　How the waves rock the beaches boisterous
山島竦峙　　　　How island mountains stand bold and marvellous

樹木叢生　　　　Trees of varying sizes grow competing for the sun
百草豐茂　　　　A hundred species of grass thrive green as one
秋風蕭瑟　　　　Whence the autumn wind blows bleak
洪波湧起　　　　Billows surge to show thunderous feats

日月之行　　　　The sun and moon revolve in good time daily
若出其中　　　　They rise and fall as if from the deep
星漢燦爛　　　　Stars from the Milky Way twinkle ever so gaily
若出其裏　　　　They always return to sea to sleep

幸甚至哉　　　　How grateful I feel to be here
歌以詠志　　　　I sing this song for memory to adhere

龜雖壽
（節選）

Tortoise Longevity
(selected part)

神龜雖壽　　Sacred tortoise live their lives long
猶有竟時　　They will not go against nature but die along
騰蛇乘霧　　Free spirit dragons rise above the clouds to glide
終為土灰　　In death they will disintegrate and return to earth to hide

老驥伏櫪　　An old horse takes its respite in its stall
志在千里　　Its determination remains to gallop speedily and tall
烈士暮年　　A brave man knows his years in decline
壯心不已　　His aspirations remain bold and high

短歌行　　　　A Short Song on the Death of My Father

仰瞻幃幕	I lift my eyes to see the screens
俯察幾筵	I lower my eyes his table is so clean
其物如故	Everything is intact as before
其人不存	Alas the master is here no more
神靈倏忽	All of a sudden his soul has flown
棄我遐遷	I am fatherless all alone
靡瞻靡恃	Who shall I look up to lead me grow
泣涕漣漣	I weep my tears incessantly flow
呦呦遊鹿	Deer bleat hither and yonder
銜草鳴麑	They nurse the young they care
翩翩飛鳥	Birds fly here and there
挾子巢棲	They protect their young in the nest
我獨孤煢	I alone am desolate and in despair
懷此百離	Severed from a father I so revered
憂心孔疚	Deep in my heart my grief overflow
莫我能知	A hurt no one but I can know
人亦有言	Behold the effects of change had been told
憂令人老	That sorrow makes us old
嗟我白髮	Behold how my hair is greying in haste
生一何早	Is it not too early for a man of my age
長吟永歎	Loudly I wail and bleakly I sigh
懷我聖考	To my father's sudden decease I inquire
曰仁者壽	They say longevity favours those who are kind
胡不是保	Why should my father die

曹植 Cao Zhi (192—232)

七哀詩   Lament

明月照高樓	Playful moonlight streams across the tower
流光正徘徊	Her soft light lingers on the tower
上有愁思婦	Wiltingly a lady lets out tender sighs
悲歎有餘哀	Lamenting heart-rending pain she cries
借問歎者誰	Who could be here in such ruth
言是宕子妻	Forsaken a love without proof
君行逾十年	Away you have been for scores of years
孤妾常獨棲	Left behind alone I live with but tears
君若清路塵	You rise like upward dust on your way
妾若濁水泥	Like muddy water I still stay
浮沉各異勢	Swim or sink we separately remain
會合何時諧	Whence we will be united again
願為西南風	How I would like to be the southwest wind
長逝入君懷	Sailing across the land to fall into your arm's wing
君懷良不開	Where your embrace is kept in unfold
賤妾當何依	Where and what could I rely to hold

七步詩　　Written on Seven Paces by Demand

煮豆燃豆其	Beans weep boiling in pot
豆在釜中泣	Being cooked fired by its own stalk
本是同根生	Growing up we stemmed from the same root
相煎何太急	Providence allows no haste you have me cooked

贈白馬王彪　　To My Brother

丈夫志四海	A man's vision extends to the four seas
萬里猶比鄰	Ten thousand miles away from home is neighbourly
恩愛苟不虧	When love is felt deep and brotherly
在遠分日親	However far the separation is like being together daily

六朝
SIX DYNASTIES
(265–618)

陶潛 Tao Qian (365–427)

擬挽歌辭 (I)

有生必有死
早終非命促
昨暮同為人
今旦在鬼錄
魂氣散何之
枯形寄空木
嬌兒索父啼
良友撫我哭
得失不復知
是非安能覺
千秋萬歲後
誰知榮與辱
但恨在世時
飲酒不得足

Elegy Song (I)

To live is to accept death in peace
The day will come when I finally breath
Last night we are together as man
This morn we are in Ghost Registrar's hand
Whither I wonder will go my soul
In a decaying box my body is a load
My children seek their father in grief
Friends see my corps cry and heave
Loss or gain I no longer care
Rights and wrongs not my affair
After ten thousand years have passed away
Who will know my glory or disgrace
I regret while living still
Mellow brews I fail to drink my fill

歸園田居 (I)　Back to Nature (I)

少無適俗韻	In youth I had little interest in worldly affairs
性本愛丘山	By nature hills and rills I care
誤落塵網中	Foolishly I later fell in mundane snares
一去三十年	And got entangled for thirty long years
羈鳥戀舊林	A bird in cage yearns to return to the woods
池魚思故淵	A fish in tank remembers its river roots
開荒南野際	In tilting the southern land into cultivating fields
守拙歸園田	Back to nature I happily feel
方宅十餘畝	A score of acres make up my estate fine
草屋八九間	There I build cots of thatched roofs eight or nine
榆柳蔭後簷	Tall elms and willows give shade to my eaves
桃李羅堂前	In the front peach and plum trees supply fruits easy
曖曖遠人村	A neighbouring village can be seen in the far distance
依依墟裏煙	Further in the market evening smokes waft on occasions
狗吠深巷中	Dogs are heard in the deep alleys now and then
雞鳴桑樹巔	Amid mulberry trees cocks crow to please their hens
戶庭無塵雜	Not a dust should my courtyard be intruded
虛室有餘閒	Plenty of leisure fills my unoccupied rooms
久在樊籠裏	After long years of abject servitude
復得返自然	Back to Nature I call this home

(III)

種豆南山下
草盛豆苗稀
晨興理荒穢
帶月荷鋤歸
道狹草木長
夕露沾我衣
衣沾不足惜
但使願無違

(III)

At the foot of the southern hills growing beans I try
Bean stalks soon wilt while grass thrive
To clear the weeds I early rise
Hoe on shoulder I return home by moonlight
Narrow are the paths where shrubs grow tall
My clothes are soaked when heavy dews fall
It matters not if I'm wet
So long as my life goals are met

飲酒詩二十首
(V)

結廬在人境
而無車馬喧
問君何能爾
心遠地自偏
採菊東籬下
悠然見南山
山氣日夕佳
飛鳥相與還
此中有真意
欲辨已忘言

Drink (20 Poems)
(V)

Amid man's haunted environs I have my chalet
Where noises of hoofs and wheels are kept away
Asked how such a place could have serenity
A detached mind can create peace naturally
At dawn I pick daisies by the fence at will
And watch the beauty of the southern hill
Whence the fresh mountain air is here to stay
Birds leave and return to their nests day after day
Herein rests the true meaning of life
If need be told no words could express my mind

無名氏 Anonymous (Six Dynasties)

敕勒歌   **Shepherd Song**

敕勒川	Along the Li Lei Rill
陰山下	Beneath the Yin Hill
天似穹廬	Like a huge cover the sky shields
籠蓋四野	While land within earth's corners yields
天蒼蒼	Blue yonder the sky hovers
野茫茫	Wilderness the land covers
風吹草低見牛羊	Winds lower tall grass grazing cattle appear

孔紹安 Kong Shao'an (577–date of death unknown)

落葉   **Fallen Leaf**

早秋驚落葉   I watch in surprise how leaves twirl in air during early fall
飄零似客心   Like a lone traveller roams with no home to call
翻飛未肯下   Every leaf twists and twirls not willing to fall
猶言惜故林   As if to show its love for the tree that bore

2

唐朝、五代

公元六一八年至九〇七年
公元九〇八年至九七九年

Part B

Tang Dynasty
(618—907)

Five Dynasties
(908—979)

唐朝
TANG DYNASTY
(618–907)

虞世南 Yu Shinan (558–638)

詠螢	**Firefly**
的歷流光小	You shed a tiny flickering light
飄颻弱翅輕	With wings weak and thin you fly
恐畏無人識	Wishing your identity to be known
獨自暗中明	You gleam in darkness alone

王績 Wang Ji (590—644)

過酒家　　　　　Passing the Tavern

此日長昏飲	This day I drink drunk all day
非關養性靈	'Tis not for keeping my body and soul in good state
眼看人盡醉	As most people are drunk every day
何忍獨為醒	Why should I alone be sober anyway

野望　　　　　Wilderness View

東皋薄暮望	On the eastern landing at dusk I come to see
徙倚欲何依	Loitering I know not wither I should be
樹樹皆秋色	Trees after trees all dressed in autumn hue
山山唯落暉	Hill on hill the setting sun paints a beautiful view
牧人驅犢返	Shepherds lead their herds home delightful
獵馬帶禽歸	Hunters and steed carry prey so plentiful
相顧無相識	Here I have no one to call my company
長歌懷采薇	I sing hermit songs from memory

無名氏 Anonymous (Tang Dynasty)

金縷衣 The Golden Gown

勸君莫惜金縷衣	Love not your gown of golden threads I say
勸君惜取少年時	Love the hours of your youthful days
花開堪折直須折	Gather flowers in full bloom while you may
莫待無花空折枝	Wait not until they turn into dry twigs I pray

雜詩 A Poem

近寒食雨草萋萋	Grass grows lush with rains from Cold Food Day
着麥苗風柳映堤	Wheat stalks wave while willows cast shadows in lake
等是有家歸不得	Concerned that my home is too far for me to return
杜鵑休向耳邊啼	I ask cuckoos not to sing their homeward songs

寒山 Han Shan (dates of birth & death unknown)

杳杳寒山道

The Cold Hill Way

杳杳寒山道	Long long the way to Cold Hill
落落冷澗濱	Inward inward the waterway chill
啾啾常有鳥	Chirp chirp I hear many a singing bird
寂寂更無人	Silent silent no one here to utter a word
淅淅風吹面	Crisp crisp winds blow across my face
紛紛雪積身	Flake after flake snow covers my body
朝朝不見日	Morning after morning I see no sun
歲歲不知春	Year after year I know no spring

無題

No Title

自樂平生道	My way of life features self-recreation
煙蘿石洞間	Living in a cave up on high mountain
野情多放曠	'Tis a natural feeling of being wild and free
長伴白雲間	With white clouds keeping me company
有路不通世	Hill paths keep me away from social bushels
無心孰可攀	To achieve a state of void I daily battle
石床孤夜坐	Alone I contemplate on a rock bed cool
圓月上寒山	On me the moon shines full

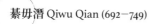

綦毋潛 Qiwu Qian (692−749)

春泛若耶溪　　Spring Boating on the Ruoye Stream

幽意無斷絕	A reclusive life I continue to cherish
此去隨所偶	Whatever nature provides I'll flourish
晚風吹行舟	The evening breeze blows my boat ahead with steam
花路入溪口	To reach the entrance of the welcoming floral stream
際夜轉西壑	By night we turn west into the vale I know
隔山望南斗	From this side of the hill I watch the Dipper aglow
潭煙飛溶溶	Above the placid pool mist rises behold
林月低向後	The moon hangs high as seen in the forest below
生事且瀰漫	As life proceeds calm and persisting
願為持竿叟	I am at peace an old man with a rod fishing

布袋和尚 Cotton Bag Monk (dates of birth & death unknown)

農夫問道　　A Farmer's Way

手執青秧種福田	I plant a rich paddy field tender shoots in hand
低頭便見水中天	In the water the sky smiles at me as I bow my head
六根清淨方為道	Keeping my mind serene I surely see the Way
退步原來是向前	Every backward step means forward progress made

問答

是非憎愛世偏多
仔細思量奈我何
寬卻肚皮常忍耐
放開笑口暗消磨
若逢知己須依分
縱遇冤家也共和
若能了此心頭事
自然證得六波羅

Question and Answer

Rights wrongs hate and love are plenty
In my mind and measures they are but empty
I bare my big tummy accepting people's jeers
I open my heart to contain every smear
Meeting a true friend I dearly keep
To any enemy I also greet
Keeping my mind free of wants and plights
I testify Buddha's truth in all nature's sights

問法號

我有一布袋
虛空無阻礙
展開遍萬方
入時觀自在

My Name

A cotton bag is my luggage
Empty it has no blockage
Whence open it reaches ten thousand spheres
Closed it contains my satisfaction and cheers

牟融 Mao Rong (?–79)

秋夜醉歸有感

銜杯誰道易更闌
沉醉歸來不自歡
惆悵後時孤劍冷
寂寥無寐一燈殘
竹窗涼雨鳴秋籟
江郭清砧搗夜寒
多少客懷消不得
臨風搔首浩漫漫

寫意二首

寂寥荒館閉閒門
苔徑陰陰屐少痕
白髮顛狂塵夢斷
青氈冷落客心存

高山流水琴三弄
明月清風酒一樽
醉後曲肱林下臥
此生榮辱不須論

Returning Home Drunk in an Autumn Night

Who says drinking hard can quell sadness in an autumn night
I return from the tavern drunk my sorrow still in bind
Feeling helpless I stare at my sword idly hung on wall
Sleepless I sit keeping company with my lamp fire in stall
Rains batter my bamboo window singing autumn songs
In cold dawn washer women beat their clothes on and on
How much pining for home am I to endure
I stand in the wind ceaselessly scratching my head forlorn

Two Poems on Feelings

At this wild deserted place my door idly shut
The shaded paths wet with moss clogs leave no mark
I wandered till my hair grey dreams of love no longer on
Under blankets far from home my heart lingers on

From high mount water falls I plug my zither time and again
In cool breezes and bright moon a jug of wine I drink
In drunken land beneath trees on my bent arm I lie
Who cares to count glories and failures in life

題破山寺後禪院

清晨入古寺
初日照高林
曲徑通幽處
禪房花木深
山光悅鳥性
潭影空人心
萬籟此俱寂
惟餘鐘磬音

A Chan Hall behind a Temple Ruin

I arrive at this ancient temple at first light
The morning sun shines into the forest lofty trees bright
A bamboo-lined path leads me to a deep serene retreat
The Chan Hall is hidden in shrubs and flowers sweet
Birds chase one another in the mountain aura displaying pleasure
In the bottom of the mountain pond I find solitude and leisure
'Tis so quiet I find no trace of heavenly sounds here
Only temple bells toll their peel linger in the air

李頎 Li Qi (690—751)

古從軍行

白日登山望烽火
黃昏飲馬傍交河
行人刁鬥風沙暗
公主琵琶幽怨多

野雲萬里無城郭
雨雪紛紛連大漠
胡雁哀鳴夜夜飛
胡兒眼淚雙雙落

聞道玉門猶被遮
應將性命逐輕車
年年戰骨埋荒外
空見蒲桃入漢家

Ancient Army March

We climb hills to watch for beacons during the day
At riverside in the evening we drink our horses in haste
Marching where winds and sands black our sight
We hear our Princess plays the pipa sigh and sigh

Tents spread ten thousand *li* no town could be found
Icy rain pounds the desert turning it into snowy ground
As northern geese honk solitary notes night after night
Tartar soldiers shed tears in a war they dare not defy

Hearing that the Jade-Gate Pass stays an impasse
We'd risk our lives pursuing the chariots fast
Buried here are skeletons of warriors killed every year
They saw no grape wine brought home from the frontier

琴歌

主人有酒歡今夕
請奏鳴琴廣陵客
月照城頭烏半飛
霜淒萬樹風入衣
銅鑪華燭燭增輝
初彈淥水後楚妃
一聲已動物皆靜
四座無言星欲稀
清淮奉使千餘里
敢告雲山從此始

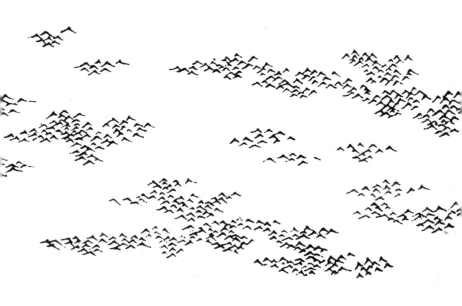

Dulcimer Music

The host has ample wine for everybody this eve
Invited the dulcimer master plays the Guangling at ease
Toward the moonlit city wall birds flying free
The frosty wind reduces the foliages of many trees
Lamps and candelabra render the room bright
The maestro plays Green Waters then the Chu Concubine
Hearing a single melody the audience sits absolutely still
In the silence even stars appear a few
My mind returns to my diplomatic post a thousand *li* away
Dare I tell the clouds and hills here I'd rather stay

李嶠 Li Qiao (644–713)

風

Wind

解落三秋葉　　　Falling leaves in late autumn blow
能開二月花　　　Early spring blooms show
過江千尺浪　　　Thousand feet waves across the river heave
入竹萬竿斜　　　Ten thousand poles punting boats weave

中秋月

Mid-Autumn Moon

圓魄上寒空　　　Up the frigid sky the moon rises round in full
皆言四海同　　　People see it shining same in all oceans
安知千里外　　　Who would know the view in a place far away
不有雨兼風　　　Heavy winds and rains may storm the terrain

宋之問 Song Zhiwen (656–712)

題大庾嶺北驛
At the Post House up Dayu Ridge

陽月南飛雁	Geese migrate south comes the fall
傳聞至此回	Folks say they will return here one and all
我行殊未已	My journey certain its date unsettled
何日復歸來	Returning home alas a future riddle
江靜潮初落	The river calm its tides ebbed
林昏瘴不開	The woods foggy as the day abate
明朝望鄉處	I shall watch at dawn where my home rests
應見隴頭梅	Wavy mume-blossoms should be in their best

渡漢江　　　Crossing the Han River

嶺外音書斷	In exile home messages in voice or writing are blocked absolutely
經冬復歷春	Through winter and spring none comes successfully
近鄉情更怯	I grow timid more and more as I approach home
不敢問來人	Dare I inquire what had happened these years and to whom

張旭 Zhang Xu (658－747)

春草

青草青青萬里餘
邊城落日見離居
情知海上三年別
不寄雲間一紙書

桃花溪

隱隱飛橋隔野煙
石磯西畔問漁船
桃花盡日隨流水
洞在清谿何處邊

Spring Grass

Spring grass greens ten thousand *li*
The sun sets at the frontier town before parting you and me
I knew we would be separated for three years overseas
I write not a single letter for the clouds to carry

The Plum Flower Stream

Shrivelling in the mist a bridge hangs high
West of the boulder I inquire a fisherman nearby
Plum petals float with the water all day long
Where in this stream dose the Paradise Cave belong

回鄉偶書

少小離家老大回
鄉音無改鬢毛衰
兒童相見不相識
笑問客從何處來

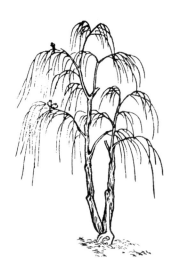

詠柳

碧玉妝成一樹高
萬條垂下綠絲條
不知細葉誰裁出
二月春風似剪刀

On Homecoming

I left home while young and return in old age
My accent remains the same while my scanty hair grows grey
Children here see me but know not my identity
Beaming they ask where I came originally

The Willow

Emeralds adorn trees tall and green
Ten thousand hanging branches wavy and thin
Would you know who cared for these fine leaves
Spring winds in February as crisp as scissors

張若虛 Zhang Ruoxu (660－720)

春江花月夜

春江潮水連海平
海上明月共潮生
灩灩隨波千萬里
何處春江無月明

江畔何人初見月
江月何年初照人
人生代代無窮已
江月年年望相似

不知江月待何人
但見長江送流水
白雲一片去悠悠
青楓浦上不勝愁

昨夜閒潭夢落花
可憐春半不還家
江水流春去欲盡
江潭落月復西斜

斜月沉沉藏海霧
碣石瀟湘無限路
不知乘月幾人歸
落月搖情滿江樹

A Moonlit Night by the River in Spring

In spring the river rises to level with the sea
The moon rises together with sea tides as she should be
Following the waves she travels thousands of *li*
Where'er the river flows there she will be

Who first saw the moon rise by riverside
Which year was man first graced by moonshine
Generation after generation man change and thrive
Year in year out the moon looks but alike

To whom the moon specially bestows her light we do not know
We see ever so clearly the Yangtze River's incessant flow
Up in sky patches of white clouds leisurely float
Down on earth green maples cluster to their sadness untold

I dreamed last night to see flowers falling on water at ease
And pity myself this late spring hour still away from thee
The river carrying all feelings of spring will not reverse its flow
The reclining moon even dwelling in water will maintain her grow

A partial moon striving to shine on can brighten a misty sea
Her luster on crimson boulders will beautify the surroundings for all to see
I know not how many of my loved ones will be home the next moon
I know for sure all trees here will boast her love very soon

陳子昂 Chen Zi'ang (661—702)

登幽州台歌　Ascending Youzhou Tower

前不見古人　Great men of history are not seen here
後不見來者　Those to follow are yet to appear
念天地之悠悠　The universe revolves in orderly motion
獨愴然而涕下　I stand here in tears feeling uncertain

送東萊王學士無競　Parting Gift

寶劍千金買　I bought this sword with a thousand pieces of gold
平生未許人　Never had I allowed anyone to hold
懷君萬里別　You are now going ten thousand *li* away
持贈結交親　I give it to you as companion on your way
孤松宜晚歲　Pines love to breathe the wintry air
眾木愛芳春　Other trees thrive in spring fair
已矣將何道　What more is there to say
無令白髮新　No words would stop my hair turning grey

張九齡 Zhang Jiuling (678–740)

望月懷遠　Pining for You in Moonlight

海上生明月　The moon's floods her brilliance over the ocean face
天涯共此時　A moment shared by people in all places
情人怨遙夜　While lovers complain the unending night
竟夕起相思　Yearning to see each other till dawn appears in sight
滅燭憐光滿　I blow out the candle the room is fully bright
披衣覺露滋　I don my coat to feel the moist dew outside
不堪盈手贈　How I love to give you a handful of moonbeams
還寢夢佳期　Better back to bed to meet you in my dream

王翰 Wang Han (687–726)

涼州詞　Up to the Front

葡萄美酒夜光杯　Fine grape wine fills agate cups so luminous by night
欲飲琵琶馬上催　Before we drank to the tune of pipa we were
　　　　　　　　　　　summoned to fight
醉臥沙場君莫笑　Scorn not whence you see us dead drunk on battle ground
古來征戰幾人回　How many warriors ever came home safe and sound

王之渙 Wang Zhihuan (688－742)

登鸛雀樓　Ascending the Heron Tower

白日依山盡　The white sun diminishes o'er the mountain top
黃河入海流　The Yellow River flows to sea non-stop
欲窮千里目　To see a grandeur view a thousand *li* from here
更上一層樓　One more flight up the tower it will be clear

涼州詞〔又名《出塞》〕
To the Frontier

黃河遠上白雲間　The Yellow River rises to meet white clouds above
一片孤城萬仞山　A lone Wall guards ten thousand mounts so proud
羌笛何須怨楊柳　The Mongol flute will not sing songs of willows
春風不度玉門關　Beyond the Jade Pass no vernal breeze blows

孟浩然 Meng Haoran (689–740)

夏日辨玉法師茅齋　　My Buddhist Teacher's Hut

夏日茅齋裏　　Inside the straw hut all summer day long

無風坐亦涼　　I sit feeling cool even no breezes come along

竹林深筍概　　New shoots sprout up in the bamboo grove

藤架引梢長　　Vines extent new growths over the spectacle

燕覓巢窠處　　Pairing swallows search for a safe nest site

蜂來造蜜房　　Busy bees turn nectars into honey sweet and fine

物華皆可玩　　All things in the universe we can appreciate

花蕊四時芳　　In all four seasons floral fragrances substantiate

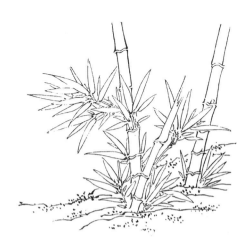

宴梅道士山房

林臥愁春盡
搴帷覽物華
忽逢青鳥使
邀入赤松家
金灶初開火
仙桃正發花
童顏若可駐
何惜醉流霞

留別王維　　Leaving Wang Wei

寂寂竟何待　　How forlornly will I wait
朝朝空自歸　　With a grieving heart day after day
欲尋芳草去　　How I wish to find my friend dear
惜與故人違　　Only to regret missing you here
當路誰相假　　People in high office will not apprehend
知音世所稀　　Bosom friends are hard to find in this land
只應守寂寞　　I should be content to lead a solitary life
還掩故園扉　　And stay behind closed doors in my native land

A Feast with Monk Mei up the Mountain

Awake in the forest I loath that spring will cease to be an entity
From the open curtain I marvel on nature's splendid beauty
A legend bluebird arrives suddenly bringing a message
Invitation for me to visit the Immortal Red Pine Village
The burning furnace is set to freely flame
The Legendary Peach is showing its bursting bloom
If you wish childhood looks to last forever
Let's be drunk with the immortal nectar

過故人莊　Visiting an Old Friend in His Farm

故人具雞黍	My old friend prepares food chicken and all
邀我至田家	Inviting me to visit him in his country hall
綠樹村邊合	His house sits on the edge of a lush green wood
青山郭外斜	Closely logged to a blue mountain foot
開筵面場圃	From his window fields and fields can be seen
把酒話桑麻	We chat between drinks on how crops grow so green
待到重陽日	Whence comes the Double Nine Festival next year
還來就菊花	I will again come to enjoy the chrysanthemums here

宿建德江　Mooring on Jiande River

移舟泊煙渚	I moor my boat by the misty rivershore
日暮客愁新	Renewing grief haunt me when the sun is seen no more
野曠天低樹	The vastness of this unending plain dwarfs tall trees
江清月近人	Deep in the crystal clear river the moon is near me

春曉　A Spring Day Dawn

春眠不覺曉	I linger in bed contentedly this spring morn
處處聞啼鳥	While birds everywhere busily chirp to warn
夜來風雨聲	After the slashing all night by winds and showers
花落知多少	Who would know the number of fallen flowers

王灣 Wang Wan (693–751)

次北固山下　　Passing by North Mountain

客路青山外　　Journeying by the green mountainside
行舟綠水前　　My boat glides on the emerald water so fine
潮平兩岸闊　　At full tide the banks are pushed wide
風正一帆懸　　Sent by helpful breezes a sail hangs high
海日生殘夜　　Washed in sunrise the sea leaves night behind
江春入舊年　　The river brings in spring to rid off the year old
鄉書何處達　　Who will carry my letter home fast behold
歸雁洛陽邊　　The wild geese are idling here in the Capital

王昌齡 Wang Changling (698–756)

芙蓉樓送辛漸

寒雨連江夜入吳
平明送客楚山孤
洛陽親友如相問
一片冰心在玉壺

出塞

秦時明月漢時關
萬里長征人未還
但使龍城飛將在
不教胡馬度陰山

塞下曲

飲馬渡秋水
水寒風似刀
平沙日未沒
黯黯見臨洮
昔日長城戰
咸言意氣高
黃塵足今古
白骨亂蓬蒿

Adieu Xin Jian

You and I arrived at City Wu in cold rain last evening
By the solitary Chu Mountain I bid you farewell this morning
If my kins in the Capital should inquire about my well being
Tell them my mind is pure as ice in a wine jar made of white jade

To the Frontier

The moon of the Chin Dynasty now shines on the gates of Han
Guarding the Great Wall a thousand *li* many warriors are yet to return
Should the Speedy General of Dragon City still abound
No Tartar steed is seen this side of Yin Mount

On the Front

My horse had its drink while crossing the autumn river
With freezing water and sharp wind it felt like having a sword sever
On the desert plain the sun remains vivid after setting
In the gathering darkness I saw the distant town Lintao looming
Battles were waged at the Great Wall in by-gone days
What noble spirit past heroes had displayed
Events old and new now buried under sand no longer pertain
Where scanty weeds grow white bones remain

劉方平 Liu Fangping (date of birth unknown-758)

夜月

更深月色半人家
北斗闌幹南斗斜
今夜偏知春氣暖
蟲聲新透綠窗紗

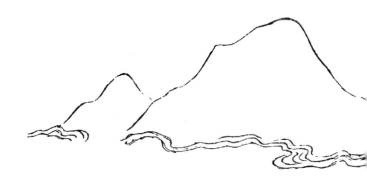

春怨

紗窗日落漸黃昏
金屋無人見淚痕
寂寞空庭春欲晚
梨花滿地不開門

A Moonlit Night

The moon keeps half my room bright at deep night
The Plough invites the North Star and the South Star to appear in dim light
Tonight I feel the warmth of a new spring
Through my window shutters insects singing

Loneliness

The setting sun seen through the window at parting day
In her gilded bower she wipes tears away
The empty courtyard shows spring slipping by
The ground filled with fallen petals the gate shut tight

王維 Wang Wei (701—761)

山中

In the Mountain

荊溪白石出　　O'er white pebbles a clear stream glides
天寒紅葉稀　　In cold days few red leaves are found on hillsides
山路元無雨　　There is no trace of rain on the hilly path
空翠濕人衣　　My clothes are moistened in green bath

竹裏館

A Cot on Bamboo Hill

獨坐幽篁裏　　I sat alone in a serene bamboo grove
彈琴復長嘯　　Playing the lute I croon with nothing to prove
深林人不知　　Here in the deep wood no one knows me
明月來相照　　The moon shines on me ever so friendly

雜詩

A Recontre

君自故鄉來　　Since you just came from my native land
應知故鄉事　　I wonder if you hold large and small events in hand
來日綺窗前　　Whence you passed by the window of my home
寒梅着花未　　Was the cold mume already in bloom

九月九日憶山東兄弟
To My Brothers on Double-Nine Festival

獨在異鄉為異客	Alone a stranger I remain in foreign land
每逢佳節倍思親	At every festival I pine for my dear ones in fervent
遙知兄弟登高處	From here I can see my brothers ascending the mountains with fun
遍插茱萸少一人	Everywhere they plant dogwood spray the team is missing one

終南別業
Retirement at South Hill

中歲頗好道	At mid-life I became a true believer of the wisdom of Dao
晚家南山陲	And retire to settle at the foot of South Hill when old
興來每獨往	Here I loiter at will with not much in mind
勝事空自知	And review in solitude the good deeds I've left behind
行到水窮處	I saunter to where the mountain stream no longer flows
坐看雲起時	I sit waiting to watch rising clouds afloat
偶然值林叟	By chance I meet a firewood gatherer as I roam
談笑無還期	We chat and cheer forgetting to return home

相思

Yearning

紅豆生南國	Red berries thrive in the southern plain
春來發幾枝	They load down trees every spring
願君多采擷	Do gather them to fill your fold
此物最相思	They fortify loving memories to hold

鳥鳴澗

A Dale Where Birds Sing

人閒桂花落	Folks enjoy their respite when sweet osmanthus fall
夜靜春山空	Spring hills become empty on quiet nightfall
月出驚山鳥	A sudden moonshine awakes birds in the hill
時鳴春澗中	Their fitful twitters will keep a spring dale filled

陽關三疊

To a Departing Ambassador

渭城朝雨浥輕塵	This quiet little town Wei is clean washed by morning rain
客舍青青柳色新	Young willows by the tavern lodge bright and green
勸君更盡一杯酒	Do down this cup of wine with me once and again
西出陽關無故人	West of the Yangguang Pass no friends will be seen

鹿柴

The Deer Place

空山不見人
但聞人語響
返景入深林
復照青苔上

The hill vacant no one is seen
Chats are heard within
Deep in the woods this reflecting scene
The moss covered ground mirrors serene

酬張少府

A Response to Prefect Zhang

晚年惟好靜
萬事不關心
自顧無長策
空知返舊林
松風吹解帶
山月照彈琴
君問窮通理
漁歌入浦深

In my old age I treasure quietude
World affairs I care nil
On self-reflection I had not a life plan in view
I enjoy recalling past events fable and real
Breezes from among the pines set my sash free
I play my zither with moon and hills in peace
You ask for wisdom to attain success failure-free
Hear how fishermen up-stream singing at ease

渭川田家　　Home at River Wei

斜光照墟落	A village bathes in the sun's slanting ray
窮巷牛羊歸	Among the lanes homeward cattle find their way
野老念牧童	Grandfather looking for the herd boy waits
倚杖候荊扉	He leans on a bamboo cane by the gate
雉雊麥苗秀	Pheasants love to flock in the wheat fields
蠶眠桑葉稀	Where silkworms rest mulberry leaves become few
田夫荷鋤至	Hoes on shoulders farm hands proudly show
相見語依依	They meet and chat forgetting to go
即此羨閒逸	For this rustic life I long
悵然吟式微	Humming my favourite Homily Song

送別　Farewell

下馬飲君酒	We dismounted our horses to have a cup of wine
問君何所之	I ask for your destination before we say good-bye
君言不得意	You say you have left your unhappy career aside
歸臥南山陲	And on your way home where South Mount stands behind
但去莫復問	I say not a word more as I see you on your way
白雲無盡時	White clouds will keep you company wherever you stay

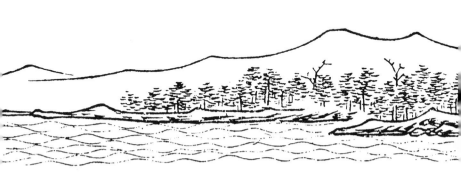

李白 Li Bai (701—762)

行路難

金樽清酒斗十千
玉盤珍饈值萬錢
停杯投箸不能食
撥劍四顧心茫然
欲渡黃河冰塞川
將登太行雪滿山
閒來垂釣碧溪上
忽復乘舟夢日邊
行路難
行路難
多歧路
今安在
長風破浪會有時
直掛雲帆濟滄海

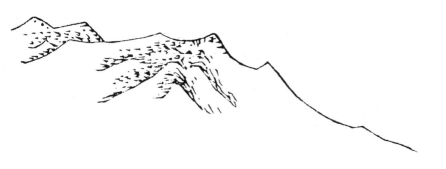

The Road of Life is Difficult

Golden bottled wine costs ten thousand coins a barrel

Choice food on jade plates the same price to follow

Drinks ceased I raise my chopsticks in vain

My sword drawn I look around only to feel empty pain

I wish to cross the Yellow River it is frozen

I wish to climb Mount Taihang it is full of snow

In idle I enjoy time fishing by the blue stream

And dream of sailing a boat into the sunny horizon

The road of life is difficult

The road of life is difficult

Full of diverting paths

Whither should I go

The time will come whence I ride strong winds to cleave the waves

I will hoist my sail tall to triumph in the high sea.

宣州謝朓樓餞別校書叔雲

棄我去者昨日之日不可留
亂我心者今日之日多煩憂
長風萬里送秋雁
對此可以酣高樓
蓬萊文章建安骨
中間小謝又清發
俱懷逸興壯思飛
欲上青天覽日月
抽刀斷水水更流
舉懷銷愁愁更愁
人生在世不稱意
明朝散髮弄扁舟

峨嵋山月歌

峨嵋山月半輪秋
影入平羌江水流
夜發清溪向三峽
思君不見下渝州

Farewell to Uncle Yun at Xuanzhou

What has deserted me yesterday I would not retain
What is disturbing me today worries not remain
See how wild geese ride the autumn wind ten thousand *li* away
A grand sight that calls for rounds of wine to celebrate
While your writings equal the powers of ancient poet saints
My essays are like little Xie's prose simple and plain
We both share the same ambitions aiming high
Wishing to pick the moon down from the sky
I try to sever the river with my sword its torrents speed up the flow
I try to drown my sorrows with wine more sorrows come on tow
My life in this world is not without despair
Tomorrow let's sail our boat freely with loosened hair

Song of Moon O'er Mount E Mei

The moon o'er Mount E Mei appears like autumn's golden brow
She casts fancy shadows on the meandering river as it quietly flows
I will set out from Clear Stream for the Three Gorges tonight
How I miss you when the tall cliffs keep you out of my sight

獨坐敬亭山

眾鳥高飛盡
孤雲獨去閒
相看兩不厭
只有敬亭山

山中問答

問余何意棲碧山
笑而不答心自閒
桃花流水窅然去
別有天地非人間

春夜洛城笛

誰家玉笛暗飛聲
散入春風滿洛城
此夜曲中聞折柳
何人不起故園情

Watching Jingting Peak in Solitude

Birds stop before reaching your majestic peak so high
Solitary clouds drift over you far and nigh
Where I can watch birds and clouds a wonderful view
Here when I'm sitting in front of you

Conversations in the Hills

I dwell in among green hills someone asks why
My mind at ease with a smile I give no reply
To watch the stream carrying peach blossoms pass my window by
This place is too wonderful for man it is a paradise

Flute Music in a Spring Night at Luoyang

From whose flute this music is stirring the air
Carried by the east wind to Luoyang it enters everybody's ear
'Tis the farewell song Willow Branches that's heard tonight
Who would not feel for our lost motherland nostalgia surge high

望天門山

天門中斷楚江開
碧水東流至此回
兩岸青山相對出
孤帆一片日邊來

下終南山過斛斯山人宿置酒

暮從碧山下
山月隨人歸
卻顧所來徑
蒼蒼橫翠微
相攜及田家
童稚開荊扉
綠竹入幽徑
青蘿拂行衣
歡言得所憩
美酒聊共揮
長歌吟松風
曲盡河星稀
我醉君復樂
陶然共忘機

A View of the Mount Heaven Pass

The Yangtze rolls on to split Mount Heaven for a gorge
Billows hurl the eastward river to turn back north
As the green riverbanks watch from opposite sides
A solitary sail appears leaving the sun behind

With Hermit Husi in the Zhongnan Mountain

I descended the green hill as dusk got hold
The moon followed me home without being told
Looking back at the path I had leisurely treaded
It winded through thickets in dark green spread
We arrived at your farmhouse holding hands
Children opened the wooden gate polite and glad
The secluded alley had lush green bamboo lined on both sides
While greenish blue vines caressed my clothing as I walked by
We chatted amiably enjoying peace of mind
And sampled fine brews our connoisseur taste so define
Fervently we sang songs of pine and wind
Stopping not until stars appeared dim and thin
How happy it was with me tipsy and you in glee
We made merry forgetting worldly strife and drudgery

月下獨酌

花間一壺酒
獨酌無相親
舉杯邀明月
對影成三人
月既不解影
影徒隨我身
暫伴月將影
行樂需及春
我歌月徘徊
我舞影零亂
醒時同交歡
醉後各分散
永結無情遊
相期邈雲漢

Drinking Alone in Moonlight

A bottle in hand amid flowers plentiful

Drinking alone with no one dear to hold

I raise my cup to invite the moon for my drinking mate

Her light casts my shadow so we have a three-some date

The moon knows not how to drink or cheer

Leaving only my shadow to follow me here and there

Together for the moment we happily play

And make merry this spring day

I sing and the moon lingers far and near

I dance and my shadow flutters hither and where

Sober we remain cheerful and gay

Drunk we part to go each other's way

We pledge togetherness for eternity

To parallel the legendary lovers in the Galaxy

將進酒

君不見　黃河之水天上來
奔流到海不復回
君不見　高堂明鏡悲白髮
朝如青絲暮成雪
人生得意須盡歡
莫使金樽空對月
天生我材必有用
千金散盡還復來
烹羊宰牛且為樂
會須一飲三百杯
岑夫子　　丹丘生
將進酒
君莫停
與君歌一曲
請君為我側耳聽
鐘鼓饌玉不足貴
但願長醉不願醒
古來聖賢皆寂寞
惟有飲者留其名
陳王昔時宴平樂
斗酒十千恣歡謔
主人何為言少錢
逕須沽取對君酌
五花馬　　千金裘
呼兒將出換美酒
與爾同銷萬古愁

Let's Drink

Behold Yellow River waters originate high from the sky
Torrents rush to sea will never return low or high
Behold grandparents before the mirror watch their grey hair sadly
Silky-black locks at dawn turned white at dusk so mercilessly
When in success we should enjoy life in great delight
And never leave golden goblets empty in a moonlit night
Nature has endowed me with talents to usefully apply
Gold spent in thousands will be regained out right
Cows and sheep finely cooked will be savoured merrily
And mellow brews will be shared a thousand round in glee
Dear friends and students
Replenish your cups
Do not interrupt
Let's together sing
Let your ears hear my soothing ring
Bells and drums are unimportant not even costly dishes
I prefer to get drunk any time I wish
Most scholars and saints are not recorded in historic books
Only wine lovers who share and cheer are remembered in documentary notes
Being host one should spare not any money
But to offer one's best wines for everybody to share generously
Stately stallions
Costly furs
My son will take them to exchange for the finest brews money can buy
Let's drink together until we are high
And leave any lingering worry behind

憶秦娥

簫聲咽

秦娥夢斷秦樓月

秦樓月

年年柳色

灞陵傷別

樂遊原上清秋節

咸陽古道音塵絕

音塵絕

西風殘照

漢家陵闕

送孟浩然之廣陵

故人西辭黃鶴樓

煙花三月下揚州

孤帆遠影碧山盡

唯見長江天際流

Tune: Remembering the Palace Maids

Her flute mute
Her dream cut short by a rendezvous at the moonlit Qin Palace
O moonlit Qin Palace
How she lamented bidding farewell to those glorious days
When year round green palace willows stayed
So much happiness is left behind in the land where autumn fests celebrate
As memories on the Xianyang ancient ways faded
O memories faded
Whence the sun sets even the west wind stood
Only the Han tombs and palace ruins continue to moot

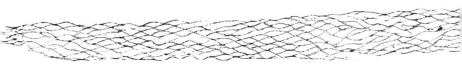

Farewell to Meng Hao Ran at Yellow Crane Tower

My bosom friend is sailing west from the Yellow Crane Tower
Destination Yangzhou where late spring flowers shower
His lone sail diminishes where the sky limit lies yonder
In the horizon the Yangtze's flow continues further

早發白帝城

朝辭白帝彩雲間
千里江陵一日還
兩岸猿聲啼不住
輕舟已過萬重山

自遣

對酒不覺暝
落花盈我衣
醉起步溪月
鳥還人亦稀

菩薩蠻

平林漠漠煙如織
寒山一帶傷心碧
暝色入高樓
有人樓上愁
玉階空佇立
宿鳥歸飛急
何處是歸程
長亭連短亭

Leaving Bai Di Town at Dawn

I left at dawn the castle town of Bai Di beneath colourful clouds
To sail round one thousand *li* of waters and canyons in a day
While monkeys on shore said adieus aloud
Their sad cries vanished as my skiff passed mountains away

Solitary Pursuit

Alone I drank unaware of dusk
While falling petals are covering my gown fast
Tipsily I rose to stroll along the gleaming brook
The birds are gone and no man looked

To the Tune of Dancing Buddhists

Over the sprawling plain teaming woods weave a misty screen
On cold mountains strays a belt of heart-rending green
Where dusk masks the tower high
Alone she lets out a sad sigh
On marble steps her futile wait is nigh
Up high homing birds fly sweeping by
Where could her heart find a source of solace
She searches far and near finding not a trace

靜夜思

床前明月光
疑是地上霜
舉頭望明月
低頭思故鄉

清平調詞三首 (I)

雲想衣裳花想容
春風拂檻露華濃
若非羣玉山頭見
會向瑤台月下逢

On a Quiet Night

Moonlight carpeted the floor before my bed
Could it be frost that had spread
Lifting my head I see the moon so bright
Lowering it I yearn to reach home tonight

Three Serene Tunes (I)

Her face looks floral her dress floats like cloud
Vernal breeze arrives to reveal a beauty proud
If not seen among the beauties in Mount Jade-Green
Will meet her at Crystal Hall in moon gleam

長幹行　Song of Wife in Chang Gan

妾髮初覆額	While my hair was cut covering my forehead straight
折花門前劇	I played with flowers plucked from my front gate
郎騎竹馬來	Riding on bamboo stilts you entered the scene
繞床弄青梅	Like a pair of green plums we played together so keen
同居長幹里	As neighbours at Chang Gan Lane
兩小無嫌猜	We shared one another's joy with no guessing

十四為君婦	I was fourteen when I became your loving bride
羞顏未嘗開	Bashful I often cast off any feelings of delight
低頭向暗壁	Lying sideways I turned to face the wall on my side
千喚不一回	Daring not to respond to your loving calls a thousand times

十五始展眉	At fifteen I opened my brows to find myself
願同塵與灰	And decided to be with you in sickness or in health
常存抱柱信	You declared to die rather than to betray our ties
豈上望夫台	Who would know then I need to look for you all my life

十六君遠行	At sixteen you left to roam afar
瞿塘灩澦堆	O'er river canyons studded with boulders large
五月不可觸	Where spring tides wreck boats sailing near
猿聲天上哀	As frightened gibbons wail asking heaven to interfere
門前遲行跡	I count your every step outside our door
一一生綠苔	Green moss now grow covering them all
苔深不能掃	They penetrate so deep no sweeping will clear them away
落葉秋風早	Early autumn winds are hurrying leaves to frail
八月蝴蝶黃	Butterflies arrive waiting not for August to appear
雙飛西園草	They pair to fly all over our garden spheres
感此傷妾心	Watching all these hurts me body and soul
坐愁紅顏老	As I sit in solitude waiting to grow old
早晚下三巴	One day you may decide to leave the gorges for home
預將書報家	Do remember to send me a message to let me know
相迎不道遠	To meet you I will walk to earth's end
直至長風沙	Stopping not where I meet persisting winds and sands

秋夕旅懷

涼風度秋海
吹我鄉思飛
連山去無際
流水何時歸

目極浮雲色
心斷明月暉
芳草歇柔豔
白露催寒衣

夢長銀漢落
覺罷天星稀
含悲想舊國
泣下誰能揮

Thoughts away from Home on an Autumn Night

Blowing across the autumn sea winds cool
I pine for my homeland feelings flew
Continuous mountain range to nowhere extend
Waters flow incessant their return who knows when

I search from the floating clouds for a signal
My heart breaks the bright moon points to no road
My love remains away gentle and beautiful
White dews will hurry her sending me winter clothes

My dream lasts so long even the Galaxy dims in wait
Whence I wake only a few stars in the blue sky stay
In grief my mind goes to my mother country
Who could help me stop from weeping heavily

崔顥 Cui Hao (704–754)

黃鶴樓

昔人已乘黃鶴去
此地空餘黃鶴樓
黃鶴一去不復返
白雲千載空悠悠
晴川歷歷漢陽樹
芳草萋萋鸚鵡洲
日暮鄉關何處是
煙波江上使人愁

The Yellow Crane Tower

The resident immortal has left with the legend yellow crane
What remains in this empty tower is only in name
Whence the yellow crane gone its soul will not return again
White clouds drift timelessly free of any concern for loss or gain
On a sunny day every tree stands on the wide plain clear
Sweet grass thrive on Parrot Islet their aroma drifts near
Where O Where is my homeland beyond the setting sun
The Han River's misty ripples make my yearning for home run

儲光義 Chu Guangxi (707-760)

釣魚灣　Fishing Bay

平釣綠灣春	I fish at Green Bay on a fine spring day
春深杏花亂	Apricots blossom wild on these late spring days
潭清疑水淺	Seeing water clear I suspect the pool to be shallow
荷動知魚散	Watching moves of lotus plants I know where fishes go
日暮待情人	I wait for my lover to appear when the sun sets low
維舟綠楊岸	And moor my boat on a bank of green willows

吃茗粥作　On Eating Tea Congee

當晝暑氣盛	The mid-day heat is at its high
鳥雀靜不飛	Birds are too lazy to fly
念君高梧陰	I fancy you resting under a plane tree shade
復解山中衣	Your hill clothes open for cooling in haste
數片遠雲度	Clouds roam far two or three
曾不蔽炎暉	They had not shaded the heat free
淹留膳茶粥	Please stay on to sample my tea congee
共我飯蕨薇	And my vegetable rice so tasty
敝廬既不遠	In a short distance lies my rusty shed
日暮徐徐歸	Together we walk home in the sunset

劉長卿 Liu Changqing (709－780)

新年作　　　Written on New Year's Day

鄉心新歲切	Approaching New Year's Day my homesickness grows
天畔獨潛然	Tears are usual in this distant land as time unfolds
老至居人下	In old age I regret being under the commands of generals
春歸在客先	Spring recurs my chance of going home unsettled
嶺猿同旦暮	How I loathe spending my days with only monkeys in sight
江柳共風煙	Amid winds and mists my only friends are willows at riverside
已似長沙傅	Captive like the prince's teacher in the Capital
從今又幾年	How long will I be bound to this place how old

尋南溪常山道人隱居
Visiting Daoist Chang by the Stream

一路經行處	Along the way I had become aware
莓苔見履痕	Footprints touched the moss ground to tear
白雲依靜渚	White clouds nestle above to shade the moor
春草閉閒門	Lush grass stopped in front of the solitary door
過雨看松色	Clean pine needles tell me about visits of rain
隨山到水源	I follow the mountain path to reach the spring
溪花與禪意	Between wild flowers and *Chan* wisdom I contemplate
相對亦忘言	No words are needed to communicate

唐玄宗 Tang Xuanzong (712－756)

經魯祭孔子而歎之
Honouring Confucius at Lu

夫子何為者	What did you strive to teach honourable sage
棲棲一代中	Busying yourself here and there in your time always
地猶鄹氏邑	This being the Lu territory in bygone days
宅即魯王宮	Palace the Duke of Lu had his family happily raised
歎鳳嗟身否	Whence the Phoenix gone did you bemoan your ill-fate
傷麟怨道窮	The Unicorn absent you might regret your ideals berate
今看兩楹奠	As we pour libations to honour you with deep bows
當與夢時同	You can rest in peace we now defend your teachings with vows

杜甫 Du Fu (712–770)

獨酌成詩　　　**Written When Drinking Alone**

燈花何太喜　　Why the lamp wicks flicker so merrily

酒綠正相親　　Emerald liqueur warms me genially

醉裏從為客　　When drunk I fuddle days away in glee

詩成覺有神　　A poem written it's because a spirit helps me

兵戈猶在眼　　Images of war are vivid before my eyes

儒術豈謀身　　Scholarship will not make life easy however one tries

共被微官縛　　I dread being bound by a humble position in office

低頭愧野人　　I lower my head before people who are free

秋興八首 (I)、(III)、(IV)
Autumn Thoughts (I), (III), (IV)

(I)   (I)

玉露凋傷楓樹林	Jade dew drops in the wilt maple woods
巫山巫峽氣蕭森	Cliffs in the Mount Wu Gorges a solemn mood
江間波浪兼天湧	Waves in the Yangtze leap high as sky
塞上風雲接地陰	Low clouds over the pass touch the earth shy
叢菊兩開他日淚	With tears I watch asters bloom and fade again
孤舟一繫故園心	My skiff anchors only on my dreamed homeland
寒衣處處催刀尺	The needs of winter clothes hurry tailors' tasks
白帝城高急暮砧	Mallet beats intensify at Fort Beidi before dusk

(III)   (III)

千家山郭靜朝輝	The town of a thousand families dawns in gleam
日日江樓坐翠微	Each day I sit on the riverside tower to dream
信宿漁人還泛泛	With scanty catch at night fishers still keep afloat
清秋燕子故飛飛	Even in autumn swallows linger flitting to and fro
匡衡抗疏功名薄	My petition to the Emperor nets me in danger and woe
劉向傳經心事違	A learned Liu in the classics I cannot be
同學少年多不賤	My schoolmates all have fortunes better than me
五陵裘馬自輕肥	In furs and well-fed steeds they ride for gaiety

(IV)

聞道長安似弈棋	I hear our Capital changes like a game of chess
百年世事不勝悲	A century of historic events forgotten at best
王侯第宅皆新主	Grand halls are now dwelled by new lords
文武衣冠異昔時	Powerful officers on formals different and odd
直北關山金鼓振	Gongs and drums at northern hills shatter the ears
征西車馬羽書馳	Decorated chariots hurry westward with no fear
魚龍寂寞秋江冷	Here in the autumn chills men of ability have no place
故國平居有所思	I pine for my old country where I used to live in peace

天末懷李白　　I Pine for Li Bai from this Earth's End

涼風起天末	A cold wind rises here at earth's end
君子意如何	I wonder where your thoughts land
鴻雁幾時到	Whence shall news from you arrive by the geese
江湖秋水多	Through rills and lakes autumn waters may hiss
文章憎命達	Good fortunes may not be a match with good writing
魑魅喜人過	Mindful midgets dislike talents thriving
應共冤魂語	If you prefer to share with a poet who died in discontent
投詩贈汨羅	To Qu Yuan in the Miluo your poem sent

夢李白二首 （I）

Two Poems Dreaming of Li Bai (I)

死別已吞聲	We sob when death renders us apart
生別常惻惻	Parting in life would wrench our hearts
江南瘴癘地	Where you are malaria is in riot
逐客無消息	Your exile down south I hear not
故人入我夢	In my dreams you occupy a rightful place
明我長相憶	You know how I pine for you always
恐非平生魂	I fear I might miss you in body and soul
路遠不可測	Being so far apart nothing can be in hold
魂來楓葉青	As your soul visits maples turn green
魂返關塞黑	Back to the dark hills the path not gleam
君今在羅網	Now that you are in the messes of law
何以有羽翼	How could you wing pass the mighty paws
落月滿屋梁	Tonight my house is lit by moonshine
猶疑照顏色	As if to show me the looks of your kind
水深波浪闊	Deep friendship is like waves high and wide
無使蛟龍得	Where dragons thrive having no need to hide

(II)

浮雲終日行
遊子久不至
三夜頻夢君
情親見君意
告歸常局促
苦道來不易
江湖多風波
舟楫恐失墜
出門搔白首
若負平生志
冠蓋滿京華
斯人獨憔悴
孰云網恢恢
將老身反累
千秋萬歲名
寂寞身後事

(II)

Clouds float travelling all day long
You have been wandering long time gone
I dream of you three nights repeatedly
Knowing you pine for me equally
Every time you take leave we hesitate
Visits are difficult you sadly state
Rills and lakes are full of waves and winds
Travelling boats could easily be turned in
At the door you scratch your hoary hair
As if to say your life unfulfilled and in despair
The Capital is full of high offices
You are only neglected in near misses
Who says the net of void is vast
Even in old age you are caught fast
Your name and deeds are everlasting
Any life regret is something to pass

秋笛　Flutes of Autumn

清商欲盡奏　Sad tunes fill the air again and again
奏苦血霑衣　The flute player has clothes in blood stains
他日傷心極　He will someday grieve even more
征人白骨歸　When a lover's remains are returned from war
相逢恐恨過　Your time together was only a short encounter
故作發聲微　You express this with low notes on the flute lever
不見秋雲動　Grieving clouds not heard in your playing
悲風稍稍飛　Laments could only sound like winds soughing

歸雁　Homebound Geese

東來萬里客　Whence will this fighting cease
亂定幾年歸　For me to return home ten thousand *li* east
腸斷江城雁　I sadly watch wild geese flying in line
高高正北飛　Soaring northward flying higher and higher

南征　Travelling South

春岸桃花水	Along the river banks peach blossoms flow in spring
雲帆楓樹林	Clouds give shades to the maple wood rings
偷生長避地	To survive I always look for a refuge place
適遠更沾襟	Tears incessant I go far away
老病南征日	'Tis time to travel south of the River
君恩北望心	Looking north my gratitude to the King no quiver
百年歌自苦	Throughout life I have been singing bitter songs
未見有知音	I've met no one who understands my song

麗春　Poppies

百草競春華	One hundred plants vie for spring glory
麗春應最勝	Poppies a sure win with no need for story
少須好顏色	Before others you are readily seen
多漫枝條剩	Beaming buds on stems strong and thin
紛紛桃李枝	Peach and plum branches profuse everywhere
處處總能移	They are transplanted here and there
如何貴此重	Why are you so precious and valuable
卻怕有人知	'Tis better few people could get to know

晚晴
(II)

州晚驚風度
庭幽過雨沾
夕陽薰細草
江色映疏簾
書亂誰能帙
懷幹可自添
時聞有餘論
未怪老夫潛

A Clear Eve
(II)

Villagers are surprised to see a sudden gust
The recluse courtyard serene with no dust
The setting sun heats the thriving grass to perfume
Bamboo curtains reflect river scenes vividly seen
Who would help me to tidy books in disarray
For wine refills I can manage right away
Gossips show people wish to know who is here
If an old man lives invisibly near

蜀相

丞相祠堂何處尋
錦官城外柏森森
映階碧草自春色
隔葉黃鸝空好音
三顧頻煩天下計
兩朝開濟老臣心
出師未捷身先死
長使英雄淚滿襟

Prime Minister Memorial

Where is the late Prime Minister's Memorial Hall
Outside Chengdu under cypress arches standing tall
The green steps reflect the thriving grass in spring
Amid thick tree leaves orioles heartily sing
Thrice the King invited him to administer his domain
For two terms the loyal minister served in the same reign
He died early before victory is ascertained
Future heroes weep recalling his respects attained

田舍

田舍清江曲
柴門古道旁
草深迷市井
地僻懶衣裳
欅柳枝枝弱
枇杷樹樹香
鸕鷀西日照
曬翅滿魚梁

My Cottage

The limpid river meanders by my cottage
My wicket door opens to an ancient passage
The nearby market is rutted with wild grass
Remote here I care not for clothes of high class
Willows sway their branches too weak to swing
Scattered loquat trees perfume the air singing
Cormorants carry the sun rays on their wings
To shine the fish ponds with golden links

卜居

百花潭水水西頭
主人為卜林塘幽
已知出郭少塵事
更有澄江銷客愁
無數蜻蜓齊上下
一雙鸂鶒對沉浮
東行萬里堪乘興
須向山陰上小舟

Searching for a Home Site

Following the Flowering Streams to its west end
Among trees and ponds I found this peaceful land
Leaving city life I put all mundane cares behind
Pristine waters will cleanse my soul fine
Dragonflies in big numbers swam high and low
Mandarin duck pairs play in water above and below
I might sail east a thousand *li* for gaiety
At Shanyin I board my boat and set myself free

春水

二月桃花浪
江流復舊痕
朝來沒沙尾
碧色動柴門
接縷垂芳餌
連筒灌小園
已添無數鳥
爭浴故相喧

登高

風急天高猿嘯哀
渚清沙白鳥飛回
無邊落木蕭蕭下
不盡長江滾滾來
萬里悲秋常作客
百年多病獨登台
艱難苦恨繁霜鬢
潦倒新停濁酒杯

Spring Swells

Water swells arrive with peach blossoms in spring
Rivers recover their water marks in an instant
At morn floods cover the sand banks showing no trail
Green torrents open my cottage door without fail
Sweet baits dangle on ends of invisible strings
Bamboo pipes keep the garden wet and singing
Birds arrive from nowhere to join in the play
They chatter and bicker as they happily bathe

Up the Mountain

High sky and swift winds send gibbons wearily cry
O'er white sand in the clear river birds recurrently fly
In the boundless wood trees shed their leaves like showers
From the long river torrents roll forgetful of the hour
Ten thousand *li* from home I grieve this autumn my plight
Surviving lengthy illness I alone climb up this platform high
Through hard times my hair is turning white
Battling poverty I now must give up wine

旅夜書懷

細草微風岸
危檣獨夜舟
星垂平野闊
月湧大江流
名豈文章著
官因老病休
飄飄何所似
天地一沙鷗

病馬

乘爾亦已久
天寒關塞深
塵中老盡力
歲晚病傷心
毛骨豈殊眾
馴良猶至今
物微意不淺
感動一沉吟

Reflections in an Inn

Short grass thrive on riverbanks cooled by breezes
Alone a tall mass stands on a boat in darkness
A sky decorated by low stars sets the plain wide
The moon bright heaves up the river's rolling tide
My fame is not built by my writings at will
Retirement from public office is natural when old and ill
How free it feels doing little I wonder
Like a water bird between sky and land hovers

To My Ailing Horse

You have followed my rein for so many years
Through snow and deep mountain passes we cheer
You have always trotted in good form wherever we go
Seeing you ill in your aging days I feel sorrow
Your coat and frame are not different from others your kind
'Tis your loyalty to me that shines
This small gesture of appreciation is definitely not shallow
I'm moved to sing you my praise from my soul

野望

清秋望不極
迢遞起曾陰
遠水兼天淨
孤城隱霧深
葉稀風更落
山迴日初沉
獨鶴歸何晚
昏鴉已滿林

兵車行（節譯）

車轔轔
馬蕭蕭
行人弓箭各在腰
耶娘妻子走相送
塵埃不見咸陽橋
牽衣頓足攔道哭
哭聲直上乾雲霄
道旁過者問行人
行人但雲點行頻
或從十五北防河
便至四十西營田

Watching the Wilderness

On this autumn day I see a boundless view
Layers of hills and trees loom in vivid hues
At a distance serene are the water and the sky
Hidden in deep mist a lone town appears from behind
Lingering leaves easily fall when swept by wind
Toward the mountain ranges a retiring sun plummets in
Why should a solitary crane return to its nest late
When black crows have thronged the woods in haste

The Conscript March (selected part)

Chariots rumble rumble
Horses grumble grumble
The conscripts march to fight armed with arrows and bows
Parents and wives run along to say goodbye
Dust from their running blind the Xianyang Bridge out right
They wail and stamp their feet trying to halt the onward march
Their heart-rending cries strike even clouds dry
A passer-by inquires what is happening
Conscripts reply that draft orders will be continuously in
Fifteen-year-olds are sent to guard the northern shore
By age forty they will be compelled to farm the wilderness on tour

秋野　Autumn Wild

易識浮生理	To know the order of life is elementary
難教一物違	To find exceptions to the rule is thorny
水深魚極樂	Deep water offers a place for fishers to merry
林茂鳥知歸	Dense woods provide homes for birds to roost safely
吾老甘貧病	In old age one accepts poverty and sickness sensibly
榮華有是非	To temper with fame and wealth invites disputes many
秋風吹幾杖	Autumn winds encourage old folks to seek tranquility
不厭此山薇	Northern hill vegetables offer tasteful diets healthily

落日　Sunset

落日在簾鈎	The setting sun hangs on my screen hook
溪邊春事幽	Early spring affairs flow in murmuring brook
芳菲緣岸圍	Riverbanks green emanating fragrance sweet
樵爨倚灘舟	Woodcutters rest on mooring boats to eat
啅雀爭枝墜	Birds bicker for falling sprigs
飛蟲滿院遊	Flying all over the courtyard are insects
濁醪誰造汝	It matters not how liqueurs are distilled
一酌散千憂	One sip will dispel hundreds of cares to nil

贈衛八處士　To Hermit Wei

人生不相見	How often in life we fail to meet
動如參與商	Moving like Orion and Scorpion on separate feet
今夕復何夕	This our night by lucky feats
共此燈燭光	Together by candlelight we sit
少壯能幾時	How many youthful days can we count
鬢髮各已蒼	Before grey hairs on our heads mount
訪舊半為鬼	Half our old friends have gone to the underworld
驚呼熱中腸	Finding them under their tombs I feel low
焉知二十載	Never had I expected after two decades
重上君子堂	We would be together in your homestead
昔別君未婚	Unmarried you were when we last parted
兒女忽成行	Today sons and daughters line up your yard
怡然敬父執	They greet me politely as their father
問我來何方	And ask my dwelling place whither
問答乃未已	Even as we continue making conversation
兒女羅酒漿	Food and wine are in preparation
夜雨翦春韭	Leeks are fetched from the garden while raining
新炊間黃粱	Yellow millets on the stove steaming
主稱會面難	You lament being together is so difficult
一舉累十觴	Raising our cups ten times we drink special
十觴亦不醉	Wines do not make me drunk in ten rounds
感子故意長	Our friendship lasting I happily found
明日隔山嶽	Tomorrow we will be separated by hills again
世事兩茫茫	Lost in mundane affairs by then

江邊星月二首
Moon and Star by Riverside Two Poems
(II)　　　　　(II)

江月辭風纜　　From above the river the moon takes leave

江星別霧船　　Viewed from the fog-veiled boat stars disappear

雞鳴還曙色　　When cocks crow to herald in the morning hue

鷺浴自清川　　Egrets bathe happily in the shimmering rill

歷歷竟誰種　　I wonder who had planted the cassia in the moon

悠悠何處圓　　And where she will share her perfect and happy mood

客愁殊未已　　In my roaming life sorrow dominates my mind

他夕始相鮮　　In another night I shall fly to sit by her side

張繼 Zhang Ji (715 – 779)

楓橋夜泊　　Mooring by Maple Bridge Overnight

月落烏啼霜滿天　Amid crow cries the moon hides behind the snowy sky
江楓漁火對愁眠　Under lofty maple trees dimly lit river boats lie side by side
姑蘇城外寒山寺　Cold Hill Temple stands outside the Gu Su city wall
夜半鐘聲到客船　Bells toll at midnight for boatmen at moor

岑參 Cen Shen (715-770)

輪台歌・奉送封大夫出師西征

輪台城頭夜吹角

輪台城北旄頭落

羽書昨夜過渠黎

單於已在金山西

戍樓西望煙塵黑

漢兵屯在輪台北

上將擁旄西出征

平明吹笛大軍行

四邊伐鼓雪海湧

三軍大呼陰山動

虜塞兵氣連雲屯

戰場白骨纏草根

劍河風急雪片闊

沙口石凍馬蹄脫

亞相勤王甘苦辛

誓將報主靜邊塵

古來青史誰不見

今見功名勝古人

A Sent-off to General Feng in His Western Expedition

Bugles blare all night on top of the Luntai walls
At the northern end all flags fall
Urgent reports from high had passed Quli last night
Hun chieftain's army is stationed at Jing Shan's west side
We see at the observation post the west dust high
Here at Luntai our regiments are prepared to fight
With the Han standard up our men march on a western campaign
Blowing up their fifes at dawn they march on a long train
The rumble of drums on all sides stirs up a sea of snow
Our triple troop make army whoops to shake Mount Yin low
The enemy's spirit stows like thick unmoving clouds
They see on grounds bleached bones with grassroots shroud
Brisk winds over the Sword River blows snows wide
On cold gravel roads horses leave their hoofs behind
The Vice-chancellor spares no hardship to serve his King
He vows to calm down all conflicts in the frontier terrain
Who does not wish to have his good deeds recorded in history
But today's success should weigh more than ancient bravery

走馬川行・奉送封大夫出師西征

君不見走馬川行雪海邊

平沙莽莽黃入天

輪台九月風夜吼

一川碎石大如斗

隨風滿地石亂走

匈奴草黃馬正肥

金山西見煙塵飛

漢家大將西出師

將軍金甲夜不脫

半夜軍行戈相撥

風頭如刀面如割

馬毛帶雪汗氣蒸

五花連錢鏇作冰

幕中草檄硯水凝

虜騎聞之應膽懾

料知短兵不敢接

車師西門佇獻捷

Seeing General Feng off on His Western Expedition

Behold the Dashing Horse River flows on a sea of snow
The desert stretches wide its expanse only the horizon knows
Up the Wheel Tower autumn gales roar throughout the night
On river bed even broken rocks are big like measuring *dou*
Carried by winds rocks fly everywhere wild
The Huns steeds are plump and strong when grass grows tall and yellow
Dust and smoke rise from battles west of Golden Mount
Where our generals lead the army fast to combat ground
Eager warriors keep their metal armours on while they rest
Ready to advance at midnight sharp spears in their best
Frigid winds like sharp swords slash faces inducing loud screams
Dashing steeds sweat their manes steam
Ice rolls down from horse back like floral shower
Inside the tent inkwells freeze the commander can only issue verbal order
Enemy cavaliers should be afraid of such a fierce campaign
They dare not cross swords with our warriors nor allowed to complain
Victory reports are expected to reach commander Feng at Westgate

司空曙 Sikong Shu (720–790)

雲陽館與韓紳宿別

故人江海別
幾度隔山川
乍見翻疑夢
相悲各問年
孤燈寒照雨
濕竹暗浮煙
更有明朝恨
離杯惜共傳

喜外弟盧綸見宿

靜夜四無鄰
荒居舊業貧
雨中黃葉樹
燈下白頭人
以我獨沉久
愧君相見頻
平生自有分
況是蔡家親

Bidding Han Shen Adieu at Yun Yang Inn

We had said adieu many times on land and at sea
Separated by hills and rills our friendship firm and free
Meeting again we wonder if it is only in dreams
Recounting our ages we console one another and beam
A dim lamp shines weak in the coolness of rain
Deep in the bamboo grove heavy mists rise again
For the impending sorrow of parting again tomorrow
Let's drink our cups empty thorough

Enjoy Passing a Night with Cousin Lu Lun

The night silent with no neighbours in sight
An old desolate house in the wild
In the rain all trees have yellow leaves
Beside a lamp we compare our grey hairs and heave
You say your life has been on the downside for a long time
How delightful are my frequent visits you reminded
We are brought together by destiny
Closely related we share each other's good company

江村即事　　　　　Village by Riverside

釣罷歸來不繫船　　　Back from fishing I moor not my boat
江村月落正堪眠　　　'Tis good time to sleep a low moon my hood
縱然一夜風吹去　　　Even if the wind overnight blows my craft astray
只在蘆花淺水邊　　　It'll be amid the reeds in the shallow waterways

錢起 Qian Qi (722—780)

歸雁

瀟湘何事等閒回
水碧沙明兩岸苔
二十五弦彈夜月
不勝清怨卻飛來

The Returning Geese

Why leave where you were for here so easily geese
Greenish blue water white sands beneath mossy river banks designed to please
As the River Goddess plays the zither of twenty-five strings this moonlit night
Will you not be touched by the many regrets each string sings nigh

湘靈鼓瑟

善鼓雲和瑟
常聞帝子靈
馮夷空自舞
楚客不堪聽
苦調淒金石
清音入杳冥
蒼梧來怨慕
白芷動芳馨
流水傳湘浦
悲風過洞庭
曲終人不見
江上數峯青

送僧歸日本

上國隨緣住
來途若夢行
浮天滄海遠
去世法舟輕
水月通禪寂
魚龍聽梵聲
惟憐一燈影
萬里眼中明

Musical Soul of the Xiang River

Drum booms harmonize with the zither to please the clouds
From yonder the Saintly Emperor's soul is aroused
Dances the Water Goddess so gay
Southerners listen in daze
Her performance induces metal and stone to sing drearily
The clear tones fuse with echoes in space merrily
The old plane tree is moved to express its admiration
Scented white reeds release perfume in saturation
The music flows with the Xiang River to its extent
Then veers across Dong Ting Lake raising a whirl of desolation
No one can be found whence the melodies ended
On upper river a few verdant peaks silently stand

Seeing a Japanese Bonze off to Home

By divine design you had come to our country to learn
The voyage you took could be part of a dreamy sojourn
The sea boundless is far like the sky's extent
Sailed on Buddhist blessings your vessel light and transcend
Water and moon are both objects of Zen tranquillity
Fish and dragon are moved by chants of the Sutra heavenly
Held high a solitary lamp can enlighten your mind with insight
Ten thousand *li* from here you will see us with eyes so bright

谷口書齋寄楊補闕

泉壑帶茅茨
雲霞生薛帷
竹憐新雨後
山愛夕陽時
閒鷺棲常早
秋花落更遲
家童掃蘿徑
昨與故人期

與趙莒茶宴

竹下忘言對紫茶
全勝羽客對流霞
塵心洗盡意難盡
一樹蟬聲片影斜

To My Friend Yang from My Study

Around my cottage a winding brook meanders
To my straw screen clouds leave their colours
Bamboos look affectionate when newly washed by rain
Hills love the sun in its setting splendour
Idle stocks roost early before eve
Autumn flowers are slow to shed their leaves
My house boy has swept clean the overgrown path for thee
A dear old friend I earnestly await to see

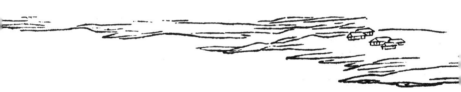

A Tea Party with Zhao Ju

Friends of Bamboo understand one another sipping tea purple
An association tighter than Daoists tipsy with Immortal Brew
Emotional cares washed clear silent words have much to say
A tree of singing cicadas precipitates but a light shade

飲茶歌誚崔石使君

越人遺我剡溪茗

采得金牙爨金鼎

素瓷雪色縹沫香

何似諸仙瓊蕊漿

一飲滌昏寐

情來朗爽滿天地

再飲清我神

忽如飛雨灑輕塵

三飲便得道

何須苦心破煩惱

此物清高世莫知

世人飲酒多自欺

愁看畢卓甕間夜

笑向陶潛籬下時

崔侯啜之意不已

狂歌一曲驚人耳

孰知茶道全爾真

唯有丹丘得如此

Tea Drinking Song for Master Cui

My southern friend sent me a gift of Shan Qi tea
In my kettle I boil the golden tender leaves
The snowy white bubbles emit a fragrance so sweet
It competes with the flower nectar the immortals eat
A first sip clears the late day drowsy head
The mind happy wandering in cosmic spreads
A second sip purifies the soul
As if a sudden rain washes away dusts of old
A third sip puts me right on the Way
No more need to dispel any worry away
This tea is pure and serene not commonly seen
People who consume wine are just self-deceiving
Recall the legend spirit drinker lying by the urn at night
Smile with poet Tao as he picks his daisy in a day fine
The great singer Cui is remembered no more
With a single song he had the ears of listeners in roar
Do find your true self in the art of tea drinking
And be in the sweet land the immortals are dwelling

飲茶歌送鄭容

丹丘羽人輕玉食
采茶飲之生羽翼
名藏仙府世空知
骨化雲宮人不識
雲山童子調金鐺
楚人茶經虛得名
霜天半夜芳草摺
爛漫緗花啜又生
賞君此茶祛我疾
使人胸中蕩憂栗
日上香鑪情未畢
醉踏虎溪雲
高歌送君出

A Tea Drinking Song for Zheng Rong

Immortals in Fairyland care not eat luxurious viands
They gather tea leaves to drink and their spirit wings
Their name unknown hidden in Never-never Land
Their bones decompose in the Cloud Palace den
An attendant in Cloud Hill makes tea with a copper boiler
The Tea Classic of Lu Yu remains a dogma
Tender tea leaves split in frosty nights
Light yellow tea buds open in the morning to thrive
A taste of this special tea rids all my ills
Such wonders linger in my mind still
Legend poets enjoy tea together with the sun on Censor Peak
In exhilaration they strolled pass the Tiger Brook limits
Laughing and singing you and I bid goodbye here

尋陸鴻漸不遇　Visiting Master Lu Hongjian to See Him Home

移有雖帶郭　I visit your dwelling in solitude away from town

野徑入桑麻　Through mulberries the wild path leads me down

近種籬邊菊　Your fence displays new chrysanthemums waiting to grow

秋來未着花　They are not yet in bloom although autumn will follow

扣門無犬吠　I knock at your door the dog is quiet wagging its tail

欲去問西家　West of your cabin I ask neighbours about your trail

報道山中去　They say you go deep up the mountain every day

歸來每日斜　On your return you bring the retiring sun in dim ray

韋應物 Wei Yingwu (736–792)

賦得暮雨送李曹　　To Li Cao in a Drizzling Evening

楚江微雨裏	A light drizzle along the Yangtze River
建業暮鐘時	The Evening toll in Nanjing sounds near
漠漠帆來重	Broad sails moving leisurely following the rain
冥冥鳥去遲	Homing birds fly slowly on laden wings
海門深不見	The sea gate is away too far to be seen
浦樹遠含滋	Nearby trees are moist with rain
相送情無限	Seeing you off I feel infinitely sad
沾襟比散絲	Tears run through my robe like silk fleece wet

喜園中生茶　　Happy to Grow Tea in My Garden

潔性不可污	Its pure character must not meet with sully
為飲滌塵煩	Drinking it could wash clean all anxiety
此物信靈味	This thing tastes really supreme
聊因理郡餘	It comes from a land of greens
本自出山原	Away from official duties I take leisure
率爾植荒園	To cultivate my garden in pleasure
喜隨眾草長	Happy to see it thrive with other vegetation
得與幽人言	With understanding it chats with me in animation

夕次盱眙縣　Mooring in Xuyi at Dusk

落帆逗淮鎮　My sail lowered I board this way-side town
停舫臨孤驛　To a lone pier my boat moors sound
浩浩風起波　Gales ruffle sending waves on shore
冥冥日沉夕　Deep into dusk the western sun is seen no more
人歸山郭暗　To the dimming hillside town I gradually return
雁下蘆洲白　Tiring geese alight on a white reed isle they earned
獨夜憶秦關　Alone a traveller to home I pine
聽鐘未眠客　Counting distant bells through this sleepless night

秋夜寄丘員外　To Master Qiu in an Autumn Night

懷君屬秋夜　I pine for you this autumn night
散步詠涼天　Strolling alone I sing of the cold season in rhyme
空山松子落　High up in the empty mountain pine cones silently fall
幽人應未眠　You my eremite friend will not be awake for long

寄全椒山中道士　　To My Friend the Daoist Hermit

今朝郡齋冷	'Tis so cold in my study this morn
忽念山中客	I think of you living deep in the mount
澗底束荊薪	Gathering dry twigs from the river bed
歸來煮白石	I boil white pebbles for soup and dine so glad
欲持一瓢酒	A gourd of my best brew for you I wish to deliver
遠慰風雨夕	In this rainy cold eve so we may share together
落葉滿空山	Fallen leaves have the hills covered slope to slope
何處尋行跡	Where could I find traces of you to fulfil this hope

李益 Li Yi (746–829)

江南曲　　A Song from the South

嫁得瞿塘賈	Since I became a roving merchant's wife
朝朝誤妾期	I miss his presence every day in my life
早知潮有信	If I knew the rhythmic trust of the tide
嫁與弄潮兒	I would choose to be a sailor's bride

敦煌曲子詞：菩薩蠻

枕前發盡千般願
要休且待青山爛
水面上秤錘浮
直待黃河徹底枯
白日參辰現
北斗回南面
休即未能休
且待三更見日頭

盧綸 Lu Lun (748—799)

送萬巨

把酒留君聽琴
難堪歲暮離心
霜葉無風自落
秋雲不雨空陰
人愁荒村路細
馬怯寒溪水深
望斷青山獨立
更知何處相尋

Lyrics from Dunhuang: Tune Buddhist Dancers

In our pillow talks we make vows thousand times over
Our love will last unless the green hills rod and fall under
Or water is able to float big lumps of lead
And the Yellow River dried exposing its bed
And stars were seen in broad daylight
The Dipper moved south to shine bright
Even then our love will not wane
Unless the sun appears at midnight again

Seeing Wan Ju off

With zither song and wine I beg you to stay
It is heart-rending to part on this year-end day
Frosted leaves fall where no winds blow
Autumn clouds rainless their shades flow
On the narrow path of this deserted village who would not grieve
Facing the deeps of this frigid river what horse would not fear
Alone I stand in search for green hills to appear
Hoping to meet you where you had disappeared

塞外曲

Frontier Songs

(I)

(I)

鷲翎金僕姑
燕尾繡蝥弧
獨立揚新令
千營共一呼

His arrows in eagle feather tufts
His pennons marked by swallows
He stands tall waving out a new order
A thousand battalions shout a united holler

(II)

(II)

林暗草驚風
將軍夜引弓
平明尋白羽
沒在石棱中

Under the dim woods grass shiver as winds howl
At night the general tests his iron bow
He looks for his arrow the next morn
It pierced a rock amid the wild thorns

(III)

(III)

月黑雁飛高
單于夜遁逃
欲將輕騎逐
大雪滿弓刀

Wild geese fly high in moonless nights
The Tartar Chieftain waits for darkness to take flight
Our cavaliers make chase their steeds fast
Their bows and swords coated with snow dust

(IV)

(IV)

野幕敞瓊筵
羌戎賀勞旋
醉和金甲舞
雷鼓動山川

By evening sumptuous banquets are wide spread
The natives feast the victors with all they have
Dancing on golden armours we drink to get drunk
The hills and rills shake at the thunders of our drums

孟郊 Meng Jiao (751–814)

烈女操　　　　A Faithful Widow

梧桐相待老　　　Plane trees of different genders grow old together
鴛鴦會雙死　　　Mandarin ducks live and die in pairs a wonder
貞女貴徇夫　　　A faithful wife stands ready to die sacrificial
捨生亦如此　　　Life lost is accepted as natural
波瀾誓不起　　　My heart is still as water in an old well
妾心古井水　　　It has no possible ripples to tell

遊子吟　　　　A Roamer Sings

慈母手中線　　　Needle and thread in mother's hand
遊子身上衣　　　Preparing clothes for a son going to far away land
臨行密密縫　　　Sewing stitches quicken as parting draws near
意恐遲遲歸　　　His return may be in delay mother fears
誰言寸草心　　　Who says a son's casual affection
報得三春暉　　　Is adequate in return for Mum's undivided devotion

韓愈 Han Yu (768–824)

山石

山石犖确行徑微
黃昏到寺蝙蝠飛
升堂坐階新雨足
芭蕉葉大梔子肥
僧言古壁佛畫好
以火來照所見稀
鋪床拂席置羹飯
疏糲亦足飽我饑
夜深靜臥百蟲絕
清月出嶺光入扉
天明獨去無道路
出入高下窮煙霏
山紅澗碧紛爛漫
時見松櫪皆十圍
當流赤足踏澗石
水聲激激風吹衣
人生如此自可樂
豈必局束為人靰
嗟哉吾黨二三子
安得至老不更歸

Mountain Rocks

The mountain path is narrow between jagged rocks craggy
Bats flutter overhead as I arrive at the temple toward eve
After the stairs I sit down my feet are wet with rain
Broad leaf banana trees grow beside fat elecampane
A monk shows me the Buddha murals on an ancient wall
He illuminates the art work magnificent and tall
My bed is prepared and a meal is carefully set
The coarse rice and vegetables keep me adequately fed
Hearing no insects I sleep sound through the quiet night
The moon rises on mountain top and enters my room bright
I leave the temple in the morning for a walk finding no road
In the hazy terrain I walk up and down not knowing where to go
Dyed in red and green the mountain and brook vie for glamour
At times I meet an old pine its girth takes ten persons to measure
I step in the running water to touch the pebbles my feet bare
The rushing water sounds pleasing the winds flap my coat flare
Life like such is wonderful indeed
Why be confined to follow other people's leads
All I need is to find friends two or three
Back to nature we live to old age happy and free

劉禹錫 Liu Yuxi (772－842)

秋詞

Autumn Song

自古逢秋悲寂寥	People drag the melancholy of autumn since old
我言秋日勝春朝	I say autumn days outshine spring morns total
晴空一鶴排雲上	A single crane sours above clouds in a fine day
便引詩情到碧霄	It evokes inspiration of green skies for poets to praise

烏衣巷

The Lane of Mansions

朱雀橋邊野草花	By the Red Bird Bridge wild grass grow
烏衣巷口夕陽斜	By the Lane of Mansions the sun sets low
舊時王謝堂前燕	Swallows which frequented painted eaves in bygone days
飛入尋常百姓家	They skim by common people's dwellings today

竹枝詞二首

Bamboo Songs Two Poems

(I)

(I)

楊柳青青江水準	Meandering through green willows the river murmurs on
聞郎江上唱歌聲	I hear you on your boat singing me a song
東邊日出西邊雨	While the sun shines in the east the west is in rain
道是無晴卻有晴	You my dear appears aloof but your love for me is plain

李紳 Li Shen (780-846)

| 憫農二首 | **Feeling for Farmers Two Poems** |

(I)

(I)

春種一粒粟
秋收萬顆子
四海無閒田
農夫猶餓死
......

A single seed planted in spring
In autumn ten thousand yields harvest bring
Where all fields are skilfully tilled
Why farmers die of hunger still
...

(II)

(II)

鋤禾日當午
汗滴禾下土
誰知盤中飧
粒粒皆辛苦
......

At noon they hoe preparing fields for planting
Their sweat drip on the rice shoots washing
Who would remember the rice in our bowls
Every grain comes from hard toils untold
...

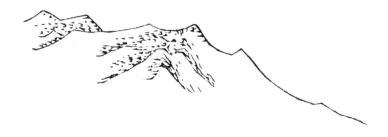

白居易 Bai Juyi (772-846)

食罷

食罷一覺睡
起來兩甌茶
舉頭看日影
已復西南斜
樂人惜日促
憂人厭年賒
無憂無樂者
長短任生涯

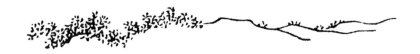

夜聞賈常州、崔湖州茶山境會亭歡宴

遙聞境會茶山夜
珠翠歌鐘俱繞身
盤下中分兩州界
燈前各作一家春
青娥遞舞應爭妙
紫筍齊嘗各鬥新
自歎花時北窗下
蒲黃酒對病眠人

After a Meal

Taking a nap after a meal
Getting up later and have two bowls of tea
I raise my head to watch the sun light
Toward the southwest the sun has reclined
Optimists feel the days pass in a hurry
Pessimists complain of remaining years
Those who are carefree for being worried or happy
Ride on life's ups and downs with natural ease

A Tea Party at Tea Hill

I hear about an evening tea party at Tea Hill
Many bejewelled maidens sing and dance at will
Guests are served with two top tea choices on the platter
In lantern lights all participants become family members
Maiden dancers move showing dazzling beauty
Two varieties of purple tea compete for best quality
With tea flowers I feel sick sitting by the window
I shall drink this herbal wine medicinal

大林寺桃花

人間四月芳菲盡
山寺桃花始盛開
長恨春歸無覓處
不知轉入此中來

賦得古原草送別

離離原上草
一歲一枯榮
野火燒不盡
春風吹又生
遠芳侵古道
晴翠接荒城
又送王孫去
萋萋滿別情

Peach Blossom at Da Lin Temple

By April flowers everywhere are all but fallen
Here on temple ground peach flowers only begin to blossom
I oft regret when spring is gone it leaves no trace
Knowing not it has come to adorn this place

Farewell by the Ancient Grass Plain

Grass grows on this ancient plain wide and far
They thrive and wither once every year
Heath fires burn but in vain
A touch of vernal breeze they thrive again
Their fragrance penetrates paths swept by wind
They adjoin towns in ruin bright and green
I've come to bid you farewell once again
Grief overwhelms like wild grass on plain

燕詩示劉叟

樑上有雙燕
翩翩雄與雌
銜泥兩椽間
一巢生四兒
四兒日夜長
索食聲孜孜
青蟲不易捕
黃口無飽期
觜爪雖欲敝
心力不知疲
須臾十來往
猶恐巢中饑
辛勤三十日
母瘦雛漸肥
喃喃教言語
一一刷毛衣

Swallow Song

A pair of swallows above our girder appear

A she bird and a he bird together they fair

For a new nest they bring bits of mud and fibre with their beaks

Soon four chicks are hedged in it so neat

The foursome baby birds grow day and night

They plead for nourishment tweeting with mouths wide

Fresh worms are far away and not easy to catch

The opening mouths are ne'er fully fed

Beaks and claws of parent birds are worn out approaching defeat

But dad and mom care not their own fatigue

They busy in relay rounds to fetch food without rest

The hunger of their nestlings must not go through any test

After a month of such laborious tasks complete

Mom is thin as chicks fat

To teach baby birds to chirp and call is no small feat

The fletching feathers also need be cleaned with Mum's beak

一旦羽翼成
引上庭樹枝
舉翅不回顧
隨風四散飛
雌雄空中鳴
聲盡呼不歸
卻入空巢裏
啁啾終夜悲
燕燕爾勿悲
爾當返自思
思爾為雛日
高飛背母時
當時父母念
今日爾應知

As soon as baby birds get ready to fly

They need be coaxed to take position on tree branches near by

Off they fly with no time to linger

The dispersed birds on wings seen no longer

The parents search in the air calling their young anxiously

Not a single baby bird returns home knowingly

To the empty nest mother and father their love prolong

They twitter grief all night long

Swallow swallow you needn't harbour any regret

To your own childhood days you must reflect

Remember those happy days you were growing up

You did also leave your parents to freely fly and hop

How your parents cared to be with you in anguish

The same caring you now know too late to appease howe'er you wish

琵琶行   Pipa Song

潯陽江頭夜送客	At river's Xun Yang Station I parted a friend one autumn night
楓葉荻花秋瑟瑟	Maple leaves and reed flowers scattered to sadly sigh
主人下馬客在船	I dismounted to greet my friend he was already on his boat
舉酒欲飲無管弦	We raised our cups to drink hearing no musical notes
醉不成歡慘將別	Without a song we drank flatly our hearts were heavy
別時茫茫江浸月	The moon in the river seemed to suggest our separation finality
忽聞水上琵琶聲	At that instant pipa music flowed from the water
主人忘歸客不發	We stood still while our boat pulled out its anchor
尋聲暗問彈者誰	We traced the source of music to find the musician
琵琶聲停欲語遲	In a moment of silence a hesitant pipa player entered our vision
移船相近邀相見	We moved our boat near to invite her over
添酒回燈重開宴	While we refurbished our party goodies for her to savour
千呼萬喚始出來	She appeared shy even after repeated calls sincere
猶抱琵琶半遮面	Holding her pipa to shield half her face as she moved to the centre
轉軸撥絃三兩聲	Twice or thrice she plucked the strings to test the sounds
未成曲調先有情	Before we heard a tune her music already touched us profound

絃絃掩抑聲聲思	The melodies revealed her deep thoughts and pathos strong
似訴平生不得志	As if telling about her unrealized wishes life-long
低眉信手續續彈	With brows lowered she played her instrument naturally
說盡心中無限事	To articulate social events and private feelings convincingly
輕攏慢撚抹復挑	Light plucks and brisk runs released all her emotions out
初為霓裳後六麼	From the scores of "Green Apparel" and "Colourful Clouds"
大絃嘈嘈如急雨	The heavy strings thrummed her theme like pattering rains
小絃切切如私語	The light strings tinkled in soft reverberating rings
嘈嘈切切錯雜彈	As loud patters and soft murmurs mixed to orchestrate
大珠小珠落玉盤	The notes and phrases resonated like pearls dropping in a jade plate
閒關鶯語花底滑	Oriole trills sliding through flower petals delightfully dinged
幽咽泉流水下灘	Sad sobs continuously trickled from a lingering spring
水泉冷澀絃凝絕	At times the cold water seems to congeal notes from the strings
凝絕不通聲漸歇	And submerge melodic sounds into fading hints
別有幽愁暗恨生	Still we heard vague grieving regrets in communicate
此時無聲勝有聲	Silence affected our souls more than loudness inundate
銀瓶乍破水漿迸	In a moment we heard the abrupt burst of a silver jar
鐵騎突出刀槍鳴	And saber clashes of soldiers riding steeds rumbling past

曲終收撥當心畫	Before the music ended she swept on the strings right across
四絃一聲如裂帛	All four strings exploded in a sound of tearing silk cloth
東船西舫悄無言	Silence reigned among listeners on boats left and right
唯見江心秋月白	At mid-river the moonshine was especially bright
沉吟放撥插絃中	Then she pensively slid the plectrum between the strings
整頓衣裳起斂容	And rose to tell us her story with a composed mien
自言本是京城女	I was born in the Capital she began to narrate
家在蝦蟆陵下住	At the foot of Toad Hill my home locate
十三學得琵琶成	At thirteen I learned to play the pipa the best way
名屬教坊第一部	My skills had put me among peers in prime place
曲罷曾教善才服	With every performance I earned warm encouraging praises
妝成每被秋娘妒	My beauty became the envy of maidens of yesterday
五陵年少爭纏頭	Young men crowded around to shower gifts on me
一曲紅綃不知數	A single performance would return rolls of fine silk free
鈿頭銀箆擊節碎	Being young I wasted my years collecting hairpins in silver
血色羅裙翻酒污	And allowed spilled wine to stain my silk gowns so improper
今年歡笑復明年	Time disappeared as I laughed my joyous life away
秋月春風等閒度	With the flow of moonlit nights in autumn and breezy spring days
弟走從軍阿姨死	With my younger brother joining the army and our servants gone

暮去朝來顏色故	My beauty began to fade as time wore on
門前冷落車馬稀	No longer were there carriages and fine steeds at my door
老大嫁作商人婦	So I married a merchant realizing my prime no longer in store
商人重利輕別離	My merchant husband cared for money more than for me
前月浮樑買茶去	He was often away doing trades on tea
去來江口守空船	Being his wife I watched time go by on a boat empty
繞船月明江水寒	In nights with shining moon my boat house was not homely
夜深忽夢少年事	I often dreamed of happy years washed away so free
夢啼妝淚紅闌幹	And woke up to find my rouge face drowned in tears

我聞琵琶已歎息	Listening to her sad music I sighed feeling pain
又聞此語重唧唧	Now hearing her story I sighed again and again
同是天涯淪落人	You and I are both in misfortune drifting from shore to shore
相逢何必曾相識	With this encounter need we have known each other before
我從去年辭帝京	I was banished from office in the Capital last year
謫居臥病潯陽城	To live a degraded life in sickness at Xun Yang near here
潯陽地僻無音樂	This place is too primitive to feature melodic songs
終歲不聞絲竹聲	I have not heard any sophisticated music all year long
住近湓城地低濕	Dwelling by the river the grounds are damp and low
黃蘆苦竹繞宅生	My house is amid scattering bamboo and wild reeds yellow

其間旦暮聞何物	What is there to hear from dawn to dusk simple
杜鵑啼血猿哀鳴	But repeating cuckoo calls and gibbon cries frightful
春江花朝秋月夜	On most spring morns and autumn moon evenings
往往取酒還獨傾	All I could do is to get drunk alone for entertaining
豈無山歌與村笛	Of course there are village pipes and mountain songs to hear
嘔啞嘲哳難為聽	But they are crude noises grate to the ear
今夜聞君琵琶語	I listen to you playing the pipa tonight
如聽仙樂耳暫明	Your divine music sooths my heart empowering me to hear fine
莫辭更坐彈一曲	It would be so pleasing if you would play us an encore
為君翻作琵琶行	In return I promise to write about your performance I so adore

感我此言良久立	She showed her gratitude by standing respectfully
卻坐促絃絃轉急	Then sat down to play the strings with quick sweeps elegantly
淒淒不似向前聲	Her superb performance produced tunes sad and dreary
滿座重聞皆掩泣	The audience was mesmerized and began to weep freely
座中泣下誰最多	Who wept the most among the people in the party
江州司馬青衫濕	None other than the host on blue robe sobbing unceasingly

錢塘湖春行 Visiting West Lake in Spring

孤山寺北賈亭西	Lone Hill north looks on the Jia Pavilion east
水面初平雲腳低	Beneath low clouds the lake water brims at ease
幾處早鶯爭暖樹	On the sun-warmed trees orioles compete to trill
誰家新燕啄春泥	With mud in beak to where goes the swallow
亂花漸欲迷人眼	Seeing so many flowers my eyes are dazzled
淺草才能沒馬蹄	On the short grass soft banks horse hooves show
最愛湖東行不足	How can I stroll the east bank enough I love so
綠楊陰裏白沙堤	Under green willow shades the White Sand Dyke glows

長相思 Tune: Eternal Pining

汴水流	The Bian River slowly flows
泗水流	The Si River chattily goes
流到瓜州古渡頭	They reach the ancient dock at Guazhou
吳山點點愁	Distant hills in the south mark my sorrows
思悠悠	My longings continue to show
恨悠悠	My complaints endlessly go
恨到歸時方始休	They will cease whence my love returns to me
月明人倚樓	Alone I stand on moonlit balcony

憶江南

江南好風景舊曾諳
日出江花紅勝火
春來江水綠如藍
能不憶江南

望月有感

時難年荒世業空
弟兄羈旅各西東
田園寥落干戈後
骨肉流離道路中
吊影分為千里雁
辭根散作九秋蓬
共看明月應垂淚
一夜鄉心五處同

Recall the South

The wonders of southern country I so highly admire
Dawn by the river bank flower blooms like red fire
In spring the river surges like gleaming sapphire
Can I not pine for the wonderful south I love

To My Brothers While Sharing the Moon

At a time of war and famine our family house lies forlorn
Brothers and sisters have freed east or west hearts torn
Gardens and fields lay fallow long after the soldiers gone
Family members strayed on hinder roads drifting on
Memories of dear ones seem like geese lost on long journey
Lineal roots dispersed wide like autumn weeds tumbly
Whence we watch the moon under separate roofs with tears
Though far apart our love for one another will keep us near

柳宗元 Liu Zongyuan (773–819)

溪居

久為簪組累
幸此南夷謫
閒依農圃鄰
偶似山林客
曉耕翻露草
夜榜響溪石
來往不逢人
長歌楚天碧

登柳州城樓寄漳、汀、封、連四州刺史

城上高樓接大荒
海天愁思正茫茫
驚風亂颭芙蓉水
密雨斜侵薜荔牆
嶺樹重遮千里目
江流曲似九迴腸
共來百越文身地
猶自音書滯一鄉

My Dwelling by the Stream

Bound by official girdles for many a year
I'm happy to be banished to this wild southern sphere
In leisure a pastoral neighbour and I make friends
I am a guest with trees in the hill end to end
At dawn I try to rid the weeds wet with dew
At dust I use my boat pole to rap the rocky hill
Walking about I often find no one in view
Loudly I sing towards a sky in shining hue

To Friends in Exile

From this high tower I see only a land untamed
Between sea and sky uneasy thoughts roam with no aim
A sudden gale ruffles the pond stirring lotus in bloom
Heavy rains beat the wall where climbers leave spotty room
Dense trees on the hills have views in a thousand *li* blocked out
Like flexuous bowels rivers meander round and about
Since coming to this uncultured land
Messages between you and I stagnant sent or not sent

漁翁　Old Fisherman

漁翁夜傍西巖宿	An old fisherman moors by the west cliff for the night
曉汲清湘燃楚竹	At dawn he boils the stream water on a bamboo fire
煙銷日出不見人	By sunrise the mist gone he is out of sight
欸乃一聲山水綠	Creaking the oars he enters a world of green admire
回看天際下中流	Down midstream he turns to view the horizon far away
巖上無心雲相逐	On cliff tops free clouds chase one another so gay

飲酒　Drinking

今夕少愉樂	Nothing joyful in view this evening
起坐開清尊	I get up to open a bottle of clear brew
舉觴酹先酒	Let me first thank the Lord of Wine
為我驅憂煩	He helps me dispel all worries in mind
須臾心自殊	A single draught makes the world different
頓覺天地暄	Everything becomes colourful and exuberant
連山變幽晦	Mountain scenes open my mind wide
綠水函晏溫	Greenish blue rivers bring warmth divine
藹藹南郭門	The southgate leads to jubilance
樹木一何繁	Flourishing trees wave arms in exuberance
清陰可自庇	Under the cool shades I feel fine
竟夕聞佳言	And hear silent advice into the night
盡醉無復辭	Should anyone say I must decline drunk with wine
偃臥有芳蓀	I lie on the perfume meadow rolling round and round
彼哉晉楚富	The rich and successful may claim with no experience
此道未必存	To say there's no joy in drunkenness

江雪

千山鳥飛絕
萬徑人蹤滅
孤舟蓑笠翁
獨釣寒江雪

晨詣超師院讀禪經

汲井漱寒齒
清心拂塵服
閒持貝葉書
步出東齋讀
真源了無取
妄跡世所逐
遺言冀可冥
繕性何由熟
道人庭宇靜
苔色連深竹
日出霧露餘
青松如膏沐
澹然離言說
悟悅心自足

River in Snow

A thousand hills where no birds fly
Ten thousand paths no man in sight
A straw-cloaked old man in a lone boat behold
Alone he fishes in a river of frozen snow

Reading Zen With Master Chao Early Morning

With cold water from the well I rinsed my mouth
Mind unperturbed I cleaned my gown any dust brushed out
Carefully I spread open the Sutra inscribed on durable leaves
To read it outside my study facing east
Buddhism truths their sources are difficult to identify
Many wisdom seekers tried hard but failed to find
Words of Zen promise the enlightened bliss in Nirvana
O How I'd love to go on way near the parameter
'Tis still and serene here in my master's terrain
Moss verdant adjoin deep bamboo paths their spirit pertain
At dawn traces of mist and dew Nature keeps
After an overnight bath demure pines attract zealous peeps
Master Chao wears a smile saying not a word
He has me enlightened although untaught

賈島 Jia Dao (779—843)

題興化園亭

破卻千家作一池
不栽桃李種薔薇
薔薇花落秋風起
荊棘滿庭君始知

Temple Garden

Against a thousand designs a single garden built
Only roses are cultivated fruit trees nil
Whence roses wither petals follow autumn winds fly
A garden of thorns remain consequences you abide

尋隱者不遇

松下問童子
言師採藥去
只在此山中
雲深不知處

Visiting a Hermit

I asked your whereabouts from your house boy in pine wood
He said you were out collecting herbs in good mood
You are surely somewhere in these hills
Who knows amid roaming clouds where you wander at will

遣悲懷

(I)

謝公最小偏憐女
自嫁黔婁百事乖
顧我無衣搜藎篋
泥他沽酒拔金釵
野蔬充膳甘長藿
落葉添薪仰古槐
今日俸錢過十萬
與君營奠復營齋

((II))

昔日戲言身後事
今朝都到眼前來
衣裳已施行看盡
針線猶存未忍開
尚想舊情憐婢僕
也曾因夢送錢財
誠知此恨人人有
貧賤夫妻百事哀

Remembering My Late Wife

(I)

Being the youngest you are the darling in your family
Marrying me in poverty you take up your new role caringly
Seeing me in tatters you empty contents of your dowry chest
With a gold hairpin you fetch wine to meet my drinking zest
Wild vegetables and herbs are made into nice dishes
They are cooked with fuels of dry tree branches
Now I earn more than a hundred thousand coins as salary
Alas I can but offer you sacrificial food and money

(II)

We joked once what you or I would do when one first died
Today this sad fact has become true for me with no deny
The clothes you had left are nearly all given away
But I loath to open your sewing box in any haste
I assure you that our servants are treated the same with your kindness
Whenever I dream of you I help needy people doing my best
Everyone must endure sorrow following a dear one's death
Couples poor like you and I suffer more than the rest

(III)

閒坐悲君亦自悲
百年都是幾多時
鄧攸無子尋知命
潘岳悼亡猶費詞
同穴窅冥何所望
他生緣會更難期
他生緣會更難期
報答平生未展眉

離思

曾經滄海難為水
除卻巫山不是雲
取次花叢懶回顧
半緣修道半緣君

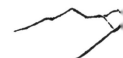

菊花

秋叢繞舍似陶家
遍繞籬邊日漸斜
不是花中偏愛菊
此花開盡更無花

(III)

Sitting alone I grieve for you and for me
My life is left with days numbered when I shall meet thee
Deng my childless friend accepts his lonely fate
Pan our neighbour widower pines for his wife words fade
Could I wish more than sharing the same tomb with you
Or be husband and wife with you through incarnation for sure
All I can do is to lie in gloom through nights with open eyes
To repay your love in a life with brows often knitted tight

To My Lover

I've crossed many seas to devote myself to water
In my heart no cloud can compare with the cloud of Mount Wu
Among flowers in profusion I've been tardy to pursue
Partly for my devotion to Dao partly because I love you

Chrysanthemum

Autumn mums adorn my cottage as they did Tao's house in days old
Along the hedge their brilliance so vivid I linger until the sun hangs low
I can't be blamed for loving this flower my appreciation partial
Whence they wither away there will be no flower to follow

金銅仙人辭漢歌

茂陵劉郎秋風客

夜聞馬嘶曉無迹

畫欄桂樹懸秋香

三十六宮土花碧

魏官牽車指千里

東關酸風射眸子

空將漢月出宮門

憶君清淚如鉛水

衰蘭送客咸陽道

天若有情天亦老

攜盤獨出月荒涼

渭城已遠波聲小

From the Han Palace the Bronze Statue Depart

The Emperor gone like an autumn breeze
His steed neighed at night by dawn no trace
In the painting laurel trees stood mute besides guarding rails
Invading moss grew covering grounds of his thirty-six palaces
The palace attendants prepared a carriage to cover a thousand *li*
At the Eastern Pass acid wind twirled to deter him from advancing

Only the moon of yesterday saw him leave the palace door
Overcame by sadness tears rolled like mercury ball
Only withering orchids said adieu to bid him farewell
If there was heavenly love it would grow old as well
For a companion a desolate moon remained on a silver plate not abate
The Capital was far behind as his gallop roars faded

許渾 Xu Hun (791−858)

塞上曲　　　　　A Frontier Song

夜戰桑乾北　　Our soldiers fought on the northern shore at night
秦兵半不歸　　Half of them returned half died
朝來有鄉信　　Messages arrived this morning
猶自寄寒衣　　Winter clothes from home will be coming

謝亭送別　　　　Farewell at Parting Pavilion

勞歌一曲解行舟　Following the farewell song the boatman let loose the boat
紅葉青山水急流　Amid red leaves and green mountains rapids flow
日暮酒醒人已遠　I awake from drunk at dusk you had gone far
滿天風雨下西樓　Beneath winds and rains I leave for home fast

秋日赴闕題潼關驛樓
Returning to the Capital in Autumn

紅葉晚蕭蕭	Crimson leaves sigh and sigh in the evening
長亭酒一瓢	I drank a full gourd of wine at the Long Pavilion
殘雲歸太華	As dwindling clouds return to West Mount up high
疏雨過中條	Light rain showers the middle ridges from behind
樹色隨關迴	I see trees in brilliant colours circle the city wall
河聲入海遙	I hear rumbles going to the distant sea river pour
帝鄉明日到	I shall be arriving at the Capital tomorrow
猶自夢漁樵	I still dream of playing a fisher or woodcutter's role

盧同 Lu Tong (795−835)

走筆謝孟諫議寄新茶

日高丈五睡正濃
軍將打門驚周公
口雲諫議送書信
白絹斜封三道印
開緘宛見諫議面
手閱月團三百片

柴門反關無俗客
紗帽籠頭自煎吃
碧雲引風吹不斷
白花浮光凝碗面

一碗喉吻潤
兩碗破孤悶
三碗搜枯腸
唯有文字五千卷
四碗發輕汗
平生不平事
盡向毛孔散
五碗肌骨清
六碗通仙靈
七碗吃不得也
唯覺兩腋習習清
蓬萊山，在何處
玉川子，乘此清風欲歸去

A Note with a Gift of New Tea

In deep slumber at high noon I feel happy
A minor officer knocks and wakes me up suddenly
To announce the delivery of a note personal
A silk-wrap box marked by three seals emerald
Opening the package to read the note at ease
I find a cake of tea with three hundred tea leaves

Closing my wicket with no one else inside
Amid vapour and aroma I brew tea to drink in delight
Clear clouds and a gentle breeze soothe continual
White flowers float to the brim of the bowl

Drinking one bowl my throat feels wet and tranquil
A second bowl drives away my solitary ills
The third bowl surges my guts thorough
To reveal five thousand volumes of words sensible
The fourth bowl induces perspiration mild
Through open pores dispel all injustice in life

The fifth bowl relaxes my bones and muscles
The sixth bowl touches my very soul
Holding the seventh bowl I could drink no more
My two arms have turned into wings on winds soar
Wherever is the land of the immortals
With my new wings I wish to pursue eternal

贈別二首

(I)

娉娉裊裊十三餘

豆蔻梢頭二月初

春風十里揚州路

卷上珠簾總不如

(II)

多情卻似總無情

唯覺尊前笑不成

蠟燭有心還惜別

替人垂淚到天明

題宣州開元寺水閣

六朝文物草連空

天淡雲閒今古同

鳥去鳥來山色裏

人歌人哭水聲中

深秋簾幕千家雨

落日樓台一笛風

惆悵無日見范蠡

參差煙樹五湖東

Parting Two Poems

(I)

Slender and graceful she is in early teens
Like a cardamom tip with growing hints
Vernal breezes warm up ten miles of scenic roads
Behind roll up curtains her beauty brilliantly shows

(II)

Deeply in love yet we appear not to be
Drinking to part we know not how a smile can begin
The candle has a wick just as we have a heart
Through the night it sheds tears for us before we part

Ruins in Splendour

The cultural splendours of the Sixth Dynasty are no more
Leisure clouds roam in the pale sky the same as yore
Birds come and go through reds and greens up wooded hills
Happy songs and sad wails mix sinking deep in murmuring rills
A thousand houses veiled behind curtains in late autumn rains
As the sun set towers and terraces heard a lone flute sing
How I miss the Sage by the lakeside in bygone days
When old trees stood in haze east of the Five Lakes

江南春

千里鶯啼綠映紅
水村山郭酒旗風
南朝四百八十寺
多少樓台煙雨中

清明

清明時節雨紛紛
路上行人欲斷魂
借問酒家何處有
牧童遙指杏花村

遣懷

落魄江湖載酒行
楚腰纖細掌中輕
十年一覺揚州夢
贏得青樓薄幸名

Spring South of the River

Orioles sing in a thousand *li* amid blooms red and green
Wine shops by hills and rills hoist banners to lure people in
Four hundred eighty splendid temples of yore still remain
Together with pagodas through years of mists and rains

Qing Ming Festival

Qing Ming day for remembering ancestors is usually in drizzles
Visitors struggle on roads to graveyards their hearts fissure
Where could I find a tavern to drown out this sad hour
A cowherd points to a village beyond the apricot flowers

Confession

Roving in rivers and lakes I indulge in pleasure and wine
Slender southern girls dance their hips in my hand fine
Awoke from a ten-year dream of roving life in action
I earned the name of a fickle lover among green mansions

泊秦淮

煙籠寒水月籠沙
夜泊秦淮近酒家
商女不知亡國恨
隔江猶唱後庭花

寄揚州韓綽判官

青山隱隱水迢迢
秋盡江南草未凋
二十四橋明月夜
玉人何處教吹簫

Mooring on River Qinhuai

Mist veils the frigid water while moonlight veils the sandbar
I moor on the Qinhuai River at dusk to sample the bars
Songstresses know not their motherland in defeat
They sing to glorify the new ruler their voice peak

To Magistrate Han of Yang Zhou

Behind the green hills water flows far
With autumn leaving southern grass is yet to wither
Whence the twenty four bridges in brilliance by moonshine
Where is your favourite lass whose flute music so fine

李商隱 Li Shangyin (812—858)

無題

來是空言去是蹤
月斜樓上五更鐘
夢為遠別啼難喚
書被催成墨未濃

蠟照半籠金翡翠
麝熏微度繡芙蓉
劉郎已恨蓬山遠
更隔蓬山一萬重

無題

相見時難別亦難
東風無力百花殘
春蠶到死絲方盡
蠟炬成灰淚始乾
曉鏡但愁雲鬢改
夜吟應覺夜光寒
蓬山此去無多路
青鳥殷勤為探看

No Title

You promise to come but gone without a hint
I wake as the moon wane to hear the dawn bell ring
I meet you in my dream when cocks crow loudly
And try to write you before the ink is ready

The candlelight kept half of our broidered bed lit
The musk scent from the censor filled the room sweet
The Fairy Mount is far beyond reach
Ten thousand mounts away you are faraway indeed

No Title

Staying together is difficult and parting even more heart-rending
Whence the east wind blows weak how could flowers not be fading
Silkworms die not until they have spun all silks so lingering
Candles burn out only when no more tears can be dripping
A morning look into the mirror you are alarmed of locks greying
Your sad croons by night makes the moon feel unnaturally chilling
'Tis not far to reach the legendary isles from here
Would the blue birds care to find the way to lead you there

無題

昨夜星辰昨夜風
畫樓西畔桂堂東
身無彩鳳雙飛翼
心有靈犀一點通
隔座送鈎春酒暖
分曹射覆蠟燈紅
嗟餘聽鼓應官去
走馬蘭台類轉蓬

嫦娥

雲母屏風燭影深
長河漸落曉星沉
嫦娥應悔偷靈藥
碧海青天夜夜心

No Title

Watching last night's starry twilight in the gentle wind
And thinking of you in your bower at the East Cassia Hall
How I wished to be with you if only I had wings
With telepathy you must have heard my inner call
Could it be when you were drinking with friends wine so warm
Or reading cup signs beside burning candles brilliant lights shone
Alas I am hearing drums to summon me to duties officially
And mount my steed to head for the Capital however unwillingly

To Cheng E the Moon Goddess

Behind the agate screen candlelight flickers vividly
As the Milky Way wanes stars fade away gradually
O Moon Goddess you ought to regret taking the elixir behind your family
By nights you are doomed to miss your dears from this side of the Galaxy

登樂遊原

向晚意不適
驅車登古原
夕陽無限好
只是近黃昏

錦瑟

錦瑟無端五十弦
一絃一柱思華年
莊生曉夢迷蝴蝶
望帝春心託杜鵑
滄海月明珠有淚
藍田日暖玉生煙
此情可待成追憶
只是當時已惘然

To Ancient Tomb Mount

Towards dusk I felt a sense of gloom
I drove my carriage to visit the ancient tombs
The setting sun shines its brilliance so sublime
How I wish this grandeur is not a sign of vanishing time

The Zither

It is not known why the zither has fifty strings
Each string and strain evokes the vanishing times of spring
In his morning dreams Zhuangzi fancied the love life of butterflies
And past emperors expressed their amorous desires through cuckoo cries
In the moonlit ocean luminous pearls sadly shed tears
Across the sun-warmed fields white vapours rise
Such beautiful feelings await future memory recalls
But I was at a loss then not knowing what it was for

利州南渡

澹然空水對斜暉
曲島蒼茫接翠微
波上馬嘶看棹去
柳邊人歇待船歸
數叢沙草羣鷗散
萬頃江田一鷺飛
誰解乘舟尋范蠡
五湖煙水獨忘機

西陵道士茶歌

乳竇濺濺通石脈
綠塵愁草春江色
澗花入井水味香
山月當人鬆影直
仙翁白扇霜鳥翎
拂壇夜讀黃庭經
疏香皓齒有餘味
更覺鶴心通杳冥

Ferrying South from Lizhou

The slanting rays of sunset shine on limpid water
Jagged islets float under a blue sky near
Horses neigh seeing the ferry moving away
People wait for returning boats in willow shades
From the sand grass tufts gulls take flight
O'er ten thousand *li* of fields a heron glides
Who would ride a skiff to find Fan Li so wise
He sailed in the misty Five Lakes leaving worldly strives behind

A Tea Song of Daoist Xi Ling

Water drips along icy columns in caves serene
Spring grass and tea creams colour the river green
Wild flowers follow streams to the well fragrance in action
Amicable pines wave in moonshine to invite appreciation
Our dear immortal waves his white feathers for breeze
As he sings the Daoist classics at night to please
Flavours of this tea brew linger in between my teeth
On crane's wings I arrive near yonder free sphere

更漏子 · 柳絲長

Tune: Water Clock Drips All Night – Willow Tendrils Lengthy

柳絲長	Willow tendrils lengthy
春雨細	Vernal drizzles plenty
花外漏聲迢遞	Beyond the flowers the water clock drips all night
驚寒雁	Startled geese take flight
起城烏	Crows on city walls high
畫屏金鷓鴣	In the painted screens partridges frolic in delight
香霧薄	Fragrant mist light
透簾幕	Penetrating the silk tapestry hung high
惆悵謝家池閣	I sit by the solitary pool to sigh
紅燭背	Behind the red candles
繡簾垂	By the closed brocade panels
夢長君不知	I dream of you if you care to know

更漏子 · 玉爐香
Tune: Water Clock Drips All Night – The Jade Censor Fragrant Usual

玉爐香	The jade censor fragrant usual
紅蠟淚	Red candle burnt tearful
偏照畫堂秋思	In the shadowy parlour autumn thoughts linger
眉翠薄	Eyebrows painted pale
鬢雲殘	Hair bun dishevel
夜長衾枕寒	In the long night cold are the quilt and pillow
梧桐樹	Lonely pine trees
三更雨	After midnight rains
不道離情正苦	They speak not of her bitter parting sorrow
一葉葉	Leaf by leaf solitary
一聲聲	Sound by sound singly
空階滴到明	They fall on vacant steps till dawn

商山早行

晨起動徵鐸
客行悲故鄉
雞聲茅店月
人迹板橋霜
槲葉落山路
枳花明驛牆
因思杜陵夢
鳧雁滿回塘

夢江南

梳洗罷
獨倚望江樓
過盡千帆皆不是
斜暉脈脈水悠悠
腸斷白蘋洲

Early Departure

Early I rise to rush to the carriage station
Pining for home I hurry to start the motion
Cocks crow while the moon is still over my inn
On the bridge frost keeps travellers from coming in
The hill path is dotted with fallen oak leaves delight
While the post-house wall gleams with orange blossoms bright
I dreamed last night of a different scene
Frolicking in my native pond mallards and geese fondly seen

Tune: Pining for Home in the South

After my morning routine affairs
Alone I watch far from up stairs
I see you not in a thousand passing sails
The setting sun silent the flow eternal
My broken heart remains on Islet of farewell

河傳

湖上

閒望

雨蕭蕭

煙浦花橋路遙

謝娘翠娥愁不銷

終朝

夢魂迷晚潮

蕩子天涯歸棹遠

春已晚

鶯語工腸斷

若耶溪

溪水西

柳堤

不聞郎馬嘶

曹松 Cao Song (828－903)

己亥歲感事

澤國江山入戰圖

生民何計樂樵蘇

憑君莫話封侯事

一將功成萬骨枯

Tune: from the River

By the lake
She watches vague
Everywhere rains
Distant beach and bridge in rainy haze
Eyebrows knit the songstress is sad as scenery prolong
All day long
She is lost in the evening tidal song
Her wandering lover is not coming home
'Tis late spring
Her heart breaks hearing orioles sing
Ask the brook
West of the brook
On the long willowy pathway
When will she hear her lover's horse neigh

The War Years

The lush countryside has been marked for battles
People here can no longer work and live without sorrow
Tell me not of glories of generals and kings
A victor's success is built on bones ten thousand soldiers slained

 羅隱 Luo Yin (833–909)

自遣　Relaxation

得即高歌失即休	Sing your accomplishments accept any failures practically
多愁多恨亦悠悠	And dispel whatever sorrow or hate for tranquillity
今朝有酒今朝醉	Fine brews on hand drink your fill today
明日愁來明日愁	Let go possible worries to come the next day

雪　Snow

盡道豐年瑞	They say abundant snow forebodes a bumper year
豐年事若何	What good is bumper harvest if distribution unfair
長安有貧者	As hungry folks linger within Capital walls
為瑞不宜多	Let's pray heavy snow does not oft fall

皮日休 Pi Rixiu (834–883)

茶舍 Tea Hut

陽崖枕白屋	A grey hut stands beneath the south cliff
幾口嬉嬉活	A small family happily lives
棚上汲紅泉	A clear spring runs through the bamboo deck
焙前蒸紫蕨	Before baking tender tea tips give a sweet sap
乃翁研茗後	Father grinds the tea leaves fine
中婦拍茶歇	Mother sings tea songs to rhyme

章碣 Zhang Jie (836－905)

焚書坑

竹帛煙銷帝業虛
關河空鎖祖龍居
坑灰未冷山東亂
劉項原來不讀書

韋莊 Wei Zhuang (836－910)

章台夜思

清瑟怨遙夜
繞弦風雨哀
孤燈聞楚角
殘月下章台
芳草已雲暮
故人殊未來
鄉書不可寄
秋雁又南回

Book Burning Pit

Smoke of burning classics rise to signal the empire's fall
Wall gates and rivers fail to guard the imperial dragon hall
Before the burning pit cooled the rebels east of the mountain is gathering speed
The leaders Liu and Xiang are not interested to read

Night Thoughts on Terrace Tower

A sighing lute laments the night being long
The string melodies sad as wind and rain
By the lamplight I hear bugles roaring on
Beyond Terrace Tower the moon steadily wanes
My best friends are on their searching ways
My old pals have yet to return with sure dates
I have no way to send messages home
The southbound geese had departed early in autumn

荷葉杯　　Tune: Cup of Lotus Leaves

記得那年花下	I recall that year we stood amid beautiful flowers
深夜	At late hour
初識謝娘時	When I first met you my sweet
水堂西面畫簾垂	In your curtained bower on west street
攜手暗相期	We held hands to promise a future meeting hour
惆悵曉鶯殘月	The moon waned and orioles cried too soon
相別	We parted
從此隔音塵	No more communication
如今俱是異鄉人	Now unknowns we are living in different places
相見更無因	There is no cause for meeting again

菩薩蠻　　Tune: Buddhist Dancers

人人盡說江南好	They all say how beautiful is southern land
遊人只合江南老	Wanderers like to stay there till lives end
春水碧於天	Water in spring green as the sky
畫船聽雨眠	On painted boats one sits in the rain to sigh
壚邊人似月	Tavern attendants are beautiful as the moon
皓腕凝霜雪	Their arms frosty white as snow
未老莫還鄉	Do not return home north before you grow old
還鄉須斷腸	To leave for home will be heartbreak for sure

金陵圖　　　　The Ancient Capital

江雨霏霏江草齊	The river in drizzles its banks covered with grass so green
六朝如夢鳥空啼	The Six Dynasties gone no bird's cry would again win
無情最是台城柳	Willows unfeeling stand on guard for all portals
依舊煙籠十里堤	They loom like mist adorning the Capital

菩薩蠻　　　　Tune: Buddhist Dance

勸君今夜須沉醉	Please get drunk tonight to drown your sorrows
樽前莫話明朝事	Wine jar in hand speak not of tomorrow
珍重主人心	I am grateful to you for this your kind advice
酒深情亦深	Your hospitality and wine are accepted with delight
須愁春漏短	Worry you may that spring is short as water-clock drips dictate
莫訴金杯滿	Complain not of full cups but take them in haste
遇酒且呵呵	Rejoice when in laughters wine comes your way
人生能幾何	Happiness appears only so sparingly you may say

聶夷中 Nie Yizhong (837－884)

田家　　　　　Peasants

父耕原上田	On the old plain fathers toil
子屬山下荒	Down hills sons cultivate land into soil
六月禾未秀	In June crops are still in blade
官家已修倉	Official granaries are busily made

張泌 Zhang Bi (842－914)

寄人　　　　　To My Love

別夢依依到謝家	I follow you in my dreams where're you are
小廊回合曲闌斜	The zigzag corridors in your courtyard in my heart here
多情只有春庭月	Impressed with my love for you the moon keeps her shine
猶為離人照落花	To uphold our longing for each other divine

崔塗 Cui Tu (854—date of death unknown)

除夜有懷　Thoughts on New Year's Eve

迢遞三巴路	Far and wide the roads to Ba country in the west
羈危萬里身	Ten thousand *li* away from home my heart knows no rest
亂山殘雪夜	Amid the snow covered hills I pass the night
孤燭異鄉人	A stranger I remain by candlelight
漸與骨肉遠	Farther and farther I stay away from my dear kins
轉於僮僕親	Servants befriend me their care needs no hint
那堪正飄泊	O how I loath to remain in this roving life
明日歲華新	On New Year's Day tomorrow I'll begin anew outright

皇甫曾 Huang Fuzeng

送陸鴻漸山人採茶
Seeing Master Lu off to Pick Teas

千峯待逋客	A thousand hills await Master Lu's visit
香茗復叢生	Fragrant tea leaves thrive featuring tender tips
採摘知深處	He knows the best picks in the mountain deep
煙霞羨獨行	Alone he pursues following scenic leads
幽期山寺遠	His mind rests in a temple far wherever
野飯石泉清	He quenches his thirst in springs bursting from boulders
寂寂燃燈夜	Comes the Lantern Fest of the year in solitude
相思一磬聲	A distant knell warms the heart in gratitude

五代
FIVE DYNASTIES
(907–960)

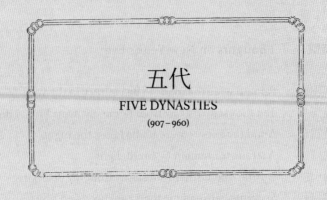

顧夐 Gu Xiong (date of birth unknown－928)

訴衷情　　　　　Tune: Revealing Inner Feelings

永夜拋人何處去　Where were you all night leaving me
絕來音　　　　　Not a word from thee
香閣掩　　　　　I kept my chamber closed tight
眉斂　　　　　　Eyebrows knit
月將沉　　　　　Till the moon out of sight

爭忍不相尋　　　How could you not long for me
怨孤衾　　　　　To this lone quilt I loath
換我心　　　　　Exchange my heart
為你心　　　　　For your heart
始知相憶深　　　You may feel for me as I feel for thee

鹿虔扆 Lu Qianyi

臨江仙（節選）　Tune: Riverside Immortals (selected part)

金鎖重門荒苑靜　Doors heavily locked this deserted garden sits still
綺窗愁對秋空　　Ornate windows face the autumn sky sad and chill
翠華一去寂無　　Once gone the royal flag leaves not a trace
玉樓歌吹　　　　Singing in the bower of jade
聲斷已隨風　　　Gone with the wind its tunes faded

張喬 Zhang Qiao

書邊事 On the Frontier

調角斷清秋	Bugle sounds cut through the austere autumn air
征人倚戍樓	Tired of fighting I lean on the watch tower for a rest
春風對青冢	Spring breezes keep graves green and fair
白日落梁州	The white sun sets toward the northwest
大漠無兵阻	The vast desert is free of troops for now
窮邊有客遊	Travellers brave to reach the far frontier
蕃情似此水	The Barbarian wishes are like rivers in this area
長願向南流	They strive to push down south year after year

牛希濟 Niu Xiji (date of birth unknown–925)

山渣子　　　Tune: Mountain Hawthorn

春山煙欲收　　Spring hills are about to rid their misty veil
天淡星稀小　　 Pale sky sees stars small and pale
殘月臉邊明　　The waning moon her face in shiny hue
別淚臨清曉　　Approaching dawn tears turn to dews

語已多　　　　Much has been said
情未了　　　　Love relations yet to be set
回首猶重道　　She turns to emphatically add
記得綠羅裙　　Keep this green skirt deep in your mind
處處憐芳草　　Where'er you roam do not leave this love behind

蝶戀花

幾日行雲何處去
忘卻歸來
不道春將暮
百草千花寒食路
香車繫在誰家樹
淚眼倚樓頻獨語
雙燕來時
陌上相逢否
撩亂春愁如柳絮
悠悠夢裏無尋處

南鄉子

細雨濕流光
芳草年年與恨長
回首鳳樓無限事　茫茫
鸞鏡鴛衾兩斷腸

魂夢任悠揚
睡起楊花滿繡床
薄幸不來門半掩　斜陽
負你殘春淚幾行

Tune: Butterfly Loves Flower

Where do you roam like floating clouds day after day
Remembering not home
Nor spring growing old
Hundreds of grass and flowers line up the Cold-Meal road
At whose residence your carriage and horse the trees hold
Drown in tears I watch from the balcony muttering regret
Visits a pair of swallows
I wonder if they had seen you along the road
They stir up love longings spreading like flakes of willow
Even in blurry dreams I could not find you high or low

Tune: Southern Country Song

Drizzles keep the running time glide at ease
Fragrant grass thrives with sorrows as years increase
Encaged here in this bower past happiness is now distant
The love-bird quilt and mirror remind me of heart-breaks this instant

In dreams my soul goes anywhere I please
Whence awake I find catkins covering my bed a million pieces
My fickle lover visits me no more my rift door invites the setting sun
For our vanishing spring I owe you tears like streams run

菩薩蠻

花明月黯籠輕霧
今霄好向郎邊去
衩襪步香階
手提金縷鞋

畫堂南畔見
一向偎人顫
奴為出來難
教君恣意憐

烏夜啼

昨夜風兼雨
簾幃颯颯秋聲
燭殘漏斷頻倚枕
起坐不能平

世事漫隨流水
算來一夢浮生
醉鄉路穩宜頻到
此外不堪行

Tune: Buddhist Dancer

Bright flowers veiled in thin mist under dim moonlight
'Tis an opportune time to venture your way my love
With torn stockings in fragrant steps
Holding slippers sown with golden threads

We meet south of the painted hall
In your firm trembling embrace I fall
'Tis not easy for me to meet you as I wish
Do caress me every way as you please

Tune: Crow Cries by Night

Raining wind soughed all night long
My door screen rustled like an autumn song
Water clock drips kept me from sleep after candlelight died
I got up from bed with a disquiet mind

All things drift gone like water in a perishing stream
Life floats like a dream
Let's frequent the road to beautiful drunkland
Nothing else is worth lifting a hand

相見歡・虞美人

春花秋月何時了
往事知多少
小樓昨夜又東風
故國不堪回首月明中
雕闌玉砌應猶在
只是朱顏改

問君能有幾多愁
恰似一江春水向東流

清平樂

別來春半
觸目柔腸斷
砌下落梅如雪亂
拂了一身還滿
雁來音信無憑
路遙歸夢難成
離恨恰如春草
更行更遠還生

Happily Together – Tune: Yu the Beautiful

Whence in cycles of spring flowers and autumn moon will time stand still
How many past events should remain on my memory wheel
Vernal breeze showed pity again warming my humble chamber last night
Down memory lane I dare not review my lost kingdom by moonlight
Jade palaces their ornate railings must still be on ground
So many fair lasses there before are no longer around

Ask how many sad memories I keep my consciousness on
They flow like spring river torrents on and on

Tune: Serene Music

Spring is half gone since we parted
My heart breaks where'er it tries to park
Mume blossoms fall like scattering snow
They cling on me though I brushed them off moments ago
The geese came bringing no message from you
Home is too far even in a dream
Parting griefs are like grass in spring
They thrive however far I walk trying to leave them behind

浪淘沙

簾外雨潺潺
春意闌珊
羅衾不耐五更寒
夢裏不知身是客
一晌貪歡
獨自莫憑欄
無限江山
別時容易見時難
流水落花春去也
天上人間

相見歡

無言獨上西樓
月如鈎
寂寞梧桐深院
鎖清秋
剪不斷
理還亂
是離愁
別是一般滋味在心頭

Tune: Waves Refining Sands

Drizzles patter outside my closed blinds
Spring feelings abound
Near dawn my quilt cannot warm my chills
I dreamed my captive life cast aside
For a moment of delight
Whence looking o'er these railings I should not solitarily stand
To reminisce about my lost empire its boundless land
'Tis easier to part than yearning for re-union again
Gone are the happy days with withered flowers and perishing flow
Same on high yonder as among man I know

Tune: The Joy of Togetherness

Silently the west tower I alone ascend
The crescent moon hangs
Lonely the plane tree in courtyard stands
Autumn is locked still
Cutting would not sever
Reasoning ne'er
'Tis the sadness of separation
A heart-rending feeling set deep in the soul

虞美人・風回小院庭蕪綠

風回小院庭蕪綠
柳眼春相續
憑闌半日獨無言
依舊竹聲新月似當年
笙歌未散尊前在
池面冰初解
燭明香暗畫堂深
滿鬢清霜殘雪思難任

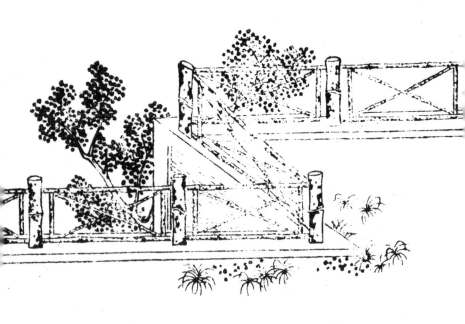

Tune: Yu the Beautiful − Wind Returns to My Small Courtyard Deplete of Green

Wind returns to my small courtyard deplete of green
The willows seem to thrive again this spring
On the railings I lean for half a day without a word
The new moon and bamboo murmur like yore
Music and songs remain with dinning and wine
Ice on pool tops melts as the weather turns mild
Candlelight and subdue fragrance keep the ornate hall alive
This greying in my temple must I abide

3

Part C

Song Dynasty

(960–1279)

宋朝

SONG DYNASTY

(960-1279)

魏野 Wei Ye (960—1019)

書友人屋壁 Written on the Wall of a Friend's House

達人輕祿位	A wise man views powerful positions not inviting
居處傍林泉	Settling house near woods and springs
洗硯魚吞墨	Washing his inkwell he feeds fishes with ink
烹茶鶴避煙	Brewing tea birds fly away to avoid smoking
閒惟歌聖代	In leisure he sings for the happy present
老不恨流年	In old age he regrets not the passing springs
靜想閒來者	Ask who knows the meaning of relaxation
還應我最偏	No other than I who shuns wealth and reputation

葉紹翁 Ye Shaoweng (1100—1151)

遊園不值 Visiting a Garden with an Absent Host

應憐履齒印蒼苔	Tender moss dislikes my clogs their teeth inflict pain
小扣柴扉久不開	I tap the door repeatedly no one answers my call
春色滿園關不住	No garden can confine the splendour of spring
一枝紅杏出牆來	A red apricot branch extends o'er the fence wall

王觀 Wang Guan (1035−1100)

卜算子・送鮑浩然之浙東

水是眼波橫
山是眉峯聚
欲問行人去那邊
眉眼盈盈處

才始送春歸
又送君歸去
若到江南趕上春
千萬和春住

潘閬 Pan Lang (date of birth unknown−1009)

酒泉子

長憶西湖
盡日憑欄樓上望
三三兩兩釣魚舟
島嶼正清秋

笛聲依約蘆花裏
白鳥成行忽驚起
別來閒整釣魚竿
思入水雲寒

Tune: Song of Divination – To a Departing Friend

Rippling waters stretch to beam the eyes
On arched brows mountains gather high
Should you ask wayfarers whither bound
Just search where beaming eyes are found

I've just seen spring depart
And now you and I must part
Down south if you should catch a spring day
Be sure to keep her with you always

Tune: Wine Spring

I shall always remember West Lake
Daily I watched leaning on the rails gazing with no break
Fish boats passed by in twos and threes
Islets in clear cool autumn breezes

Amid the flowery reeds flute songs rose
Startled white birds swiftly flew in rows
Departed I now repair my fishing rod in my leisure
Lost in thoughts of water and clouds with quiet pleasure

古成之 Gu Chengzhi (968–1038)

憶羅浮

憶昔羅浮最上峯
當年曾得寄仙踪
憑欄月色出滄海
欹枕秋聲入古松
採藥靜尋幽澗洗
寄書閒仗白雲封
紅塵一下拘名利
不聽山間午夜鐘

Remembering Mount Luofu

I recall the highest peak of Mount Luofu in days old
Up there dwelled immortals their presence known
By the rail I watch the moon emerging from the sea
On my pillow I hear autumn winds amid old pines hiss
I quietly pick medicine herbs and wash them on stream
And write to dialogue with white clouds on my staff I lean
Why should I battle for gains of money and fame
And miss hearing the twilight peals in the mountain

范仲淹 Fan Zhongyan (969–1052)

御街行　　　　Tune: Strolling on Royal Walk

紛紛墜葉飄香砌	On fragrant ground green leaves shower
夜寂靜	In a night so still
寒聲碎	Bricking sounds chill

真珠簾卷玉樓空　　Behind rolled up blinds an empty bower
天淡銀河垂地　　　From a pale sky the Milky Ways lower

年年今夜　　　　　This night every year
月華如練　　　　　Bright moonlight near
長是人千里　　　　We are a thousand *li* apart

愁腸已斷無由醉　　A broken heart allows me not to get drunk
酒未到　　　　　　Before wines arrive
先成淚　　　　　　Tears have my face covered

殘燈明滅枕頭倚　　I rest on my pillow alone in flickering light
諳盡孤眠滋味　　　To feel the sorrow of a lonely night

都來此事　　　　　Griefs as they appear
眉間心上　　　　　On brows or deep in the heart
無計相回避　　　　Unavoidable they are

漁家傲　　Tune: Fisherman's Pride

塞下秋來風景異　Autumn scene in the frontier looks extraordinary
衡陽雁去無留意　Wild geese leave with no love to stay
四面邊聲連角起　From all four corners bugles repeatedly roar

千嶂裏　　Walled in by peaks
長煙落日孤城閉　The town gates are lowered before sun-fall

濁酒一杯家萬里　I hold a cup of unstrained wine knowing home is far away
燕然未勒歸無計　Short of a clear victory any plan to return home is in sway
羌管悠悠霜滿地　On frosty grounds foreign flutes tune only doleful says
人不寐　　No one could sleep
將軍白髮征夫淚　Seeing the general's hair grey soldiers weep

蘇幕遮　Tune: Behind Silk Screens

碧雲天	White clouds pale the blue sky
黃葉地	Yellow leaves fill the grounds high
秋色連波	Waves on waves of autumn colours flow
波上寒煙翠	Tethering green mists aglow
山映斜陽天接水	On shiny hills sun rays vividly spray
芳草無情	In the horizon water and sky a single display
更在斜陽外	Whither are you my unfeeling lover
黯鄉魂	Beyond the setting sun hover
追旅思	My soul is homebound
夜夜除非	Following dreams around
好夢留人睡	Night after night present and past events meet
明月高樓休獨倚	Sweet dreams prolong slumbers so neat
酒入愁腸	Up on the high bower in moonlit nights
化作相思淚	'Tis better not to lean on rails alone
	As wines touch bowels in sorrow
	Nostalgic thoughts heave and tears roll

柳永 Liu Yong (987-1053)

望海潮

東南形勝
江吳都會
錢塘自古繁華
煙柳畫橋
風簾翠幕
參差十萬人家
雲樹繞堤沙
怒濤捲霜雪
天塹無涯
市列珠璣

戶盈羅綺
競豪奢
重湖疊巘清嘉
有三秋桂子
十里荷花
羌管弄晴
菱歌泛夜
嬉嬉釣叟蓮娃
千騎擁高牙
乘醉聽簫鼓
吟賞煙烟霞
異日圖將好景
歸去鳳池誇

Tune: Watching the Tides

Southeast scenic splendour
Capital of ancient Kingdom Wu
Qiantang thrives today as ever
Misty willows along painted bridges
Breezy windows their curtains green
To adorn a hundred thousand dwellings
Cloud-crowned trees surround the sandy banks
Roaring waves roll up a sky of snowy sands
This river extends to land's end
Mounts of pearly jewels on display at the daily fair

Homes filled with splendid silk and satin array
Folks here compete in magnificent opulence
Layers of lakes reflect the peaks and serene towers
Autumn fragrances linger with osmanthus flowers
Ten thousand *li* of blooming lotus
Northern pipes play with sunshine
Water chestnut songs sung on starry nights
Old fishermen and native maidens beam with delight
A thousand stallions hoisting flags to bid your arrival
Tipsy you may best appreciate melodies of flutes and drums
Chanting praises for this wonderful land beneath the sun
On a future date you might render this grand scene in flowery narrations
And boast your experience to the court with warm affection

憶帝京

薄衾小枕涼天氣
乍覺別離滋味

輾轉數寒更
起了還重睡
畢竟不成眠
一夜長如歲
也擬待
卻回征轡
又爭奈
已成行計
萬種思量
多方開解
只憑寂寞厭厭地
繫我一身心
負你千行淚

Tune: Recalling the Imperial Capital

In meagre quilt and small pillow when weather is cold
I begin to suffer the parting sorrow

Tossing in bed I count the chilly hours
Getting up only to return to bed however
Can't sleep
The night feels lonely as year
How I wish to return to you for perpetual stay
But I'm already far away
A thousand deliberations entertained
Mounts of excuses said in vain
They only accentuate my loneliness as much as I hate
My heart is tied to you my remaining years
Not enough to compensate for all your tears

雨霖鈴

寒蟬淒切

對長亭晚

驟雨初歇

都門帳飲無緒

留戀處

蘭舟催發

執手相看淚眼

竟無語凝噎

念去去

千里煙波

暮靄沉沉楚天闊

多情自古傷離別

更那堪冷落清秋節

今宵酒醒何處

楊柳岸

曉風殘月

此去經年

應是良辰好景虛設

便縱有千種風情

更與何人說

Tune: Bells Drowned by Rain

Cicadas tuned dreary in the cold
We sojourned at the pavilion till the evening is old
Showers over
Under the city gate we drank in dull mood
As we linger
Your departing boat tooted
Hand in hand we gazed at each other in teary eyes
With congealed sobs words come not to say goodbye
Ahead as you go
A thousand *li* of waves and mist lie
Clouds are heavy in the boundless southern sky
Those deep in love must suffer parting sorrows since days of old
Especially parting in the autumn cold
Where will I be after tonight when sober
On banks of willows
The moon wanes in day-break breezes
With you away for years
All bright days and pleasing scenery here will exist in vain
If I should ever coquette in a thousand ways
To whom could I show my feelings anyway

八聲甘州

對瀟瀟暮雨灑江天

一番洗清秋

漸霜風悽慘

關河冷落

殘照當樓

是處紅衰綠減

苒苒物華休

惟有長江水

無語東流

不忍登高臨遠

望故鄉渺邈

歸思難收

歎年來踪迹

何事苦淹留

想佳人

妝樓顒望

誤幾回

天際識歸舟

爭知我

倚欄杆處

正憑凝愁

Tune: Eight Beats from Ganzhou Music

Against the incessant late showers river and sky stand

Cleanly washed autumn looks new again

Gradually fierce gales blow dreary and chill

Few souls stay by hill or rill

In my lonely lodge only fading sunlight remains still

All vegetations green or red have withered

No more splendour

Only currents of the Yangtzi River

Flow steadily east silent as ever

I dare not ascend high to look far and around

In search of my lost native land where to be found

Homesickness abound

To my roving I sigh

Lingering here and there I know not why

My beloved

Watching from her bower with longing eyes

How oft had she mistaken

A returning boat on horizon to be mine

Little would she know

I am also watching from this balcony rail

Pining for her my heart frozen in sorrow

木蘭花

龍頭舴艋吳兒競
笋柱鞦韆遊女並
芳洲拾翠暮忘歸
秀野踏青來不定

行雲去後遙山暝
已放笙歌池院靜
中庭月色正清明
無數楊花過無影

Tune: Magnolia

Dragon Boat glade men of Wu compete to gain speed
On swings fair maidens move gayly to and fro
Women picking vegetables delightfully forget to leave the mead
Treading on green fields folks freely come and go

With clouds gone the distant hills appear in pale hue
With flutes mute silence returns to the garden pool
Bathed in crystal moonlight the middle court is still
Catkins dance in great numbers leaving not a shadow in view

天仙子

水調數聲持酒聽
午醉醒來愁未醒
送春春去幾時回
臨晚鏡
傷流景
往事後期空記省

沙上並禽池上暝
雲破月來花弄影
重重簾幕密遮燈
風不定
人初靜
明日落紅應滿徑

Tune: Songs of Immortals

Cup in hand I listen to parts of the Water Song
Waking from mid-day intemporance sorrows keep me tipsy on
Whence will spring return now it is sent away
Watching the mirror at dusk
I'm alarmed how time had passed
To recall bygone events is but in vain

On the poolside sands a pair of love birds perch happily
Freed from clouds the moon induces flowers to play with dancing shadows
Indoor lights are veiled by multiple layers of screens
No steady wind
The night feels serene
Tomorrow fallen red petals on paths will be seen

建茶

北苑中春岫幌開
里民清曉駕肩來
豐隆已助新芽出
更作歡聲動地摧

蝶戀花

檻菊愁煙蘭泣露
羅幕輕寒
燕子雙飛去
明月不諳離恨苦
斜光到曉穿朱戶

昨夜西風凋碧樹
獨上高樓
望盡天涯路
欲寄彩箋無尺素
山長水遠知何處

Jian Tea

Hills in Fujian are showing signs of mid-spring
Farmers carry baskets to train up the slope for tea picking
Thunders and rains are hurrying tender leaves to thrive
Chorus of joy shattering the earth here and there rise

Tune: Butterfly Loves Flower

Orchids tear dews while asters in doleful misty grey
Silk curtains could not allay this cold
Pairing swallows take hasty go
The moon could not know our parting grief
It shines till dawn its slanting light strayed into crimson windows

Last night western gales got green trees withered
Alone I ascended the tall tower
To search all the roads under the sky
How I wish to send you my darling comforting messages on ornate paper
But where would it go amid long mountain ranges and meandering rivers

浣溪沙

一曲新詞酒一杯
去年天氣舊亭台
夕陽西下幾時回

無可奈何花落去
似曾相識燕歸來
小園香徑獨徘徊

Tune: Silky Brook Sands

I wrote a new poem and drank a cup of wine
In the old pavilion last year's weather remained fine
When will you come back to celebrate the sun its ray decline

Helplessly I see flowers fade and fall
Happily these swallows I seem to know are back on my wall
Round the fragrant path in my cosy garden I loiter alone

張昇 Zhang Bian (992–1077)

離亭燕

一帶江山如畫
風物向秋瀟灑
水浸碧天何處斷
翠色冷光相射
蓼岸荻花中
隱映竹籬茅舍

雲際客帆高掛
門外酒旗低垂
多少六朝興廢事
盡入漁樵閒話
悵望倚危欄
紅日無言西下

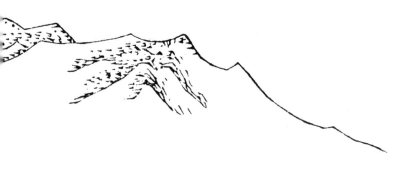

Tune: Swallow Vacated Pavilion

My motherland is so picturesque in a grand sweep
The view in autumn is especially splendid and sweet
Water merge with sky as one leaving no slack in space
The sun's cooling rays match the evening hue with grace
Where on the islets tall reeds thrive like hay
Bamboo fences keep my thatched cabin under shade

Under distant clouds a white sail stands tall
Beyond the mist tavern flags hang low to call
What of events recording the Six Dynasties their rise and fall
Fishermen and loggers weave stories to tell them all
I watch in melancholy the multi-story tower our glorious past
Saying not a word the sun sets westward fast

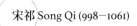

宋祁 Song Qi (998–1061)

玉樓春

東城漸覺風光好
縠皺波紋迎客棹
綠楊煙外曉寒輕
紅杏枝頭春意鬧

浮生長恨歡娛少
肯愛千金輕一笑
為君持酒勸斜陽
且向花間留晚照

余靖 Yu Jing (1000–1064)

雙松　　　Double Pines

自古詠連理	Poets since old like to sing for diverse vegetation growths
多為豔陽吟	And the brilliance of colourful sky shines they loaf
誰知抱高節	Those who hold fast to their integrity
生處亦同心	They group together into a like-mind community
風至應交響	Singing in the wind their sounds orchestrate
禽棲得並陰	Trees with roosting birds give plenty of shade
歲寒當共守	They crowd together to wait for the new year to dawn
霜雪莫相侵	The warmth dispels frosty colds on any individual don

Tune: Jade Pavilion in Spring

Approaching town east the scenery is renowned
Rippling waters greet visiting boats up and down
In the morning chill green willows dance delight
On pink apricot branches spring riots high

In our floating life we regret having few pleasures
But we value gold more than hearty laughter
With this wine let me on your behalf ask the setting sun to stay
To leave among the awaiting flowers its most warming ray

暮春　　Late Spring

草帶全鋪翠	The pasture belt is green through to the end
花房半墜紅	The hothouse is half-filled with red petals
農家榆莢雨	A farmer dons on a bamboo coat against the rain
江國鯉魚風	Schools of carp occupy the river as kings
堤柳綿爭撲	Willow tendrils dance to present a wavy dyke
山櫻火共烘	Wild berries cover the hills red as if on fire
長安少年客	Would youngsters in the Capital know
不信有衰翁	There are fishermen in bamboo coats

黃龍慧南禪師 Huanglong Huinan (1002−1069)

趙州吃茶　　Zhao Zhou Eat Tea

相逢相遇知來歷	People meet and inquire each other's credentials
不揀親疏便與茶	I serve tea regardless of relationship far or close
翻憶憧憧往來者	Searching my memory on all people in my encounter
忙忙誰辨滿甌花	How many knew the quality of a bowl of tea I wonder

介石 Jie Shi (1005−1045)

歲晏村居　　Village Life towards Year End

歲晏有餘糧	Foods are plenty even towards year end
杯盤氣味長	Platters of wines and meats are prepared on hand
天寒酒腳落	Folks drink full cups of wine in cold day meals
春近朧頭香	Anticipating spring fragrant meaty broths are procured
菜色青仍短	Cooked vegetables remaining green are eaten keen
茶芽嫩復黃	Tender tea leaves in yellow broth filled to the brim
此中得深趣	These are foods and drinks for happy sharing
真不羨膏粱	No one envy fine cuisine in lavish feasting

歐陽修 Ouyang Xiu (1007–1072)

踏莎行　　　　Tune: Treading on Grass

候館梅殘	Mume blossoms by the roadside are fading
溪橋柳細	Willow trees near the small bridge greening
草熏風暖搖征轡	Amid warm air and fragrant grass a rider is set to go
離愁漸遠漸無窮	The farther he roams the heavier his parting grief grows
迢迢不斷如春水	On and on like torrents in the spring river flow
寸寸柔腸	Tender guts hurt inch by inch
盈盈粉淚	On her teary face longing eyes are locked in
樓高莫近危欄倚	Against the railing up high she must not lean
平蕪盡處是春山	To the end of the plain lie the spring hills
行人更在春山外	Her rider husband is already beyond her view

浣溪沙 · 堤上遊人逐畫船
Tune: Silky Sand Brook – People on the Dyke Follow the Ornate Boat

堤上遊人逐畫船	People on the dyke follow the ornate boat
拍堤春水四垂天	Spring tides caress the shore their froths unfold
綠楊樓外出鞦韆	From outside the green wall a swing occasionally shows
白髮戴花君莫笑	Aging poets wear red flowers on their hairs grey
六麼催拍盞頻傳	Listening to the Liuyou song and drinking to celebrate
人生何處似樽前	What could be happier in life than drinking till late

蝶戀花

庭院深深深幾許
楊柳堆煙
簾幕無重數
玉勒雕鞍遊冶處
樓高不見章台路
雨橫風狂三月暮
門掩黃昏
無計留春住
淚眼問花花不語
亂紅飛過鞦韆去

夢中作

夜涼吹笛千山月
路暗迷人百種花
棋罷不知人換世
酒闌無奈客思家

Tune: Butterfly Loves Flower

Deep deep the mansion and courtyards so deep
Willows wave smoke rising to veil
Countless screens ensure mystry keep
Where her master is roaming on jade saddles she knows not
Standing in her balcony she seeks his whereabouts seeing naught
Fury gusts and rain pours rage the late spring dusk
She closed all windows and doors to shut out the evening
Spring departs despite her wish for it to remain
Tearfully she asks flowers what to do flowers answer not
Only a flurry of pink petals fly past by her swing

Written in My Dream

My flute tunes invite the moon to shine on a thousand hills
The roads a maze with hundreds of flowers bloom in goodwill
Whence our chess game ends the world has changed we know it not
Drinking in leisure does not keep me from pining for home a lot

曾鞏 Zeng Gong (1019－1083)

寄獻新茶

種處地靈偏得日
摘時春早未聞雷
京師萬里爭先到
應得慈親手自開

司馬光 Sima Guang (1019－1086)

西江月

寶髻鬆鬆挽就
鉛華淡淡妝成
青姻翠霧罩輕盈
飛絮遊絲無定
相見不如不見
有情還似無情
笙歌散後酒微醒
深院月明人靜

Sending a Gift of New Tea

They grow in terrains where sunrays visit first
Leaves are picked in early spring before thunder bursts
Ten thousand miles to the Capital they hurry to deliver
Only mother can do the brewing right with loving care

Tune: Moon on West River

She has her hair done up in a bun fluffy
Wearing simple makeup she appears happy
Delightful as engulfed in a purple mist
Her graceful steps light as willow downs I shall miss
Before we part we already wish to meet
Our love appears casual it is by no means weak
Tipsiness overcomes there are no more songs
Nobody around in the deep courtyard the moon shines on

王安石 Wang Anshi (1021–1086)

漁家傲

平岸小橋千嶂抱
柔藍一水縈花草
茅屋數間窗窈窕
塵不到
時時自有春風掃
午枕覺來聞語鳥
欹眠似聽朝雞早
忽憶故人今總老
貪夢好
茫然忘了邯鄲道

元日

爆竹聲中一歲除
春風送暖入屠蘇
千門萬戶瞳瞳日
總把新桃換舊符

Tune: Fisherman's Pride

Small bridges linking smooth banks on the lap of hills
Sapphire water meanders through floral and grass mazes in a rill
Thatched cots stand around their windows so neat
No dust here
Vernal breezes sweep them away thither and hither
From my noonday noose I wake to hear birds sing
Their chirps loud like cocks crowing the dawn in
I realize in a flash people do pass away when old
'Tis alright to have dreams to hold
They help me forget that one day I too have to go

Lunar New Year's Day

On a sound of firecrackers we bid farewell to the year old
As vernal breezes warm up the Tu Su brew we welcome the new
The sun shines visiting thousands of family doors
Every door displays new couplets to celebrate the new year for all

勘會賀蘭山主
Meeting the Master of Mount Helan

賀蘭山上幾株松　　How many pines are growing in Helan Mount
南北東西有幾峯　　How many peaks stand in all directions around
買得往來今幾日　　You dwell in here since how many days ago
尋常誰與坐從容　　Who sits with you at ease in days usual

對棋與道源至草堂寺
To My Friend on Chess and Dao

北風吹人不可出　　With the attack of north winds people venture out not
清坐且可與君棋　　What a pleasure to play chess when doing naught
明朝投局日未晚　　Not even continuing till tomorrow time is at our disposal
從此亦復不吟詩　　'Cause we can forget writing poems in this life mortal

桂枝香－金陵懷古
Tune: Fragrance of Laurel Branch – Pining for Old Capital

登臨送目	I climb up high to cast eyes far
正故國晚秋	In this late autumn the old country marvellous
天氣初肅	The weather sublime and cool
千里澄江似練	The limpid river like a belt winds a thousand *li*
翠峯如簇	Emerald peaks tower in vivid relief
歸帆去棹斜陽裏	Sails rush home as the sun sets in diminishing heat
背西風	Against west winds
酒旗斜矗	Fluttering tavern banners compete
彩舟雲淡	'Neath pale clouds painted boats merrily float
星河鷺起	Towards the Milky Way egrets sour up to note
畫圖難足	A grand sight no artist can capture in brush strokes
念往昔	Gone are past
繁華競逐	Opulence that saw people vie
歎門外樓頭	Sighs heard outdoors and in bowers high
悲恨相續	Griefs and hates never go in demise
千古憑高	Many historic events viewed from a stand this high
對此漫嗟榮辱	Successes and failures in subdue murmurs nigh
六朝舊事如流水	Deeds of the Sixth Dynasties fade washed by river tides
但寒煙　衰草凝綠	Memories of cold mists and withered grass kept in mind
至今商女	How songstresses today joyfully sing
時時猶唱	And sing
後庭遺曲	Songs composed by the captive King

書湖陰先生壁

茅簷長掃靜無苔
花木成畦手自栽
一水護田將綠繞
兩山排闥送青來

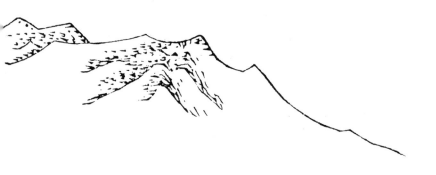

Written on the Wall of Master Hu Yin

The cabin is swept spotlessly clean no moss will grow
Shrubs and flowers line the yard he planted with a single hoe
A stream nurtures the paddy fields blazing ever so green
Distant hills open the door their verdant beauty dwells in

晏幾道 Yan Jidao (1030-1106)

臨江仙

夢後樓台高鎖
酒醒簾幕低垂
去年春恨卻來時
落花人獨立
微雨燕雙飛
記得小蘋初見
兩重心字羅衣
琵琶絃上說相思
當時明月在
曾照彩雲歸

鷓鴣天

彩袖殷勤捧玉鐘
當年拼卻醉顏紅
舞低楊柳樓心月
歌盡桃花扇底風

從別後　憶相逢
幾回魂夢與君同
今宵剩把銀釭照
猶恐相逢是夢中

Tune: Immortals by the River

Awake from my dream the tower locked tight
Heavy curtains hang low a sober sign
Whence last year's spring sorrows visit and grow
Alone I stand amid flower beds unfold
In the drizzle a pair of swallows left leaving no trace to follow
I still remember when I first met lovely Ping
Her silk dress embroidered with two hearts locked in a ring
She played the pipa to sing her love for me
The moon was our witness
She brought me clouds of colourful brilliance

Tune: Partridge Sky

With colourful sleeves you pour me wine again and again
Those were the days when we sang and drank not caring to think
You danced like willows keeping the moon in the tower
You sang in tune with breezes stirred up by peach flower

Ever since we parted I've been recalling our togetherness
Time and again I dreamed of being with you
Tonight I gaze at you in candlelight it seems
Being together with you is only possible in my dreams

蘇軾 Su Shi (1037—1101)

滿江紅・寄鄂州朱使君壽昌
Tune: River All Red – To Officer Zhu

江漢西來	The Yangtze and Han rivers from the west meet
高樓下	Right at the tall Crane Tower's feet
葡萄深碧	Waters green as grapes
猶自帶	They carry
岷峨雲浪	Cloud floats from Mount Omei
錦江春色	To display spring in scenic beauty
君是南山遺愛守	You are the benevolent officer from South Mountain
我為劍外思歸客	I am roamer longing for my native Sichuan home
對此間	On this encounter
風物豈無情	All events and times are rich in affection
殷勤說	To dialogue in satisfaction

江表傳	The legend classics of Wu
君休讀	You had missed reading
狂處士	Deeds of ancient brave heroes
真堪惜	Stay with respect in memory total
空洲對鸚鵡	Where Parrot Sands stood in solitude
葦花蕭瑟	Reed flowers quietly flew
不獨笑書生爭底事	We laugh at today's scholars striving to achieve
曹公黃祖俱飄忽	Glories of past kingdom lords buried beneath
願使君	I wish for you
還賦謫仙詩	To write lines in tune with Li Bai poems immortal
追黃鶴	Free as a crane yellow

汲江煎茶

活水還須活火烹
自臨釣石取深清
大瓢貯月歸春甕
小杓分江入夜瓶
茶雨已翻煎處腳
松風忽作瀉時聲
枯腸未易禁三碗
坐聽荒城長短更

Ladle the River to Make Tea

Vital water requires vigorous fire to boil
I ladle water from river deeps squatting at a fishing point
With a big dipper I pluck the moon to an empty carafe
With a small scoop I guide the river to flow into my pitcher
Tea leaves turn and churn in snow white bubbles powered by heat
Like hissing among pines they sound gentle and sweet
After three bowls of tea my empty guts are at ease
I sit in this forgotten town enduring nights short or lengthy

望江南 · 超然台作
Tune: Viewing River South – Transcendent Platform

春未老	Spring not yet old
風細柳斜斜	In gentle breezes willows sideways flow
試上超然台上看	I ascend the Transcendent Platform to behold
半壕春水一城花	The moat carries flowers around the city so beautiful
煙雨暗千家	A thousand families live in hazy shadow
寒食後	Pass the Cold Food Festival
酒醒卻諮嗟	Awake from drunkenness I sigh in sorrow
休對故人思故國	Longing for home in my old country is of no avail
且將新火試新茶	Better to brew new tea with a new fire temporal
詩酒趁年華	To drink and write poems in days youthful

中秋月　　The Mid-autumn Moon

暮雲收盡溢清寒　Clouds gone at dusk the world cool and serene
銀漢無聲轉玉盤　The Man of Galaxy moves the moon on a charming sheen
此生此夜不長好　I recall not a happier night than this you and I hold
明月明年何處看　Where you and I will view this same moon next year
　　　　　　　　　who knows

東坡　　The East Slope

雨洗東坡月色清　Washed by rain the east slope a beauty under moonshine
市人行盡野人行　I arrive to survey the terrain people had left behind
莫嫌犖确坡頭路　Do not dismiss this deserted slope leading to nowhere
自愛鏗然曳杖聲　Here I stick my staff heavy its resonance loud and clear

紅梅

怕愁貪睡獨開遲，
遲自恐冰容不時。
故作小紅桃杏色，
尚餘孤瘦雪霜姿。
寒心未肯隨春態，
酒暈無端上玉肌。
詩老不知梅格在，
更看綠葉與青枝。

Red Plum Blossom

She prefers to drown her grief in sleep so she blooms late

It matters not what her icy look has to say

Imitating peach and apricot roughs on her face

To maintain her uniqueness a slender and frosty grace

Her serene character cares not for the brilliance of spring

Her jade skin carries the hue of a subdue wine stain

Alas the old poet knew not how to describe her noble beauty

Only sang songs of peach leaves and apricot boughs ordinary

蝶戀花　Tune: Butterflies Love Flowers

花褪殘紅青杏小　Colours fade on receding blooms apricots yet to grow
燕子飛時　Gliding pass are swallows
綠水人家繞　The garden walls girded by vermilion flow
枝上柳綿吹又少　Willow catkins mostly gone carried by vernal blows
天涯何處無芳草　Everywhere else sweet green grass grow
牆裏鞦韆牆外道　Swing standing inside out of the walls winds a road
牆外行人　A man walks by
牆裏佳人笑　While inside a laughing maiden behold
笑漸不聞聲漸悄　As ringing laughter fades silence follows
多情卻被無情惱　How enchantment dims as enchantment gets hold

題西林壁　Written on the Wall of Westwood Temple

橫看成嶺側成峯　Viewed directly it is a mountain its peak seen from one side
遠近高低各不同　Its view differs when perceived from near far low or high
不識廬山真面目　If you failed to recognize Mount Lu its true face
只緣身在此山中　Just know you are in the heart of the very place

念奴嬌　　　　　　Tune: Charm of a Maiden Dancer

憑高眺遠　　　　　I stand high on platform to look wide and far
見長空萬里　　　　The sky an expanse of ten thousand *li* vast
雲無留迹　　　　　Clouds left leaving not a strand of white
桂魄飛來光射處　　The moon glints with her soul pure and bright
冷浸一天秋碧　　　Water reflects the sky in autumn green divine

玉宇瓊樓　　　　　Palaces and towers of ornaments and carve jade
乘鸞來去　　　　　They come and go carried by legendary crane
人在清涼閣　　　　He who lives in dwellings of cool simplicity will appreciate
江山如畫　　　　　Our motherland picturesque like art in display
望中煙樹歷歷　　　Through diligent stride these are seen with no delay

我醉拍手狂歡　　　I get drunk and clap my hands in great delight
舉杯邀月　　　　　To the moon I raise my cup to invite
對影成三客　　　　Together with my shadow three good friends we might
起舞徘徊風露下　　We dance and dance till dews alight
今夕不知何夕　　　Unconcerned what day and year this night

便欲乘風　　　　　O wind may I ride on your wings
翻然歸去　　　　　To home in a wink
何用騎鵬翼　　　　Who needs the big bird its wide-spread wings
水晶宮裏　　　　　Inside the crystal palace
一聲吹斷橫笛　　　A single tune shatters my flute into two pieces

沁園春・赴密州早行馬上寄子由

孤館燈青

野店雞號

旅枕夢殘

漸月華收練

晨霜耿耿

雲山攤錦

朝露溥溥

世路無窮

勞生有限

似此區區長鮮歡

微吟罷

憑征鞍無語

往事千端

當時共客長安

似二陸初來俱少年

有筆頭千字

胸中萬卷

致君堯舜

此事何難

用舍由時

行藏在我

袖手何妨閒看

身長健

但優遊卒歲

且斗樽前

Tune: Qin Garden Spring – To My Brother on My Way to Exile

In this lone inn the lamp burns a dim green

Cock crows are heard too early in morning

Breaking my lingering dream

Quietly the moon recedes its cold rays

Enters the morning frost here to stay

Clouds and hills together weave fine brocades

Morning dews their pearly drops on display

Worldly affairs go on without limit

Man's toiling likes are but short visits

How I had led a life joyless and oft in defeat

After singing this song

I mount my saddle in silence to go on

Brooding over a thousand past events as I ride along

Remember our days together in the Capital

Somewhat like the young Lu brothers in literary fame

On our brush tips essays of a thousand words easily attained

Knowledge in ten thousand volumes within our rein

We advise great emperors in history

With no difficulty

Careers can only advance on the right time

Decisions are mine

Why not stand aside to watch how the world goes by

May we keep in good health

To pass our days and years in tranquillity

And don't forget to drink wine urns empty

行香子 · 過七里灘
Tune: Joy of Union Eternal – Passing through the Seven-league Shallows

一葉舟輕	A boat light as a leaf on water glides
雙槳鴻驚	Its dipping oars frighten wild geese nearby
水天清	Water and sky serene
影湛波平	Clear shadows follow gentle waves green
魚翻藻鑒	In and out of water-plants fishes play
鷺點煙汀	An egret dots the misty space
過沙溪急	I go thru sandy rills rowing bold
霜溪冷	On frigid water enduring the cold
月溪明	On moonlit rivers serene
重重似畫	Every turn presents me with picturesque scenes
曲曲如屏	Every bent appears a screen
算當年	I recall those years past
虛老嚴陵	Empty days spent
君臣一夢	In the emperor's dreams
今古空名	Then as now deeds and fame existed but empty
但遠山長	Distant hills stay eternal
雲山亂	Cloudy hills in dishevel
曉山青	Morning hills ever so green

江城子・乙卯正月二十日夜記夢
Tune: Riverside Town – Remembering My Deceased Wife in Dream

十年生死兩茫茫	Ten years since your death you and I drifted in worlds so vague
不思量	Even as I try not to contemplate
自難忘	Your death I can't negate
千里孤墳	With you in a lonely grave ten thousand *li* away
無處話凄涼	To whom could I my grief convey
縱使相逢應不識	If we should by chance meet you may know me not
塵滿面	Face dusty
鬢如霜	Hair frost-grey
夜來幽夢忽還鄉	At last in a dream I returned home in haste
小軒窗	Sitting by the little window
正梳妝	You were doing make-up with so much grace
相顧無言	We met with not a single word to say
惟有淚千行	Only tears rolled a thousand lines astray
料得年年腸斷處	I recall I visited your lone grave every year in grief
明月夜	At moonlit nights
短松岡	On a pine wood rise

水調歌頭

明月幾時有
把酒問青天
不知天上宮闕
今夕是何年
我欲乘風歸去
又恐瓊樓玉宇
高處不勝寒
起舞弄清影
何似在人間
轉朱閣
低綺戶
照無眠
不應有恨
何事長向別時圓
人有悲歡離合
月有陰晴圓缺
此事古難全
但願人長久
千里共嬋娟

Tune: Prelude to Water Melody

Whence will the moon shine this way again
I ask in earnest a wine-cup in hand
Where up the palaces in sky
What year could it be tonight
I'd love to return there riding the wind
But I fear where these towers and jade palaces are in
The chill and altitude are too much for my liking
Dancing with my shadow in tow
I feel 'tis a better place here with people I know
In the ornate mansion red
Behind lowered drapes embroidery spread
Such glare kept me sleepless in bed
I should have no lingering spite or hate
O Moon why do you always shine when people separate
Among men sorrow joy separation or togetherness are but normal life state
For you Moon there are times of shade or shine wane or full
None had always been perfect since time immemorial
Let's keep our love true everlasting
And share the moon bright and trusting

定風波

莫聽穿林打葉聲
何妨吟嘯且徐行
竹杖芒鞋輕勝馬
誰怕
一蓑煙雨任平生
料峭春風吹酒醒
微冷
山頭斜照卻相迎
回首向來蕭瑟處
歸去
也無風雨也無晴

Tune: Calm Wind and Water

Fear not the forest wind and rain beating on leaves

Advance surely forward singing aloud your mind at ease

More than horses straw sandals and cane I depend

No fear

A straw cloak is all I need to battle life's mist and rain

Drown in shrill drink I welcome the warmth of venal breezes to make me sober

Chills I feel

The sun on hill top its enduring ray envelops me all over

I turn to reassess all events of my dreary past

Home now

Storm wind or shine imperious

念奴嬌・赤壁懷古

大江東去

浪淘盡

千古風流人物

故壘西邊

人道是　三國周郎赤壁

亂石崩雲

驚濤拍岸

捲起千堆雪

江山如畫

一時多少豪傑

遙想公謹當年

小喬初嫁了　雄姿英發

羽扇綸巾談笑間

強虜灰飛煙滅

故國神遊

多情應笑

我早生華髮

人生如夢

一尊還酹江月

Tune: Remembering Palace Maids Memory at Crimson Cliff

The big river flows east
Awashed with its waves
Gone are so many heroes forgotten in history
Where on the west bank the old fortress stands
Premier Zhou Yu of the Three Kingdoms won at the Crimson Cliff his fame append
Jagged boulders extend high to pierce the overhanging clouds
Thundering waves surge to carve out the river banks
Rolling up a thousand mound of froths white as snow
For a motherland with such picturesque beauty
Many a gallant soul braved battles to show loyalty
I recall Premier Zhou Yu in yore
His new bride present he beamed with his personality people adore
Wearing a silk hood and waving his plume fan he watched amid laughters
In witness of his planned victory the enemy boats were reduced to ashes
On a revisit in mind and spirit this land so eventful
Only the heroes' premature grey hair made his loved ones feel regretful
Life is but a passing dream
O moon to you I drink
For your witnessing history with your crystal gleam

和子由澠池懷舊

人生到處知何似
應似飛鴻踏雪泥
泥上偶然留指爪
鴻飛哪復計東西
老僧已死成新塔
壞壁無由見舊題
往日崎嶇還計否
路長人困蹇驢嘶

李之儀 Li Zhiyi (1038－1117)

卜算子

我住長江頭
君住長江尾
日日思君不見君
共飲長江水
此水幾時休
此恨何時已
只願君心似我心
定不負相思意

A Duet with My Younger Brother on the Good Old Days

Who could fore-see how life goes settling hither and wither
It would be like a migrant goose running on snow-wet ground
If by chance a mark is left on the cold muddy ground
Would the flight-bound bird take note so it may later titter
Gone is our good friend the monk now resting in a dagoba
The poems we wrote on the temple wall are seen no more with decay
You may recall the arduous journeys we together made
They were so distant and weary our donkey brayed to say it would not bother

Tune: Song of Divination

I live by the Yangtze's upstream and you downstream
Night by night of you I dream
Day in day out you are not in sight but deep in my mind
The same water we share to drink
Whence will this stream of longing cease
Whence will my pain and sorrow ease
Let's hope that our hearts are alike
Then not in vain we each other pine

黃庭堅 Huang Tingjian (1045–1105)

清平樂 · 晚春　　Tune: Music Serene – Late Spring

春歸何處　　　　O Where did spring go
寂寞無行路　　　By herself alone she knows no road
若有人知春去處　If ever anyone knows her dwelling place
喚取歸來同住　　Please call her back together we'll stay

春無踪迹誰知　　Who's sure spring has left no trace
除非問取黃鸝　　Ask the oriole
百囀無人能解　　It sings a hundred tunes for none to know
因風吹過薔薇　　On wings with wind they fly past the rose

水調歌頭 · 遊覽

Tune: Prelude to Water Melody – Seeing As I Go

瑤草一何碧	Divine Grass green all over
春入武陵溪	Spring at Peach Flower Valley hover
溪上桃花無數	Where peach flowers bloom in huge numbers
枝上有黃鸝	Orioles on every branch linger
我欲穿花尋路	I try to find my path through the flowers
直入白雲深處	To enter where clouds flow
浩氣展虹霓	And feel the grandeur of the rainbow
只恐花深裏	My concern rests with the flowers
紅露濕人衣	Their red dews may wet my clothes
坐玉石 倚玉枕	Reclining against a boulder I sit
拂金徽	And adjust notes melodic
謫仙何處	Where is Li Bai the legend poet
無人伴我白螺杯	Who would drink with me this minute
我為靈芝仙草	I seek for herbal grass immortal
不為朱唇丹臉	Not for fame or worldly materials
長嘯亦何為	I croon to no avail
醉舞下山去	Tipsy I walk down the hill merrily
明月逐人歸	The moon follows me home caringly

踏莎行・茶詞

畫鼓催春
蠻歌走餉
雨前一焙誰爭長
低株摘盡到高株
株株弯是閩溪樣
碾破春風
香凝午帳
銀瓶雪滾翻成浪
今宵無睡酒醒時
摩圍影在秋江上

Tune: Treading on Grass – Tea Poem

Beating colourful drums to celebrate spring
Minority people eat in the fields while they sing
Tea leaves are baked before the Cold Meal Festival
Picking tea leaves from low shrubs and tall trees joyful
Tall tea trees boiled by the Min Stream usual
Grinding Spring Breeze leaves into fine dust
Their fragrance fills shading tents set up for the task
In the silver kettle snow-white ripples churn
Sleeping not this night I stay awake and frequently turn
To see Mount Mowei sleeping in the autumn river

秦觀 Qin Guan (1049 –1100)

鵲橋仙

纖雲弄巧
飛星傳恨
銀漢迢迢暗度
金風玉露一相逢
便勝卻人間無數
柔情似水
佳期如夢
忍顧鵲橋歸路
兩情若是久長時
又豈在朝朝暮暮

Tune: The Magpie Bridge Immortal

Clouds float creating wonders like artist feats

Stars fleeting regret repeats

Across the Milky Way the Cowherd goes to his annual reunion meet

A single moment together in jade dew and golden breeze

Can eclipse all human affections in multiple heat

Their love flows tenderly as water

This happy date seems but a dream

They had to leave the Magpie Bridge to go each their own way

When lovers promise to love forever

Need they measure togetherness by days or hours

滿庭芳　　　　Tune: Fragrant Courtyard

山抹微雲	Laced clouds touch the mountains high
天黏衰草	Widely spread bristle grass reach the sky
畫角聲斷譙門	The painted bugle sound fades from inquisitive sight
暫停征棹	Halt the venturous boat
聊共引離尊	Let's drink together before parting sadness takes hold
多少蓬萊舊事	How many past events come to mind
空回首	'Tis no use to remind
煙靄紛紛	Let them vanish with passing mists and sighs
斜陽外	As the setting sun beyond hides
寒鴉萬點	Crows appear dotting the dimming sky
流水繞孤村	Girding the lonely village the river quietly glides
銷魂　當此際	My soul stirs
香囊暗解	As I loosen your fragrant pouch with a frisk search
羅帶輕分	And untie your silk girdle on urge
謾贏得青樓	My actions helped me to earn a name of fame
薄倖名存	A fickle lover of brothel lane
此去何時見也	Now a rover I know not whence we'll meet again
襟袖上　空惹啼痕	On your sleeves tears leave wasted stains
傷情處	Where sorrow remains
高樓望斷	Beyond your high bower
燈火已黃昏	City lights quietly mark the looming dusk

江城子　　　　　Tune: A Riverside Town

西城楊柳弄春柔	Willows play with the vernal breeze in west town
動離憂	I pine for you
淚難收	Tears anew
猶憶多情	Remember how I express my love for thee
曾為繫歸舟	Holding your boat not letting it leave
碧野朱橋當日事	The fields green and bridge red like yore
人不見	I see you not again
水空流	Water flows in vain
韶華不為少年留	Time passes retaining not our youthful days
恨悠悠	Lingering regrets
幾時休	Not to forget
飛絮落花時候	Whence willow catkins fly with falling flowers
一登樓	I climb up the city tower
便做春江都是淚	If the river flows with my tears in spring I say
流不盡 許多愁	It will not suffice to carry my sorrow away

千秋歲 · 水邊沙外
Tune: Ten Thousand Years – At Water Front away from Sands

水邊沙外	At water front away from sands
城郭春寒退	The city turns warm as vernal cold wanes
花影亂	Flower shadows flicker in disarray
鶯聲碎	Fragments of oriole songs in sway
飄零疏酒盞	Wandering I now seldom drink
離別寬衣帶	Suffering from separation my coat needs a tight string
人不見	My dearest not seen
碧雲暮合空相對	I face the empty sky where fine clouds dwelt in
憶昔西池會	How I remember our togetherness at West Pond
鵷鷺同飛蓋	Winging together in the air love birds so fond
攜手處	Where we held hands
今誰在	Now I look for you only in vain
日邊清夢斷	Dreams rise and break whence the sun disappears
鏡裏朱顏改	In the mirror a different person now appears
春去也	Spring is gone total
飛紅萬點愁如海	Ten thousand petals waft over a sea of sorrow

米芾 Mi Fei (1051–1109)

浣溪沙 · 野眺
Tune: Silky Sand Brook – Watching the Wild

日射平溪玉宇中	The sun shines on a namelass brook against a wide sky
雲橫遠渚岫重重	Clouds line up mountain ranges with no divide
野花猶向澗邊紅	Wild flowers decorate the stream banks in red light
靜看沙頭魚入網	I watch leisurely how trapping nets invite fish in
閒支藜杖醉吟風	Leaning on my cane tipsily I sing to the wind
小春天氣惱人濃	This unpredictable weather has my mind unsettling

賀鑄 He Zhu (1052-1125)

鷓鴣天

重過閶門萬事非
同來何事不同歸
梧桐半死清霜後
頭白鴛鴦失伴飛
原上草
露初晞
舊棲新壠兩依依
空床臥聽南窗雨
誰復挑燈夜補衣

青玉案

凌波不過橫塘路
但目送　芳塵去
錦瑟華年誰與度
月橋花院
瑣窗朱戶
只有春知處
飛雲冉冉蘅皋暮
彩筆新題斷腸句
試問閒愁都幾許
一川煙草
滿城風絮
梅子黃時雨

Tune: Partridge Sky

On revisiting the Capital I feel things are no longer the same
You and I came as a couple why can't we leave together again
The plane trees nearly wilt after suffering the frost
My hair grey 'tis hard to endure a companion lost
On the plain grass grow anew
They thirst for drying dew
How I drag to leave our old home and your grave new
On this unshared bed I pine for you listening to pelting rain
Who will be mending my clothes by this midnight lamp again

Tune: Green Jade Server

Will your ripple-like steps ever come this way again
My eyes followed the fragrant dusts raised by your passing
With whom will you spend your youthful years in delight
On moonlit bridges and flower-filled courts
Inside blinded windows and crimson door
A dwelling known only to spring
When fleeting clouds fly past the green plain at dusk
I wave my brush once again to write heart-broken verses
Asked how deep and wide my lovesickness is
Misty river banks where grass thrive
All o'er town catkins carried by wind fly
Pattering drizzles urging plums to ripe

周邦彥 Zhou Bangyan (1057−1121)

西河 · 金陵懷古
Tune: West Rill – Remembering the Ancient Capital

佳麗地	The land of exceptional beauties
南朝盛事誰記	Who records the prosperity of the Six Dynasties
山圍故國繞清江	Rills meander round hills in the old country
髻鬟對起	A pair of green hills guards the river flow
怒濤寂寞打孤城	Surging billows pound the city walls powerful
風檣遙度天際	Toward the horizon tall sails steadily go
斷崖樹	Trees growing on cliffs
猶倒倚	Hanging branches and leaves
莫愁艇子曾繫	Boats from Lake Mo Chou had moored here before
空餘舊跡	They are seen no more
鬱蒼蒼	A sky in vivid green
霧沉半壘	Fallen fords their remains seen
夜深月過女牆來	The moon passes over the walls at night
賞心東望淮水	To the east she watches over River Qin Hui
酒旗戲鼓甚處市	To whom wine banners and drum beats invite
想依稀 王謝鄰里	Vaguely I recall the two legend wealthy families nigh
燕子不知何世	Swallows knew not human affairs
入尋常巷陌人家	To ordinary families in common lanes they nest
相對如說興亡	To hear stories of dynasties told
斜陽裏	In sunset glow

蝶戀花 · 商調秋思
Tune: Butterfly Loves Flower

月皎驚烏棲不定	Nesting birds are startled by a moon too bright
更漏將殘	The water-clock drips out the dwindling night
轆轤牽金井	As the Wind Maid draws water from the Well of Gold
喚起兩眸清炯炯	You wake me up and gaze my face with pearly eyes
淚花落枕紅棉冷	Tears roll down our pillow wetting its cotton cold
執手霜風吹鬢影	We hold hands as frigid air lifts locks on beside your brow
去意徊徨	We loathe knowing our time together is running out
別語愁難聽	Words of farewell are too sad for the ear
樓上欄杆橫斗柄	Beyond the upstairs rails the Plough appears
露寒人遠雞相應	On frosty dews you are far as cock-crows fill the air

朱敦儒 Zhu Dunru (1081–1159)

相見歡   **Tune: Joy of Meeting**

金陵城上西樓	At the West Tower on Jinling city wall
倚清秋	I stand alone on a clear day in the fall
萬里夕陽垂地	In ten thousand *li* the setting sun hangs low
大江流	Where the Big River continues to flow
中原亂	Our central plain in savage war
簪纓散	Noble officers scatter and fall
幾時收	Whence shall our motherland be like yore
試倩悲風吹淚	I ask the winds of sorrow how tears should travel
過揚州	Back through Yangzhou our Capital

好事近 · 漁父詞
Tune: Happy Events Are Near – Fisherman's Song

搖首出紅塵	I leave the world behind with a shake of head
醒醉更無時節	Choosing no particular day or month to be inebriate
活計綠蓑青笠	I make a living fishing in straw hat and cloak
慣披霜衝雪	Wearing frost or braving snow is but habitual
晚來風定釣絲	At night when winds lull my fishing line is quiet
閒上下是新月	The crescent moon appears high and low a duet
千里水天一色	Where sky and water converge in a thousand *li*
看孤鴻明滅	A lone swan appears and vanishes as it pleases

趙佶〔宋徽宗〕Zhao Ji (1082–1135) [Emperor of Song Dynasty]

宴山亭 · 北行見杏花
Tune: Hillside Pavilion – To Watch Apricot Flowers in the North

裁剪冰綃	Like finely cut silk petals
輕疊數重	Layers of ice-white sensual
淡着燕脂勻注	Light evenly touched shades
新樣靚妝	Your new make-up so beautiful
豔溢香融	Fragrance augments charm
羞殺蕊珠宮女	Rendering palace maids shy
易得凋零	How easily time and events fade
更多少	Large and small
無情風雨	Through heartless wind and rain
愁苦	Sad and pain
問院落淒涼	Ask the dreary courtyard
幾番春暮	How many springs had been spent in vain
憑寄離恨重重	My heart is laden with breaking grief
者雙燕何曾	This pair of swallows
會人言語	Could they understand what was said on sorrows
天遙地遠	Distance boundless between earth and sky
萬水千山	Ten thousand streams and a thousand hills high
知他故宮何處	Where could my loved palace be on hide
怎不思量	How could I not pine and sigh
除夢裏有時曾去	In dreams my native land I not often find
無據	Not for sure
和夢也新來不做	Not even dreams occur like usual

李清照 Li Qingzhao (1084–1156)

訴衷情　　Tune: Revealing Inner Feelings

夜來沉醉卸妝遲　Heavily drunk I undress late last night
梅萼插殘枝　　Keeping the withered mume in my hair nigh
酒醒熏破春睡　　Sober the sweet scent wakes me from sleep
夢斷不成歸　　In dream my homeland not even in memory keeps

人悄悄　　Silently silently I remain
月依依　　Lingering the moon stays
翠簾垂　　Lowly the blinds unrolled

更挪殘蕊　　I crush dry petals in my fingertip
更拈餘香　　To keep the sweet scent in hold
更得些時　　Waiting for time to go

永遇樂 — Tune: Eternal Happiness

落日熔金	The sun sets like molten gold
暮雲合璧	Evening clouds marbling cold
人在何處	Darling where are you
染柳煙濃	Dense smoke keeps willows in dye
吹梅笛怨	Sad plum blossom tunes the flute sighs
春意知幾許	Whence will spring arrive
元宵佳節	On Lantern Festival
融和天氣	Weather agreeable
次第豈無風雨	Wind and rain will follow
來相召	I thank poet friends and wine
香車寶馬	Sending scented carriage steeds divine
謝他酒朋詩侶	In vain they invite
中州盛日	Remember happy days in the Capital
閨門多暇	Gathering in my home so pleasurable
記得偏重三五	Bosom friends few and valuable
鋪翠冠兒	Heads topped with emerald
撚金雪柳	Filigree in gold
簇帶爭濟楚	Fashions vied invariable
如今憔悴	Now in languid air
風鬟霜鬢	With grey dishevelled hair
怕見夜間出去	I fear being seen in eve affairs
不如向簾兒底下	Preferring to sit behind window screen
聽人笑語	To listen others chat and laugh unseen

攤破浣溪沙

病起蕭蕭兩鬢華
看殘月上窗紗
豆蔻連梢煎熱水
莫分茶
枕上詩書閒處好
門前風景雨來佳
終日向人多醞藉
木犀花

Tune: Silk – Washing Stream, Broken Form

Following extended illness grey hair on my temples seen

In sick bed I see the waning moon through the window screen

Why boil water burning twigs with cardamom seeds

For taking medicine no need

On pillows poetry books sit for convenient reading

Outside my door the scenery is best when raining

I enjoy my neighbour's wines and caring

Osmanthus flowers

聲聲慢

尋尋覓覓
冷冷清清
淒淒慘慘戚戚
乍暖還寒時候
最難將息
三杯兩盞淡酒
怎敵他　晚來風急
雁過也
正傷心
卻是舊時相識
滿地黃花堆積
憔悴損
如今有誰堪摘
守着窗兒
獨自怎生得黑
梧桐更兼細雨
到黃昏　點點滴滴
這次第
怎一個　愁字了得

Tune: Adagio

I search and search

Feeling cold and lonely

Dreary hurtful and pain

Whence the weather alternates between warm and cold

'Tis most difficult to forget and hold

Drinking by cups and carafes alone I float

Cannot dispel the gloom of dusk suddenly blow

I watch geese flying pass

In grief

Could they be the ones I used to know

Yellow flowers pile up all over

Faded

Who would care to pick any ever

I sit by the window in solitude

Waiting counting how long will night befall

Of plane trees and drizzles

They patter and grizzle at dusk

For all these

How could the word sorrow my feelings narrate

一翦梅

紅藕香殘玉簟秋
輕解羅裳
獨上蘭舟
雲中誰寄錦書來
雁字回時
月滿西樓
花自飄零水自流
一種相思
兩處閒愁
此情無計可消除
才下眉頭
卻上心頭

如夢令

昨夜雨疏風驟
濃睡不消殘酒
試問捲簾人
卻道海棠依舊
知否
知否
應是綠肥紅瘦

Tune: A Twig of Mume

Pink lotus its fragrance fades on a mat of jade
I doff my silk robe
To board alone on an orchid boat
From among the clouds who had sent me a letter on brocade
Whence the geese return
Moonlight will fill my bower
Flowers drift as water flows
One single agog
Heartbreaks in two places
How to dismiss this sorrow I know not
It may disappear from eyebrow knit
Or sink into my aching heart deep

Tune: Like a Dream

Last night intermittent rain fell with sudden blows
I slept soundly without finishing my brew
This morning I ask my maid rolling up the screen
The begonias are fine she says with a beam
Don't you know
Don't you know
They ought to grow leaves thick green and stems red lean

漁家傲

天接雲濤連曉霧
星河欲轉千帆舞
彷彿夢魂歸帝所
聞天語
殷勤問我歸何處
我報路長嗟日暮
學詩謾有驚人句
九萬里風鵬正舉
風休住
蓬舟吹取三山去

醉花陰

薄霧濃雲愁永晝
瑞腦消金獸
佳節又重陽
玉枕紗廚
半夜涼初透
東籬把酒黃昏後
有暗香盈袖
莫道不消魂
簾捲西風
人比黃花瘦

Tune: Fisherman's Pride

Waves of cloud and morning mist adjoin to paint the sky
The Milky Way turns to elicit a thousand sails dance
Dreamy my soul seems to have returned home in heaven
From voices on high
I was asked in earnest where I wish to go
I say 'tis far far place I would go till its day old
My poems are full of verses that shake people's souls
The legend big bird sails the wind to go ninety thousand *li*
O wind don't you stop
My boat will sail through three mountains to the divine sea

Tune: Drunk under Flower Shade

Amid thin mist and thick clouds my sorrows linger all day
The inlaid animals on my censer play with incense so gay
'Tis Double Nine Fest season again
Behind the translucent drapes my jade pillow lay
Midnight chills mercilessly invade
In evening end I drink by the eastern flower hedge
My sleeves filled with fragrance
Who could say this life is not bright and easy
Whence wind from the west uprolls my curtains
Behold I am thin as yellow flower

陳與義 Chen Yuyi (1090-1138)

臨江仙 · 夜登小閣，憶洛中舊遊
Tune: Immortals by the River: Remembering Friends Travelling Together in Old Times

憶昔午橋橋上飲	Remember on the Noon Bridge we used to drink
坐上多是豪英	Bright wits of the day joined in
長溝流月去無聲	The crescent moon waned in silence
杏花疏影裏	Sitting 'neath lacy shadows of apricot flowers
吹笛到天明	We played flute music till the dawn hours
二十餘年如一夢	Twenty odd years gone dream in a whistle
此身雖在堪驚	Alive I'm surprised knowing none be immortal
閒登小閣看新晴	Carefree I ascent the tower to watch the new moon shine
古今多少事	How many events past and present could survive
漁唱起三更	Hear the fishermen sing after midnight

張元幹 Zhang Yuangan (1091–1161)

賀新郎 · 送胡邦衡待制赴新州
Tune: Celebrating with the Bridegroom – Seeing Hu Quan off Banished South

夢繞神州路	Haunted by dreams of lost country and shame
悵秋風	Autumn winds complain
連營畫角	Among tents bugles drearily blow
故宮離黍	The palace deserted weeds overgrow
底事昆侖傾砥柱	How could the kingdom fall in such a sudden
九地黃流亂注	On nine towns the Yellow River wildly flows
聚萬落千村狐兔	Ten thousand villagers overrun by Jerchen foes
天意從來高難問	This will of heaven we should never question
況人情老易悲如許	Humiliation easily forgotten sadness knows no relief

更南浦
South You Go

送君去	I bid you adieu
涼生岸柳催殘暑	Cool river willows drive summer heat away
耿斜河	The Milky Way in sway
疏星淡月	Stars sparse and moon pale
斷雲微度	Broken clouds quietly go
萬里江山知何處	Where have ten thousand *li* of rivers and hills gone
回首對床夜語	I seek answers from our past chatting not forlorn
雁不到	No geese go your way
書成誰與	How will I send letters your way
目盡青天懷今古	I search the sky for thoughts of yore and today
肯兒曹恩怨相爾汝	On hardship and ease our love and hate
舉大白	Let us be plain and abide
聽金縷	Listen to this song of my mind

楊無咎 Yang Wujiu (1097–1169)

玉樓春 · 茶　　Tune: Jade Bower in Spring – Tea

酒闌未放賓朋散	As dinner approaches the end I ask my guests to stay
自揀冰芽教旋碾	I grind white tea shoots to brew for the day
調膏初喜玉成泥	The boiling broth turns into jade white cream
濺沫共驚銀作線	It spills and churns silver lines approach the brim
已知於我情非淺	We all know each other well our affection not shallow
不必寧寧書木宛面	No need to write down details on the bowls
滿嘗乞得夜無眠	Everyone drinks on forgetting the night is ending
要聽枕邊言語軟	Contented to listen to intimate chats so soothing

岳飛 Yue Fei (1103−1141)

滿江紅

怒髮衝冠

憑欄處

瀟瀟雨歇

抬望眼

仰天長嘯

壯懷激烈

三十功名塵與土

八千里路雲和月

莫等閒白了少年頭

空悲切

靖康恥

猶未雪

臣子恨

何時滅

駕長車踏破賀蘭山缺

壯志飢餐胡虜肉

笑談渴飲匈奴血

待從頭收拾舊山河

朝天闕

Tune: A River in Red

Wrath stood my hair to throw off my hood

On railings I stood

Seeing the rain ceased

I cast my eyes high

To the sky I crooned long sighs

To express my patriotic devotion clear and bright

Like dust and soil thirty-year achieved honour I regard

Eighty thousand *li* of cloud and moon I tread

Youthful powers must not be wasted in idle

Forever regret

Humiliation of our Capital

The defeat is yet to erase

A general's hate must be expressed in actions haste

I will ride my chariot fast

To break through the He Lan Mountain Pass

Let's will to dine with the enemy's flesh for meat

With the Hun's blood we quench our thirsts in laughter repeats

Whence we recover our lost land

We will report to our Royal Court to celebrate

小重山　Tune: Manifold Hills

咋夜寒蛩不住鳴	Incessantly autumn cricket sounds stir the night
驚回千里夢	Breaking my dream a thousand *li* my home nigh
已三更	'Twas well after midnight
起來獨自繞階行	Up alone I paced the yard round and round
人悄悄	Not a soul around
簾外月朧明	Outside the window the moon was bright
白首為功名	For glory I paid my life
舊山松竹老	The bamboos and pines at home thrived
阻歸程	Homebound journey is on hold
欲將心事付瑤琴	To my lute I confide what's in my mind
知音少	No listener
弦斷有誰聽	Who would hear broken strings expressing feelings

陸游 Lu You (1125–1210)

蘭亭道上　　Flower Dock Tea from the Orchid Pavilion

湖上青山古會稽	Up from the lake stands this ancient green hill
斷雲漠漠雨淒淒	Intermittent clouds gather to spread rains chill
籃輿晚過偏門市	A bamboo sedan passes this remote temple in the evening
滿路春泥聞竹雞	Above the hilly muddy road of spring birds sing
蘭亭步口水如天	It is water all over at the Orchid Pavilion station
茶市紛紛趁雨前	Tea traders rush to the market ahead of rain
烏笠遊僧雲際去	In a bamboo hat a roving monk chases the clouds
白衣醉叟道傍眠	A drunken old man lies on roadside totally passed out
陌上行歌日正長	Wayfarers on the winding field paths sing as they go
吳蠶捉績麥登場	Cocoon farmers join grain peddlers to the market carrying loads
蘭亭酒美逢人醉	The Orchid Pavilion wine spares no drinker from intoxication
花塢茶新滿市香	New tea from the Flower Dock fills the market with fragrant sensation

訴衷情

Tune: Of Innermost Feelings

當年萬里覓封候	Alone I rode ten thousand *li* long ago
匹馬戍梁州	To the call in arms at frontier Leung Zhou
關河夢斷何處	Now in fading dreams I know not where to go
塵暗舊貂裘	My cavalier coat of sable worn and old
胡未滅	The invaders not defeated yet
鬢先秋	My hair no longer black
淚空流	Tears shed in vain
此生誰料	Who could expect in this my life
心在天山	My heart still at Tian Shan
身老滄洲	My body here at home getting old

十一月四日風雨大作

During a Storm on the Fourth Day of the Eleventh Moon

僵臥孤村不自哀	I grieved not lying forlorn in a village hut
尚思為國戍輪台	Plans to reclaim our lost frontier loomed in my heart
夜闌臥聽風吹雨	Listening to how stormy winds hurry the pouring rain
鐵馬冰河入夢來	I dreamed how our steely steeds braved the frozen river on free rein

釵頭鳳	Tune: Phoenix Hairpin
紅酥手	Tender hands fine
黃藤酒	Well aged wine
滿城春色宮牆柳	In a spring-filled city willows confined
東風惡	Harsh east winds
歡情薄	Happy feelings thin
一懷愁緒	My heart filled with misery
幾年離索	Yearnings years too long
錯　錯　錯	Wrong Wrong Wrong
春如舊	Spring like last year remains
人空瘦	I see you are so thin
淚痕紅邑鮫綃透	Your red kerchief soaked with tears
桃花落	Peach blossoms fall
閒池閣	By the deserted hall
山盟雖在	Our love oaths still true
錦書難托	Messages could not get through
莫　莫　莫	No No No

詠梅 — In Praise of Mume (Tune: Song of Divination)

驛外斷橋邊	By the fallen bridge outside the post hall
寂寞開無主	A flower is in bloom forlorn
已是黃昏獨自愁	She stands in self-imposed dreary by evening
更着風和雨	And endures the thrashing of wind and rain
無意苦爭春	She lays no claim to possess spring
一任羣芳妒	And remains indifferent what envy other flowers bring
零落成泥碾作塵	Even when her petals fall in mud to become dust
只有香如故	Her fragrance will long last

示兒 — To My Son

死去元知萬事空	I know death negates many a worldly deed
但悲不見九州同	Still I grief to see our country not united
王師北定中原日	Whence our royal force resumed command of the central plain
家祭無忘告乃翁	Tell me in a special rite so my mind will be in peace again

唐琬 (1124－1156)

釵頭鳳　　　　Tune: Phoenix Hairpin

世情薄	Fairness has worn thin
人情惡	Relations belligerent
雨送黃昏花易落	Rain-filled eves hasten flowers to fall
曉風乾	Morning breezes fuss
淚痕殘	Traces of tears fade
欲箋心事	I wish to write you my feelings
獨語斜闌	Only to lean on rails alone
難　難　難	Hard Hard Hard
人成各	You and I have gone different ways
今非昨	'Tis no more like yesterday
病魂常似秋千索	Hanging tight my injured soul continues to groan
角聲寒	Time-horns their frigid notes blow
夜闌珊	Nights persist refusing to grow old
怕人尋問	To dispel any query
咽淚妝歡	Tears swallowed I appear cheery
瞞　瞞　瞞	Hide Hide Hide

范成大 Fan Chengda (1126—1193)

冬日田園雜興
(III)

屋上添高一把茅，
密泥房壁似僧寮。
從教屋外陰風吼，
臥聽籬頭響玉簫。

(IV)

松節然膏當燭籠，
凝煙如墨暗房櫳；
晚來拭淨南窗紙，
便覺斜陽一倍紅。

Winter Songs

(III)

Adding a layer of rushes to my roof the house looks taller
With clay-cast on the walls it is now warm as a monk dweller
Who cares how winds outside tear and roar
Lying in bed I enjoy the flute music from next door

(IV)

Burning pine cream for light is better than candles
Smoke aroma scents the room and blackens the portico
At dusk I cleaned the paper cover of the south window
The setting sun red the brilliance double

(VII)

撥雪挑來踏地菘，
味如蜜藕更肥醲。
朱門肉食無風味，
只作尋常菜把供。

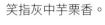

(VII)

榾柮無煙雪夜長，
地爐煨酒暖如湯。
莫嗔老婦無盤飣，
笑指灰中芋栗香。

(VII)

Wiping away the snow we collect the cabbage on frosty ground
It tastes succulent like lotus roots sweet and round
Rich folks in big mansions know only meat on their tables
They regard this heavenly vegetable only as eatable

(VII)

Warmed by short wood logs the snowy night is long
Buried under earth a jar of wine is hot as broth
Don't blame the old wife preparing no fine food
Smiling she fetches roasted taros and chestnuts smelling good

楊萬里 Yang Wanli (1127−1206)

戲筆
Brushing Fun

野菊荒苔各鑄錢	Wild daisies and mosses appear round like coins
金黃銅綠兩爭妍	Gold and copper shine to vie for joy
天公支與窮詩客	Nature rewards poets with such pays for recognition
只買清愁不買田	To purchase sorrow and not lands for cultivation

曉出淨慈寺送林子方
Seeing Lin off from the Temple in the Morning

畢竟西湖六月中	'Tis West Lake in mid-summer fully shown
風光不與四時同	Scenery no other season has known
接天蓮葉無窮碧	Green lotus leaves reach far into the boundless sky
映日荷花別樣紅	Pink lotus blooms soaked in sunshine a radiant dye

朱熹 Zhu Xi (1130–1200)

觀書有感　Insight from Reading

半畝方塘一鑑開	To the small glassy pond I plunge
天光雲影共徘徊	To experience how light and shadows play for fun
問渠哪得清如許	Asked how ideas in the pond could be so deep and clear
為有源頭活水來	The water comes from bustling springs far and near

張孝祥 Zhang Xiaoxiang (1132–1169)

西江月　Tune: Moon over the West River

問訊湖邊春色	Is the lakeside spring scenery still the same
重來又是三年	It's been three years now I've come again
東風吹我過湖船	Thanks to east wind my boat crossed the lake at ease
楊柳絲絲拂面	Strands and strands of willow caress my face like breeze
世路如今已慣	I am used to life as it floats high or low
此心到處悠然	My heart is at peace where'er I go
寒光亭下水連天	Water merges sky beneath the Pavilion Cold Light
飛起沙鷗一片	Where a flock of water birds take flight

念奴嬌

洞庭青草
近中秋
更無一點風色

玉鑒瓊田三萬頃
着我扁舟一葉

素月分輝
明河共影
表裏俱澄澈

悠然心會
妙處難與君說

應念嶺表經年
孤光自照
肝膽皆冰雪
短髮蕭疏襟袖冷
穩泛滄溟空

盡吸西江
細斟北斗
萬象為賓客

扣舷獨嘯
不知今夕何夕

Tune: Charm of a Maiden Dancer – On Dongting Lake

Green is Dongting Lake
Mid-autumn approaching
No wind stirring

On thirty thousand acres of wild space white as jade
A tiny dot my leaf-light skiff glides gay

Stars and moon each show brilliance subdue
Shadows vividly in view
Their pure clean essence emanate

Calm and free I feel
In awe I wish but unable to share this felicity with you

My exile in the southern town I strive to forget
As I self-reflect
I did everything in order and clean as ice nugget
In thin short hair I now wear clothes simple and plain
My skiff and I glide with no worry in this immense expanse

How I'd like to take the Yangtze for cooking water
And wield the Dipper my spatula
To share a feast wildly with my celestial roomer

I beat my bulwark in tune with loud bowls
What date is this night I care not know

辛棄疾 Xin Qiji (1140−1207)

西江月 　　Tune: Moon over West River

萬事煙雲忽過	Ten thousand affairs gone like clouds and haze
一身蒲柳先衰	A hundred years of willows withered away
而今何事最相宜	What is best for me to do at present
宜醉	To get drunk
宜遊	To travel
宜睡	To sleep
早趁催科了納	It is better to pay the tax levies duly
更量出入收支	And balance income and expenses
乃翁依舊管些兒	This old man still cares for some business
管竹	To savour bamboos
管山	To appreciate hill greens
管水	To enjoy water serene

定風波 · 暮春漫興
Tune: Calm Wind and Wave – Late Spring

少日春懷似酒濃	Spring felt like aged brew in days youthful
插花走馬醉千鍾	Playing games on horseback I drank wine a thousand cups filled
老去逢春如病酒	In old age all springs evoke wine rueful
唯有	Exception
茶甌香篆小簾櫳	A bowl of fragrant tea behind drapes low
卷盡殘花風未定	Winds continue to sweep away fading flowers
休恨	No aversion
花開元自要春風	Flowers bloom in spring natural
試問春歸誰得見	Ask who can foresee the return of spring
飛燕	Swallows
來時相遇夕陽中	They came from an encounter in sunset

水龍吟·登建康賞心亭

楚天千里清秋
水隨天去秋無際
遙岑遠目
獻愁供恨
玉簪螺髻
落日樓頭
斷鴻聲裏
江南遊子
把吳鈎看了
欄杆拍遍
無人會登臨意
休說鱸魚堪膾
盡西風
季鷹歸未
求田問舍
怕應羞見
劉郎才氣
可惜流年
憂愁風雨
樹猶如此
倩何人喚取盈盈翠袖
搵英雄淚

Tune: Water-Dragon Chant – At Jiankang Riverside Tower

A thousand *li* of autumn color in southern sky

Water meets sky in endless autumn dye

I gaze on far-off northern hills

Feeling sorrow mixed with hatred still

Seeing spiral shells and hair décor of jade flowers

The sun sets behind the tower

A swan song came and gone early

This lone wanderer is in southern territory

With my precious long sword

I bang on every railing

But no one understands why I am up this tower

Tell me not the river perch is good for cooking

When west winds are blowing

Is it not time for going home to settle

To seek for land a cot and cattle

I fear to meet my old folks

Ashamed to claim a patriot for our country

I sigh for the time lost plenty

In driving winds and rains

Even an old tree has its fears

To whom could I ask for a pink kerchief or green sleeve

To wipe off this my heroic tears

西江月 · 夜行黃沙道中

明月別枝驚鵲
清風半夜鳴蟬
稻花香裏說豐年

聽取蛙聲一片
七八個星天外
兩三點雨山前
舊時茅店社林邊
路轉溪橋忽見

破陣子 · 為陳同甫賦壯詞以寄之

醉裏挑燈看劍
夢迴吹角連營
八百里分麾下炙
五十弦翻塞外聲
沙場秋點兵
馬作的盧飛快
弓如霹靂弦驚
了卻君王天下事
贏得生前身後名
可憐白髮生

Tune: Moon over West River on My Way Home through the Yellow Sand Ridge

My presence startled magpies leaving the moon-lit trees
Cicadas shrill at midnight in gentle breezes
The sweet fragrance in the rice fields promises a bumper year

In celebration frogs croak their chorus I happily hear
High in the sky seven or eight stars twinkle
This side of the hill two or three raindrops sprinkle
I recall a small tavern near the village woods
There it appears where the path leads to the bridge over the brook

Tune: Dance of Cavalry in Response to Chen Liang

Drunken we till lamps bright to check our resting glaives
Bugles reverberate from tent to tent in our dreams
Our warriors ate beef grilled on hot sand in banner shades
They sent martial airs beyond the frontier by fifty strings
'Twas an autumn maneuver in combat exercise
Gallant steeds galloping at top speed
Our bows twanged in thundering heat
We recovered lost sovereign land for empire glory
And won fame for ourselves in life as in death
Grey hair ours to keep

菩薩蠻・書江西造口壁

鬱孤台下清江水
中間多少行人淚
西北是長安
可憐無數山
青山遮不住
畢竟東流去
江晚正愁餘
山深聞鷓鴣

鷓鴣天・博山寺作

不向長安路上行
卻教山寺厭逢迎
味無味處求吾樂
材不材間過此生

寧作我
豈其卿

人間走遍卻歸耕
一松一竹真朋友
山鳥山花好弟兄

Tune: Buddhist Dancer – Written on the Wall of Zaokou

'Neath the Gloom Terrace two rivers flow
The water contains tears of refugees on the road
To the northeast I gaze looking for our lost Capital
Sadly I see but hills
Hills verdant block not my view
Eastward the rivers continue
Would they care for my heart's ills
I hear partridges cry in distant hills

Tune: Partridge Sky – At the Bo Shan Temple

Road to the Capital I no longer seek
Toward the temple friendly monks are shy to meet
I've learned to derive taste from foods brand
And lead a life unconcerned if my talent its use grand

Myself I am
Not a servitor of fame

Leaving worldly affairs I've now returned to till the land
Every pine and bamboo is a true friend
Wild birds and flowers my brothers and sisters hand in hand

青玉案 · 東風夜放花千樹

東風夜放花千樹
更吹落
星如雨
寶馬雕車香滿路
鳳簫聲動
玉壺光轉
一夜魚龍舞
蛾兒雪柳黃金縷
笑語盈盈暗香去
眾裏尋他千百度
驀然回首　那人卻在
燈火闌珊處

西江月 · 遣興

醉裏且貪歡笑
要愁那得工夫
近來始覺古人書
信著全無是處
昨夜松邊醉倒
問松我醉何如
只疑松動要來扶
以手推松曰去

Tune: Green Jade Server – Lantern Festival

A thousand trees aglow with flowers and breezes
Everywhere laughter hisses
We bring down stars like a shower
The road fragrant with prized steeds hurrying carriages through
The air filled with music vibrating from ringing flutes
Wine jars of jade pour and turn in good mood
Through the night lanterns of fish or dragon danced in best moves
Wearing blouses embroidered with golden moths and white willow
Delightful maidens sweep by giggling leaving a trail of scent mellow
I looked for my maiden a thousand rounds in the crowd
Whence I turned my head
There she was amid lantern lights subdue

Tune: Moon over the West River – Self-reflection

I love to laugh in delight even when drunk
No time to grieve
Books of ancient saints may say their fill
Those words should ne'er be taken seriously still
I got drunk beside a pine tree last night
It asked me why I like being drunk
I sensed the tree was trying to hold me right
Keep off I said and pushed away its trunk

劉過 Liu Guo (1154—1206)

臨江仙 · 茶詞　Tune: Immortals by the River – Tea Ci

紅袖扶來聊促膝	Helped by your maid to visit we fondly chat
龍團共破春溫	Warmed by Dragon-Ball tea we share spring yet
高標終是絕塵氛	In high rectitude we rid off worldly bustles
兩箱留燭影	Two of us share these candle shadows
一水試雲痕	A bowl of tea we sip until clouds go
飲罷清風生兩腋	After drinking tea our arms turn into wings on wind
餘香齒頰猶存	Between our teeth fragrance remain
離情淒咽更休論	Parting grieves and tears we must not hint
銀鞍和月載	We share the moon in silver saddles we saunter
金碾為誰分	But which of us shall keep the golden grinder

糖多令 · 重過武昌
Tune: Sugar Rich Song – Passing through Wu Chang Again

蘆葉滿汀州	The marshland is filled with thriving reeds
寒沙帶淺流	Cool sands underlie the shallow water's leads
二十年重過南樓	It's been twenty years since I last visited the south tower
柳下繫船猶未穩	My boat tied to the willows it moors not proper
能幾日	In days few
又中秋	The Mid-autumn Festival in view
黃鶴斷磯頭	The Yellow Crane marks the cliff of the Yangtze River
故人曾到否	Were you here
舊江山渾是新愁	To recall the old reign evokes sorrows new
欲買桂花同載酒	To make a laurel brew I must gather sweet flowers still
終不似	No longer like yore
少年遊	In youth we toured

揚州慢

淮方名都
竹西佳處
解鞍少駐初程

過春風十里
盡薺麥青青

自胡馬窺江去後
廢池喬木
猶厭言兵

漸黃昏
清角吹寒
都在空城

杜郎俊賞
算而今

重到須驚
縱豆蔻詞工
青樓夢好
難賦深情
二十四橋仍在
波心蕩冷月無聲

念橋邊紅藥
年年知為誰生

Tune: The Yangzhou Adagio

To the left of River Huai stands this famous capital town
West of scenic Bamboo Mount
I alight for a short break in my long journey

Behind me was ten *li* of bounty land
Green with thriving wheat strand

Ever since the northern land was overrun by Jurchen steeds
Even tall trees around the wayward ponds
Are tired of hearing war deeds

Approaching dusk
Bugles sounded cold
From vacant towns young and old

This place the poet Du Mu praised with monumental say
Alas he would have a big surprise visiting today

His famed verses on cardamoms and sprig
And dreams in green brothels so sweet
Would be counterpoints in expressing my deep distress
Yangzhou's twenty-four bridges still remain a public interest
Beneath them water swirls continue to churn and crest
The cold moon says not a word

Ask the peonies beside these proud bridges
To whom they show their brilliance year after year

元德明 Yuan Deming (1156−1203)

好事近 · 次蔡丞相韻 · 中州樂府

夢破打門聲
有客袖攜團月
喚起玉川高興
煮松檐晴雪

蓬萊千古一清風
人境兩超絕
覺我胸中黃卷
被春雲香徹

崔與之 Cui Yuzhi (1158−1239)

揚州官滿辭後土題玉立亭

天上人間一樹花
五年於此駐高牙
不隨紅藥矜春色
為愛霜筠耐歲華
四塞風沉天籟寂
半庭月冷市塵睹
臨行更致平安祝
一炷清香十萬家

Tune: Good News Near – Rhyme with Prime Minister Cai

Door knocks wake me up from dreams
The visitor brings in a gift of Full Moon beams
Recalling the legend poet's advice
Tea is brewed with pinewood fire in days fine
Paradise is a cool breeze since ancient time
Man and scenes are transformational
I recall the contents of worn-out books in my mind
They compete not with the Spring Cloud fragrance so fine

On Retirement from Office at Yangzhou

Humanity and the universe is one flowering tree
For five years I led the local office in this community
There is no amusement with spring blooms and gaiety
Like bamboo greens I respond to calls of natural duty
With peace in the frontier and stability in the country
People thrive even when they are not above poverty
Before I depart I wish health and contentment for citizens
To ten thousand families I offer my blessing with lighted incense

史達祖 Shi Dazu (1163–1220)

詠燕 · 雙雙燕

過春社了
度簾幕中間
去年塵冷
差池欲住
試入舊巢相並
還相雕樑藻井
又軟語商量不定
飄然快拂花梢
翠尾分開紅影
芳徑
芹泥雨潤
愛貼地爭飛
競誇輕俊
紅樓歸晚
看足柳暗花暝
應自棲香正穩
便忘了天涯芳信
愁損翠黛雙蛾
日日畫闌獨憑

Tune: Pairs of Swallows – Swallow Song

Spring is half gone
Between curtains and screen on my door
Last year's nest stays its mud cold
Wishing to test on a ready made home
A pair of swallows visit to see on their own
Painted ceilings and carved beams they know
Twittering they debated their decision not known
O'er flower beds they wing to and flow
Their fork tails cast moving red shadows
Along the welcoming way
Where rain has moistened clods of clay
The pair flies low in a happy race
Competing on their swift flights so gay
On the evening they return late
Flying between willows and floral maze
They perch in the nest now fragrant and save
Forgetting a message they were to convey
Her anxiety from longing shown on knitted eyebrows
The resident lady waits for her lover by day and by hour

劉克莊 Liu Kezhuang (1187−1269)

玉樓春：戲呈林節推鄉兄

年年躍馬長安市
客舍似家家似寄
青錢換酒日無何
紅燭呼盧宵不寐
易挑錦婦機中字
難得玉人心下事
男兒西北有神州
莫滴水西橋畔淚

吳文英 Wu Wenying (1200−1260)

西山

絕頂遙知有隱君
餐芝種術塵為羣
多應午灶茶煙起
山下看來是白雲

Tune: Jade Pavilion in Spring – To Jester a Friend

Galloping through the Capital years in a row
Away from home you linger in brothels as usual
Sparing no coins you drink your days away
By candlelight your nights are sleepless but gay
Words from your faithful wife you forsake readily
To fathom the feelings of a mistress is not easy
Remember your motherland while you roam north and west
Waste no tear parting a wayward mistress

West Hill

High up the mountain zenith lives this hermit
Eating fungi and herbs he and animals keep no limit
Vapours rise every noon when he brews tea
From downhill they look like white clouds flee

八聲甘州：陪庾幕諸公遊靈岩

Tune: Eight Beats of Gangzhou – On a Visit to Star Cliff with Friends

渺空煙四遠	Mists masked all sides of sky
是何年	Whence
青天墜長星	A comet trailed down in dark night
幻蒼崖雲樹	Like a tall cliff of towering trees
名娃金屋	A golden bower perched here built for Lady Xi Shi
殘霸宮城	Now in ruins a pile of debris in the royal palace
箭徑酸風射眼	On Arrow Lane acid winds blind the eye
膩水染花腥	Fallen petals in the dead moat an odorous plight
時靸雙鴛響	I fancy hearing broidered sleepers tottering at the door
廊葉秋聲	'Tis but autumn leaves hissing on the floor
宮裏吳王沉醉	In his palace the King of Wu is stranded in a drunken state
倩五湖倦客	He envies his retired general travelling the Five Lakes
獨釣醒醒	Fishing leisurely to stay awake
問蒼波無語	I ask the sky it remains silent
華一奈山青	Could black hairs endure like green mountains
水涵空	Waters contain space
闌杆高處	By the rail on high I pace
送亂鴉	To watch crows fly frivolous
斜日落漁汀	The slanting sun touches the fishery
連呼酒	I call for rounds of the finest wine
上琴台去	Up Lute Terrace I climb
秋與雲平	Where autumn and clouds intertwine

風入松　　Tune: Wind through Pines

聽風聽雨過清明	Hearing the wind and drizzles in Qing Ming
愁草瘞花銘	Amid wild grass and flowers your elegy rings
樓前綠暗分攜路	We parted on the dark-green road by the bower
一絲柳	Each thread of willow
一寸柔情	Each measure of tender feeling
料峭春寒中酒	I drown my grief with wine this chilly spring
交加曉夢啼鶯	Drowsily I awake as orioles sing
西園日掃林亭	I sweep the West Garden grounds clean every day
依舊賞新晴	To watch the fine view with you like in old days
黃蜂頻撲秋千索	Even wild wasps kiss the swing ropes where they alight
有當時　纖手香凝	The sweet scent of your tender hands remain
惆悵雙鴛不到	In grief I look for traces of your broidered shoes in vain
幽階一夜苔生	The vacant steps gathered moss through the night

鷓鴣天 · 室人降日，以此奉寄
Tune: Partridge Sky – To My Wife on Her Birthday

去歲今辰卻到家	This day last year home I was not near
今年相望又天涯	Today this year I pine for you from faraway here
一春心事閒無處	My love for you floats like a spring with no dwelling
兩鬢秋霜細有華	Like autumn frost my hairs are greying
山接水	Hill and rills link
水明霞	Waters shine in evenings
滿林殘照見歸鴉	Dyed by sunset the forest welcomes crows returning
何時收拾田園了	Whence our country is united in permanence
兒女團圞夜煮茶	Our family will brew tea together every evening

柳梢青 · 春感
Tune: Green Willow Tendrils – Spring Thoughts

鐵馬蒙氈	Armoured steeds and woollen Mongol tents heavy
銀花灑淚	In memory silver lantern lights tears many
春入愁城	This spring the Capital is in captivity
笛裏番腔	Mongol flutes toot out songs northern
街頭戲鼓	Drums roll at random on streets sudden
不是歌聲	They are music heathen
那堪獨坐青燈	How could I sit beside a lonely lamp
想故國　高台月明	And pine for the moonlights of my native land
輦下風光	Prominent happiness in the Capital
山中歲月	Dwelling these years deep in the mountain
海上心情	My heart joins the spirit of heroes fighting in the ocean

李冶 Li Yan (1232–1303)

唐多令　　　Tune: Vibrant Melody

雨過水明霞	The water is clean and sublime after rain
潮回岸帶沙	Returning tides add to the bank's sandy rims
葉聲寒	Leaves rattling cold
飛透窗紗	Through curtains behind the window
懊恨西風催世換	How regretful the west wind had changed the reign
更隨我	Following me
落天涯	To yonder horizon
寞古豪華	Bygone glories are in desolation
烏衣日又斜	Royal settlers follow the sun fallen
說興亡	To detect the rise and fall of dynasties
燕入誰家	Just find where swallows are happy
只有南來無數雁	Left are countless southbound geese
和明月	Pursuing moon light
宿蘆花	Sleeping amid flowering reeds

文天祥 Wen Tianxiang (1236－1282)

除夜 New Year Eve

乾坤空落落	Heaven and earth exist wide and high
歲月去堂堂	My years gone my spirit freely ride
末路驚風雨	Winds and rains foretell the end of my road
窮邊飽雪霜	In the frontier I had endured stormy snows
命隨年欲盡	My life will terminate in this year-end
身與世俱忘	It matters not what loss and gain had been on hand
無復屠蘇夢	I dream not drinking another cup of Tosu wine
挑燈夜未央	Only to keep my lamp bright through this night

過零丁洋 Crossing the Lonely Ocean

辛苦遭逢起一經	Moved by the *I Jin* I built my good character working hard
干戈寥落四周星	For four long years I fought the enemy with all my heart
山河破碎風飄絮	Now my motherland is shattered into pieces like drifting leaves
身世浮沉雨打萍	I swim or sink much like duckweed under heavy rain
惶恐灘頭說惶恐	For feelings of peril I sigh on Perilous Beach
零丁洋裏歎零丁	Crossing Lonely Ocean I feel dreary and lonely
人生自古誰無死	Since days of old man lived but die
留取丹心照汗青	I live loyal to my country eternally fine

張弘范 Zhang Hongfan (1238–1280)

南鄉子

深院日初長
萬卷詩書一炷香
竹掩茅齋人不到
清涼
茶罷西軒讀老莊
今古都輸夢一場
煞利名途上客
乾忙
千丈紅塵

劉敏中 Liu Minzhong (1243–1318)

浣溪沙

虢虢清流淺見沙
沙邊翠竹野人家
野人延客不堪誇
旋掃太初岩頂雪
細烹陽羨貢餘茶
古銅瓶子蠟梅花

Tune: Southern Country Song

Deep where I dwell summer days prolong
Reading ten thousand volumes incense burn long
No one visits this humble dwelling in bamboo shades
Cool and serene
I read Lao-Zhuang after tea in the west wing
Today as at all times life is but a dream
We laugh at people steep in pursuing wealth and fame
Occupied only
In thousands of bustling days not homely

Tune: Silky Sand Brook

A river flows chattering on sands clear
A family lives at riverside where bamboo shades waver
Serving visitors tea is a simple matter
The host uses his best tea the Cliff Top Snow
On open fire the broth simmers slow
Breathing plum aroma they drink with antique bowls

八聲甘州 —— 記玉關踏雪事清遊

記玉關　踏雪事清遊

寒氣脆貂裘

傍枯林古道

長河飲馬

此意悠悠

短夢依然江表

老淚灑西州

一字無題處

落葉都愁

載取白雲歸去

問誰留楚佩

弄影中洲

折蘆花贈遠　向尋常野橋流水

待招來 不是舊沙鷗

空懷感

有斜陽處

卻怕登樓

Tune: Eight Beats of Ganzhou – I Remember Our Trip through Snowy Jade Gate

I remember our trip through snowy Jade Gate
Our sable coats stiff in the cold
Woods were bare on the ancient road
We drank our horses in every running stream
Every detail is vivid in my dreams
Fleeting dreams alive are fond to narrate
How we shed tears for departed comrades out west
Nowhere to put words down to attest
Even fallen leaves joined in to mourn
You went home carried by a white cloud
Forgetting to whom your pendants should be left proud
Pride is but shadow in mid country
Alone I break reeds to send away under bridge flows
But the gulls that appear are not those we used to know
In vain I sigh
Where the sun sets
A high tower I dare not ascend

蔣捷 Jiang Jie (1245-1305)

梅花引 · 荊溪阻雪
Tune: Plume Melody – Strand at Jin Stream by Snow

白鷗問我泊孤舟	A white gull asks me while I moor my skiff
是身留	Is your body staying
是心留	Is your heart staying
心若留時	If it is your heart
何事鎖眉頭	Why show a knit brow
風拍小簾燈暈舞	Lamp shadows dance with wind on the window
對閒影	Watching the aimless shadows
冷清清	Cold intensifies cold
憶舊遊	As I recall past travels
舊遊舊遊今在否	Could past travels be alive today
花外樓	A bower towering floral ways
柳下舟	A skiff tied under willows
夢也夢也	O dream O dreams
夢不到	None of you could reveal
寒水空流	How currents aimlessly flow
漠漠黃雲	Yellow clouds widely float
濕透木棉裘	Keeping my double coat wet through
都道無人愁似我	They say no one grieves like me
今夜雪	Snowing this night
有梅花	Plums flowering bright
似我愁	To characterize my plight

馬致遠 Ma Zhiyuan (1260－1334)

天淨沙 · 秋思
Tune: Sky over Clear Sand – Autumn Thoughts

枯藤老樹昏鴉	Dry vines old trees a confused crow
小橋流水人家	Small bridge flowing water a cosy family
古道西風瘦馬	Ancient road west wind a skinny horse
夕陽西下	The setting sun goes down west
斷腸人在天涯	A broken-heart traveller stays afar

王實甫 Wang Shifu (1260－1336)

正宮 · 端正好 · 長亭送別
Tune: Calm Dignity – Parting

碧雲天	Blue sky with clouds
黃花地	Yellow flowers aground
西風緊	West wind gust
北雁南飛	Northern geese southbound
曉來誰染霜林醉	Drunk at dawn whose face flushes like autumn woods
總是離人淚	'Tis tears of lovers drown in parting mood

萬俟詠 Wansi Yong

昭君怨

Tune: Lament of Princess Zhao Jun

春到南樓雪盡	Snow gone when spring arrives at Southern Tower
驚動燈期花信	Flower Fest and Lantern Days are here
小雨一番寒	A light rain brings back the chill
倚欄杆	I lean on the rail
莫把欄杆倚	To what avail do I lean on the rail
一望幾重煙水	I see only multiple folds of misty hills
何處是京華	Where is my old Capital
暮雲遮	Behind the veil of evening clouds hanging tall

長相思 · 雨

Tune: Eternal Longing – Rain

一聲聲	Drip after drip
一更更	Hour after hour
窗外芭蕉窗裏燈	By candlelight I listen to banana leaves outside
此時無限情	I long for you every night
夢難成	No dreams
恨難平	Nor ease of sorrow
不道愁人不喜聽	Rains care not how I dislike sounds they make
空階滴到明	They beat the marble steps till morning

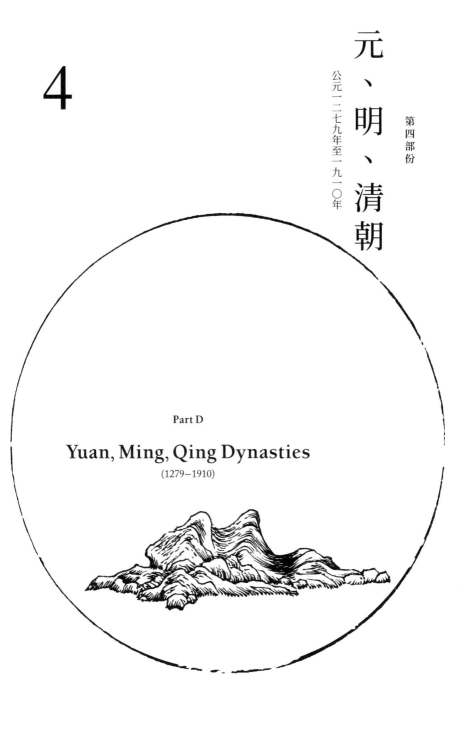

4

元、明、清朝

第四部份

公元一二七九年至一九一〇年

Part D

Yuan, Ming, Qing Dynasties

(1279–1910)

元朝

YUAN DYNASTY

(1271–1368)

曾允元 Zeng Yunyuan

點絳唇	Tune: Rouge Lips

一夜東風　　　　East winds blew all night
枕邊吹散愁多少　They disperse grief on my pillow right
數聲啼鳥　　　　Intermittent bird-cries
夢轉紗窗曉　　　My dream ended as I see dawn through blinds

來是春初　　　　You came in early spring
去是春將老　　　You left in late spring
長亭道　　　　　The road along scattered pavilions
一般芳草　　　　Same grass green
只有歸時好　　　Upon your return I will feel what spring means

張可久 Zhang Kejiu (1270–1348)

山居春枕 (二)：雙調‧青江引
Tune: Prelude to Clear River – Spring in the Mountain (II)

門前好山雲佔了　From my door I see clouds veil many a mountain green
盡日無人到　　　No one comes in
松風響翠濤　　　Through pine trees the wind gives rise to songs of green
槲葉燒丹灶　　　Fuelled by oak leaves the stove burns red
先生醉眠春自老　I drink and sleep awaiting spring to rid

喬吉 Qiao Ji (1280−1345)

山坡羊 · 自警
Tune: Sheep on Slope – Singing to Myself

清風閒坐	I sit relaxed in cool breezes
白雲高臥	White clouds high at ease
面皮不受時人唾	To people's critical views I defy
樂跎跎	Happily I sigh
笑呵呵	Laughingly I peal
看別人搭套項推沉磨	Watching people slave in hustling deals
蓋下一枚安樂窩	In my dwelling of comfort and peace
東	East
也在我	I sit free
西	West
也在我	I do as I please

憑欄人 · 金陵道中
Tune: Leaning on Railings – On My Way to Jinling

瘦馬馱詩天一涯	Like a skinny horse burdened by poetry I strayed
倦鳥呼愁村數家	Weary birds wailing pass lone villages on their way
撲頭飛柳花	Willow catkins shedding all over my head
與人添鬢華	As if my hair greys too slowly yet

百字令 · 登石頭城
Tune: Hundred Words Song – Ascending Jin Ling City

石頭城上	Up on Jin Ling City
望天低吳楚	The sky low over the southern territory
眼空無物	I find nothing more of history
指點六朝形勝地	The many lands of glory in the Six Dynasties
唯有青山如壁	Standing strong are but green hills in dignity
蔽日旌旗	Banners covered sun rays
連雲檣櫓	Sails and oars join the cloud ways
白骨紛如雪	Bones scattered like white snow seen on sunny days
一江南北	North and south of the Big River
消磨多少豪傑	On test were the wills of how many warriors
寂寞避暑離宮	The summer palaces of kings vacant
東風輦路	Royal carriage roads silent
芳草年年發	Green grass thrive year after year
落日無人松徑裏	Paths through pines are cold in sunset
鬼火高低明滅	Shadowy flames appear now and then
歌舞樽前	People sing and dance and drink
繁華夢裏	They depict past glory in dreams
傷心千古	Times in sorrow
秦淮一片明月	The moon shines the Qin Hui as usual

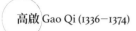

高啟 Gao Qi (1336−1374)

友之越贈以惠泉　A Gift of Hui Spring in Parting

雲液流甘漱石牙	Rain drops from clouds keep tea buds tender
潤通錫麓樹增華	Given moisture mountain trees flower
汲來曉冷和山雨	In early morning I scoop water cool with mountain rain
飲處春香帶間花	Drinking it I savour the fragrance of blooms in spring
合契老僧煩每護	The old monk busies with how best to treat his gathering
修經幽客記曾誇	The scripture scholar remembers his excessive boasting
送行一斛還堪贈	I give you a gourd of this special water in parting
往試雲門日鑄茶	Home in the Cloud Door you will brew tea every morning

釋中峯 Shi Zhongfeng (Yuan Dynasty)

行香子

Tune: Fragrance Songs

短短橫牆	Surrounding the place is a low wall
矮矮疏窗	Windows intermittent and small
一方兒　小小池塘	Nearby sits a tiny square pond
高低迭嶂	Distant hills stand low and tall
曲水邊旁	A brook meanders through them all
也有些風	Wind there is
有些月	Moon there is
有些香	Fragrance there is
日用家常	Daily utensils handy
竹幾藤床	Bamboo table and rattan bed ready
盡眼前	Before our eyes
水色山光	Water colours reflect scenic hill beauties
客來無酒	Visitors welcome with no wine
清話何妨	Chatting casually on nothing divine
但細烘茶	We brew tea caringly
淨洗盞	Bowls are washed neatly
滾燒湯	Tea broth simmers in no hurry

李道源 Li Daoyuan (Yuan Dynasty)

遊大理崇聖寺　A Visit to Chong Sheng Temple at Da Li

把茗對山雲戀戀	I sip tea facing the hill where clouds linger
看花着履雨毿毿	To view flowers in drizzles on clogs I wear
唐家舊迹今無幾	Relics of Tang Dynasty now remain few in glamour
彈指興亡可盡談	Dynastic rise and fall can be dismissed in a flicker

戴昺 Dai Bing (Yuan Dynasty)

嘗茶　Savouring Tea

自汲香泉帶落花	I draw spring water carrying fragrance of fallen petals
漫燒石鼎試新茶	To boil new tea to savour on stone stove
綠陰天氣閒庭院	My courtyard under green shades stands serene
臥聽黃蜂報晚衙	I lounge listening to bees doing their routine

明朝

MING DYNASTY

(1368–1644)

陸容 Lu Rong (1436–1494)

送茶僧

江南風致說僧家
石上清香竹裏茶
法藏名僧知更好
香煙茶暈滿袈裟

唐寅 Tang Yin (1470–1524)

題事茗圖

日長何所事
茗碗自賚持
料得南窗下
清風滿鬢絲

For a Tea Connoisseur Monk

Monks from south of the river their charisma special
Often seen with stone grinds and fragrant tea in a bamboo bowl
The learned master from the grand temple is a tea connoisseur
His robe marked with stains his chamber with tea aroma

For the Brewing Tea Painting

What could I do on a long day
Holding a tea bowl to appreciate so gay
In the southern window I expect to see
My hair floating with the vernal breeze

文徵明 Wen Zhengming (1470–1559)

煎茶詩贈履約

嫩湯自候魚生眼
新茗還跨翠展旂
穀雨江南佳節近
惠泉山下小船歸
山人紗帽籠頭處
禪榻風花繞鬢飛
酒客不通塵夢醒
臥看春日下松扉

暮春齋居即事

經旬寡人事
蹤跡小窗前
瞑色連殘雨
春寒宿野煙
茗杯眠起味
書卷靜中緣
零落梅枝瘦
風吹更可憐

Tea Making

The simmering tea awaits fish eyes to appear
Boiling leaves dance showing flags green
In south China the Grain Rain Fest is approaching
I collect the famous spring water from Mount Hui for tea brewing
This tea lover enjoys the steam aroma in the pantry
His hairs flicker amid the Zen bed and the tea fume flurry
Wine drinkers understand not the wonders of dreams
Like watching my pine door light up by the sun in spring

On Simple Living in Late Spring

Long has been an absence of human affair
No people before my window appear
In gloomy weather rains fall with no ending
In the wilderness it is cold in late spring
In and out of bed I enjoy a cup of tea
The same as reading a book in peace
Plum branches are lean and scanty
In winds they appear rather melancholy

楊慎 Yang Shen (1488–1559)

臨江仙

滾滾長江東逝水
浪花淘盡英雄
是非成敗轉頭空
青山依舊在
幾度夕陽紅
白髮漁樵江渚上
慣看秋月春風
一壺濁酒喜相逢
古今多少事
都付笑談中

Tune: Immortal by the River

To the east the Yangtze's rumbling rapids incessantly roll
Its multiple froths reflect the deeds of many a hero
Rights wrongs wins and defeats all pass in peril
Hills remain green their foliage thrive perpetual
Crimson sunsets shine their brilliance monumental
On the river islet stands a fisherman his hair is grey
In his experience autumn moons and vernal breezes integrate
With a jar of unstrained wine we gladly congregate
On the many events ancient and recent
We dismiss them in our laughter as we drink

吳承恩 Wu Chen'en (1501–1582)

樵歌子　　A Woodcutter Song

觀棋柯爛	Watching a game of chess I drop into a timeless sphere
伐木丁丁	As a woodcutter I fell trees in spree
雲邊谷口徐行	At the valley where clouds edge I stroll
賣薪沽酒	Selling firewood I go
狂笑自陶情	Laughing to echo the spirit of poet Tao
蒼徑秋高	Deep in autumn the hill paths are still green
對月枕松根	On a pine root pillow I lie to sleep under moonshine
一覺天明	Till dawn I wake up feeling fine
認舊林	Up this old forest
登崖過嶺	I scale cliffs and cross ridges
持斧斷枯藤	To cut down withered creepers
收來成一擔	Gathering enough to make up a load
行歌市上	I carry my goods to market singing
易米三升	For three pints of rice in exchange
更無些子爭競	No bargaining
時價平平	It is a fair pricing
不會機謀巧算	I have no interest in using tricks to make gains
沒榮辱	And care not to win or loose in a game
恬淡延生	Leading a simple life my days and years extend long
相逢處	In my encounters
非仙即道	Daoists and immortals gather
靜坐講黃庭	To expound the art of happiness as I quietly savour

舟行　On a Gliding Boat

白鷺羣翻隔浦風　Where the river enters the sea white cranes frolic
斜陽遙映樹重重　The sun's slanting rays render distant tree shadows vivid
前村一片雲將雨　Clouds over the distant village signal rains to pour
閒倚船窗看掛龍　I recline on my boat to watch how a rainbow takes form

楊柳青　Green Willows

村旗誇酒蓮花白　Village tavern banners feature white lotus brew
津鼓開帆楊柳青　Roaring drums hurry sails green with willows
壯歲驚心頻客路　Young and fearless I roamed on all roads
故鄉回首幾長亭　Now I pine for my homeland long pavilions show
春深水漲嘉魚味　In late spring fishes thrive in swelling waters
海近風多健鶴翎　Near the sea cranes brave winds in their flutters
誰向高樓橫玉笛　To whom up the tower the flutist sings
落梅愁絕醉中聽　Grieving with falling plums I listen in drunken sheen

戚繼光 Qi Jiguang (1528–1587)

曉征

霜溪曲曲轉旌旗
幾許沙鷗睡未知
笳鼓聲高寒吹起
深山驚殺老闍梨

陳繼儒 Chen Jiru (1558–1639)

浪淘沙・茶園即事

絕壁翠苔封
岃崱危峯
半山雲氣織芙蓉
怪鳥啼春聲不斷
躑躅花紅
茅屋掛嵱嵷
十里青松
茶園深處掛孤築
知得清明今欲到
茗綠東風

To War at Dawn

Banners undulate we marched along the frigid winding stream
Not even the sleeping waterbirds were aroused from their dreams
Suddenly our drums thundered and bugles shrilled
The deafening roar frightened even the old monks deep in hills

Tune: Waves Refining Sand – On Scenes of Tea Plantation

Moss growths block the way to cliffs remote
Sky high rise up the zenith
Clouds change colours to beautify the mountain
Rare birds make spring calls incessant
Flowers loiter in crimson
Straw huts in hills suspend
Ten miles of verdant pines present
Deep in the tea plantation my cane hangs
Do I know today is Festival Qing Ming
Featuring green tea and the spirit of spring

劉維 Liu Wei (Ming Dynasty 1368–1644)

感通寺與僧舊話
Past Chats with a Monk at Gan Tong Temple

竹居瀟灑白雲邊　　A bamboo cabin stands next to cloud's edge
僧話留連茗熏煎　　With a monk brewing tea repeatedly I chat
海山久思惟有夢　　In dreams one can handle national affairs at ease
心中長住不知年　　And forget about the passing of past years

吳偉業 Wu Weiye (1609–1671)

意難忘 · 山家
Tune: Unforgettable Memory – Mountain People

村塢雲遮	The village tower is hidden by the clouds
有蒼藤老幹	Dark verdant vines hover about
翠竹明沙	On sandy soils green bamboos tower
溪堂連石穩	Streams and pebbles seemingly hidden
苔徑逐籬斜	Mossy paths lead to fences fallen
文木幾	Finely carved tables
小窗紗	Silky curtains
是好事人家	Home for a family noble
啟北扉	Opening the northern window
移床待客	Preparing the guest chamber
百樹梅花	Hundreds of plum flowers appear
衰翁健飯堪誇	An old man his appetite large
把癭尊茗碗	He drinks tea with a bowl carved in fine roots
高話桑麻	And talk about farming matters
穿池還種柳	Willows line up ponds in rows
汲水自澆瓜	Mellon fields irrigated natural
霜後橘	After frosts tangerines quickly ripe
雨前茶	Prior to rains tender teas thrive
這風味清佳	They taste purely heaven
喜去年	Good cheers for last year
山田大熟	Hillside fields their harvest crest
爛漫生涯	Life and Nature shine their conditions finest

竺庵大成 Zhu'an Dacheng (1610－1666)

伯勞　　　Swallow

伯勞西去雁東來	Swallows leave westward when geese return east
李白桃紅歲歲開	White plum and red peach flowers bloom year after year
萬事無過隨分好	Treat all encounters naturally staying away from extremes
人生何用苦安排	Life is natural no need to plan for painful dreams

永覺元賢 Yongjue Yuanxian (1576－1657)

臥　　　Lying Down

山深蓮漏水	Deep in the mountain lilies drip overnight
一室風俏然	Gentle breezes visit my cabin delight
繩床方七尺	My seven-foot knotted bed waits for me to retire
曲肱伴雲眠	Lying down on bent arms I watch clouds high
有無渾不計	I care not whether I have or have not
凡聖亦都捐	Nor to become a saint or stay an ordinary lot
莫謂全無物	People say nothing exist in life
孤明一鏡懸	Behold a lone mirror hangs nigh

王夫之 Wang Fuzi (1619−1692)

更漏子・本意
Tune: Time Dipper Song – Real Intention

斜月橫	The moon hangs across the sky
疏星炯	Scattered bright stars shine
不道秋宵真永	Who says autumn nights are not infinite
聲緩緩	Dripper drops mark time in limits
滴泠泠	They also appraise space systemic
雙眸未易局	My eyes do not easily close
霜葉墜	Frosty leaves fall
幽蟲絮	Insects incessantly call
不道秋宵真永	Drinking thriftily leads not a drunken state
天下事	Worldly affairs
少年心	Kept my youth mind busy
分明點點深	They sink in my heart deeply

長亭怨・與李天生冬夜宿雁門關作
Tune: Parting Laments – Staying a Night at Geese Pass

記燒燭	Remember together we burned candles
雁門高處	High on Wild Geese Pass we settled
積雪封城	Heavy flurries had the town buried in snow
凍雲迷路	Beneath frozen clouds roads not recognizable
添盡香煤	To the stove we kept adding coals
紫貂相擁	We cuddle in mink coats
夜深語	The night through chatting
苦寒如許	Such bitter cold
難和爾	How could I echo
淒涼句	Your verses of sorrow
一片望鄉愁	To our native land we pined
飲不醉	Drinking without drunk

爐頭駝乳	Camel milk warmed on stove
無處	Nowhere is the master seen
問長城舊主	Not builders of the old Great Wall
但見武靈遺墓	But the tomb of Yue Fei standing tall
沙飛似箭	Sands fly like arrows
亂穿向	Darting in all directions
草中狐兔	To kill animals hiding in grass burrows
那能使	How could we
口北關南	Revive these frontier passes north and south
更重作	To rebuild
並州門戶	Gateways for our country imperial
且莫吊沙場	Do not morn the battlefield hero
收拾秦弓歸去	Reclaim our homeland with bows and arrows

清朝

QING DYNASTY

(1644–1911)

廖燕 Liao Yan (1644–1705)

祝月

竹管簫疏起夜涼
行看秋月滿輪霜
殷勤好照今宵夢
一路遙飛到故鄉

Moon Wishes

The night cool when pipes sing an isolate song
I watch the frosty full autumn moon on
With affection it shines on my dream tonight
And helps me home in speedy flight

辭諸生詩

四十年前事既非
那堪還着舊藍衣
年來著述心徒在
老去功名願已違
四海浪平龍獨臥
一天雲淨鶴高飛
須知富貴非吾願
願抱琴書伴釣磯

Bidding Farewell to Students

Events in forty years are gone to naught
A blue coat for scholars on me until it rots
Writing these years my thoughts sit still
My wish for recognition has remained years few
In the windless four seas a lone dragon lies
Cranes soar high in a cloudless sky
It should be known I had never wished to be rich
To have my zither by my side as I fish is all I wish

俍亭挺 Liang Tingting (1615−1684)

水檻　　　　　　Rail by the River

水檻沙平冷石台	From the riverfront rail I see a cold boulder on a sand landing
清風細雨雜香來	Gentle breezes and drizzles carry fragrance varying
臨風三弄江城笛	I play my flute again and again where winds blow
魂斷湘裙掃落梅	My music moves the Xian beauty to sweep up fallen peach petals

納蘭性德 Nalan Xingde (1655−1685)

長相思　　　　　Tune: Longing for You

山一程	Hills legging far
水一程	Rills legging far
身向榆關那畔行	Toward lands outside the Pass I go
夜深千帳燈	Past midnight a thousand tents aglow
風一更	Winds incessantly blow
雪一更	Snows incessantly show
聒碎鄉心夢不成	Pining for home keeps me awake no dream possible
故園無此聲	These sounds unheard in my native folds

菩薩蠻 · 過張見陽山居賦贈
Tune: Buddhist Dancer – Passing a Friend's Mountain Home

車塵馬跡紛如織	Horses and carriages cross here like knitting
羨君築處真幽僻	I envy you dwelling in a serene place hiding
柿葉一林紅	Passimo leaves top its woods red radiant
蕭蕭四面風	Gentle breezes pass from all sides pleasant

功名應看鏡	Success and fame exist like mirror images
明月秋河影	Moon shadows and Milky Way mirages
安得此山間	How I wish to have a cot with you in the mountain
與君高臥閒	To live a life of respite caring for nothing important

浣溪沙 · 身向雲山那畔行
Tune: Silky Sands Brook – Towards Cloud Hills in Horizon

身向雲山那畔行	We ride toward looming clouds far in the horizon
北風吹斷馬嘶聲	Horse neighs are silenced by powerful winds northern
深秋遠塞若為情	Autumn in the far frontier permits no emotions

一抹晚煙荒戍壘	Gentle smokes rise from army camps in the evening
半竿斜日舊關城	Slanting sunset keeps this ancient military pass shining
古今幽恨幾時平	Whence will these endless tribal conflicts abate

南鄉子‧何處淬吳鉤

何處淬吳鉤
一片城荒枕碧流
曾是當年龍戰地
颼颼
塞草霜風滿地秋

霸業等閒休
躍馬橫戈總白頭
莫把韶華輕換了
封侯
多少英雄只廢丘

Tune: Southern Country Song – Ancient Battle Ground

Where is the ancient battle ground
This vast deserted land seen along a river town
Ruins of the legendary battles of dragon kings
Washed by winds and rains
Tall grasses and frosty winds signal an autumn reign

Ambitious campaigns await imminent termination
Life with horses and spears leads to no satisfaction
Waste not youthful days to trade
For nobility
So many heroes buried in neglected graves

金縷曲 · 慰西溟

何事添淒咽
但由他　天公簸弄　莫教磨涅
失意每多如意少
終古幾人稱屈
須知道　福因才折
獨臥藜床看北斗
背高城　玉笛吹成血
聽譙鼓
二更徹

丈夫未肯因人熱
且乘閒　五湖料理
扁舟一葉
淚似秋霖揮不四　灑向野田黃蝶
須不羨　承明班列
馬迹車塵忙未了
任西風　吹冷長安月
又蕭寺
花如雪

Tune: Song of Golden Tread Comforting a Friend

Why reinforce misery
Leave it to the power on high insist not in being sully
Life is more disappointing than satisfactory
Most people complain not in history
Heaven dislikes the able and favours the ordinary
I relax on my rude couch to watch the Dipper
Beyond the city wall a flute laments its cadence bitter
A drum booms out the hour from the watchtower
The night is darkest in small hours

A man ought not to seek patronage
On a boat light as a leave I sail the five lakes for food tasty
'Tis useless to waste tears copious like autumn rain
Let sad feelings loose on a wide plain for butterflies to wing
Do not envy people in government office
Trapped in the dizzy whirl of endless business
Let the west wind blow in the Capital by moonlight
O solemn temples
Floral snow

憶秦娥 · 龍潭口
Tune: Remembering Qin Maiden – Black Dragon Pool

山重疊	Mountains fold
懸崖一線天疑裂	Between cliffs a line seen like a crack in the sky
天疑裂	A crack in the sky
斷碑題字	On a broken monumen stone inscriptions show
古苔橫嚙	Old vines tangle hiding words old
風聲雷動鳴金鐵	Battling spears cross like gales thunder
陰森潭底蛟龍窟	Down in the deep the dragon's cave lies under
蛟龍窟	The dragon's cave lies under
興亡滿眼	The rise and fall of our motherland in memory
舊時明月	Moonshines of yore in company

水調歌頭・題岳陽樓圖

Tune: Prelude in Water Melody – For a Painting on Yue Yang Tower

落日與湖水	The lake in sunset
終古岳陽城	Together with the Yue Yang City yet
登臨半是遷客	Half the visitors had been banished officers
歷歷數題名	They left their laments in poems here

欲問遺踪何處	If you asked their whereabouts
但見微波木葉	Just watch the fallen leaves on tiny ripples
幾簇打魚罾	And the cast fishing net suspended on a bamboo pole
多少別離恨	Separation sorrows are plenty
哀雁下前汀	The grieving geese plunge down a sand bar of memory

忽宜雨	Time for rain
旋宜月	Time for moon
更宜晴	Time for a fine day
人間無數金碧	So many colourful paintings adorn humanity
未許著空明	Comparing not the beauty of Nature's serenity

淡墨生綃譜就	Just wet the brush in pale ink
待俏橫拖一筆	And touch the paper with a horizontal stain
帶出九嶷青	Mount Jiu Yi stands out in a powerful state
彷彿瀟湘夜	At night on the romantic Xian River
鼓瑟舊精靈	The legendary Music Spirit appears

如夢令 · 萬帳穹廬人醉
Tune: Like a Dream – Ten Thousand Woollen Tents Make Us Feel Exhilarating

萬帳穹廬人醉	Ten thousand woollen tents make us feel exhilarating
星影搖搖欲墜	Starry shadows wave as if they are falling
歸夢隔狼河	The Wolf River spoils my wish for homecoming
又被河聲攪碎	Its torrents awake me from dreaming
還睡	Back to sleep
還睡	Back to sleep
解道醒來無味	Nothing is meaningful when awake

山花子 · 風絮飄殘已化萍
Tune: Mountain Flower Song – Petals Drift Like Water Lily

風絮飄殘已化萍	Petals long on air fell to drift like water lily
泥蓮剛倩藕絲縈	Emerging from mud lily silks tied us closely
珍重別拈香一瓣	You held a fragrant flower when we last said goodbye
記前生	Marking our life reverting
人到情多情轉薄	When love is total devotion there is no more addition
而今真個悔多情	I now wish I had kept some reservation
又到斷腸回首處	It's time again for me to grieve for my total loss
淚偷零	Tears come no more

霜天曉角 · 重來對酒
Tune: Morning Bugles on Frosty Day – We Happily Drink

重來對酒	Reunited we happily drink
析盡風前柳	Breaking willow wickers in the wind
若問看花情緒	How we love to appreciate flowers you ask
似當日	Like our time together
怎能彀	Not enough

休為西風瘦	Do not be disturbed by west winds
痛飲頻搔首	Drink to your fill to rid off worrying
自古青繩白璧	Black flies had always dirtied white walls
天已早	In daybreak
安排就	Your journey calls

采桑子 · 誰翻樂府淒涼曲
Tune: Gathering Mulberries – Song of Misery

誰翻樂府淒涼曲　　Who sings this song of sheer misery

風也蕭蕭　　Wind singing

雨也蕭蕭　　Rain singing

瘦盡燈花又一宵　　Lamp wicks burnt the night is passing

不知何事縈懷抱　　What worldly worries fill my embrace

醒也無聊　　Lanquid when awake

醉也無聊　　Lanquid when drunk

夢也何曾到謝橋　　I reach you not even in my dream

采桑子 · 明月多情應笑我
Tune: Gathering Mulberries – The Caring Moon Should Laugh at Me

明月多情應笑我	The caring moon should laugh at me
笑我如今	Laugh the way that is me
辜負春心	Oblivious of this beautiful spring
獨自閒行獨自吟	Alone I stroll and alone I sing
近來怕說當時事	Reluctant to recall the way we were
結遍蘭襟	Our friendship truthful and adored
月淺燈深	The midnight lamp burning deep the moon fading
夢裏雲歸何處尋	In my dream I ride on clouds not knowing wherein

清平樂 · 憶梁汾
Tune: Serene Music – Remembering My Friend

才聽夜雨	Night rains ring
便覺秋如許	Feeling deep autumn in
繞砌蛩螿人不語	Amid cricket chirps silence reign
有夢轉愁無據	I saw you in my dream were you in
亂山千疊橫江	Hills piled along the river at random
憶君遊倦何方	I remember your career services not blithesome
知否小窗紅燭	Don't you know with the red candle I sit by the window
照人此夜淒涼	Thinking about you all night in sorrow

蝶戀花 · 出塞
Tune: Butterfly Loves Flower – Out the Frontier

今古河山無定據	Our motherland boundaries change in days old and new
畫角聲中	Bugle sounds in review
牧馬頻來去	Herding horses frequently come and go
滿目荒涼誰可語	In dreary territories who could decree
西風吹老丹楓樹	Maple trees grow old in winds westerly
從來幽怨應無數	Ancient hatred and conflicts too many
鐵馬金戈	Battling horses and metal spears busy
青塚黃昏路	How many soldiers ended up underground buried
一往情深深幾許	Must we continue to tread deep on battling roads
深山夕照深秋雨	Deep in the mountain sunsets shine on autumn squalls

蝶戀花 · 眼底風光留不住
Tune: Butterfly Loves Flowers – Happy Days Gone Cannot Be Retained

眼底風光留不住	Happy days gone cannot be retained
和暖和香	Warmth and fragrance in harmony gained
又上雕鞍去	They pass away like galloping horses
欲倩煙絲遮別路	My wish to see you blocked by distant dusts
垂楊那是相思樹	Willow thickets witness my longing thrust
惆悵玉顏成間阻	It is painful to recall your beautiful face from screens
何事東風	Why ye east wind
不作繁華主	Helps not to bring back fond memories of yore
斷帶依然留乞句	Do not bring back fond memories of yore
斑騅一繫無尋處	Words faded the verses are no more

琵琶仙 · 中秋	Tune: Pi Pa Immortals – Mid-Autumn
碧海年年	Green ocean clear sky year by year
試問取	I ask
冰輪為誰圓缺	For whom the moon crests and fully appears
吹到一片秋香	Autumn fragrance in the winds blow
清輝瞭如雪	The moon shines white as snow
愁中看	Watching in a mood sorrowful
好天良夜	This beautiful sky in a night so peaceful
知道盡成悲咽	Why I hear all songs of sorrow
只影而今	Alone at present
那堪重對	I do not dare to recall
舊時明月	The bright moon shines of yore
花徑裏	In the midst of rows of flowers
戲捉迷藏	You and I play hide and seek
曾惹下蕭蕭井梧葉	Kicking up fallen leaves from the plane tree by the well
記否輕紈小扇	Don't you remember we waved small fans together
又幾番涼熱	And felt hot and cool shared by one another
只落得	All gone
填膺百感	Leaving hundred emotions
總茫茫	All gloom and unknown
不關離別	Not only because of separation
一任紫玉無情	The flute will tell
夜寒吹裂	Its sound shutters the bamboo in the cool night

尋芳草・蕭寺記夢

客夜怎生過

夢相伴

綺窗吟和

薄嗔伴笑道

若不是恁淒涼

肯來麼

來去苦匆匆

準擬待

曉鐘敲破

乍偎人　一閃燈花墜

卻對着琉璃火

Tune: Looking for My Lover – Recording a Dream at a Temple

How could I pass the night in this inn
With you in my dream
Sharing poems by the window
You cajole in a giggle
Were it not for pitying your yearning
Would I've come into your dream
You and I come and go in too much rush
When we are surely together
To last till bells toll in the morning
I wake to recall you fell off my arms lights dim
A radiant world confronts me in beam

劉悟元 Liu Wuyuan (1673−1725)

悟道詩

堪破浮生一也無
單身隻影走江湖
鳥飛魚躍藏真趣
大夢場中誰覺我
綠水青山是道圖
千峯頂上視迷途
終朝睡在鴻蒙竅
一任時人牛馬呼

金農 Jin Nong (1687−1764)

憶茶

草鋪綠罽地無塵
朝日熹微榆火新
兩串春團三道印
不知茶宴赴何人

A Poem of Insight

Matters and wealth are but void in a life floating in space
Roaming about I alone pace
Amid flying birds and leaping fishes truth is seen
I find no self in the vast terrains of dreams
In green hills and blue waters paths of humanity inwardly lie
Atop mountain peaks awry roads are clearly seen
Deep in the endless hole of unknowns I timelessly sleep
Caring not how others enjoy hurrying their cattle steep

Recalling Tea

Green grass covers the ground like a carpet free of dust
In the twilight wood fires are burning red and fast
Two balls of tea in a package with three seal marks
I recall not to whose tea party I took part

鄭燮〔鄭板橋〕Zheng Xie [Zheng Banqiao] (1693−1765)

雪景

一片二片三四片
五片六片七八片
九片十片無數片
飛入蘆花看不見

小廊

小廊茶熟已無煙
摘取寒花瘦可憐
寂寂柴門秋水闊
亂鴉揉碎夕陽天

寄松風上人

豈有千山與萬山
別離何易來何難
一日一日似流水
他鄉故鄉空依闌
雲捕斷橋六月雨
松扶古殿三食寒
笋鋪茶油新麥飯
幾時猿鶴來同餐

Snow Scene

One flake two flakes three four flakes
Five flakes six flakes seven eight flakes
Nine flakes ten flakes eleven flakes
Into reeds is seen no more flakes

Small Chamber

In the small chamber tea is brewed free of vapour
I pick a chrysanthemum lean and piteous
From the open wicket the autumn river appears wide
The brilliant sunset sky is dotted by crows passing by

To Master Pine Breeze

Separation matters not if by a thousand or ten thousand hills
To part is easy to re-unite difficult
Each day goes by like water flows
To pine for home from a foreign land is to no avail
In a summer rain clouds could mend a broken bridge with shadows
Pine trees can warm an old temple for many cold seasons
New wheat rice blended with tea broth makes a good meal
To dine together once again do you remember the deal

曹雪芹 Cao Xueqin (1715−1763)

紅樓夢・黛玉葬花吟
（節譯）

花謝花飛花滿天
紅消香斷有誰憐
遊絲軟系飄春榭
落絮輕沾撲繡簾

閨中女兒惜春暮
愁緒滿懷無釋處
手把花鋤出繡閨
忍踏落花來復去
……

花開易見落難尋
階前悶殺葬花人
獨倚花鋤淚暗灑
灑上空枝見血痕
……

杜鵑無語正黃昏
荷鋤歸去掩重門
青燈照壁人初睡
冷雨敲窗被未溫
……

願奴脅下生雙翼
隨花飛到天盡頭
天盡頭
何處有香丘

From *The Saga of the Red Chamber* – Lin Daiyu's **Flower Burial**
(selected part)

Flowers fall wandering flying all over the sky
Red colours fade and fragrance ceases no one can deny
Floating gossamers softly enter her scented bower
Willowdowns waltz attaching to broidery blinds

The maiden grieves in her chamber watching spring to leave
She knows not where to send her heavy heart for relief
Garden hoe in hand she steps out of her portal
Taking care not to step o'er fallen petals as she goes
...
Flowers in bloom are seen their fallen petals difficult to find
Musing by the steps her heart aches as she performs the burials
Tears silently roll witnessed only by the garden hoe
They leave blood stains on naked branches behold
...
At night fall cuckoos are mute however they like to sing
The maiden returns home to keep her doors in bolt
As she sleeps lonely accompanied by a dim light
Her quilt feels chilly as cold rain slashes the window
...
How she wished to fly on wings this very night
Following wandering petals to the end of sky
The end of sky
Where could she find a fitting fragrant burial site

未若錦囊收艷骨
一抔淨土掩風流
質本潔來還潔去
強于污淖陷渠溝

爾今死去儂收葬
未卜儂身何日喪
儂今葬花人笑痴
他年葬儂知是誰

試看春殘花漸落
便是紅顏老死時
一朝春盡紅顏老
花落人亡兩不知

袁枚 Yuan Mei (1716—1797)

馬嵬驛

莫唱當年長恨歌
人間亦自有銀河
石壕村裏夫妻別
淚比長生殿上多

Why not fill a silk bag with petals so fair
And bury them under earth with their romantic affairs
In purity they came and in purity they go
They must not be contaminated in dirty gutter flows

Oh flower you are buried today upon your demise
Who could foretell the time that I too shall die
People laugh at my folly in burying fallen flowers
I know not who will perform same come my final hour

Observe how flowers whither when spring is due to go
All beautiful beings will surely die when old
Once spring ends and young life turns old
Gone are both flowers and maiden no one takes note

Beauty Legend

Sing not the Long Regret Song of days gone
The Milky Way on earth happily lives on
When at an ordinary village man and wife separate
More than in the Palace of Long Life tears are shed

落葉詩二首

(I)

清晨鹿跡冷蒼苔
殘籜份份卷作堆
萬點烏鴉盤陣起
四山風雨逼秋來
看如老將成功退
悟到高僧解脫回
刪盡繁蕪存質乾
不應枯槁比寒灰

(III)

水墨蕭摻老筆道
畫家酷似李營丘
江湖一白浮魚艇
煙月空青見寺樓
倦客晚來宜望遠
枯禪定後不驚秋
天公收拾林巒淨
要放梅花出一頭

Falling Leaves Two Poems

(I)

At clear morning deer footprints on moss path cool
Dry leaves many twirl together to pile up full
Crows take to the air in ten thousand dots
Rains and winds in four hills delay autumn not
Approaching old age I ought to resign
Inspired by an old monk I am resolved in life
My writings neat in substance read pure and refine
They will live unlike cold ashes lingering behind

(III)

Thick and thin water inks test the art of blush painting
This artist's style is similar to the famous blush saint
In lakes and rills a fishing boat floats white
Temples vivid beneath a partly veiled moon in grey sky
The tired visitor from afar is comforted by destination nigh
Zen master regards the passage of time but sublime
Heavenly powers bestow serenity to all mountain forests
To allow a plum flower shine bright in verdant wilderness

文祚嫻 Wen Zuoxian (1812–1861)

登大容山

一峯相送一峯迎
千里崎嶇路不平
峭壁泉聲晴亦雨
懸崖雲影暗還明
嵐拖翠黛重重綠
澗瀉深溪隱隱清
回首夕陽迷舊徑
耳邊猶聽鷓鴣鳴

張佩綸 Zhang Peilun (1848–1903)

晚香

市塵知避俗
兀坐玩春深
火爐茶香細
書橫竹個陰
惜花生佛意
聽雨養詩心
傲吏非真寂
虛空喜足音

Climbing Mount Darong

Leaving one peak another welcomes us in
A thousand *li* of bumpy roads therein
A series of springs gush beneath sharp cliffs creating drizzles
Cloud shadows between mountain crags now dark now seen
Carried by winds hills present folds and folds of greens
Waters plunge deep into a pool conceiving diverse feelings
I turn to find my lost path in the sunset
My ears ring with songs of partridge singing

Evening Fragrance

Living in city bustles I remain serene
Sitting quietly to savour the deep meaning of spring
Silky vapor rises when tea brew acts are at ease
For my bookmark I use pieces of bamboo leaf
Following Buddha's wisdom I love flowers
Listening to the rains my mind broadens with poetic power
My humble self loves no isolation
In this emptiness I await footsteps of visitation

谷隱啟 Gu Yinqi (Qing Dynasty 1636–1912)

興至　　　Interest Arrives

興至持竿駕小舟	Moved by interest I row my skiff go fishing
乘風泛入五湖秋	Early morning at the Five Lakes winds send us speeding
櫓聲驚起蘆花鴈	My oars frighten the geese among tall reeds
卻逐流沙過別洲	I steer my skiff to visit other sandy islets

自聞宣 Zi Wenxuan

風敲　　　Knocks

風敲月戶屏同冷	Midnight winds knock cooling my screen
雨打茅堂暑亦寒	Rains beat my thatched hut sending summer heat in spin
高臥懶尋人事俗	A sound sleep helps me to care not matters mundane
詩腸僅比酒腸寬	My love for poems is deeper than my love for drinks

遠庵禮 Yuan Anli

一樣　　　　Same

一樣花溪一樣紅　Red flowers line up this stream and that stream the same
千株桃李千株穠　Thousands of peach trees and plum trees fragrance pertain
何人識得春風面　He who recognizes the face of spring
五色芳菲處處逢　Will appreciate its many colours wherever in

撫松 Fu Song

黃梅　　　　Ripe Plums

黃梅時節家家雨　Drizzles day after day when plums ripe
春草池塘處處蛙　Amid spring weeds in ponds flogs cry day and night
白鷺下田千點雪　White cranes alight at the fields like snows fall
黃鸝上樹一枝花　Yellow orioles flock on trees like attending floral balls

靈潤機 Ling Runji

一片　　　　　Sounds

一片潮聲下石頭　A boat sails for Shi Tou amid sounds of high tide
江亭送別使人愁　Sadly I arrive at the pavilion to bid my friend goodbye
可憐垂柳絲千尺　Pity the willow tendrils hang in thousand feet long
似為春江縮去舟　As if trying to bind the boat from sailing on

笠山寧 Li Shanning

涼夜　　　　　A Cool Night

涼夜霜飛天地秋　After a night of frost autumn is here
凋殘木葉見江流　Fallen leaves drift in the river far and near
一時體露金風裏　Whence all things are enveloped in autumn winds
月落澄潭不可求　Deep down in the pool the moon is not easily seen

江立 Jiang Li (1732-1780)

憶舊遊 · 秋窗茗話
Tune: Recalling Old Travels – Tea Talks in Autumn

正松風灑翠	Green pine needles fall in the wind
石鼎飛紅	Beneath stone stoves red flames spin
來問君家	I arrive at your home visiting
冷客偏多事	Infrequent guests must be treated warmly
笑秋將過半	Laughing at how fast autumn is vanishing
還鬥春茶	As we brew spring tea
自憐買山無計	I know a a farmer I could not be
棲泊向天涯	On a skiff I venture out to sea
願乞研箋愁	With ink and paper I create heart-rending poetry
移床借夢	Sleeping in strange beds I borrow dreams free
閒送年華	My life measuring in days let leisure be

 范學儀 Fan Xueyi

登獨秀峯 **Peak of Solitary Charm, Guilin**

一柱鎮南天	A majestic pillar stands guard for the southern sky
登臨四望懸	I ascend the cliff to view the beautiful sceneries from all sides
風雲生足下	Winds and clouds rise beneath my very feet
星斗落胸前	Stars and constellations embrace my chest so neat
拔地山千仞	Hills shoot up from the land a thousand measures tall
環城水一川	Round the town a river meanders providing water for all
憑高發長嘯	On this mountain top I croon free and happy
聲徹萬家煙	The sound waves echo chimney smokes of ten thousand families

5

Part E

Modern Period

(1911—present)

現代
MODERN
(1911–Present)

林則徐 Lin Zexu (1785−1850)

高陽台：和嶰筠前輩韻
Tune: Tall Sun Terrace – Rhyme with Zhe My Senior

玉粟收餘	Jade opium a hefty harvest
金絲種後	Golden tobacco leaf they cultivate
蕃行別有蠻煙	British ships bring in smoking evils
雙管橫陳	Lying down with a double smoking gun at ease
何人對擁無眠	Who would not fall into sleeping peace
不知呼吸成滋味	One knows not enticing tastes lead to addiction
愛挑燈	Lighting a fire happy
夜永如年	The night eternity
最堪憐	Most pitiful
是一丸泥	A tiny opium ball
捐萬緡錢	Coin strings ten thousand fall
春雷歘破零丁穴	A spring thunder shatters concaves in Ling Ding Ocean
笑蜃樓氣盡	To turn frolic mirage into true perception
無復灰然	Power trades deadly terminate
沙角台高	On high grounds at Sandy Cape near Tiger Gate
亂帆收向天邊	Fleeing ships hurry toward the horizon
浮槎漫許陪霓節	Whence the Jade Staff joins the Legend Pole
看澄波	Behold the glimmering froths
似鏡長圓	Like reflective mirrors in perfect focus
更應傳	Time has to change
絕島重洋	Back toward the enervate islands
取次回舷	Ships flurry in new altered directions

與纖　　Tug Ropes

山行也學卜灘舟　Climbing a hill is like rowing an up-current boat
牽挽因人不自由　One is not free without pulls unlike walking on flat roads
一線劃開雲徑曉　A silk rope cuts through fogs to open a path tiny
千尋曳入洞天秋　Lengthy strings send us into a world of scenic beauty
漫疑負弩經巴蜀　They say I'm bound for Sichuan to fight with bow and arrow
便當浮槎到女牛　Or to reach the home of Love Stars using the legend pole
不為絲繩標正直　If not tested by the straight measures of justice
此身誰致萬峯頭　Dare I aspire to mount a thousand zeniths to be free

李鴻章 Li Hongzhang (1823–1901)

池上篇　　From the Pond

十畝之宅　In ten acres a house I dwell
五畝之園　A garden occupies half the dell
有水一池　A pond water beaming
有竹千竿　A thousand bamboos surrounding
勿謂土狹　It is not a place too small

勿謂地偏		Not away from a port of call
足以容膝		Suffice for me to sit
足以息肩		Suffice to quell my worry wisp
有堂有庭		With a hall and a yard to stroll
有橋有船		With a bridge and a boat to row
有書有酒		Books and wines
有歌有弦		Songs and strings
有叟在中		An old man sits in peace
白須飄然		His white beard flows at ease
識分知足		He knows himself and satisfaction
外無求焉		And cares little about other nations
如鳥擇木	姑務巢安	Like a bird roosting in a chosen secure tree
如龜居坎	不知海寬	Like a hare in its hole caring not the wide sea
靈鶴怪石		With a garden of spirited rock cranes
紫菱白蓮		A pond nurturing nuts and white lilies
皆吾所好		These my likings
盡在吾前		All in my presence
時飲一杯		Now I take a drink
或吟一篇		Now I write and sing
妻孥熙熙		My wife and family in harmony
雞犬閒閒		My dogs and hens living happily
優哉遊哉		Ah leisure and serendipity
吾將終老乎其間		I shall grow old here heavenly

入都 (I)

丈夫只手把吳鈎
意氣高於百尺樓
一萬年來誰著史
三千里外欲封侯
出山志在登鰲頂
何日身才入鳳池
倘無駟馬高車日
誓不重回故里車
即今館閣須才日
是我文章報國年
馬足出羣休戀棧
燕辭故壘更圖新
遍交海內知名士
去訪京師有道人
他日燕台南望處
天涯須報李陵書

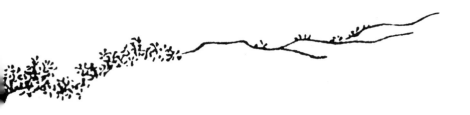

In the Capital (I)

I stand a man with a long hook my feat
A will high as a tower of one hundred feet
Ten thousand years of history who will write
Three thousand miles away who be knights
Leaving this hill I aim to climb a higher summit
Whence shall I be in the pond of the legend phoenix
Until I command a carriage drawn by four steeds
I vow not to stay in this tiny old cart domestic
At this time when motherland needs men of capability
Time has come for me to serve my country
A steed exceeding its herd should not be inactive
Swallows giving up old nests look to a new perspective
I shall join aspiring comrades within the seas
And venture to learn from gurus their minds free
The day when I look back home from the learned hall
I shall answer to my famed ancestor poet cum hero and all

樊增祥 Fan Zengxiang (1846−1931)

中秋夜無月　　Moonless Mid-Autumn Festival Night

互占清光徹九州	Your pristine lights shine all over China since old
只今煙霧鎖瓊樓	Today mist and fog cover your palace whole
莫秋遮斷山河影	Do not let your shadows dim our motherland bit by bit
照出山河影更愁	Dividing our hills and rills their parts no longer fit

黃遵憲 Huang Zunxian (1846−1905)

八月十五夜太平洋舟中望月作歌
Singing to the Moon from My Boat in the Pacific Ocean on the Fifteenth Night of the Eighth Moon

大千世界共此月	A thousand worlds in the cosmos share this moon
世人不共中秋節	Not everyone celebrates the Mid-autumn Festival
泰西紀歷二千年	The Western world marks its time in two millennial
祇作尋常數圓缺	And notes the moon's crest and fullness in cycles

到香港 　　Visiting Hong Kong

水是堯時日夏時	Water and sun are from dynasties ancient
衣冠又是漢官儀	Clothing styles are of Han tradition
登樓四望真吾土	Watching from the tower all lands are our own
不見黃龍上大旗	I see no yellow dragon on the flags flown

夜起 　　Getting up at Night

千聲檐鐵百淋鈴	The iron-horse wind chime a thousand times ring
雨橫風狂暫一停	The assault of Eight Western Powers halted for the time being
正望雞鳴天下白	As we yearn to enjoy peace and security all over
又驚鵝擊海東青	Russia invades our north-east arousing fear
沉陰噎噎何多日	Gloomy stay remains day after day
殘月暉暉尚幾星	Under a dim moon how many people stay sane
斗室蒼茫吾獨立	In the confines of my small study I stand alone
萬家酣睡幾人醒	Ten thousand families in dreams could pundits keep awake

春愁

春愁難遣強看山
往事驚心淚欲潸
四百萬人同一哭
去年今日割台灣 *(一八九五年四月十七日)

離台詩

宰相有權能割地
孤臣無力可回天
扁舟去作鴟夷子
回首河山意黯然

元夕無月

三年此夕月無光
明月多應在故鄉
欲向海天尋月去
五更飛夢渡鯤洋

Spring Sorrow

Spring sorrow lingers I look up the mountain
Past events frightful tears ready to fountain
Four million countrymen cry in unison
A year ago this day Taiwan was in cessation *(17 April 1895)

Leaving Taiwan

The Prime Minister has the power to make gifts of land in cessation
Patriotic legions helpless in reversing the traitorous decision
On a leafy skiff toward drunken land I am sailing
I look back to my motherland feeling sad and unavailing

A Moonless Lantern Festival

For three years the moon emits no light on Lantern Fest Eve
It chooses to shine where our homes used to be
To catch the moon in sky above the wide sea
Fly pass the Taiwan Strait in a predawn dream you will see

山村即目

一角西峯夕照中
斷雲東嶺雨濛濛
林楓欲老柿將熟
秋在萬山深處紅

孫中山 Sun Zhongshan (1866－1925)

挽劉道一 (1907)

半壁東南三楚雄
劉郎死去霸圖空
尚餘遺孽艱難甚
誰與斯人慷慨同
塞上秋風悲戰馬
神州落日泣哀鴻
幾時痛飲黃龍酒
橫攬江流一奠公

Mountain Village

The setting sun shines on a corner of the west mount
Over the east hills clouds break rains falling down
Before the maples turn yellow and red persimmons ripe
Deep in ten thousand mountains autumn is in radiant dye

Remembering a Martyr (1907)

Half of China south east stood three countries since ancient
Your death leaves a vacuum in our revolution intentions
What is left to do is difficult to say the least
Who could match your leadership in this task mighty
The frontier is full of enemies readying to invade
Our land has a sunset government and people are in sway
Whence we have this inept government overthrown
We will enshrine your deeds with wine wherever rivers flow

水調歌頭 ── 甲午　　**Tune: Prelude to Water Melody – 1895**

拍碎雙玉斗	A pair of national gems shattered
慷慨一何多	How very generous
滿腔都是血淚	A song made up by tears and bleeding
無處著悲歌	Nowhere to sing songs of grieving
三百年來王氣	Three hundred years of imperial comforts
滿目山河依舊	Hills and rills in same old consort
人事竟如何	Why change the governing set up
百戶尚牛酒	Hundreds of nobles in hard drinking
四塞已干戈	All four frontiers in fighting
千金劍	Swords in gold
萬言策	Lengthy plans on hold
兩蹉跎	They are but shows
醉中呵壁自語	When drunk one engages in rambling
醒後一滂沱	When awake drown in heavy raining
不恨年華去也	Care not time and life energy gone
只恐少年心事	Fear youthful thoughts and acts revolutionary
強半為銷磨	Half exerted void of productivity
願替眾生病	I accede to bear the ills of our people
稽首禮維摩	I bow to Buddha for wise counsel

自勵二首 (II)   Self-exhortation Two Verses (II)

獻身甘作萬矢的　　Dedicating to improve society I fear not ten thousand darts

著論求為百世師　　Writing to awaken my people I aim to win generations' hearts

誓起民權移舊俗　　I vow to remove obsolete habits to celebrate civil liberty

更研哲理牖新知　　And organize reasons and wisdom to enrich new knowledge

十年以後當思我　　Ten years hence my deeds should be put in review

舉國猶狂欲語誰　　Among a boisterous people what will be the burning issues

世界無窮願無盡　　Our wishes are unlimited in a world of infinite possibilities

海天寥廓立多時　　To the vast expanse of sky and sea I stand timelessly

吳佩孚 Wu Peifu (1874−1939)

春感

載酒看花興未慵
韶光又是隔年逢
只憐烽火連江右
愁聽寒山寺裏鐘

贈楊雲史

與君抵掌論英雄
煮酒青梅憶洛中
雪裏出關花入塞
至今詩句滿遼東

Spring Thoughts

Admiring spring blooms with warm wine time continues
How quickly a year gone we meet for friendship renewal
Pity to see war flames west of the river raging ample
Sadly I listen to the toll from the Honshen Temple

To Yang Yunshi

We touch palms to exchange views on who are heroes
And cook plum wine to remember our times in the Capital
We left the Pass to pursue flower blooms away from the frontier
And leave poems all over the north-east for people to savour

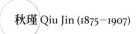
黃海舟中日人索句並見日俄戰爭地圖

萬里乘風去復來
隻身東海挾春雷
忍看圖畫移顏色
肯使江山付劫灰
濁酒不銷憂國淚
救時應仗出羣才
拼將十萬頭顱血
須把乾坤力挽回

有懷 ── 遊日本時作

日月無光天地昏
沉沉女界有誰援
釵環典質浮滄海
骨肉分離出玉門
放足湔除千載毒
熱心喚起百花魂
可憐一幅鮫綃帕
半是血痕半淚痕

Written on Board at Yellow Sea to a Japanese Friend Who Show Me a Map of Russo-Japanese War on Chinese Soil

Ten thousand miles to and return I ride the wind
Travelling alone to the East Sea thundering in spring
So sad to see the Chinese map in changed colour markings
What government would allow its land reduced to war ashes
This cheap wine drowns not tears grieving for my homeland
To be helpful we must unite many more able and devoted men
I vow to brave my head with hundred thousand others to participate
To turn around the ill fate of our motherland we must act before too late

Thoughts – Written in Japan

In gloom neither sun nor moon sheds any light
A woman's world is in deep water with no help in sight
I sold my jewellry to go overseas to see the world
And left my family at home east I go
Unbinding my feet I rid off years of poisons in tradition
With a burning heart I stir up women's spirit in motion
Behold this kerchief delicate as it appears
Half soaked with blood half with tears

日人石井君索和即用原韻

漫雲女子不英雄
萬里乘風獨向東
詩思一帆海空闊
夢魂三島月玲瓏
銅駝已陷悲回首
汗馬終慚未有功
如許傷心家國恨
那堪客裏度春風

廖仲愷 Liao Zhongkai (1877−1925)

壬戌六月禁錮中聞變 (1922)

珠江日夕起風雷
已倒狂瀾孰挽回
徵羽不調弦亦怨
死生能一我無哀
鼠肝蟲臂惟天命
馬勃牛溲稱異才
物論未應衡大小
棟樑終為蠹蠛摧

Reply to a Japanese Friend

They say in tradition no woman could be a hero
For ten thousand leagues on winds I alone rode
My poetic thoughts extend I sail the sky and the sea
In my dreams your island country is beautiful and free
I grieve to note my traditional country has changed hands
Ashamed to know I've not done enough to prevent
My heart bleeds with so much remiss and hate to apprehend
How could I enjoy a peace of mind to be a guest in your land

Thoughts in Prison (1922)

Winds and thunder may blunder over the Pearl any day
The tide to counter the revolution rises and prevails
The musical notes in disharmony the strings in acrimony
To live or die is no longer my worry
Those who know not their identity surrender to destiny
Weeds grown in barren land claim their lives a mystery
We may not measure deeds on a dimensional scale
The country's future is ruined by a termite siege

留訣內子

(I)

俊事憑君獨任勞
莫教辜負女中豪
我身雖去靈明在
勝似屠門握殺刀

(II)

生無足羨死奚悲
宇宙循環活殺機
四十五年塵劫苦
好從解脫悟前非

胡漢民 Hu Hanmin (1879-1936)

秋女俠墓

見說椎秦願已酬
那知滄海尚橫流
我來風雨亭邊過
不是愁時也欲愁

To My Wife in My Imprisonment

(I)

When I am gone your responsibility is imminent
I am confident you will not be less than a heroine
My spirit will remain alive even when body is no more
It will continue to fight mightier than a butcher's knife

(II)

To live is not an envy death not dreary
The universe revolves creating many an opportunity
Forty-five years of worldly toil is a bitter affair
This liberty in death would resolve any wrongs I might fair

The Tomb of Qiujin

Was assassin of the Qing Emperor an accomplishment
Our present society is still full of uncertain elements
How I like to honour you at the Wind and Rain Pavilion
I lament even though the time is not for lament

哭執信

豈徒風誼兼師友
尾共娘危識性情
關塞歸魂秋黯淡
河梁揾手語分明
盜猶僧主誰之過
人盡思君死大輕
衷語追華終不是
鈣金牢得似早生

魯迅 Lu Xun (1881−1936)

無題二首 (1931)
(I)

大江日夜向東流
聚義羣雄又遠遊
六代綺羅成舊夢
石頭城上月如鈎

(II)

雨花台邊埋斷戟
莫愁湖裏餘微波
所思美人不可見
歸憶江天發浩歌

Weeping for a Martyred Friend

We are not mere acquaintances and school partners
We understand each other doing difficult tasks
Leaving the frontier for home in autumn we felt sad
Before parting we held hands planning to connect
Who is responsible for confusing thieves and master
We believe your death a signal revolutionary matter
Using sad words to register our grief will not do you justice
Recording your good deeds is better than performing rituals

Two Untitled Poems (1931)
(I)

The Great Yangtze flows east day and night
Daring youngsters gather to go abroad for insight
The spirit of the Six Dynasties alive not in dreams
O'er this Rock City the crescent moon shines half dim

(II)

Revolting braves are buried at Nanjing's Yu Hua Terrace
On Mochou Lake the revolution spirit survives
Heroes I admire are seen no more
In their memory I sing loud to adore

送增田涉君歸國 (1931)

扶桑正是秋光好
楓葉如丹照嫩寒
卻折垂楊送歸客
心隨東棹憶華年

一・二八戰後作 (1932)

戰雲暫斂殘春在
重砲清歌兩寂然
我亦無詩送歸棹
但從心底祝平安

Seeing Hiloshi Masuda Home to Japan (1931)

Autumn tints are splendid in old Fusang
Bright red maple leaves bring gentle cold along
I break a willow twig to bid you farewell
My heart sails with you to recall my youthful days happy and well

Written after the 1932.01.28 Battle (1932)

War clouds clear in a dwindling spring
Heavy gun fires and spirited songs in silence sing
I have no poem for our soldiers coming home
From the depth of my heart I wish them safe at home

無題 (1934)

萬家墨面沒蒿萊
敢有歌吟動地哀
心事浩茫連廣宇
於無聲處聽驚雷

自題小像

靈台無計逃神矢
風雨如磐闇故園
寄意寒星荃不察
我以我血薦軒轅

Untitled (1934)

Amid the brambles ten thousand gloomy faces hide
Their sorrow songs shatter the earth day and night
Bound to my homeland's conditions my mind finds no rest
In silence I hear shattering thunder arrests

Inscription on My Photo

My heart has no escape but to care like darting arrows
While my homeland is hit by rocks of stormy sorrows
I speak to stars on high they don't seem to care
I will spare no blood to save my motherland I dare

蘇曼殊 Su Man Shu (1884–1918)

春雨

春雨樓頭尺八簫
何時歸看浙江潮
芒鞋破缽無人識
踏過櫻花第幾橋

朱德 Zhu De (1886–1976)

古宋香水山芙蓉寺題詩 (1911)

已饑已溺是吾憂
急濟心懷幾度秋
鐵柱幸勝家國任
銅駝慢著棘荊遊
千年朽索常虞墜
一息承肩總未休
物色風塵誰作主
唯看砥柱正中流

Spring Drizzles

I stand on the terrace playing my long flute in spring drizzles
Longing to return home to watch the Qiantong tides in loud whistles
In straw sandals and holding a begging bowl my identity here is a nullity
Amid flourishing cherry blossoms how many bridges need I cross
  before eternity

To the Hibiscus Temple at Fragrant Hill (1911)

Care for the perennial hunger and torment in motherland
To help uplift this common fate I had in years lent a hand
We rejoice our culture supports the upholding of responsibilities
And our traditional foundation helps us to ease the adversity
A thousand-year cable in decay often fails in suspension
Devotion for duty once shown will not cease in action
Who is in charge of shifts in winds and dusts since old
Just watch the rapid flows how a column mightily holds

望雨 (1963)   Waiting for Rain (1963)

風急天低雨不來   In a sky low with brisk winds no rain will arrive

迷天雲霧自徘徊   Clouds and haze in the spheres lingering slight

農夫喜雨風吹去   The rains farmers love gone with the wind

臨夜晴明月色開   At dusk the sky remains bright a moon winks

悼陳毅同志 (1972)   Remembering Comrade Chen Yi (1972)

一生為革命   For revolution you have devoted your entire life

蓋棺方論定   With your coffin closed your deeds confirmed bright

重道又親師   To your teachers and the Way you showed respects

路綫根端正   The roads you have travelled are rooted deeply in red

浪淘沙・雪中過邯鄲 (1954)
Tune: Waves Refining Sands – Passing Handan in Snow (1954)

飛雪滿山川	Flying snows covering hills and rills
淨化平原	Keeping the plain pure
融融暖氣卻春寒	In spring warm airs we still feel cold
嫩綠新苗逢瑞雪	Green shoots in spring crops welcome the benevolent snow
萬姓同歡	People of all surnames celebrate the celestial show
乘興百人團	In groups of one hundred common interest shown
巡視江南	To inspect the river south in new looks
長征彈指十餘年	The Long March long ago passed by a click of fingers
景物全新驚世變	Scenes and materials now new the world changed in surprise
天上人間	Heaven and humanity ever so nice

蔣介石 Jiang Jieshi (1887–1975)

述志 (1909)

騰騰殺氣滿全球
力不如人萬事休
光我神州完我責
東來志豈在封侯

出發校閱撰歌二則 (1928)

五月三日是國仇
國亡豈許爾優遊
親愛精誠
團結一致
快來共奮鬥
革命革命
犧牲犧牲
黑鐵赤血
求我國家獨立平等與自由
獨立、平等，中華民國乃得真自由
北伐雖完志未酬
男兒壯志報國仇
革命未成死不休
北伐雖完志未酬

My Determination (1909)

Hot is the killing spirit in a world so ill
Inferior to powers ten thousand matters stand still
Duty bound I vow to keep motherland secured
Coming to study in Japan noble laurels not my will

To Review My Army Force Two Poems (1928)

The third of May is our national rancour
Losing a nation allows no one to leisure
Caring and truthful
Unite in one mind
Together we hurriedly strive
Revolution again revolution
Sacrifice more sacrifice
Black iron in red blood out
For motherland's independence equality and freedom
Independence Equality The Chinese Republic will be truly free
Concluding the Northern Expedition I stand unfulfilled
To quell our motherland's rancour is a man's will
Revolution is the only action to treat our national ills
Until a success in revolution to death I shall not sit still

遊峨嵋口占二首 (1935)
Touring Mount E Mei Two Poems (1935)

步上峨嵋頂	Up the Omei peak I climb
強消大卜憂	Leaving all worldly concerns behind
逢寺思慈母	Visiting every temple I bear my mother in mind
望兒感獨遊	Touring alone I am my mother's pride

六三自箴 (1949)　　Reflection on 63rd Birthday (1949)

虛度六三	Sixty three years I lived days trivial
受恥招敗	Shames and failures endured
毋惱毋怒	Neither regret nor wrath
莫矜莫慢	No boasting no indolence
不愧不怍	No remorse nor deceit
自足自反	Self-sufficient and in frequent reflections
小子何幸	Lucky is this person
獨蒙神愛	Grateful to God's affection
惟危惟艱	Meeting crisis and challenges
自警自覺	Self-awake and self-conscious
復興中華	Striving to revitalize China
再造民國	For Republic reconstruction

養天自樂箴　Nurture Longevity in Happiness

淡泊沖漠　Keep the mind pure and simple as uncultivated lands

本然自得　Direct all instincts to achieve self-fulfillment

浩浩淵淵　Treat life wide as wilderness and deep as ravine

鳶飛魚躍　As birds fly and fishes glide

優遊涵泳　Swim leisurely and acknowledge the deeps

活活潑潑　Be active and happy

勿忘勿助　Remember past and present to enrich self-sufficiency

時時體察　Always care for others with empathy

陳寅恪 Chen Yinke (1890–1969)

甲申除夕病榻作時目疾頗劇離香港又三年矣 (1945)

雨雪霏霏早閉門
荒園數畝似山村
攜家未識家何置
歸國惟欣國尚存
四海兵戈迷病眼
九年憂患蝕精魂
扶床稚女聞歡笑
依約承平舊夢痕

庚寅元用東坡韻 (1950)

過嶺南來便隔天
一冬無雪有花妍
山河已入宜春檻
身世真同失水船
明月滿床思舊節
驚雷破柱報新年
魚龍寂寞江城暗
知否姮娥換紀元

In My Sick Bed on New Year's Eve (1945)

I shut my door early seeing rain and snow approach
Acres of abandoned land sit like a mountain village
Taking my family I know not where to settle in
Back to motherland I rejoice my country is surviving
Wars in the four seas are misery for my blind eyes
Nine years of suffering drags my spirit behind
What a joy to hear my daughter laughing by my bedside
Just as she appears in my dreams every night

New Year's Eve on Su Shi Rhymes (1950)

The sky is different on this side of the hill
A snowless winter sees flower blooms still
Hills and rills are ready to knock on the spring door
My lot runs like a boat sailing on a waterless course
I pine for festivities of yore lying on a moon-flood bed
A blitz shatters the building column heralds in another new year yet
Folks in this river-side town remain in individual forlorn
Would anyone know a new century is set to march on

五十六歲生日三絕 乙酉仲夏五月十七日

去年病目實已死
雖號為人與鬼同
可笑家人作生日
宛如設祭奠亡翁
鬼鄉人世兩傷情
萬古書蟲有歎聲
淚眼已枯心已碎
莫將文字誤他生
女癡妻病自堪憐
況更流離歷歲年
願得時清目復朗
扶攜同泛峽江船

My 56th Birthday

My eyes blinded last year a dead man was I
Living as man I was a ghostly sight
I laughed when my family held a birthday party for me
As if an oblate act to enliven an old dead man to be
Both ghostly and human homes care for feelings
Since antiquity book worms exaggerate moans of acrimony
My tearless eyes dry and my heart broken in pieces
I will not allow my writings to mislead future generations
My daughter in stress my wife sick what a pity
Years of fleeing and separation have hurt us deeply
How I wish peace comes and my sight is back with me
We will hold hands to sail home together a family

歸國雜吟 (II) (1937)

又當投筆請纓時
別婦拋雛斷藕絲
去國十年餘淚血
登舟三宿見族旗
欣將殘骨埋諸夏
哭吐精誠斌此詩
四萬萬人齊蹈厲
同心同德一戎衣

登南岳 (1938)

中原龍戰血玄黃
必勝必成恃自強
替把豪情寄山水
權將餘力寫肝腸
雲橫萬里長纓展
日照千峯鐵騎玻
猶有鄴侯遺迹在
寇平重上讀書堂

Random Thoughts on Way back to China (II) (1937)

Time again for me to postpone my writing to join the army
Leaving my wife and children behind is not easy
Away from my country for three years tears and blood linger
Three days on board home I once again see red banners
Glad I am to bury my bones anywhere in my motherland
With this poem I weep to declare my patriotic intent
Four hundred million people sing in unison
With unbending will to fight the Jap dwarfs we are one garrison

Ascending Mount Heng (1938)

Dragons battle in the central plain blood flows throughout motherland
Each warlord attempts to claim his territory on hand
For the moment I rest my passions on the beauties of our hills and rills
My inner feelings pour on poems and essays like torrents under keel
Clouds cross ten thousand *li* of sky above spears held high
The sun shines on a thousand peaks where iron steeds ride
Here I find the ruins home of a Prime Minister of Tang Dynasty
Whence peace comes I shall visit his Emperor's hall of study

毛澤東 Mao Zedong (1893-1976)

沁園春 · 長沙 (1925)
Tune: Qin Garden Spring – Changsha (1925)

獨立寒秋	Alone I stand in the autumn cold
湘江北去	Turning north the Xiang River gently flows
橘子洲頭	Where the Orange Isle on behold
看萬山紅遍	Ten thousand hills in crimson hue
層林盡染	Serial woods dyed in blazing red
漫江碧透	Where greenish blue waters reflect a crystal view
百舸爭流	Hundreds of barges vie to get ahead
鷹擊長空	Eagles sour up the expanding sky
魚翔淺底	Fishes in the shallows happily glide
萬類霜天競自由	In this frigid world all creatures strive to be free
悵寥廓	Brooding over this immensity
問蒼茫大地	To the boundless land I ask

誰主沉浮　　　　　Who is in command of human destiny

攜來百侶曾遊　　　Gathering here for reunion we a throng of peers

憶往昔崢嶸歲月稠　Vivid in memory are those crowded vibrant years

恰同學少年　　　　In youth we studied side by side

風華正茂　　　　　Our aspirations flowering high

書生意氣　　　　　By our bookish insight and ambitions

揮斥方遒　　　　　We boldly cast all restraints aside

指點江山　　　　　To wage new plans to build a better nation

激揚文字　　　　　Using torrid words to set people afire

糞土當年萬戶侯　　We condemned those powerful lords to mere muck in demise

曾記否　　　　　　Do you remember

到中流擊水　　　　How reaching midstream we met the surging torrents

浪遏飛舟　　　　　Waves overtook boats

采桑子・重陽 (1929)

人生易老天難老
歲歲重陽
今又重陽
戰地黃花分外香
一年一度秋風勁
不似春光
勝似春光
寥廓江天萬里霜

憶秦娥・婁山關 (1935)

西風烈
長空雁叫霜晨月
霜晨月
馬蹄聲碎
喇叭聲咽
雄關漫道真如鐵
而今邁步從頭越
從頭越
蒼山如海
殘陽如血

Tune: Picking Mulberries – Double Nine Festival (1929)

Man's life ages easy the universe goes on
Year after year the Double-Nine Festival comes along
Now it is again here
In the battle ground yellow flowers their fragrance thorough
Once a year autumn winds strongly blow
Unlike spring song
Better than spring song
The universe bright with ten thousand *li* of frosts on

Tune: Remembering Qin Maid – The Luishan Pass (1935)

The west wind brisk
Under the frosty morning moon wild geese disquiet
The frosty morning moon
Horses' hooves sound like gentle breakings
Bugles gently roar
The idle road along this grand pass metalic
With steady strides we are crossing the summit
Crossing the summit
The hills sea-blue
The setting sun blood-red

清平樂・六盤山 (1935)

天高雲淡
望斷南飛雁
不到長城非好漢
屈指行程兩萬
六盤山上高峯
紅旗漫捲西風
今日長纓在手
何時縛住蒼龍

長征 (1935)

紅軍不怕遠征難
萬水千山只等閒
五嶺逶迤騰細浪
烏蒙磅礡走泥丸
金沙水拍雲崖暖
大渡橋橫鐵索寒
更喜岷山千里雪
三軍過後盡開顏

Tune: Serene Music – The Six-turn Mount (1935)

Faint clouds hang in high sky
Southbound geese yonder fly
Whoever has not been to the Great Wall is not truely tall
We have travelled twenty thousand *li* by a count of fingers
The peak up the Six-turn Mount mightily high
Red banners flap in the west wind a great sight
Today long spears in our hands we hoist high
Whence will we have the wild dragon tied

The Long March (1935)

The Red Army has no fear for the Long March trials
Leaguing ten thousand streams and hills is usual
Heavy gusts from the Five Ridges are but gentle breezes
The grand Wumeng we tread like clay globules
The steep cliffs on the Jinsha is warmed by lapping waves
The Dadu iron-chain bridge is crossed with no regard for its cold
Mount Min's snows a thousand *li* are greeted in delight
The three troops march on victorious their spirits high

沁園春 · 雪 (1936)

北國風光

千里冰封

萬里雪飄

望長城內外

惟餘莽莽

大河上下

頓失滔滔

山舞銀蛇

原馳蠟象

欲與天公試比高

須晴日

看紅裝素裹

分外妖嬈

江山如此多嬌

引無數英雄競折腰

惜秦皇漢武

略輸文采

唐宗宋祖

稍遜風騷

一代天驕

成吉思汗

只識彎弓射大雕

俱往矣

數風流人物

還看今朝

Tune: Qin Garden Spring – Snow (1936)

The scenic charm of northern country

A thousand *li* of land frozen in ice

Ten thousand *li* of wilderness in snowdrift

North and south of the Great Wall

Rests an uncultivated domain looming

The Big River pours from its source to sea

Its winding course set on silent rolling

Mountain ranges dance like slithering silver snakes

The highland roams a spectra of elephant herds charging

All contend with the sky for stature

On a clear sunny day

Cladding in pure white and radiant red

The world's natural beauty finds no match

To a motherland of such awesome enchantment

Her sons and daughters bow to offer heroic feats

Alas regret the pioneer emperors of Qin and Han

Showed a lack of literary grace

The hailed leaders of the great Dynasties Tang and Song

Had not much poetic imagination in their souls

And the Great Genghis Khan

Favoured son of Heaven in his day

Loved too much to bow down hawks for revelry

Gone are these heroes of history

When you seek men of abiding respect and true worth

Meet them today

水調歌頭・游泳 (1956)

才飲長沙水
又食武昌魚
萬里長江橫渡
極目楚天舒
不管風吹浪打
勝似閒庭信步
今日得寬餘
子在川上曰
逝者如斯夫

風檣動
龜蛇靜
起宏圖
一橋飛架南北
天塹變通途
更立西江石壁
截斷巫山雲雨
高峽出平湖
神女應無恙
當今世界殊

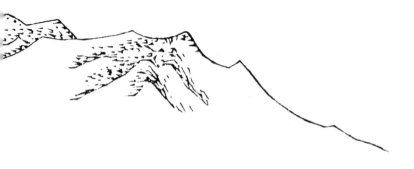

Tune: Prelude to Water Melody – Swim (1956)

Water of Changsha I drank moments ago
Fishes of Wuchang I enjoyed so
Across the Yangtze ten thousand *li* I swim through
On backstroke I search the sky for Chu State of old
Winds and waves no matter
Just like pacing my courtyard in leisure
Today at ease
I hear Confucius by a stream said long ago
How time incessantly flows
A wall of sails in the wind
Tortoise and Snake hills stand in
Grand plans in hold
Spanning north and south a bridge flies through
Nature's deep chasm becomes a road
On river west stands a cliff wall
Holding Mount Wu's winds and rainfalls
To create a calm lake up the gorges
Should the legend goddess stays watch
She would marvel what changes are shaping our world

蝶戀花 · 答李淑一 (1957)

我失驕楊君失柳
楊柳輕揚直上重霄九
問訊吳剛何所有
吳剛捧出桂花酒
寂寞嫦娥舒廣袖
萬里長空且為忠魂舞
忽報人間曾伏虎
淚飛頓作傾盆雨

為李進同志題仙人洞照 (1961)

暮色蒼茫看勁松
亂雲飛渡仍從容
天生一個仙人洞
無限風光在險峯

Tune: Butterfly Loves Flower – Reply to My Friend Li Shuyi (1957)

I lost my beloved Poplar you lost your dearest Willow
Our loved souls will rise up the Nine Leagues for sure
Asking Wu Gang on the moon what is available
He readily serves his prized laurel brew
The lonely Moon Goddess swings her swift sleeves free
To dance for all loyal souls across the sky infinitely
On hearing news from earth that people have subdued the menacing tiger
Her joyful tears turn into mighty rain to fill the land with welcome water

Inscription on a Photo of Comrade Li Jin at the Fairy Cave (1961)

In the gloom of dusk I watch pines hardy
Riotous clouds sweep past in tranquility
Nature has given birth to a Cave for Fairies
Up the perilous peaks dwell scenes in endless variety

卜算子・詠梅（1961 年 12 月）
**Tune: Song of Divination – Ode to the Plum Blossom
(December 1961)**

風雨送春歸	Wind and rain sent spring away
飛雪迎春到	Snowflakes welcome spring back to stay
已是懸崖百丈冰	When icicles a thousand feet hang on cliffs high
猶有花枝俏	There a single flower stands cute and bright
俏也不爭春	Cute and bright she intends not to possess spring alone
只把春來報	But content serving as harbinger for the first season
待到山花爛漫時	When the hills are filled with other flowers in bloom
她在叢中笑	She will smile in their midst satisfaction owned

水調歌頭・重上井崗山 (1965)
Tune: Prelude to Water Melody – Revisiting Mount Jing Gang (1965)

久有凌雲志	To ride the clouds I have always aspired
重上井岡山	Up Mount Jin Gang I again climb
千里來尋故地	Coming ten thousand *li* to revisit this old place
舊貌變新顏	I see new scenes in the old territory
到處鶯歌燕舞	Everywhere orioles sing and swallows glide
更有潺潺流水	Streams bubble as they wind
高路入雲端	High roads meet the clouds in sky
過了黃洋界	Once we crossed the Huangyang Divide
險處不須看	No perilous terrain lies
風雷動	Winds and thunders stir
旌旗奮	Flags and banners fly
是人寰	Human activities comply
三十八年過去	It has been thirty-eight years
彈指一揮間	A moment like a snap of fingers
可上九天攬月	We can embrace the moon in the Ninth Sphere
可下五洋捉鱉	And catch the Tortoise down the Five Seas
談笑凱歌還	To home singing victory at ease
世上無難事	Nothing is impossible
只要肯登攀	If only we dare to scale high

有所思 (1966)

正是神都有事時
又來南國踏芳枝
青松怒向蒼天發
敗葉紛隨碧水馳
一陣風雷驚世界
滿街紅綠走旌旗
憑欄靜聽瀟瀟雨
故國人民有所思

訴衷情・贈周恩來同志 (1975)

當年忠貞為國籌
何曾怕斷頭
如今天下紅遍
江山靠誰守
業未就
身軀倦
鬢已秋
你我後輩
忍將夙願
付與東流

Desires for Change (1966)

A time when unease is disturbing the Capital
I came south to seek plans inspirational
Green pines express ideals piercing the sky
Fading leaves drift with river flows in demise
A sudden thunder arouses the country into a stormy sea
On all streets colourful banners parade to take siege
I stand by the rail to watch the rapid rains
People in motherland turn desires into change

Tune: Revealing Inner Feelings – To Comrade Zhou Enlai (1975)

In years gone by we served our motherland loyal
No fear for losing our head for the revolution
Today our country is red all through
To whom the prosperity be entrusted in good will
National construction still in progress
Body and soul in no rest
Grey hairs prolific
You and I and succeeding generations
Must we let our perennial aspirations
Go naturally with the eastern flow

葉劍英 Ye Jianying (1897−1986)

油岩題壁 (1915)　Written on Oil Cliff (1915)

放眼高歌氣吐虹	My will a rainbow I sing my aspirations high
也曾拔劍角羣雄	Before this I had followed revolutionary men with pride
我來無限興亡感	Here I study to understand the rise and fall in history
慰祝蒼生樂大同	I will work with my people towards equality and harmony

劉伯承同志伍拾壽祝 (1942)
Wishing Comrade Liu Bo Cheng a Happy 50th Birthday (1942)

細柳營中寂不嘩	In the disciplined camps calm and alone
槍垣炮堵即吾家	Gun shots and cannon fire mark our home
將軍五十人稱健	A general vital at fifty years old
新得倭酋不自誇	You recently defeated the dwarfs deeds untold

遊新疆 (1956)　Visiting Xinjiang (1956)

老子青牛去不還	On his buffalo Laozi gone from here to wherever
而今鑽探滿天山	In Tianshan today excavations in numbers ever
自從鐵道通西域	Whence the railway reaches at this western territory
百萬青年唱出關	Millions of youths will come for new opportunities

長江大橋 (1957)　　The Yangtze River Bridge (1957)

龜蛇對峙　　The Tortoise and Snake hills guard on opposite sides
千年濁浪排空起　　Perennial churning waves in midair fly
折戟沉沙　　To submerge worn-out spears under sands
英雄淘盡　　Testing how many heroic deeds hence
都無覓處　　No count can depend

天公歎服　　Heaven praises
地上神仙　　This earthly immortal achieves
長橋飛架　　A long bridge of flying metals hangs
南北東西無阻　　Spanning to connect every direction in motherland

遙想銀河　　My thoughts go to the Galaxy up far
斜窺牛女　　To see how the Weaver and Cowherd lovers are
端的乍驚還妒　　With dismay and envy my heart beats fast

江心獨立　　I stand alone at mid-river
看巫峽巫山　　To behold Mount Wu and Gorge Wu
頭吳尾楚　　Between the ancient divides of Wu and Chu
任我從容指顧　　Now before me in full commanding view

流水不關情　　Incessant waters flow independent
讓它滾滾東去　　Boiling as they hurry to their eastward mission

鹿回頭 (1959)

海灘拾貝趁朝霞
風捲浪堆沙
境到登山臨水
伊人望望天涯
椰漿消渴
咖啡醒目
南島韶華
擷得一枝紅豆
思量寄與誰家

回梅縣探老家 (1980)

八十三年一瞬馳
木窗燈盞憶兒痴
人生百歲半九十
萬丈霞光值暮時

At Deer Turn-head Point (1959)

The best time to gather shells on the beach is at dawn
Winds stir up waves carrying sands on
Up the hill top by the water edge I climb
To the far horizon my eyes and mind find
Coconut milk quenches thirst fine
A drink of coffee brightens up the eyes
South-sea Island times merrily go by
A red bean twig on my hand
I ponder to whom it be sent

Visiting Home at Meixian (1980)

A brink of time in eighty years three
With a lamp by the window childhood memories glee
One hundred years of life approaching ninety
These evening hours shine bright and mighty

周恩來 Zhou Enlai (1898–1976)

送蓬仙兄返里有感 (1916)
(I)

相逢萍水亦前緣
負笈津門豈偶然
捫虱傾談驚四座
持螯下酒話當年
險夷不變應嘗膽
道義爭擔敢息肩
待得歸農功滿日
他年預卜買鄰錢

(II)

東風催異客
南浦唱驪歌
轉眼人千里
消魂夢一柯
星離成恨事
雲散奈愁何
欣喜前塵影
因緣文字多

Seeing Peng Xian Homebound (1916)

(I)

We met by chance predestination
Classmates in Tianjin not an accident
Your eloquence stuns even intimate friends
O'er wines and crabs we scruitinize every current event
Hardship and suffering we endure to rid off our foes
For our motherland no one is afraid to fight and defend
Whence enemy gone we promise to turn to the land
Plots of land rented we will be neighbouring farm hands

(II)

As the east wind hurried passengers on board
We sang parting songs from the south shore
You are a thousand *li* away in a twinkle
In dreams our souls tingle
Stars gone confirming separation regrets
Clouds dispersed sorrows stay intact
Fond are images of being together merry
We talked and wrote words never too many

次皡如夫子傷時事原韻 (1916)

茫茫大陸起風雲
舉國昏沉豈足雲
最是傷心秋又到
蟲聲唧唧不堪聞

無題

大江歌罷掉頭東
邃密羣科濟世窮
面壁十年圖壁破
難愁蹈海亦英雄

春日偶成 (1914)

極目青郊外
煙靄布正濃
中原方逐鹿
博浪踵相踪
櫻花紅陌上
柳葉綠池邊
燕子聲聲裏
相思又一年

Reply to Master Kao Ru Grieving over Current Events (1916)

Winds and clouds whirl over our motherland
Need it be said that our countrymen are dozy and indolent
The biggest torment is that autumn is again here
Whence noisy insects their chirps pierce the ear

No Title

The Grand River roared to resolutely turn back east
Having searched in vain wise clues to better our country
Ten years I contemplate facing a wall to make a breakthrough
I vow to tread the seas and take any daring action necessary

Thoughts on a Spring Day (1914)

I cast my eyes on the suburb green
Everywhere thickening fog seen
Power struggles occupy the heartland in heat
Assassin strikes repeated
Cherry blossoms flush o'er a winding path
Green willows by the pond hush
Amid the twitters of swallows
My thoughts spent a new year to follow

陳毅 Chen Yi (1901–1872)

憶亡 (1932)

Remembering My Wife (1932)

泉山渺渺汝何之	Under hills with the yellow spring how are you
檢點遺篇幾首詩	Among papers you left are poems in view
芳影如生隨處在	Your images alive on pages here and there
依稀門角見玉姿	By the door I seem to see a cold beauty hither
檢點遺篇幾首詩	Among papers you left are poems in view
幾回讀罷幾回痴	Whenever I read them I am with you
人間總比天堂好	Compare to heaven earth is a better place to be
宿願能償連理枝	With you in wedlock my wish has become real
依稀門角見玉姿	By the door I seem to see a cold beauty hither
定睛知誤強自支	The shadows gone I know not whither
送葬歸來涼月夜	Home from your funeral a cold moon this night
泉山渺渺汝何之	Under hills with the yellow spring how you might
革命生涯都說好	People say revolution is a life so good
軍前效力死還高	Devotion to the army death a noble toot
艱難困苦平常事	Hardship and confinement are days so normal
喪偶中年淚更滔	Losing spouse at mid-age tears torrentially flow

三十五歲生日寄懷 (1936)
On My 35th Birthday (1936)

大軍西去氣如虹　Going west our army spirit like a rainbow
一局南天戰又重　Beneath the south sky a battle again unfold
半壁河山沉血海　Half of our motherland is in a bloody sea
幾多知友化沙蟲　Many a bosom friend killed and buried beneath
日搜夜剿人猶在　Searched in days and attacked by night we survived
萬死千傷鬼亦雄　Ten thousand dead and wounded as ghosts we are alive
物到極時終必變　Tested to the limits events must surely change
天翻地覆五洲紅　Whence heaven and earth turns motherland crimson

佳期 (1940)

燭影搖紅喜可知
催妝為賦小喬詩
同心能償運蹇夢
注目相看不語時
一笑艱難成往事
共盟奮勉記佳期
百年一吻叮嚀後
明月來窺夜正遲

「七七」五週年感懷 (1942)

即今抗戰艱難日
累累新墳啓我思
五年碧血翻滄海
一片丹心照漢旗
國中忍見兒皇立
朝內惟謀其豆炊
九仞為山爭一簣
同仇敢與億民期

Wedding Day (1940)

Red candlelight flickers to greet this happy day
Undoing your make-up you busy with poetry
How grand it is our hearts join could this be a dream
Eyes meet in silence our love showing in gleams
In a smile we put all past hardships away
We vow to love with mutual support in future days
We kiss to tell one another ours is a hundred-year affair
The moon peeps in at late night her well-wishes fair

Thoughts on the 5th Anniversary of Japanese Invasion (1942)

Today marks the difficult war against the Japanese invasion
Increasing new tombs inspire me to find a viable solution
Five years of bloodshed awake people in our motherland
Sons and daughters defended our Han tradition at length
We tolerated a child-emperor on a false throne
Fighting between siblings readily condoned
We struggle to fight for nine league hills
All of our billion people will rise to eliminate the common foe

祝朱總司令六旬大慶（1946 年 11 月）

高峯泰岳萬山從
大海盛德在能容
服務人民三十載
七旬會見九州同

長江大橋（1956）

大江波浪兼天湧
南北難逾萬古同
而今建設開新面
鐵橋飛架似長虹
鐵橋飛架似長虹
江北江南一軌通
待首五洲通一軌
共慶寰球進大同

Wishing Commander Zhu De a Happy 60th Birthday (November 1946)

The high peak of Mount Tai leads ten thousand hills
Your virtues of wide tolerance like seas and rills
Serving the people continuously for thirty years
We all look forward to be with you for ten more years

The Yangtze River Bridge (1956)

Torrents of the Yangtze soar high near the sky
North and south of China are perennial divides
Today's construction opens a perspective new
A bridge of iron flies like a rainbow
A bridge of iron flies like a rainbow
North and south of the river connected by a rail
Whence this rail links all of China in transportation
A unified world of harmony and equality in celebration

蘇步青 Su Buqing (1902－2003)

南雁蕩愛山亭晚眺（1940 年回鄉）

愛山亭上少淹留
煙繞村耕欲漸休
牛背只應橫笛晚
羊腸從此入山幽
雲飛千嶂風和雨
灘響一溪夏亦秋
長憶春來芳草遍
夕陽渡口繫歸舟

憶秦娥：從台歸國（1946）

台灣峽
深藍一片波聲歇
波聲歇
孤機遙指
浙東甌北

白雲開處山重疊
晴空萬里歸時節
歸時節
紅樓幽夢
菱花新雪

Gazing Afar from the Love Hill Pavilion (Returning to Hometown in 1940)

I linger on this Love Hill Pavilion in childhood days
Watching villagers work and rest in so many ways
Riding home on my cow's back before the sun sets
Through narrow winding paths the hills quiet
Clouds pass giving thousands of pictures of wind and rain
Streams sing as summer goes and autumn comes to reign
I've always loved spring when fragrant green pastures weave
And welcome returning boats to moor on piers in eves

Tune: Remembering the Qin Maid–Returning Home from Taiwan (1946)

Taiwan Strait
On the deep blue ocean tidal songs quiet
Tidal songs quiet
My lonely airplane points far
To China coast cities north and east of the river

Where clouds disperse mountain ranges roam
On the vast clear sky 'tis time to go home
'Tis time to go home
Red towers I know
Hard bean flowers white as snow

望大小金門島 (1981)

鷺島南來秋正濃
危台東望思無窮
為何衣帶眼前水
如隔蓬山一萬重

世紀絕戀 (寫於 2002 年百歲生辰)

人去瑤池竟渺然
空齋長夜思綿綿
一生難得相依侶
百歲原無永聚筵
燈影憶曾搖白屋
淚珠沾不到黃泉
明朝應摘露中蕊
插向慈祥遺像前

Watching the Jinmen Islands (1981)

I come south to the Eaglet Island when autumn is full
Looking east from this dangling platform thoughts roam
Why should this tiny strand of water before my eyes
Divide my motherland like ten thousand hills far and high

A Century of Love (Written on My 100th Birthday in 2002)

To the yonder world you have quietly gone
In my empty study I pine for you nights on and on
Through many difficulties we stayed together for life
Even age one hundred togetherness will not forever thrive
By lamplight I recall you busy keeping our house clean
My tears incessant you will not see at Yellow Spring
I will pick a dewy flower tomorrow morning
And place it before your likeness kind and serene

浙江大學

重到武林春已闌
如來殿下水潺潺
千風萬雨都過盡
依舊東南第一山
古木參天寶殿雄
萬方遊客浴香風
勸君休坐山門等
不再飛來第二峯

悼亡妻

望隔仙台碧海天
悲懷無計寄黃泉
東西曾共萬千里
苦樂相依六十年
永記辛勞培子女
敢忘賢惠佐鑽研
嗟餘垂老何為者
兀自棲棲戀教鞭

Zhejiang University

Returning to the university spring has arrived
Learning flows like murmuring streams in halls bright
Tens of thousands of winds and rains had come and gone
Here in the south-east this university stands mountain tall
Sky high old trees give shades to the Grand Hall
Bathing in the fragrance are scholars from many shores
Do not idle around the mountain gate to guess the future
No second peak of wisdom will be a match for nurtures

Remembering My Wife

I look for paradise blocked by blue seas under a green sky
In grief I find no way to Yellow Spring to bare my mind
East and west we had together weathered millions of strives
In hardship or happiness we kept together for sixty years
Forever I will remember your labour bringing up our children
And dare not forget the many tasty meals you offer on the table
Why am I left to be old alone I sigh
Only to keep up with teaching as days roll by

懷故鄉諸老友

(I)

暈似彩雲原易散
淡如白水卻難忘
不堪閱盡風霜後
猶自逢春各一方

(II)

不緣名利動征途
卻為友朋戀故磯
漫說浮雲出山久
鄉心依舊繞山飛

Remembering Old Chums Back Home

(I)

Chums like colourful clouds disperse easily
Tasteless like plain water yet difficult to forget
I learned with grief many of you suffered inhuman threats
Now rectified I regret we are still wide spread

(II)

I embark on my life path not for money nor fame
My heart with you my friends and home-soil remains
People say a floating cloud enjoys staying up the hills
My heart flies over the hills homeward still

登衡山祝融峯 (1961)

名山南峙此登臨
絕頂融峯敢摘星
眼底奔流湘水碧
巒巔追逐白雲深
我歌紅日經天麗
誰遣豪情仗劍行
莫道兩洋波浪闊
乘風飛去搏長鯨

贈曾志 (1969)

重上戰場我亦難
感君情厚逼雲端
無情白髮催寒暑
蒙垢餘生抑苦酸
病馬也知嘶櫪晚
枯葵更覺怯霜殘
如煙往事俱忘卻
心底無私天地寬

To the Summit of Mount Heng (1961)

To the south side of this famous mount I arrive
On the summit I dare to pick a star raising hands high
Beneath my eyes the greenish blue River Xian swiftly flows
To the depths of white clouds mountain ranges follow
For the red sun in a glorious sky I loudly sing
His mightiness shown his sword in swing
Fear not the roaring waves in the two oceans wide
To battle the whales there on winds I ride

To My Wife from Prison (1969)

To return to battle ground I am unable
Indebted I am to your love tall as clouds float
Grey hairs hurry the passing of years with no concession
Falsely indicted my life will continue to face oppression
A sick horse knows justice will not come even with calls
Withered palms are surely afraid to face biting frosts
Gone are past deeds forgotten like smoke in wind
My heart magnanimous my sky wide

張學良 Zhang Xueliang (1910-2001)

無題

自占英雄多好色
好色未必皆英雄
吾輩雖非英雄漢
唯有好色似英雄

遊華山感懷

極目長城東眺望
江山依舊主人非
深仇積憤當須雪
披甲還鄉奏凱歸

柳老渡台來訪

十載無多病
故人亦未疏
餘生烽火後
唯一願讀書

No Title

All heroes love beauties since old
Not all beauty lovers are mighty and bold
Though a hero I am not
I love beauties as a hero ought

Touring Huashan

I gaze far eastward from the Great Wall
The same hills and rills my Governor reigns not
Sources of deep hatred and anger must be retorted
In armours I will return home victory songs resonant

Elder Liu Visits Me in Taiwan

For ten years I ill not for an instant
Old friends have not left me distant
Surviving war and seizure my life goes on
My only wish is to read till dawn

鄧拓 Deng Tuo (1912–1966)

一嵐清玩

茫茫山海雲深處
鬱鬱松峯夕陽紅
望斷飛鴻天外影
花魂詩思伴西東

魯迅兩週年祭 (1938)

當年長夜度春時
苦戰人間滿鬢絲
荷戟孤征誅腐惡
投槍萬眾望旌旗
傷心兩載風雲色
咽淚重刊吶喊詩
再祭他年烽火後
血花一綴自由衣

To My Wife Yi Lan

Deep amid clouds overlooking hills and rills wide
Serene pine tips remain crimson till sunset time
I look for shadows of wild geese beyond the sky
Floral souls and poetic thoughts stay by my side

On the 2nd Anniversary of Lu Xun's Death (1938)

You spent many a dark year striving for social spring
To improve human affairs your hair added grey strings
Alone you use your pen to vindicate corruption
And call all citizens to hoist banners for better options
Two years of mourning our motherland is still in confusion
With tears we strive to republish your poems in Loud Calls
We will repeat the oblation after the end of this civil war
Our bloodsheds will stain the coat of freedom in red

定情 (1942)　　Love Devotion (1942)

戰地青衫侶　　In cotton clothes we are a couple in battling lands
風沙北國春　　Spring winds whirl up sands in northland
白雲浮終古　　White clouds float as always been
江水去長東　　The eastward river flows like ever since
身世三生劫　　We had endured cosmic tests in three incarnates
心天一向紅　　Our hearts remain red like sunshine immaculate
高情為爾我　　We share life with the same lofty goals
天地自無窮　　Together we will go forward till time eternal